Settle the Score

About the author

Sam Tobin was born in Recife, Brazil and ended up in Manchester, England. He's been a BAFTA nominated producer, worked in kebab shops and studied law. He's lived in Moss Side, Brixton and Hollywood.

For more from Sam Tobin, head to www.samtobincrime.com.

Settle
the Score

Sam Tobin

HODDER &
STOUGHTON

First published in Great Britain in 2024 by Hodder & Stoughton Limited
An Hachette UK company

This paperback edition published in 2024

1

A CIP catalogue record for this title is available from the British Library

Paperback ISBN 978 1 399 71387 0
ebook ISBN 978 1 399 71389 4

Typeset in Monotype Plantin Light by Manipal Technologies Limited

Printed and bound in Great Britain by Clays Ltd, Elcograf S.p.A.

Hodder & Stoughton policy is to use papers that are natural, renewable
and recyclable products and made from wood grown in sustainable forests.
The logging and manufacturing processes are expected to conform to the
environmental regulations of the country of origin.

Hodder & Stoughton Limited
Carmelite House
50 Victoria Embankment
London EC4Y 0DZ

www.hodder.co.uk

To FEMH

Prologue

As soon as the older man came out of the bathroom it would be time to rob him.

Jake lay back on the bed and enjoyed the smell of freshly laundered sheets. His clothes were still scattered all over the floor of the bedroom. The darkly stained jeans and filthy anorak. Trainers held together with duct tape. They lay in jarring contrast to the pristine white of the hotel room carpet.

The older man had insisted Jake shower first. Jake didn't object – it had been nearly two weeks since he'd showered at his former sheltered accommodation. He had to sneak in after being banned for stealing from the other residents.

Jake let his battered body sink into the mattress as he looked up at the ceiling. The sex hadn't been anywhere near as rough as it usually was. But then usually this would happen in a side alley or if he was lucky the back seat of a car, parked on some deserted North Manchester industrial estate. To be taken to a swanky hotel, paid three times his rate and then get to do it on a king-sized bed was a rare luxury.

The older man's aftershave had imprinted itself on the pillows. It smelled expensive and respectable. A dark, floral bouquet that spoke of wealth and solidity. The man's clothes were folded neatly over a nearby chair, beside the large suitcase he'd brought up to the room with him.

Jake assumed he must be visiting Manchester for business. Maybe he had a wife and family and was taking advantage of being away to spend time with someone like Jake. Between the sheets, Jake had already given him one experience he wouldn't forget, and when he came out of the bathroom Jake would get his knife and make sure he got another.

The older man had been in there for nearly ten minutes now. If he hadn't taken his wallet in with him Jake would already be gone. But he could wait.

He looked round the room. There was a football theme. On the wall a framed Manchester City shirt bore Yaya Touré's name and what looked like his signature.

Jake's knife was in his bag on the floor with his clothes. He could get it whenever he wanted. There was plenty of time and it didn't seem like the older man was coming out of the bathroom anytime soon.

He rose off the bed to take a closer look at the shirt. It was the 2013 season. Back then Jake had been only nine years old. He lived and breathed football. His parents had got him the home and away kits just so he had a spare kit to wear while the other one was in the wash. Jake was always out in the street kicking a ball. The Etihad was only down the road. It seemed inevitable that one day he'd be playing there himself.

That was before the drugs.

Jake heard the toilet flushing and he hurried back to the bed, lying down and doing his best to make his battle-scarred nineteen-year-old body look as inviting as possible.

He draped one arm over the side of the bed, ready to reach into his bag for the knife. He'd let the old man come back onto the bed, naked and vulnerable, ready for round two. Then before he knew what was happening Jake would have a knife at the man's throat. By the time Jake was done the man would be heading back to wherever he came from, desperately inventing a story as to how he lost his wallet and phone and money. A story he could tell his wife and kids.

The bathroom door opened and, despite the best efforts of the extractor fan, a cloud of sweet-smelling white smoke wafted into the room. There in the middle of it, the older man stood for a moment looking at Jake. He was nearly good-looking but then there was something about his face, a haunted quality that lent him a darker air. He'd never once smiled since he'd picked Jake up by the canal-side.

Jake guessed he must be in his fifties but he looked younger. Where Jake's body was rail-thin and riddled with scabs and tattoos, the man's body was toned and lightly tanned. When they had sex, Jake almost enjoyed it.

Jake wasn't gay, but to feel that kind of gentle intimacy wasn't something that featured heavily in his line of work.

The older man started to approach. His bare feet padding across the thick pile of the carpet. The smell of his aftershave mingled with the clouds of white smoke. A decadent, heady aroma.

As the man knelt on the bed, Jake remembered himself. Unseen, his hand slid over the side of the bed, into his bag, searching for his knife. He kept eye contact with the older man, smiling seductively as his fingers rooted through the detritus of his bag. The half-drunk bottle of vodka, the shoplifted make-up palettes and phone cases. Where was that knife?

The older man was kneeling over Jake now. He stroked Jake's sunken chest with one hand and – for the first time Jake could recall – smiled.

The man's teeth were brown and rotten.

'Looking for this?' he said as Jake's knife suddenly appeared in the man's other hand.

Before Jake could even begin to panic, the man had slid the knife deep into his side.

Jake thought how strange it was that he barely felt the blade going in. He tried to look up into the face of the man who was murdering him but all he saw was a smothering darkness as the light in the room dimmed to nothing.

3

1

'No offence, son, but you seem like you're out of your fucking depth here. You understand what I'm saying, Dean?'

Dean did his best to nod politely as Janet Farr came to the end of yet another long, rambling monologue. Janet was pure south Manchester. Every other word out of her mouth was 'fuck' and she always made sure to end her sentences with a question to confirm the listener was following her free-form train of thought.

The Farrs lived in a house in Bredbury, just outside of Stockport. At one time, long ago, the place must have been some kind of farmhouse. Out in the open country with only a collection of strange, half-built outbuildings for company. Over time it had been enlarged and added to. Round the back of the house the garden was covered by a large, ground-floor extension with a grey uPVC conservatory and brand-new matching windows, the yellow expanding foam still visible around the joins.

But just as the house had grown, so too had Stockport, and now the Farrs' ramshackle collection of buildings with its small plot of land dotted with several rusted-out cars, a dented Jaguar and other assorted junk was overlooked by a tower block to its rear while, across the road, a newly built estate of over fifty homes stood in sharp contrast to the amateurish chaos of the Farr homestead.

The effect was completed by the fact that every single one of the windows to the front of the house had been put through at one time or another and now three sheets of chipboard filled the gaps where the glass once was. If it wasn't for the constant comings and goings, late-night parties and loud music, you'd be forgiven for thinking the place was abandoned.

This was where the Farrs called home.

The large, ground-floor extension had been built to accommodate a western-saloon-themed pub. Swing doors led from the front of the house into a room covered in wood panelling with various Confederate flags, guitars and posters hanging up on every available surface. Behind the bar there was a tap serving Budweiser and a shelf with nothing but Jack Daniel's. The centrepiece of the room was the only wall free of clutter, which had been given over to a giant mural of a cowboy wrestling a steer to the ground.

The Farrs were thieves, opportunists and – of late – drug dealers and this was what they spent their ill-gotten gains on.

'See, when we came to you we thought we were getting the other bloke. The coloured one,' said Janet, leaning back into the built-in seating that ran along the walls of the 'bar'. She was thin, almost boyish, but the way she held herself left no one in any doubt that she was far stronger than she looked. And if there was any doubt they had only to look at her face. A lifetime of corralling her family, augmented with Botox and fillers, had twisted Janet Farr's face into a permanent scowl.

Dean had never seen her in any colour other than black. She was currently in head-to-toe black Balenciaga. It matched her mood perfectly.

The man she was talking about was Dean's boss, Craig Malton. For the last three months Malton had been locked up in Strangeways prison on remand for murder. Malton had ignored Dean's multiple requests for a visiting order or phone call and so, without any further instructions, Dean had done his best to carry on business as usual.

Day to day that meant managing Malton Security. A firm that employed nearly sixty people and ran doors for half the nightclubs, restaurants and bars in the city. On top of that, Malton Security guarded high-worth individuals' homes, provided close protection and any other service you could imagine that lay in the grey area between lawful vigilance and semi-legal violence.

But what Malton was really known for was what Dean was currently engaged in. It was why Janet Farr had reached out in the first place. The security work was the official business, but what Malton really did was far darker.

Malton solved crimes for criminals. People who for whatever reason didn't want to get the police involved. Kidnapped drug dealers, unsolved gangland killings, missing product. Whatever the issue, the Manchester underworld knew that if you had the connections and you had the cash there was nothing Malton wouldn't do, nowhere he couldn't go, no one he wouldn't lean on, just so long as it produced results.

Malton had lived in Manchester his entire life. From a scrappy kid in Moss Side through to the power behind a multi-million-pound security firm. In that time he'd forged connections with the people who made Manchester work. The gangsters, the dealers, the slumlords, the corrupt politicians and the crime families who were the real power behind the city.

But Dean wasn't Malton. Malton was a middle-aged, eighteen-stone, mixed-race wrecking ball of a man whose reputation alone got people talking without saying a word or lifting a fist. Dean was a nineteen-year-old, six-foot beanpole with good manners and a face that made people want to mother him. On the other side of the room the tinny sound of a karaoke track started up. Words appeared on the large TV hanging on one wall and Janet Farr's daughter, Marie, got ready to sing.

Far from being distracted, Janet turned and cheered at the sound.

'Go on, Marie!' she hollered, clapping in support. Janet's face shone with maternal delight through her perma-glare.

Despite how much trouble they were giving him, Dean found it very hard to dislike the Farrs.

Marie was built like her mother, slight but with a natural fighter's posture. Always on the front foot. Fearless. Like her mother, her face was plumped up with fillers, but unlike Janet,

Marie had led a life of having her every whim indulged by her mum. When Marie smiled it didn't look like a prelude to violence.

Behind the bar, Carl Farr, Janet's son, looked up from his phone – half interested. The most striking thing about Carl was his head, a giant, shaved boulder plastered with a permanently stunned-looking face. Carl was hugely fat but clearly terrifyingly strong with it. His hands were like paving slabs, stubby fingers fumbling at his smartphone.

As Marie started to sing, Carl went back to listlessly staring down at his phone and Janet turned back to Dean. Her face stopped smiling.

'Over three months now since we was robbed. And what the fuck have you got to show for it?'

The truth was, with everything else he had on his plate, the Farrs and their missing drugs had fallen very low down his list of priorities. Right up until he'd been doorstepped at the Malton Security offices by Carl Farr with an offer to meet with his mum that Dean just couldn't refuse.

Dean racked his brains. What did he have to show for it? The Farrs sat slap bang in the middle of the pecking order of Manchester's drug economy. They were far below the rarefied air at the top where a handful of gangs and individuals with a global reach negotiated with South American cartels and European crime gangs to bring millions of pounds of uncut drugs into the country. But they were also several rungs above the hand-to-mouth street dealers who would be found in every part of the city, their pockets stuffed with tiny individual wraps and the filthy cash taken from the junkies they sold to.

From what Dean understood, the Farrs bought their cocaine in wholesale quantities from a UK-based seller, but they were responsible for bringing the product into the country.

The Farrs owned a garage, which gave them the perfect excuse to be shipping high-performance tyres into the UK. High-performance tyres that arrived stuffed full of drugs.

8

In order to keep at arm's length from the risk of importing the kind of quantities of cocaine that would see you locked up for the rest of your adult life, the Farrs employed a courier who travelled to Rotterdam where he would pack the tyres with the drugs before heading back to the UK and awaiting the arrival of the delivery.

Once the shipment had cleared customs the courier's job was then to remove the drugs before sending the tyres on their way to the Farrs' garage in Manchester. Then, at a later date, he could deliver the drugs to the Farrs.

This way the Farrs had a plausible explanation as to why they were involved in bringing things into the country but could stay one step removed from the illegality of the process. Should the drugs be found before the tyres had passed through customs, they could plead ignorance. Should the courier be caught with the drugs on either side of the Channel, assuming he kept his mouth shut, there was nothing to tie him to the Farrs.

That was the plan, but three months ago, on the UK side of the Channel, someone had robbed the courier of the drugs from the latest shipment. Out of pocket to the tune of a couple of hundred grand, first the Farrs had blamed the importer, but when a number of subtle and not-so-subtle threats had failed to get them a refund, the Farrs had hired Malton to find those drugs. A week later Malton had been arrested and sent to Strangeways.

'It would help if you could give me the name of the man you buy from,' said Dean as politely as possible. This had become something of a sticking point.

'And I fucking told you, I'm not a grass.'

Dean appreciated the Farrs' respect for the basic tenets of criminality but it didn't make his job any easier. Malton never let something like that get in his way. He thrived on the unknown. He told Dean that he'd rather people didn't give him the information. People lied, people omitted, people had their own agendas. When Craig Malton got information out of someone, he knew that information was true.

Dean wished he could say the same. Where Malton relied on reputation and menace, Dean relied on curiosity and smarts. Unfortunately for Dean, two hundred grand of missing cocaine was a drop in the ocean as far as Manchester was concerned. Alongside the supercharged growth of the city's skyline, cocaine consumption had skyrocketed. Coke was the Mancunian drug of choice and whoever had stolen the Farrs' drugs would have had no problem whatsoever in moving the product on.

With the missing drugs yet to make their presence felt in the underworld economy, Dean was left with nothing.

Malton had taken a chance on Dean, given him a job, and trained him up as his second in command. In the time he'd been working for Malton, he'd been shot in the face, nearly beaten to death and he'd saved Malton's life at least once. Malton had seen past Dean's age and looks and recognised someone just as adept as he was at navigating the dangerous currents of Manchester's criminal networks.

However much he wanted to walk away from the Farrs and their missing drugs, he couldn't let Malton down.

'I told them, move on. It happens,' came a voice from behind Dean. He turned to see Janet's son-in-law, Martin Farr, awkwardly negotiating the saloon doors that led into the room.

Marie was halfway through a Shania Twain number and turned, flirtatiously directing her singing towards Martin.

'Fuck off, Martin,' said Janet. 'I tell you what, if my Mickey were here now he'd fucking slap you for that.'

Martin sat down across from Dean but with a safe distance between himself and his mother-in-law. That he'd ended up taking the Farr surname and working for the Farr business told Dean everything he needed to know about where Martin stood in the Farr family hierarchy.

Martin caught Dean's eye and shared a look of patient exasperation. From the three months Dean had been dealing with the Farrs, he'd come to rely on Martin as the voice of reason.

As much as Janet rode her son-in-law, since Mickey Farr had got locked up for punching out a female police officer at a derby match it had been Martin running the show. The Farrs sold to a string of gangs who in turn supplied the street-level dealers. They were close to the violent, free-for-all of the lower levels but with just enough of a buffer to not get involved.

'This is costing us money. For what?' said Martin.

Martin obviously used steroids. His arms bulged out of his T-shirt, swarming with tattoos. His hairline was in retreat to the back of his head but he still had a youthful optimism about him, which showed in how he dressed – tight jeans, fashionable T-shirts and a padded gilet.

Despite all his toned muscle, Dean imagined the chubby, untoned arms of Carl Farr would snap Martin like a twig.

Dean hadn't brought up just how much the Farrs now owed. Without results he felt guilty even mentioning it. One more thing that Malton would have easily taken in his stride.

'Some cunt's robbed me and I'm fucked if I'm letting that go. I want my fucking drugs, Martin. You understand?' said Janet, turning on her son-in-law. 'I paid for Craig Malton and I get this fucking kid?' She turned back to Dean. 'No offence, son,' she said.

Dean nodded and kept quiet.

'Thing is, I think you're not even fucking trying. So I've had to take matters into my own hands. Sorry, love.'

For a moment Dean felt a flood of relief. Right now he was single-handedly running Malton Security. This side of the business was too much to be doing on top of all of that. If Janet Farr could help this along then he wasn't too proud to accept assistance.

'I had a word with my Mickey,' said Janet with a smile.

On the other side of the bar, Marie missed the high note by miles.

'See, he's banged up with your boss – Craig Malton,' Janet carried on. 'No point giving you a kicking. Need you to get the fucking job done.' She smiled. 'But your boss, sat on his arse in Strangeways? I reckon he could stand to have a little reminder of who it is he's fucking about with. Give you a bit of an incentive to get off *your* arse and find my fucking drugs.' Janet turned to her son-in-law with a wickedly pointed Botox grin. 'If that's all right with you, Martin?'

Marie finished her song with a flourish. Carl kept on looking at his phone. Janet turned and applauded wildly. Dean said nothing. If what she was telling him was true, then things were about to get messy.

He almost felt sorry for Mickey Farr.

2

Malton had forgotten how much he enjoyed the flat, airless calm before the violence.

It had been three months since his arrest for murder and in that time the outside world had faded to an indistinct blur somewhere at the back of his mind.

It was a murder he hadn't committed, but now that seemed somehow irrelevant. As did the events that had led up to his arrest. Now all that mattered was contained within the walls of HMP Manchester, the prison known to the world as Strangeways.

All his life Malton had lived in the shadow of Strangeways. As a young kid growing up in Moss Side he'd seen friends and family carted off behind the walls of the notorious Victorian prison. He'd later come to realise how it was only sheer luck that he hadn't wound up there himself. Between stealing car radios and never backing down from a fight, there were more than enough reasons to send a sullen, mixed-race kid away to teach him a lesson. But he'd never been caught. Working first as a bouncer and then running his own security firm, he'd become well versed in exactly what it takes to walk the fine line between legal violence and illegal brutality.

Malton closed his eyes and listened to the din. The constant background noise of prison. That had been his first surprise. After the six hours or so it took to check him in through the modern visitors' centre that had been built on the side of the old prison, he'd been led back several centuries to the true Strangeways. The sprawling Victorian gaol made of brick and steel. A tiny city-state of convicts within spitting distance of Manchester city centre. Hundreds of prisoners, bored, scared, angry, frustrated. All shouting themselves hoarse. Laughter, screams, threats and bestial noises. And outside the rain kept up its relentless drumbeat. The whole cacophony echoed off the hard surfaces, meaning that every waking moment was awash with hostile white noise.

It was impossible to make out any one sound in amongst the din. But Malton knew they were coming.

Back when he was on the outside he made it his business to know every movement of Manchester's criminal classes. He was a living encyclopaedia of the Manchester underworld. From the drug gangs in North Manchester replaying the darkest moments of Nineties Moss Side, to the warring criminal firms of Salford flaunting their armed violence just as much as their wealth. All of Manchester existed in Malton's head as a lurid map of sin, greed, brutality and money.

Thirty years entangled in that world had taught him that beyond violence and intimidation it was knowledge that carried the day. Knowing who had stolen from whom. Who was planning violent retribution and who was looking to get out for good. Knowledge let Malton stay one step ahead. It let a lone man navigate the lethal currents of the underworld and live to tell the tale. Malton was just one man. He had no muscle, no gang. He didn't carry a gun. Malton had something far more important: knowledge.

But that was on the outside. In Strangeways there were only criminals. Murderers, rapists, drug dealers, wife beaters and worse. Every colour of human atrocity, packed together in a crumbling Victorian building. Locked away from the world but not locked away from each other.

Since his arrival Malton had started again. He had recreated his life outside in microcosm. Discovering prison gossip. Solving beefs and mediating between factions. The reputation he had outside carried inside the walls of Strangeways, gilded with the belief that he was now a murderer.

Malton didn't correct that impression. It served him well. His cell was testament to that.

The room was small, smaller still for a man of Malton's size. A stack of instant noodles was piled up on his dresser alongside tea, coffee, sweets and other small luxuries. He had no fewer than five different mobile phones hidden around the cell. Every cell now had a landline, but with calls monitored and numbers restricted, mobile phones were essential for prisoners who wanted to pick up their life outside while behind bars. But Malton didn't eat his food or use his phones. He traded them and rented them and made sure that he was at the centre of prison life.

If the guards knew, they left him alone. Better to have someone like Malton keeping things calm than to crack down on him and upset the equilibrium. S Wing, where Malton found himself, had never been more peaceful.

Until today. Until he'd heard the rumour of what was coming his way. Three men, armed and under instructions to send a message by beating him to within an inch of his life.

The thought amused him.

He gave his neck an experimental flex. The thick, cable-like muscles stood to attention as they flowed down into his vast back and off to the thick, dense curves of his arms. His flimsy grey prison tracksuit could barely hold him. His hands rested on his knees, two broken cudgels that bore witness to a lifetime of conflict.

Malton stared at the wall opposite his bed. His expression was blank, almost meditative. His head was shaved, his features nearly delicate but then not quite. His skin a light brown – the mixed-race heritage that had made him who he was. A man always apart. Never belonging. Under his right eye was a thick scar. A memento from when he was starting out and had yet to become such good friends with brutality.

Outside, buried in Southern Cemetery, was the young man Stephen Page. The boy he was meant to have killed. He hadn't seen that coming. He'd been too consumed with his own dead boy – James, his lover.

Malton had slept with men and women in his time but had only ever truly loved two people. One of them was his childhood sweetheart who, the last time they'd met, had tried to kill him. The other was James.

James who made Malton feel like he belonged somewhere. James who made Malton feel at home in his skin. James who was butchered. James whose killers Malton had been pursuing when he was arrested. He had been so blinded by his quest for vengeance that all the knowledge and insight that had kept him alive up to that point had simply fallen away to be replaced with all-consuming rage.

But that was outside. Inside, Malton didn't have to worry about any of that. Inside, the world was far more simple, straightforward and nasty.

The heavy metal door to his cell opened and, without saying a word, three men entered, the final one closing the door behind him.

They were young, two white, one black. Barely in their twenties. Their bodies still slight and delicate, their youthful egos more than compensating for what their physicality could not do.

Malton saw that they each carried some kind of weapon. A prison knife made from a sharpened toothbrush, a block of wood, a jagged shard of Perspex from one of the countless broken windows.

'Mickey Farr's got a message for you,' said the first man in the room. A blond kid with curly hair and the makeshift knife.

Malton stood up and for the first time a look of doubt crossed the men's faces. Malton wasn't tall but he was wide, his bulk filling the small cell. An immovable object. But he was more than that. His face was blank, a dark slab on which their fears were written for all to see.

'I've got a message for Mickey Farr,' said Malton, and flew at the three men.

3

Police tape surrounded Piccadilly Basin. A few minutes' walk from the train station, the area had once been a hub for goods coming in along the canals on their way to the warehouses of Manchester. It had been the beating heart of the city's trade.

Now it was a car park. The canals were still there, winding around the old warehouse buildings before disappearing beneath the city centre to emerge back into daylight in the Gay Village, but all that remained of Piccadilly Basin's glory days was the large, stone archway that led to the scruffy patch of land where you could leave your car for just ten pounds a day.

Uniformed officers were doing their best to patrol the perimeter and keep back the handful of curious onlookers. It didn't help that in the past few years several tower blocks and hotels had been built on the land surrounding the basin and now dozens of faces peered down from the flats and hotel rooms.

A small white tent had been erected alongside the canal, just before it headed underground, and a crime scene van announced that something serious was afoot.

Ruth Porter stood on a raised footbridge over the canal, which gave her a perfect view of everything going on. She saw the police vans that had brought uniform out to guard the scene. And she clocked the unmarked police car that had two plain-clothes detectives stood beside it, both urgently talking into their phones.

She held up her own phone and took some photos as a crime scene officer dressed head to toe in protective clothing emerged from the tent clutching several bags of evidence.

Ruth was late for work but this felt like the sort of thing that her work ought to be all about.

Ruth wrote for *Mancunian Ways*, a local online news platform that in reality was owned by a larger, national news agency. Growing up watching her dad write for the *Manchester Evening News*, Ruth had never wanted to be anything other than a journalist. She'd seen how hard he had worked, how doggedly he'd gone after politicians and the police. How he'd been able to go anywhere in the city and be either welcomed like a brother or shunned like a pariah. Love him or hate him, her dad's journalism meant something to people.

Even when watching him leave the paper after huge cuts to the newsroom left him doing little more than rewriting press releases, Ruth hadn't been put off. Her dad had told her to do anything else, do whatever she wanted. Just don't be a journalist. But it was too late. Ruth was hooked.

Mancunian Ways was her first job after university and she loved it. They were a team of ten people. Half a dozen journalists all her own age, an older woman – Helen – who ran the office, and a handful of admin staff. It wasn't the hard-hitting investigative journalism Ruth dreamed of doing but it was a start.

She pressed record on her phone and turned it on herself. She'd been making videos of herself since she was a little girl. It came utterly naturally. Her face appeared on the screen. She looked younger than her twenty-three years. A soft round face with large brown eyes and a small mouth. She still got ID'd at the supermarket when buying alcohol. But those eyes shone with a steely intelligence. Something else she inherited from her father.

'It's half eight, I'm at Piccadilly Basin and as you can see,' said Ruth turning the phone round, 'there's a heavy police presence. That tent over there suggests a body. Whatever it is, the police seem keen to keep people back.'

'Can I ask you to move along, please?'

Ruth swung the camera round to catch a young man in police uniform. He had a goatee beard and rectangular glasses. He couldn't have been much older than Ruth. She continued filming, unfazed, her camera now pointing at the officer.

'Good morning, officer, can you tell us a little bit about what's going on here?'

The young officer shook his head. 'I'm sorry, you're going to have to move. We're sealing off the whole area.'

'Is that because of the murder?' chanced Ruth.

'I can't talk about that,' said the officer, unwittingly confirming Ruth's suspicion.

Ruth began to slowly walk away, filming the whole time.

'Do you have to film me?' pleaded the officer.

'I'm Ruth Porter, *Mancunian Ways*. This is right up from the Gay Village and next to the canal underpass, which is a known hotspot for male sex workers. Can you comment on whether this is yet another dead young man?'

'I can't comment on that,' said the officer, again fleshing out Ruth's suspicions.

In between writing articles for *Mancunian Ways* on a new bar where you could play battleships while you drank or a restaurant that served everything on toast, Ruth liked to work her own stories. She knew that *Mancunian Ways* was little more than a hub for recycling articles that came down from the parent company. Adding local flavour by letting themselves be the mouthpiece of half a dozen Manchester PR firms. But she'd never forgotten the look on her dad's face on the days when his stories were front-page news. He'd bring an immaculate copy home with him and they'd read it together, Ruth quizzing her father and learning all the tricks of the trade.

Ruth's current obsession was the idea that there was a serial killer stalking the streets of Manchester, knocking off young men.

'Can you tell us *anything* about the victim?'

The officer shook his head again.

'Careful,' he said and caught Ruth's arm before she walked backwards off the top of the steps down from the footbridge.

Ruth finally stopped filming and got her balance. 'Thanks.' She smiled.

'You're welcome,' said the officer, blushing a little.

Ruth put her phone away and turned to go. The police were indeed extending the perimeter. Officers with tape chased pedestrians further and further back.

Whether or not there really was a serial killer was up for debate. What was indisputable was that in the past five years there had been an unusual number of young men turning up dead. The problem being they were drug addicts, sex workers and runaways. The kind of people you'd expect would meet an untimely end. Either way it could be a fun story. And if *Mancunian Ways* didn't want it, maybe there was a podcast in there. A calling card for Ruth to go on to bigger things.

She was definitely late now. Helen would be having words.

Ruth turned and started to walk off towards the *Mancunian Ways* offices in the Northern Quarter. As she skirted the edge of Piccadilly Basin something caught her eye.

A few metres away a policeman with tape was extending the cordon to the very edge of Piccadilly Basin. But Ruth was already speeding up.

Ahead of her, nestled beside a pile of rubbish, was a mobile phone.

The officer with the tape was getting closer now but had stopped to remonstrate with a driver who seemed to be under the impression that he had some sort of special permission to drive into a crime scene.

With the officer distracted Ruth kept walking, got up to where the mobile phone was lying, and in one smooth movement feigned bending down to tie her shoelaces, pocketed the phone and kept going.

Behind her the officer taped off the bags of rubbish but Ruth didn't look back.

If she could have seen herself she'd recognise the look on her face. It was the same look her dad used to get when he knew he was about to crack a story wide open.

4

A red bullet tore through the sun-baked greens and browns of the Ibiza countryside. The sound of its eight-cylinder engine met the aggression of the driver and echoed out over the hillsides as the sleek MGB GT sports car wound its way around the snaking coastal road.

Every turn was attacked. Every hairpin bend a test of nerve as the driver relentlessly threw the tiny car around the edge of the island.

Behind the wheel, the driver never once flinched. Her thick black curls bounced along in the breeze while a pair of large dark sunglasses hid her face, leaving her small, tight smile the only sign that maybe she was enjoying her game of chicken with death.

It wasn't like Keisha had anything to lose.

She'd been in paradise for nearly a year now and yet it still felt like something was missing.

With the windows down and her foot on the accelerator, Keisha felt weightless as she cut through the mid-morning heat. She was wearing a thin, white cotton dress; her arms bare; light, rope-soled espadrilles on her feet. The air whipped through the small sports car, cooling Keisha's skin, which in her time here had turned a dark shade of brown. Very different to back home.

A lifetime spent under a pale, watery Mancunian sun had left her caught between her Irish mother and her Ghanaian father. But Ibiza had transformed her. She loved to look in the mirror and revel in her newfound blackness. It felt like someone new staring back. Someone whose life could be anything she wanted it to be.

But still sometimes she'd wake at night, the windows to her bedroom wide open in a futile gesture against the constant heat. Lying there in the warm embrace of the Mediterranean climate she felt a fluttering in her chest, a nagging feeling like there was something she'd forgotten.

She'd lie there in the dark as her restless brain dragged itself back over the inventory of her life.

She'd grown up in Hulme and lived long enough to see her home demolished not once but twice as the council clumsily tried and failed to tackle the chronic deprivation that characterised her upbringing. It had taught her that there was no Manchester. Not really. Nothing that couldn't be knocked down and rebuilt again and again.

It was a lesson she took to heart. As a mixed-race kid in Hulme she stood out, and so she made it her business to fit in wherever she went. It didn't take long for Keisha to realise the deck was always going to be stacked against people like her, so she decided she was going to play her own game.

She threw the small car round a bend before mounting a straight that took her uphill. To her right, the flawless blue ocean stretched away to a glittering horizon, while to her left, isolated white villas dotted the hillside. Some simple and crude, others grand play-palaces. Keisha floored the accelerator and as the car rose towards the baby blue sky it felt like she might take off.

No matter how fast she went she knew it would never be enough. A couple of decades of grinding her way through the Manchester underworld had seen her involved in everything from theft to wholesale drug dealing via several murders. In all that time Keisha had been careful to never be the one getting her hands dirty.

But that kind of dirt has a way of catching up with you.

With nowhere left to run, Keisha had finally broken free of Manchester. The rain and history and suffering. She'd run all the way to Ibiza but still it felt like there was something that had slipped her mind. Something she'd left behind.

Some nights she wondered if it was the boy she'd grown up with in Hulme. Another mixed-race outcast. She'd met him filled with doubt and self-loathing and she'd made him into a man who could take on anyone. But then he'd left her and, despite her threatening to burn the city down, he hadn't come back.

Last she heard of Craig he'd been arrested in Liverpool. Charged with the murder of some kid. She surprised herself when her only response to the news was to shrug and pour out another drink.

Since arriving in Ibiza she'd not wanted for male company. There was the young Swedish DJ. He'd lasted a month before she got bored and sent him packing. Then there was the older man with the yacht. For all his money and confidence, he was still in his sixties. Yacht or not, Keisha needed someone who could challenge her, not someone who was winding down in gilded retirement. They were just the highlights. Freed from the constant scrutiny of the incestuous cliques of Manchester, she had thrown caution to the wind and enjoyed herself.

As her car reached the top of the hill, suddenly the entire island was beneath her. For a thrilling moment she could see it all. The sun enveloped her whole body, dazzling her through her glasses. She looked to the sky and was surprised to find her thoughts turn to Anthony. Anthony, the child who'd been stillborn. Anthony who was buried and then exhumed from Southern Cemetery. Anthony who she'd laid to rest, cremated in a final act of catharsis before she fled Manchester and everything it meant to her. If Anthony was up there somewhere beyond the blue then Keisha hoped he understood.

Now the road dipped and, with gravity on her side, Keisha pushed the engine for all it was worth. The speedometer nudged over a hundred and the countryside became a thrilling blur. But still there was that feeling in the back of her mind. Matching her speed, following her every step and just out of sight.

At the bottom of the hill Keisha slammed the brake and hauled the MGB into a tight, ninety-degree turn up the dirt track that led to her villa. She'd been down into the town picking up supplies. As glad as she was to leave behind the cold and the rain and the lifetime of dirt, she did still miss some things from home. The spices she cooked with, readily available in multicultural Manchester, were like gold dust on Ibiza. So too the craft gin made under railway arches just outside the city centre that she'd discovered a taste for in later life. And she missed the bulla cakes she used to buy in bulk from a bakery out in Old Trafford. And so every month she had arranged a delivery to be sent to a post office box in the nearest town.

Keisha cut the engine and the silence of the island enveloped her. She took the box of groceries off the back seat of the MGB GT and headed into the house.

For what she could afford, Keisha's villa was small. It sat high up and surrounded by acres of land that ranged over several steep cliffs. It was no accident that she'd chosen to make her home somewhere impossible to overlook and dangerous to approach from any direction but head on.

The villa itself was a circular building in the style of the island. Thick, cool walls and dozens of small windows to let the sun in and keep the heat out. A spiral staircase ran up the centre of the villa with a living area on the ground floor and bedroom on the top two floors. In the middle was Keisha's favourite part. The kitchen.

She kicked off her espadrilles and felt the heat coming up from the tiled floor on her bare soles.

Whatever it was that was troubling her it surely wouldn't be able to withstand the joint onslaught of gin and Jamaican baking. She broke a tray of ice over the kitchen counter, scooping up the cubes into a tall glass. The ice felt intensely refreshing against her sun-warmed skin. She popped a cube in her mouth and fetched tonic from the fridge, setting it next to the glass on the counter.

Keisha noisily crunched on the ice cube as, with a kitchen knife, she cut away the packaging.

She was about to open the box when her phone rang. She picked it up with one hand while with the other began unpacking all her Mancunian goodies.

'Yes. Yes, that's me. How did you get this number? Oh. I see. No. That can't be right. Keisha. Bistacchi. My maiden name? McColl. My father's name? What do you want to know that for?' Keisha paused a moment, her mind scrabbling. Then she said, 'Boateng.'

Keisha let out an audible gasp. Suddenly the phone felt heavy in her hands. The words coming out of it distant and indistinct.

'Yes. I understand. Of course. Yes. Thank you.'

She heard her voice but it sounded lost, passive, scared. Keisha hung up and looked at the phone as if somehow it might tell her something new. Add details to what she'd just heard.

Her dad was dead. Harold Boateng, the father she hadn't seen since she was a little girl. It had been over four decades since she last saw him but according to the man on the other end of the line, in his will he had appointed her the executor of his estate.

As she stood staring down into the box, Keisha realised something. The feeling of having forgotten something was gone. In its place a concrete certainty.

She was going home.

5

'I told him. You can't be here. He spits at me. I told him again. He downs his drink, swears at me and runs into the toilets. I tell the bar manager I will remove him; I go into the toilets. I remove him.'

The man sitting across from Dean measured his words carefully. A combination of his naturally silent nature and English being his second language.

Illian was originally from Serbia, a kick-boxer and one of Malton Security's most trusted doormen. Illian wasn't a talker. He didn't charm punters or defuse situations with banter. Illian looked exactly like what he was: someone you didn't want to end up on the wrong side of.

But now it was Illian who found himself in trouble.

'The CCTV in the bar completely backs up your story,' said Dean. 'Right up until he goes in the toilets. No CCTV in there.'

At one time the cocktail bar in the Northern Quarter had been a hipster hangout for those in the know. Now that the Northern Quarter had become just another buzzword for developers to entice overseas investment into the city, the clientele of the bar had gone from cool, young creatives to coke-fuelled scallies and their girlfriends keen to go somewhere that looked good on the socials. That was when they had contracted Malton Security to keep a lid on things.

Illian frowned and looked down at his lap. Dean had seen first-hand what Illian could do working a door. He'd watched Illian take down half a dozen drunks single-handedly. Stepping into the midst of brawls and surgically removing punters, one at a time. Using just enough force to do the job.

Dean had also seen what Illian could do if he *really* wanted to hurt someone. The results were terrifying.

So when he got a call from a police officer about an assault by a Malton Security employee, the last person he expected to be involved was Illian.

Illian was tall and slender. Built like an action man, he was well over six foot. But now he was up against an opponent he couldn't defeat: the council licensing committee.

The police had declined to press charges due to lack of evidence but the customer claiming Illian had beaten him up in the toilet was now both suing Malton Security and had reported Illian to the licensing committee.

Illian's hearing was coming up in a few days. It was yet more work for Dean.

'OK,' said Dean, trying to sound optimistic. 'I've got everything I need.'

He got up. Illian rose too. Dean was tall but Illian had a few inches on him. Not to mention a couple of stone of muscle. He looked worried.

'It'll be fine,' said Dean. 'I promise.'

A brief look of hope came over Illian. He gave a small nod and left the office.

As soon as he was alone, Dean felt guilty. He was making more promises he wasn't sure he'd be able to keep.

Dean had been working in Malton's office ever since Malton went inside. In one corner of the room stood Malton's weight bench, untouched. When Malton was here he and Dean would talk over work while Malton lifted improbable amounts of weight as if they were nothing.

A battered leather sofa sat against one wall where Dean would perch and watch Malton bench.

Malton didn't use computers and so Dean had got himself a laptop, which sat on the large, leather-topped desk where Malton used to hold court.

Behind Dean was a map of Greater Manchester made up of four different ordnance survey maps tessellated together.

It was filled with pins, each one representing a job Malton had undertaken for someone. The anxious father whose drug profits paid for Malton to find his missing daughter. The club owner who wanted to discover who was behind the extortion on his club. The Chinatown card game organiser who had been robbed by someone foolish enough to believe they could get away with it.

And there, stuck in Bredbury, was the pin representing the Farrs.

Dean looked over at the weight bench and wished he had Malton here to discuss his theories with and to share the load. But he was alone. There was the business, there was Illian's hearing, there were the Farrs. It was too much for one man. If only he could reach out to Malton.

At first he'd taken Malton's silence as some kind of personal rejection. But as the days turned into weeks turned into months, Dean had convinced himself that Malton's silence must be part of some greater plan. Malton putting a firewall between Dean and himself. Protecting both him and the business from the murder charge hanging over him.

But Malton hadn't just cut Dean out of the loop. Dean learned he'd not been in contact with his lawyer – business partner and former girlfriend Bea Wallace. Bea was Manchester's top criminal lawyer. A petite, five-foot-nothing blonde Geordie with an expensive taste in shoes and a client list that included some of the heaviest criminals in the North West.

Something had happened a few months ago between them, something Malton had never shared with Dean. Whatever it was, it seemed that when Malton most needed someone like Bea he had decided to cut her loose.

That raised the possibility that Malton's silence wasn't a tactic at all. Malton had simply given up. Finally broken and fallen into the abyss he spent so much of his life peering down into.

Whatever had happened, Dean wouldn't give up on Malton. The most valuable thing he could do right now was keep things ticking over until the police finally realised they'd got the wrong man.

Dean wondered what exactly Mickey Farr would be saying to Malton over in Strangeways. He was less worried about Malton – he could easily take care of himself – and more concerned about getting further jammed up with the Farrs. They were mid-tier drug dealers but that didn't mean they could be taken lightly. Patriarch Mickey Farr had already done time for murder, and his son Carl was a chip off the old, violent block.

In truth, he'd had the Farrs on the backburner. With so much else on, they had seemed like a distant priority.

His train of thought was derailed by his mobile phone going off with the alarm he had set for himself. It was eleven o'clock. A smile came over Dean's face as he got up and swiftly locked the office door.

Sitting back down at his desk, he opened his laptop.

Eleven o'clock, the one time that everything else stopped and he and Vikki talked over Skype.

His girlfriend Vikki had been down in London for nearly nine months now. Her fashion course was only a year long, but it seemed like forever since she went. The plan had been for Dean to come and visit and for her to come back up to see him. Somehow neither of those had happened. Vikki found the world of her course filled with distractions. London was rich with people and places and experiences. All of which Dean was painfully aware made sharing a terrace in Moss Side with him seem rather pedestrian. For his part he'd been busy enough before Malton had simply upped and left for Liverpool chasing down James's killers. But after Malton got arrested, suddenly the workload overtook him.

That meant eleven o'clock was sacred. The one time of the day he kept for himself.

Dean listened to the Skype tone as he waited for Vikki to pick up. In truth, rather than bringing them together, the daily call was having the exact opposite effect. Doing it every day meant they had quickly run out of topics of conversation.

Vikki talked about fashion and Dean talked about crime and it seemed like they were on totally different planets.

That didn't stop Dean breaking into a smile as Vikki's face filled the screen. She was athletic, with a strong jaw and skin that glowed beneath her dirty blonde hair. Even confined to a tiny laptop screen, Dean could sense her near-six-foot frame.

'You working?' asked Vikki, an uncertainty in her voice.

Dean could see Vikki's room behind her. She was living in a shared house with a couple of other students. The walls were covered in artwork, mood boards, mirrors, ribbons, fabric and anything else that could be thrown up. A riot of creativity.

'Always,' said Dean with a smile. 'You?'

Vikki smiled and nodded. Dean couldn't help notice her eyes dart sideways and for just a moment focus on something off screen.

'But that's why I always make sure eleven is free,' said Dean.

Vikki looked back down the camera and smiled a little too much. Immediately Dean got the sense that there was something going unsaid.

'Are you OK?' he asked quickly. 'The course and everything?'

'Course is fine. Great. Doing great,' said Vikki too quickly. 'To be honest I wanted to talk to you about the course.'

'Always interested,' said Dean, hoping he hadn't betrayed the sudden sick feeling that the phrase 'I wanted to talk' stirred up in him.

'It's the eleven o'clock thing,' said Vikki apologetically.

'I can do another time,' blurted Dean. 'Eleven o'clock was just the first time we got.'

Again Vikki's eyes glanced to the side and Dean could swear she gave the tiniest shake of her head to someone off frame.

Dean had been so excited for Vikki to go to London. True, he missed her like crazy, and true, there was a part of him that worried she'd never come back, but despite all that he loved her drive and ambition. He'd first met her when searching for her father Leon Walker – a notorious Manchester headcase who had set his sights on Malton. But long before Leon ended

31

up behind bars for life, Dean had fallen for Vikki. She was tough, resourceful and made Dean feel fearless.

Which was ironic because right now he was terrified.

'I still want to talk,' said Vikki. 'Just maybe not every day. I've got a lot on down here.'

'I get that,' said Dean. 'I'm run off my feet up here. There's a licensing thing and this job for a family called the Farrs and with Malton banged up . . .'

'Yeah,' said Vikki, only half listening. 'Look, I've got to go but I'll give you a ring later, OK?'

'Are you sure you're OK?' asked Dean. Even though he knew Leon Walker was locked away in Wakefield with all the worst monsters in the British Prison Estate, her father had made more than enough enemies in his time. Enemies who would think nothing of going after his daughter.

'It's fine,' said Vikki. Then just before she hung up she looked to the side again, about to say something, but the call cut out and Dean was left looking at the Skype interface.

Nothing of what he'd just seen made sense. He was pretty sure someone was there with Vikki. And she wanted to cut off contact? Or rather, scale it back. Was she in trouble? Was this something to do with her father? If she was in danger she knew she only had to say the word and he'd be driving down to London. Farrs be damned.

Or was he the one in trouble? Had it finally happened, had Vikki decided that she was staying in London? Staying in London with someone else?

Dean took another breath. This was too much. Vikki was in London. There was nothing he could do right now even if he knew what it was he was dealing with. However, the Farrs were right here in Manchester and breathing down his neck. One problem at a time.

If he could get the Farrs out of his hair then maybe he could take a couple of days off. Head down to London. Find out what was going on. But if he wanted to do that he needed to find those drugs.

32

Leaving the licensing paperwork on his desk, Dean pulled on his blue Ventile raincoat and headed out into the relentless Mancunian rain to talk to the last person who had handled the Farrs' missing drugs.

6

Mancunian Ways was an open-plan office spread across the upper floor of a small Victorian warehouse in the Northern Quarter. From her window Ruth used to be able to see Shudehill coach station but now a giant glass tower block obstructed the view. Every day Ruth now looked out on the face of new Manchester. Steel and glass and money. Manchester was growing almost by the week. Ruth felt the pace of change all around her and itched to be part of this new movement in the city.

The phone she'd found this morning was safely at the bottom of her bag. She'd already locked herself in the toilet and with trembling hands tried to turn it on, only to discover the battery was flat. She'd get a charger in her lunch break. Whether it was anything to do with the murder or simply a phone that had fallen from the pocket of a drunken nightclubber, Ruth suddenly felt energised.

First she took a brief look on Twitter and Instagram as well as trawling the city centre Facebook groups. It was enough to convince her that what she had seen this morning was a murder scene. The young officer moving her on had all but admitted it.

Across the office floor, various enthusiastic journalists wrote articles about new hamburger bars and pop-up boutiques while in the only private office on the floor, her boss Helen was still in some kind of meeting with someone Ruth recognised as an executive from their parent company down in London.

Ruth had managed to slip in without anyone noticing she was late. She set up in the corner of the open-plan office as far away as possible from her co-workers while, with her laptop angled so that only she could see her screen, she went over everything she'd already collected about this would-be serial killer.

There were eight men in all that she had found. All discovered within the city centre or thereabouts. The furthest out had been Gorton, which was only a five-minute drive out down Hyde Road. The oldest was twenty-six, the youngest only seventeen and they were all known to be drug users and sex workers.

A couple of them had been stabbed, four strangled, one beaten to death and one had been found in the canal in such a state that police hadn't released a cause of death.

What really excited Ruth was that, as yet, it seemed like no one else was looking at these deaths as being connected. There was no online talk about a serial killer. No one had put the pieces together. Yet.

She felt her heart racing as she spooled through her notes on her laptop. Maybe this *was* a podcast? Maybe this was what would get her out of *Mancunian Ways* and on to some proper journalism. Just like her dad.

There was one problem. Up until now she thought she had her killer. A few months ago the police had arrested a man called Craig Malton over in Liverpool and charged him with the murder of a boy called Stephen Page. Malton ran a security firm in Manchester but that was about all Ruth could find out about him. He didn't seem to exist anywhere online. That just made Ruth even more curious.

With Malton behind bars this new body brought up the prosaic possibility that the murders were simply unrelated. Bad things happening at random.

She gazed out of the window to where the giant glass column blocked the view and threw the entire street into shade. A two-bed apartment in the building cost four hundred thousand pounds. On what *Mancunian Ways* paid her she could never dream of owning somewhere like that.

None of her friends could. Creatives, bar staff, trainee teachers, even a junior doctor. Everyone she knew her own age was barely getting by. It cost most of your salary to rent in the city centre; buying was an impossibility. The young blood that made Manchester more than simply a collection of roads and buildings were being priced out of the very city that thrived on their vitality.

Then it hit her. The angle! What if Malton had been wrongly accused of murder? What if there was a serial killer and he was still out there? She could make a podcast about proving Malton's innocence. It could be the next *Serial!* Better, it would see her exposing the real killer.

'That doesn't look like "Ten Phrases Every Mancunian Will Know the Meaning Of",' said Helen, peering over Ruth's laptop.

Helen wasn't much older than Ruth, early thirties she guessed. Her hair was a dark auburn and hung in a neat, shoulder-length bob. Today she was wearing a blue chore jacket and matching work trousers over a ribbed T-shirt.

It wasn't that Helen wasn't a nice person; she was a journalist herself. But faced with managing the wafer-thin margins of a media start-up she had been forced to become the constant bearer of bad news.

Ruth instinctively shut the laptop. 'I've nearly finished,' she lied with a smile.

'It needs to go up in the next half hour,' said Helen without smiling. She turned to the office. 'That goes for everyone here. Three pieces a day is the new schedule. At least one up before lunch. OK?'

A listless chorus of voices rang out.

Helen continued. 'I've just been in with someone from head office. Our ad revenue is down this month. If that happens again then there's no other option but to look at staff cuts.'

Morbid silence hung in the air. Realising that perhaps she'd gone too far, Helen added, 'So let's show them what *Mancunian Ways* is made of!' to a few stray cheers.

'Done!' came a voice from the other side of the office. Ruth looked over. It was Damion. He always got his stories out first. The other month he'd had an interview with someone from the London office. There was talk of him moving down there.

'If Damion can do it so can the rest of you!' said Helen, and hurried back to her office, closing the door behind her to resume hearing more bad news from down in London.

Damion saw Ruth looking and smiled, embarrassed. He was a good-looking guy. He had that lantern-jawed, athletic thing that so many posh boys seemed to have. And with it an invincible confidence.

Ruth turned away and opened up her laptop. That had settled it. If her days at *Mancunian Ways* were numbered then she was going to jump before she was pushed. And what better parachute to land a brand-new job in than an award-winning podcast about Manchester's very own serial killer and the wrongful imprisonment of Craig Malton?

7

'Have you ever thought about self-harm or suicide?' said Governor Cunningham, sounding bored by her own questions.

While one overall senior governor ran the prison, beneath them were several junior governors, each in charge of their own area. Some ran wings, others oversaw aspects of the prison regime. Tricia Cunningham was the governor in charge of safeguarding. Something of a dark joke within the walls of Strangeways.

Malton didn't say a word. He sat quietly staring across the desk at Cunningham. As part of the ongoing attempt to fix the chronic levels of violence and criminality within Strangeways, all of the governors' offices had been moved on to the wings. Now the staff who ran the prison were locked up alongside the prisoners.

'One of those boys is going to need long-term rehabilitation,' said Cunningham, changing tack.

Malton knew exactly what he'd be needing. He'd been in that cell when they came for him and he'd shown them just what a bad idea that was. Outside, Malton would have held back. He would have talked those boys down. Let them imagine the fate that would befall them if they really did try and attack him. Outside, it seemed like a failure to resort to violence.

Inside was a different story. Malton had stamped down on the kneecap of the lead boy, crippling him instantly. Then he'd stepped over the screaming body, grabbed the next boy by the back of the head and pulled his face down into Malton's knee. The lad's face exploded in snot, blood and teeth, by which point all that was left was a weeping young man, limply holding out his makeshift weapon, too scared to use it. Malton had let him go. It never hurt to have someone to spread the word about what happens if you stepped to Craig Malton.

'Lucky for you it happened in your cell,' said Cunningham. 'Hard to argue against self-defence when they come looking for you.'

Cunningham gave a little smile. She was in her late thirties. In another life Malton could imagine her as the kind of high-maintenance woman who got up an hour early to do her hair. She was still striking and obviously worked out. But whatever vanity Cunningham had she left on the other side of the thick, brick walls. Her hair was pulled back in a pony-tail, her face scrubbed clean.

'As governor for safeguarding, it's my job to pick up on vulnerable prisoners before things get out of hand,' she said. 'I gather from intelligence that Mickey Farr has some kind of issue with you?'

Malton said nothing. Inside or out, some things never changed. You don't grass.

'Mickey's quite a handful. You don't want to be on the wrong side of someone like him,' said Cunningham, aiming for an encouraging tone.

Malton silently shrugged.

Finally Cunningham tried becoming stern. 'Thing is, I know you're not in any danger. I've visited the infirmary, seen what you did to those two lads. That third lad? He wasn't hard to find – just follow the trail. He was so scared he shit himself.'

Cunningham couldn't help giving a small smile. Malton recognised it for what it was: the coping mechanism of some-one who works knee-deep in human misery and has to find the funny side in the darkness or else they'd never be able to get up in the morning.

Malton had never seen the funny side. He remembered being a kid back in Moss Side and being teased about his alcoholic father and absent mother. As far as Malton was con-cerned, in life, there was nothing to laugh about.

Cunningham looked Malton up and down from the other side of the desk. In the silence Malton became aware of the prison noise. It never stopped; you just got used to it, zoned it out when you needed to. He could smell Cunningham's antiperspirant. She wouldn't wear perfume, not in a prison – that was asking for it. But in amongst the stink of shit and piss and blood and vermin that made up Strangeways, the gentle feminine fragrance was like an oasis.

'I can put you in the VPU,' said Cunningham, breaking the silence.

Malton's jaw clenched. The VPU. Vulnerable Prisoners Unit. Home to the snitches and the child molesters. The prisoners who even their fellow convicts despised.

He saw Cunningham reading his reaction. Whatever else Cunningham was, she wasn't a lightweight. She knew how a prison worked and wasn't afraid to get her hands dirty.

'I'm not in danger,' said Malton plainly.

'I'm thinking more about the rest of S Wing,' said Cunningham.

She let that hang for a moment before standing up and blowing out her cheeks.

'But for now let's just see how it goes, eh?'

Malton stood up to leave.

'Oh, before you go,' said Cunningham. 'That young journalist has been back in touch asking to speak to you. Apparently now she doesn't think you're some kind of serial killer. Thinks you might be innocent.'

'No visitors,' said Malton flatly.

'OK. Most of the guys in here would love to sit down with a pretty young thing and brag about all the stuff they got up to. Plead their case.'

'No visitors,' said Malton and turned to go.

Malton headed along S Wing, past rows of doors on either side and on to the staircases that took him all the way up to his cell on the third-floor landing. The sound of the rain hammering against the outside of the building filled the space, echoing off the whitewashed brick walls.

The thought of talking to the press appalled Malton. He knew he was innocent. Being in prison for something he didn't do didn't bother him. What bothered him was just how used to being inside he was getting and how, with every passing day, the outside world became less and less real. Outside, James was still dead. His killers still at large and Malton powerless to find them.

But inside, all he had to do was survive.

'Hello, sunshine!' a voice rang out from the third-floor landing.

Malton looked up to see a small, compact man in his sixties – with a face that had never lost its boyish mischief – leaning over the railings.

'Be seeing you around, pal,' said Mickey Farr and gave Malton a wink.

8

It had been raining the day Keisha left Manchester. It was raining the day she returned. Grey, sullen skies pouring forth a seemingly unending torrent of water over the city. Rain washing over stone and brick and glass, cascading over broken pavements and collecting in the potholes of the fractured streets.

From her room high up in the Midland Hotel, Keisha looked out over St Peter's Square. Down below, bodies hurried across the open spaces, making for the relative cover of the tram stop. A handful of figures stood dotted about, oblivious and immobile as the rain came down around them.

The rain was still there but everything else had changed. The offices built where once the Odeon cinema squatted now loomed over the square, taller even than Manchester Town Hall across the other side of the precinct. The war memorial had been moved out of the way of the new tram platforms to where it now stood just behind the town hall, thronged with soggy garlands of paper poppies. Even the library had got in on the act, wrapping itself with a brand-new glass walkway to cover the alley between itself and the town hall.

Keisha turned back to her room. It felt like an affront to know that Manchester, however much she had rejected it, had continued in her absence. Time moved on as if the city didn't even need Keisha Bistacchi.

Keisha pulled the blanket she'd taken from the bed tighter around her shoulders. She hadn't expected the cold to be quite so much of a shock. The feeling of being warm to her bones was already a distant memory.

She crossed over to the desk and helped herself to a chip from the meal she'd had room service bring up.

Keisha had never stayed in the Midland. She never had a reason to. But growing up in Manchester she knew it was there – a gigantic, grand hotel bedecked in ornate, Victorian detail that promised something impossibly opulent within. In all her time in the city she'd avoided the Midland. It seemed like something from another time. She went to the boutique hotels, she drank in the bars halfway up brand-new skyscrapers and ate in restaurants opened by footballers and Michelin-starred chefs. Keisha chased the elusive vision of what Manchester was becoming and never had time for anything as stolid as the Midland.

But when she was booking her return, suddenly she was seized with the desire to stay there. To find something of the Manchester she remembered. The bars and restaurants and boutique hotels had come and gone but the Midland was still standing. That spoke to Keisha.

The paperwork from the solicitor covered the desk. He hadn't been able to add much more than what he'd said on the phone. Harold Boateng had died in a car accident and Keisha had been named as the executor of his estate.

The details were sparse. Harold had been living somewhere on the coast. There was no one else mentioned in his will. Only Keisha. The man who had walked out on her when she was still a child had never forgotten her. So why had he never got in touch? Why had he let her mum struggle alone? Why hadn't he been there for her?

More importantly, after all this time why had he picked Keisha to settle up his affairs?

Keisha had long ago cut her father out of her heart and cauterised the wound. She didn't need nor want him. But something about his sudden reappearance intrigued her. Could this be what was missing back in Ibiza? Every other part of her life in Manchester had been wound up, packed away or buried somewhere no one would ever find it. Was this the last loose end?

Keisha shivered. Even with the radiators on full blast it felt cold. The rain hammered on the window. It sounded like someone throwing bucketfuls against the pane. It was like the world was trying to wash Manchester off the face of the earth.

As far as Keisha was concerned that was no bad thing. There was nothing left here for her. As soon as she'd sorted out her dad's estate she'd be gone and never look back.

But first she had to claim his body.

9

Ruth scrambled to turn the phone volume down as it beeped again and again with incoming messages.

She'd headed out at lunch to the small phone shop round the corner where, behind a counter thronged with phone cases of every imaginable colour, the young man was more than happy to help her locate an appropriate charger as well as asking her if she was single.

Returning to the office having lied about an imaginary boyfriend, Ruth left the phone to charge for the rest of her lunch break, meaning to head to the toilets for the last ten minutes of lunch to try and turn it on.

As it was, she'd got caught up in a lively debate about whether or not there were too many middle-aged people going to raves at the Mayfield Depot. Everyone in the office, it seemed, had a cache of candid shots they'd taken of various over-thirties gurning and sweating their way through into the early hours, surrounded by a sea of people at least a decade younger.

So, by the time Helen emerged from her office to chase everyone back to work, Ruth had run out of time.

It took all her patience to wait another fifteen minutes before sneaking off to the toilet with the phone.

The toilet was a large room with a lock on the door and the toilet in one corner. Ruth hated using the office toilet. The room was freezing and the paper translucently thin. Worse, with the toilet in one corner away from the door, she could never quite relax without imagining she'd forgotten to turn the lock and someone was about to walk in and find her with her knickers down on the other side of the room.

45

This time she made sure she'd locked the door before she turned the phone on. Her heart was vibrating nearly as hard as the phone as message after message came up.

It had only occurred to her while shopping for a charger that if this phone did indeed have something to do with a murder, not only had she taken it from a crime scene, but now her prints were all over it. But the voice of reason was barely audible up against the excitement Ruth felt about this potentially explosive lead.

Telling herself that, if need be, she could wipe it clean and drop it back where she found it, Ruth opened the phone with a simple swipe and began to dig through this treasure trove of clues.

Almost instantly, she felt sick to her stomach.

JAKE, WHERE ARE YOU?

YOU BACK YET?

NOT HEARD FROM YOU. YOU OK?

JAKE I'M WORRIED CALL ME.

As they piled up, the messages became more frantic.

JAKE, YOU DICKHEAD TURN ON YOUR PHONE NOW!

WHERE THE FUCK ARE YOU?

PLEASE JUST CALL.

JAKE?

At least five different numbers sending over twenty messages. All of them asking where whoever owned the phone was. Like they were expecting him back. Whoever Jake was, there were a lot of people very worried about him.

Ruth thought back to the white tent over in Piccadilly Basin.

'Are you in there?' came Damion's voice through the door.

'Just a minute,' shouted Ruth. Even though she wasn't actually on the toilet, it felt embarrassing to be caught in here by Damion.

'I can wait,' joked Damion from behind the door.

Without much time left, Ruth scrolled past all the incoming messages, looking for the last thing sent by Jake.

The messages asking if Jake was OK started coming in around eleven o'clock the night before.

Two hours before that, Jake had sent his last message. It was a photo.

It looked like it was taken in a hotel room. A man taken from behind as he walked into the bathroom. It didn't look like he knew his photo was being taken. For one thing, he was facing the other way. For another, he was naked.

Ruth clicked on the photo and it filled the phone screen.

'Are you going to be much longer?' said Damion through the door.

Ruth ignored him. She was too busy looking at the photo. There was a mirror in the bathroom and if she enlarged the picture just enough she could see the face of the naked man, looking right back at her.

10

Despite having an entire company to run, a workforce of over fifty bodies to manage, a girlfriend in London who may or may not be about to dump him and a boss who was locked up for murder and refusing to take his calls, Dean found his mind perfectly clear. Thanks to his morning visit to the Farrs, he was focused on one thing and one thing only: finding the Farrs' missing drugs.

There are several stages between the hidden cocaine factories of South America and the streets of the UK. Each stage brings with it its own risk and its own experts willing to take those risks for the right price. While the Farrs' supplier had direct connections to cocaine producers in Venezuela, he had no desire whatsoever to get involved in the business of smuggling the product into the country. That was a totally different set of skills with a totally different set of pitfalls.

Hence the Farrs and their tyre garage and the courier they employed to take all the risk, handling the product. An air-gap in the fractured supply chain of international narcotics. The courier had dealt exclusively with Martin Farr and Martin had known him only as Ray. Ray, a fall guy who, should the police ever discover something amiss, would take the heat while the Farrs could very convincingly plead ignorance. It was simple but effective.

Of course there was the chance that, if arrested and threatened with a double-digit jail term, Ray might turn on the Farrs, but for the Farrs that was an acceptable risk when placed against the hundreds of thousands of pounds profit. It didn't hurt that this Ray would know exactly what kind of retribution awaited him should he decide to turn on the Farrs.

Whoever had robbed Ray either didn't know or didn't care.

If Malton had been around, Ray would have been the first person he'd have looked into. It made sense. An inside job. The courier sets up the robbery, plays dumb and takes a cut. It was obvious to the point of cliché. But with all the other demands on Dean's time, following up that lead had simply not happened. Until now.

Janet Farr had given Dean an address and not much else. As per the arrangement the only thing the Farr's knew about their courier was the name 'Ray' and the address where they had arranged to store the drugs.

That address was a house just off Langworthy Road in Salford. A strange, once-new estate built on the road to the local tip. Formerly pristine new houses, now overgrown and isolated, stuck between the terraces of Langworthy Road and the brownfield debris that surrounded the tip.

According to Janet, when the drugs went missing the Farrs were thinking along the exact same lines. Find Ray, find the drugs. But after Carl had been sent round to kick the door off the hinges and ask some very rough questions, he'd discovered the house empty.

Dean just hoped that he could find something that had slipped the forensic attention of Carl Farr. Having met Carl, he was optimistic.

It was easy enough to find the house. The front door had been replaced with a metal screen by the council, screwed into the frame around the door.

Dean parked across the road and, in the driving rain, made his way over to the house. Since taking over running Malton Security, Dean had begun driving a dark blue BMW owned by the business. It was powerful but old, the interior starting to look a little shabby, but as far as Dean was concerned it was like driving around in a palace.

For once Dean was glad of the rain. This was already a remote bit of Salford with no reason for anyone to linger any longer than they absolutely had to. With the addition of driving rain he could be sure that no one was watching as he kicked open the flimsy gate round the side of the house and made his way to the back of the property.

The garden was small, the grass nearly head height, and several black bin liners had been dumped in one corner. One of the panels that made up the fence surrounding the garden had been kicked out, revealing the scrubland beyond the back of the houses. Dean wondered if that was someone getting in or someone making themselves a discreet way out.

Already he was feeling better. This was why he did this job. The thrill of intruding into the unseen parts of the city. The bits that hadn't got the memo about a thrusting new future. Salford had always been a few steps behind Manchester, but now with the Quays and the Lowry and the development on the edge of the city boundaries, it was running to catch up.

And just like its more prosperous neighbour, beneath the surface were hundreds of thousands of secrets, all boiling away waiting to be dragged into the light.

Keeping close to the house, Dean reached the French windows and removed the hammer from his pocket. From the age of the houses he'd guessed the locks would have a plastic surround to the handles, a critical weakness that could easily be exploited. Without hesitation he took the hammer and smashed the rectangular plastic cover that encircled the handles of the door. He was halfway to smashing it out when the entire lock mechanism simply fell away, still attached to the plastic.

Dean turned the handle and slipped inside. He wasn't ready for what he found.

Nothing.

First the back room, then the dining room and kitchen. The whole house was furnished. Every room was immaculate. There were signs in the hallway of Carl Farr kicking the door open but apart from that everything was untouched. It was like a show home. Nothing on the walls, no food in the cupboards, no milk in the fridge, no books or records. Nothing.

Dean stood still in the hallway and listened. Despite the rain, the sound of him breaking in would have carried through the house. If there was anyone there they'd have heard.

Dean heard only silence.

This was the right address. The front door was missing. This is where Janet Farr believed the courier lived and yet, from what Dean had found, it was like no one had ever been here.

The bathroom was just as clean as downstairs but finally in the front bedroom Dean found something. The bed was unmade. Someone *had* slept here.

He walked over and put his hands on the sheets. They were cold. Whoever left this bed, they didn't do so recently.

Dean crossed the room and opened the free-standing cupboard in one corner. Like all the furniture in the house, it was neat and new and didn't quite fit. As if the entire house had been furnished by someone who wasn't planning to ever stay there any length of time but needed to at least keep up appearances.

There, hanging up in the cupboard, was an old, blue anorak.

Dean was taking it off the hanger when he heard the unmistakable metallic clink of keys. He started rifling through the pockets. As he did so, he noticed it smelled faintly of laundry; whoever had worn it had washed it. Kept it neat just like the rest of the house.

He found the keys in the front pocket. A whole bunch. The other pockets yielded some loose change and a receipt and that was it.

Dean stood in the middle of the bedroom floor and examined the keys. There were a couple that looked like they could have been keys to the door Carl kicked in. One of them had its own fob with M7 written on it. Dean wondered what M7 could refer to. Maybe a safety deposit box? But finding out which one based on a two-digit reference was as good as impossible. More promising, there was an electronic car key.

Dean wandered to the window and looked out on the street. There were several cars parked on the road, as well as his own. He held up the keys and pressed the unlock button. Two doors down, a red Toyota Yaris winked its lights back at him.

***

Dean stood in the rain looking at the car. An unremarkable Toyota. The perfect car to anonymously ferry hundreds of thousands of pounds of drugs in.

Walking to the side that faced away from the house, Dean saw something he hadn't initially seen in the rain. The passenger-side window was missing. Someone had taped a black bin liner over the empty gap in the door.

Janet had said that the courier had been held up at gunpoint by two masked men. They'd boxed Ray in, dragged him out and taken the drugs.

Looking at the makeshift repair, Dean wondered if they'd smashed the window doing it.

Taking a quick look round to confirm he was the only person stupid enough to be out in this weather, Dean set to the repair and quickly peeled away the black plastic.

The interior of the car smelled like the house had. Clean, neutral. Not new but definitely cared for. From what Janet had said the courier was an older man. Who would suspect a retiree in a neat Toyota? Even with a broken window. And then there were the modifications that Carl had made to the car.

Dean leaned in, opened the door and climbed in.

He didn't have time to enjoy being out of the rain. Working quickly, he remembered what Janet Farr had told him and turned the air conditioning button all the way to the left before pulling on it hard.

Rather than coming off in his hand the button had weight to it. Dean could feel something connected to it as he pulled it out nearly an inch before he heard a solid thud and a hidden shelf dropped down from under the passenger's side of the dashboard.

This was the hidden compartment that Janet said Carl had put in the car. It wouldn't stay hidden if police stripped the car down but as long as the courier kept his nerve it was more than enough for a casual search.

It was empty.

Dean didn't think he'd have found it without Janet's help. So how did the robbers know it was there? Had the courier given it up?

He leaned over, closed the compartment and sat for a moment thinking.

Wherever Ray was, he'd left the car. Whoever robbed him had found the secret compartment. Or perhaps they already knew about it. In fact, they knew everything. They knew the car he drove; they knew his routes.

But still they'd smashed the window.

Dean had a thought. He leaned forwards and very carefully felt the carpet in the footwell with his fingertips.

It didn't take long to find what he was looking for. First one, then two then several small cube-like shards of broken window.

Taking immense care not to cut himself on the broken glass, Dean gathered up all the shards and laid them out on the dashboard.

Then he got out his phone, turned on the torch and crossed his fingers.

Shining the light on the bits of broken window, Dean saw what he was looking for. They were covered in dried blood.

The blood of whoever had smashed the window to rob the courier.

11

Malton never forgot the feeling of James's body against his own. Unlike Malton, James was slight, skinny even. But when he held James close that first time, he was shocked at how strong he felt. A lifetime of poverty, which had come to an end with the unnerving rise of his brother Callum through the criminal ranks of Merseyside, had kept James lean but tough.

Lying there next to James, Malton felt like he'd found a kindred spirit. Someone who, forged by circumstance into a dogged survivor, was now doing their best to become some-one new. Someone better.

James had been a club promoter. Going from small, cli-quey gay nights to full-blown student clubs. Backed with the money and reputation of his brother, James had made the city his own. While Callum threatened you, James made you fall in love with him.

He was funny and generous and brought any room to life.

He was also long dead.

But if Malton closed his eyes for a few seconds then he could nearly trick himself that the young man who was lying next to him in his cell was James.

It only lasted a few seconds. It was impossible for Malton to think of James without thinking back to how he found him. He'd been kept alive as long as possible. Made to suffer in a way that had no equal.

At the sight of it, Malton felt like he had somehow absorbed all of James's pain. A pain he carried around, stored away for the day when he got to pay it back.

The young man lying on the bed next to him was Connor. He was nineteen. He'd been caught red-handed stealing from one of the houses built along the canal in Ancoats. Ten years ago the canal was home to junkies and muggers. Today it was lined with properties worth millions. What was Connor meant to do?

He had been in prison for nearly a year, in which time he'd dried out in the drugs-free wing and then been moved into S Wing where he met Malton.

Malton wasn't looking for a relationship. People who got close to Malton had a bad habit of ending up dead or worse. But Connor had sought Malton out. As if attracted to Malton's air of defiant solitude.

Outside, Malton wouldn't have given the time of day to someone like Connor. He was just a kid. And he was loud too. James was loud but he knew when to shut up. Connor had no such survival instincts. He walked the wing with a reckless disregard for his own safety. Teasing, bullshitting and flirting.

Malton wrapped an arm around Connor. He felt the sharp outline of Connor's back against his bare chest. He knew Connor wasn't asleep but neither of them much wanted to talk. They'd just had sex, and in the post-coital come-down, Malton was experiencing a rare moment of clarity.

His mind was back on the outside. The hand-to-mouth survival of prison was gone and instead he was roaming far and wide over Manchester. Freed from the walls of his cell, he turned over the events that had brought him here.

He'd been tracking down the first solid lead he'd had on James's killers in over a decade. A single line of a witness statement. A second-hand report of a prison confession. But it was enough to send Malton tearing through Liverpool.

Malton dealt with the street. With paid rumours and extracted confessions. The information he worked with was earned with trust and violence. In the normal course of things he'd never have access to court documents, much less the time or inclination to trawl through them looking for clues. The lead had come from Bea Wallace, a deceptively ruthless legal genius, lawyer to some of the heaviest figures in the Manchester underworld and Malton's former lover.

The prospect of a solid lead after all this time had overwhelmed Malton. He did something he never normally did. He put his trust in someone. Took Bea at her word and followed that clue all the way to Liverpool and the pub where he'd been arrested at gunpoint.

Since then he'd had ample time, locked up in Strangeways, to think about that clue. About the chances of Bea coming across it. About how convenient it had been for Bea to have something like that to hold over him. To lead him on, to manipulate him with.

If he ever got out he would be having words with Bea Wallace.

But Bea was the least of his problems. While he was away chasing shadows in Liverpool a youth named Stephen Page had been murdered in East Manchester. Strangled and left in the back seat of a minicab. Slumped over in full view. Malton had never met Stephen, never been in the minicab where he was found but somehow his DNA was in that car. His and his alone.

A minicab should be a nightmare for forensics but someone had made sure it was spotless save for hair matched to Malton.

It wouldn't even have got that far if there wasn't a witness. A confidential police informant had placed Malton in the cab. Led the police to what was clearly a staged scene.

The rest was history.

'What you thinking?' said Connor, not turning around. He was from Moston, his accent a bastardised mixture of Oldham and Manchester. Always with a soft charm underneath. As much as it surprised him, Malton found himself getting very fond of Connor these past few months.

He held Connor tighter and the clarity began to fade as the noise of Strangeways reasserted itself. The hollering, shouting, screaming pageant of madness.

Before Malton could answer there was a knocking at the door. By now the guards had worked out that, for the sake of making their lives easier, it was better to have Malton onside than against them.

Malton got up, shrugging off Connor without a second thought.

'I was only asking,' complained Connor wryly.

Malton pulled on a sweatshirt and went to answer the door, ignoring Connor completely.

The outside world was gone again. All that existed was within the walls of Strangeways.

***

He opened the door to see a young officer looking nervous. He was not much older than Connor.

'Sorry to interrupt,' he said, Malton's look causing him to immediately regret his choice of words. 'I mean . . .' he stammered.

Malton didn't say anything – he just stared, leveraging the silence to leave the officer in no doubt where the power lay.

The guard swallowed and composed himself before he said, 'You've got a visitor.'

12

The man on the table in front of her was dead. But all Keisha could see was the staff member, standing solemnly in the corner, his hands crossed in front of him, his head bowed.

He was the man who had come to meet her at the reception of the Clinical Sciences Building, one of several university and research buildings on the Manchester Royal Infirmary Campus. After confirming her details he had offered his condolences and led her to the room where her father's remains were waiting.

That morning, before coming to view her father, Keisha had a taxi take her out in the driving rain to Selfridges where she spent a couple of thousand getting some more suitable clothing.

She now wore some expensively distressed jeans and a thick, shaggy jumper in a muted grey. Over the top she'd gone for a man's heavy parka with a hood large enough to fit her hair. She'd bought three identical pairs of black Nike Air Force trainers, one pair of which she was now wearing.

The cold and the rain and the circumstances of her visit sapped any enthusiasm Keisha might have had for dressing up for the occasion. She wanted to be warm and dry and gone as soon as possible.

Outside the room the attendant had warned Keisha about the injuries her father had sustained in the crash. The car had run him over as he was crossing a road. He'd been sent flying while the driver had carried straight on. Police had yet to trace them. The upshot – what was left of Harold Boateng wasn't pretty. She waited quietly until he'd finished before confirming that she still wanted to see him.

Whether it was the building or the rain or the cold or knowing that the father she hadn't seen in over forty years was lying dead in the next room, Keisha didn't argue, didn't make demands. She just let herself be shown into the room.

But then the attendant had followed her. And now he was standing there in the corner. Wearing green hospital scrubs. His lanyard was in Manchester United colours. On his feet were scuffed-up Crocs and he hadn't shaved that morning.

The moment she'd waited for all these years and all she could see was that man.

Harold lay on the slab but somehow he kept slipping in and out of Keisha's vision. As if when she looked at him her mind instantly blanked out what she saw. Instead she kept going back to the man in the corner. The man intruding on her moment. The man who hadn't even bothered to shave this morning of all mornings. The day when he would be tasked with taking Keisha to see her dead father.

She closed her eyes for a moment and swallowed hard. She could smell the room. The polite, neutral, disinfected air.

She opened her eyes and calmly said, 'I'm here to see my fucking dad. He's fucking dead so I don't know what you think I'm going to get up to in here on my own, but if you don't get the fuck out right now you're going to be joining him on that fucking slab. Do you understand what I'm saying?'

The attendant looked lost. His eyes went from side to side, looking for help that wasn't coming.

'I asked you a fucking question,' growled Keisha.

'I'm sorry,' blurted out the man, already halfway to the door.

'You'll know I'm done 'cos I'll be fucking done,' said Keisha after him.

Finally she was alone in the room. Her heart was racing. She didn't usually talk to strangers like that. Losing her temper wasn't a victory she was willing to give to anyone. Least of all some jumped-up hospital porter. But she had snapped and got what she wanted.

She was alone with her father.

59

Finally, she turned to face the table.

Harold looked old; his dark skin had a grey tinge to it, the hair on his head run through with silver and white. His lower half was covered with a sheet, but from what Keisha could see, the accident had been severe.

Harold's right arm had been discreetly covered with its own blanket while his face was still swollen and bruised.

Keisha took a breath and approached the table.

Despite the years and the damage, the face that looked up at her was her own. There were her nose and her lips. There was the delicate chin. There was her blackness.

Before she knew what she was doing she was reaching out to touch him.

His skin was cold but somehow that felt right. Like touching a photograph. It didn't feel like Harold was still here but instead this artefact that looked like he once did. Something inert and dead that would require something from Keisha to bring it to life.

She closed her eyes and struggled to reanimate him in her mind. Her memories were so old. So much had happened since he left. Her mother had raised her single-handed, filled her with joy and confidence and passion. She'd gone out and made Manchester her own. But there, right at the start, lingered this man. The man who had left her and now had finally found her again.

Keisha opened her eyes. There was nothing. This was just a dead old man. Whatever reasons he had for making her his executor were his and his alone.

Keisha had never needed him and she didn't need him now.

All that was left was to put him in the ground and leave this city for good.

13

'Can you believe the queue? It's all these lazy bastards getting their McDonald's on Just Eat, jamming up the kitchen.'

The woman in the driving seat next to Dean hammered the horn of her black Peugeot 208 to no obvious effect on the line of cars slowly crawling into the drive-thru. Dean cringed a little but DI Benton seemed oblivious.

Benton was Malton's police contact. They went way back, further than Dean dared ask and much further than Malton had ever offered to elaborate on. Benton had a love-hate relationship with the Greater Manchester Police. She loved working for them and they hated her. Luckily for Benton she was far too good at what she did to be side-lined, no matter how hard they tried.

Benton had told Dean to meet her at the Fort retail park in Cheetham Hill. Where once had stood a crumbling disaster of urban planning – ironically nicknamed 'The Fort' by locals – now stood a giant retail park, slowly sucking what blood was left out of the city centre.

Waiting in his car, he'd got the call to come and meet Benton in the queue for the McDonald's drive-thru. Dean had dutifully got back out into the rain and with his collar turned up in a futile gesture against the elements, had waded across the car park to find Benton's car in a long line of vehicles that spilled out into the nearby road, blocking the oncoming traffic.

Benton's car was roasting hot. The heating had been turned all the way up. Dean was beginning to steam.

'Hope you don't mind a bit of a working lunch,' said Benton, inching her car forward in line.

Benton was wearing a dark green fleece top over a white shirt and cheap-looking office trousers. It looked like she was growing her hair out. Or hadn't had time to deal with it. Benton cut her own hair.

'It's not a problem,' said Dean. He needed a favour from Benton and was in no position to complain.

'To be honest, I'm amazed you're still doing this,' said Benton, turning to Dean.

'This case?'

'No. Any of it. I know you're a clever lad. And believe me, I know you don't mind getting your hands dirty, but why bother?'

'I need to keep things going. For when Malton gets out,' said Dean honestly.

Benton shook her head. 'You spoken to him since he went in?'

Dean looked away, embarrassed.

'Me neither,' said Benton. 'He'd already gone off the deep end, pissing off to Liverpool chasing ghosts. Now he's banged up, it's like he's a different person.'

'Maybe,' said Dean. 'Or maybe it's deliberate. Damage control. He's in there so why get messed up with what's happening out here?'

Benton smiled condescendingly. 'He's really done a number on you, hasn't he?'

The car in front started to move. Benton impatiently ground the accelerator down and they moved forward a few inches, her car filling with the toxic smell of a burning clutch.

'What you do,' said Benton, 'why not just do it for someone legit? Someone who doesn't work for the kind of fuck-ups Craig does. He does his thing. Did his thing,' she corrected herself. ''Cos that's who he is. It's his world. It's not yours.'

Dean knew everything she said made sense, but there was more to it than that. He loved working for Malton. Dean's teenage years were spent fucking up at school and bouncing through shitty jobs to help his mum pay for the tiny flat they had moved into after his parents divorced. He was adrift. Malton had not just given him purpose, he'd also given him a sense of pride. He had started to see Manchester just how Malton saw it. A sordid series of interconnecting deals, favours, threats and bribes. A messy, complicit tangle of self-interest and venality. Dean couldn't get enough.

Benton sensed Dean's silence and said, 'But I'm guessing you didn't come to me for career advice. What you got for me?'

Dean dug in his pocket and produced a bag containing the shards of glass.

'Please don't tell me you're going to ask me to run some DNA,' said Benton as she edged ever closer to the speaker where she could place her order.

Dean frowned. 'I need you to run some DNA.'

Benton shook her head. 'So what's in it for me? Apart from buying my lunch, obviously.'

'What you want?'

Benton thought for a moment.

'You know what, love? 'Cos it's you, and 'cos I'm getting soft in my old age, let's just say I've got a massive favour on account.'

'Whatever you need,' said Dean quickly.

Benton laughed. 'Bless. I mean with the big man. Once he gets out. If he ever gets out.'

'He's innocent,' said Dean.

'Never stopped GMP before,' said Benton jauntily. 'Whose blood is this?' said Benton, holding up the plastic bag of broken glass.

Dean quickly went through all the details in his head, removing anything incriminating.

'A family who buy product in bulk. From overseas. Got their own route into the country. Someone robbed them. I think that blood might be the robber.'

'Well,' said Benton. 'Sounds like you're a very busy boy running around taking care of Craig's business while he's on his hols in Strangeways. Hope you're making time for that girl-friend of yours. What's she doing up in London again?'

'Fashion,' said Dean. He'd not thought about Vikki all morning and now suddenly she came rushing back. The look on her face when she'd told him she wanted to call a halt to their daily calls. The strong impression he had that someone was there with her. Things that Dean didn't have the time or energy to worry about started to fill his head.

Benton was still talking, oblivious, 'Fashion? Interesting. Always need people at Primark. Send her my love. Actually, don't. Fewer people know I'm spending my time with the likes of you, the better.' She laughed at her own joke and then, sensing Dean wasn't quite as amused, added, 'Soon as I get something on this blood I'll let you know. You just keep me in the loop yeah?'

Dean knew he could trust Benton. But he also knew that DNA would take time. Benton would have to contrive a reason to search for it. Every time she did Malton a favour she put herself at risk. In her own way she was just like Malton. Doing whatever it took to get the job done. While Malton did it for money and reputation, Benton did it out of a genuine sense of justice.

It made him feel guilty about not telling her the other lead he'd found in the house. At first the keys had him stumped but then he thought to check on the receipt. Once he saw where it was from, suddenly the fob with M7 written on it made complete sense.

They finally reached the speaker. Benton wound down her window.

'Can I take your order?' said a fuzzy voice through the rain and static.

'Two Quarter Pounder with Cheese Meals, large, Coke, two apple pies.' As an afterthought, she turned to Dean and said, 'You want anything?'

14

'I need you to confirm for the tape that you have refused legal representation.'

It had been nearly a month since Malton had last seen DCI Priestly. He was young for a DCI. Priestly had the polite air of someone who'd never been the kind of places Malton had been. Never made the kind of hard choices Malton had made.

It was Priestly who'd led the operation to arrest him in Liverpool. An operation that ended up with a kid getting shot dead. Apparently Priestly had managed to sidestep that particular clusterfuck and convince the CPS to charge Malton with murder.

'I don't want legal representation,' said Malton. He didn't need it. He was already in prison. Already charged with murder. A lawyer just meant someone else he'd have to trust and, after what had happened with Bea, Malton wasn't in the mood to trust anyone anymore.

'OK,' said Priestly warily. 'I've come here today to give you a final chance to put forward your side of the story.'

As a DCI, Priestly was already one foot out of the door of day-to-day policing. Malton knew that for a DCI to be talking to him in person there must be something more going on.

But he stayed silent. The prison interview rooms had been recently refurbished. They still smelled faintly of new carpet. Malton wondered how long it would be before they smelled just like every other inch of Strangeways.

Priestly continued, 'Stephen Page, aged nineteen, was found dead in a white Ford Tourneo parked up in Collyhurst on the 17th of November last year.'

Priestly paused again. Malton wondered if he honestly expected him to talk.

'He had been manually strangled and his body left propped up on the back seat. A witness places you in that car and subsequent forensic investigation found your DNA in that car.'

Priestly stopped again. Malton didn't dignify the silence with a response.

'Bear in mind that if you choose to plead guilty pre-trial that will significantly affect your sentencing options.'

Malton knew this was a lie. No one is ever in the mood to excuse an honest murderer. Besides, he was innocent.

'Can you account for your DNA being in that car?'

Malton said nothing.

'Can you account for the witness placing you in that car?'

'What's his name?' said Malton, finally speaking even though he already knew the answer.

'The witness is a confidential police informant and as such I'm not at liberty to disclose his identity.'

Malton knew how it looked. When Stephen was murdered, Malton had been AWOL in Liverpool. Alone and out of contact with anyone as he chased down the lead into James's murder. But he also knew how the law worked. He'd spent enough of his life staying just the right side of the line.

He leaned forward and fixed Priestly in the eye. 'CPS have charged me with murder. Whatever you told them, they thought there was a case to answer. That you've come back now, a DCI no less, to ask me this tells me that maybe what you told them wasn't quite as watertight as maybe you made it out to be.'

Priestly swallowed and tried to speak but Malton cut him off.

'Your case rests on the word of a grass, a grass who can't tell you how, when or where I met Stephen Page. And with some DNA evidence. Body hair. Not blood, not spit, not semen or even skin cells. Body hair. The DNA that anyone who had access to me could have conceivably obtained. There's no

CCTV putting me at the scene. There's no other witnesses. There's nothing to connect me to Stephen Page. And, when you came to arrest me, your boys with MP5s shot a kid dead.'

The furore over the shooting had easily eclipsed Malton's arrest. With the police not releasing any details to the press, the shooting had dominated the news until the next atrocity. Malton's arrest had passed almost unnoticed.

Priestly made a valiant attempt to look unruffled. 'Are you claiming that someone is setting you up?' said Priestly indignantly.

Malton shook his head. 'If I were you I'd be more worried about who's setting you up.'

15

The walls of the Nag's Head were covered in framed photographs. Every inch of space taken up with photos of old Manchester, football memorabilia and seemingly whatever the landlords could get their hands on.

It took all of Ruth's resolve not to check the phone sitting at the bottom of her bag. Throughout the afternoon the messages kept coming for Jake. Going from the panicked urgency of the night before to a weary resignation, as if whoever was sending them knew exactly what had happened.

From the tone of the messages and the photos she'd found on the phone she had begun to piece together a picture of who he was.

Jake Arnold was a teenager, barely out of school, long, curly hair, shaved at the sides and a cute face with chubby lips and a button nose. There were hundreds of selfies. Some clothed, many more naked and even explicit. Jake was into drugs. He was into sex work. He was into a lot of dark places. Scrolling through his phone, Ruth felt a pang of guilt at what she was doing. Intruding on the privacy of someone she hadn't even met. Someone who, deep down, she knew at that very moment was lying dead in the mortuary.

At the back of her mind, looming over it all, was that face in the hotel mirror. The body was toned and tanned, youthful even. But the face was very different. The face told on the body. The skin was brittle and thin, lines worn into the tanned flesh. The eyes peeled back and bloodshot, alert like an animal ready to fight to the death. But what stuck in Ruth's mind most was the teeth. Brown and crooked. Resting in rotten gums and totally at odds with the rest of the man's appearance.

It gave him the look of a man possessed by something truly evil.

'Two pints of Carling,' said her dad, returning from the bar and setting the glasses down on the corner table.

Ruth had been so caught up in her investigation she'd forgotten her dad Glen was in town and that she'd agreed to meet up for a drink that evening. He'd taken her by surprise turning up at her office just as she was leaving for the day.

Glen was short and bald with an unruly beard making up for the lack of hair on his head. He had a restless energy that seemed far younger than his years. He and her mother lived out in the Peak District in the small pub they'd bought for their retirement.

Glen took a sip of his pint and looked around the room.

'What have they done to this place?' he joked. 'Bad enough they shut down the Press Club, now the Nag's Head's gone all bougie.'

Ruth smiled. Her dad was a great complainer. He never meant any of it; he just liked to bitch and moan and joke. All part of the newsroom culture that had stayed with him long after he'd left the newsroom.

'What you working on?' he asked.

Ruth knew what her father thought of *Mancunian Ways*. She thought the same thing. But he was her dad and he was immensely proud of her and so whatever reservations he might have had about the kind of journalism she was doing, he kept them to himself and instead heaped lavish praise on everything she did.

'A new bar opening, profile of a food truck and ten phrases every Manc will Know the Meaning Of.'

'Fucking hell,' muttered her dad before he could stop himself.

'That wasn't one of them.' Ruth smiled.

'It's good, three pieces a day, that's a work rate. Used to be we'd spend weeks on the one piece. Of course, that was back then,' he said quickly catching himself. 'Not like now with the internet and TikTok and . . .' He trailed off and took a drink.

Ruth wished she could tell him that she was digging into a serial killer. That she had evidence of a murder victim and a wrongful arrest and a huge story that no one else had picked up on. But until she was sure what it was she was dealing with, she decided to keep quiet. As much as she craved her dad's approval, she knew that if she told him what she had he would pepper her with questions, interrogate the story, testing it for weaknesses. She wanted his feedback but she wanted to be ready for it.

'How's Mum?' she asked.

'Working,' he said. 'I told her, running a pub is a shit retirement. But no one listens to me.'

He looked around the room again. Settling into his surroundings.

'We're dead proud of you. Me and your mum. Not a lot of jobs left in journalism these days. No one wants to read the news. They just want lies and bullshit.'

'It's OK,' said Ruth, hoping her dad hadn't been back on the tinfoil hat Facebook groups he seemed drawn to in his later years.

Her dad leaned forward with an earnest look in his eyes. 'It's a start. When I was your age I was out on the *Oldham Chronicle* covering school fetes and pool winners. But I worked my way up. Like I know you'll do.'

He finished speaking and started to stand.

'Excuse me, joys of middle age,' he said. 'Let's hope they've tarted up the loos too.'

He headed off to the toilets, moving as confidently as if he were in his own front room.

Ruth watched him go and finally her resolve caved. Her hand went into her bag and she pulled out the phone.

There were a couple of new messages but Ruth wasn't interested in these. She had already worked out her next plan of action. She needed to delve into Jake's life. Find out who he was and who the man was in the photo from the hotel room.

Ruth pulled up the photo. Jake had sent it to someone called Eddie, via WhatsApp. What she was about to do was a risk, but then she remembered all the times her dad had told her about doorstepping murder suspects, trailing gangsters' wives and going through the bins of dodgy politicians. If you wanted to be a proper journalist you had to get your hands dirty.

She composed a message.

IT'S JAKE. WE NEED TO MEET.

Ruth looked down at the message. She'd toyed with the truth. That she'd found the phone and now wanted to return it. But that carried the risk that this Eddie simply told her where to take it or just outright ignored her. She needed Eddie's attention and she needed to get him to meet her.

If Jake had sent him that photo, that meant that Eddie was someone he trusted. Someone who would go looking if he went missing. Someone who would want to meet him.

On the other side of the bar her dad emerged from the toilet and started chatting to the barmaid.

Ruth looked down at the phone and pressed SEND.

16

'Our job is to make this as easy as possible for you,' said the woman sat across from Keisha.

Everything in the office was tasteful and understated. Not quite an office, not quite . . . the place where you went to talk about the business of burying the dead.

The funeral director was younger than Keisha but spoke with the trained sympathy of a true professional.

Keisha was dripping with water as she sat listening. It ran off her parka to be soaked up in the dark beige carpet of the funeral director's office. Keisha had her sunglasses firmly on and sat leaning back slightly, taking the woman in.

'I want my father buried in Southern Cemetery. You've got his death certificate for his name. I want a stone. Nothing fancy. Nothing cheap. I want a priest to do a committal service. That's it.'

The funeral director wrote all this down, nodding away as she did so.

'And how many will be in attendance?'

'The priest,' said Keisha.

'Just the priest?'

'Yes.'

The funeral director was clearly thinking what to say next. Beside her on the desk, Keisha saw the stack of brochures. Coffins, headstones, horses and carts. All the extras that quickly added up.

Keisha felt a twinge. She wasn't sure if it was grief or guilt. Harold had chosen her to arrange this. It didn't change forty years of neglect, but despite him being a cold, mangled corpse on a gurney back at MRI, something inside Keisha didn't want him to think that he'd won. That somehow he'd been in her head all this time and now his cheap, unattended funeral was her revenge.

'And a horse-drawn carriage,' said Keisha out of nowhere.

The funeral director sat up a little straighter and did a bad job of hiding her excitement. 'A horse-drawn carriage is a very popular option but it is a little more expensive.'

'And flowers, loads of flowers. Spelling out his name. Harold. And fuck it, let's stick him in the most expensive coffin you have. Sort of thing that costs more than a terrace house in Harpurhey. Can you do that?'

'We have a lot of options.'

'You're not listening. I didn't ask for options. I asked can you do that. For, say, twenty grand,' said Keisha, tossing out a figure that felt large enough to put a few ghosts to bed.

'Yes,' said the funeral director without hesitation.

'Twenty grand it is then,' said Keisha. 'I don't care what you do, just spend twenty grand doing it.'

The funeral director seemed to have recovered sufficiently to understand what Keisha was telling her. Her hands went back to resting on the desk in front of her and she gave a little nod.

'We good?' said Keisha. This was it. She'd done what her father had asked her to do. More than he had ever done for her. Putting him in the ground for more money than he'd probably ever seen in his whole life.

'When do you want the burial?'

'Tomorrow.'

The funeral director gave a gentle frown. 'I'm afraid the quickest we can do for a burial in Southern Cemetery is five days.'

Five days of rain and memories and dodging ghosts. Keisha wasn't going to attend. But she wanted to know it was done before she was back on that plane.

'I need it sooner. How much?'

'It's not a question of money, it's just scheduling.'

Keisha stared at the funeral director through her dark glasses. The young woman was on the heavy side but solid. Like a sportswoman. Keisha briefly wondered if threats might speed things up but then she caught herself. This was the straight world. Where threats got the police involved. Straight people got scared and they stopped thinking straight.

'Five days,' said Keisha firmly.

'One more thing,' said the funeral director as Keisha was about to get up to leave. 'Would you like to write down some things about your father? Something the priest could use at the graveside. Let him know something about the man he's burying?'

Keisha thought for a moment. What did she know? He had left her. He had never reached out. And now he was dead.

'Born in Manchester. Died in Manchester,' said Keisha.

17

Malton felt unusual as he walked back into S Wing. Priestly had offered him a way out. A final chance to put his side of the story before it was all dragged out in the harsh daylight of a trial. And yet Malton had simply taunted him, snapped like a sullen teenager and then demanded to return to his cell.

As he climbed the stairs to the third-floor landing, something felt wrong. He looked around the wing and it felt like he'd always been here. Inside these walls.

Passing the second-floor landing, Mickey Farr was saying something to him. Smiling, nodding, threatening in his own nasty, cheerful way. But Malton couldn't hear the words. He couldn't hear anything. Mickey's creased, leathery face twisted and contorted but the words were lost to Malton. His whole world had shrunk to fit inside Strangeways and now it felt like it had shrivelled down into the small, poisonous space inside his own head.

He knew why he hadn't challenged Priestly. Why for three months he'd not even tried to look into who was setting him up. In his heart Malton knew he belonged here. Not for a murder he hadn't committed but for the sin of being Craig Malton.

His parents were dead. James was dead. Keisha was gone. Bea had betrayed him. Once upon a time he'd imagined that if he tried hard enough he'd be able to fool the world. Fool people into caring for him. Trick them into not seeing what he really was. But he knew what he was. And eventually so did everyone he ever cared about. The miasma that had hung around him since the day he was born was too strong to ever be overcome with good intentions. It swirled about him, repelling anyone who got too close, and if they didn't take the hint it would consume them.

Outside, every day was a struggle to stay one step ahead of the darkness. But inside these walls there was only darkness. Nowhere to run, no reason to hide. A perverse feeling of ease among the violence and privation.

Mickey Farr was waving at Malton as he climbed the final stairs to the third-floor landing.

Malton was dimly aware that the landing was empty. No men leaning over the barrier talking. No one perched in the doors to their cells staring at the same patch of brick wall for hours on end. He was alone.

He stopped for a moment and reached out to the barrier at the edge of the landing to steady himself. It was a long way down. Metal netting strung over the gaps to prevent suicides or worse. Various bits of rubbish from cells had been chucked onto the netting and left there, no one caring enough to bother removing them. The metal rail in Malton's hand felt cold to the touch. He finally realised what he'd done.

He'd given up. His entire life had been one long struggle to belong, but now he was locked up with all the other animals he had told himself he'd finally got what he wanted. He was where he belonged.

The revelation was a body blow. Malton let go of the barrier and staggered the short distance to his cell. Suddenly desperate to shrink the world down even further.

Connor would be waiting for him and maybe he'd fuck him, maybe he'd beat him up, maybe he'd just lie there. He couldn't say. He felt unlike he'd ever felt before. Finally, he'd admitted defeat. Decades spent holding on for dear life had left his insides in a permanent clench. Waiting for the next blow to come. But now it felt like he was melting. Robbed of any reason to continue.

He smelled it before he got into the cell. The sweet stink of cooked meat.

Connor was lying on the floor of the cell, his limbs splayed out unnaturally.

His face was gone.

The kettle, still warm with the mixture of sugar and boiling water, lay discarded on the bed. The careless signature to a studied act of brutality.

A pitiful, wet sound came from where Connor's mouth used to be.

Connor was only nineteen. He had no family, no prospects. All he had was his youth. His pretty face and his too-easy confidence. Now all he had was suffering and pain. He was as good as dead.

Malton looked down at the bloody, blistering mess and suddenly his entire world sped into sharp focus.

Months inside had softened him. Lulled him into a false sense of ease. Hidden the reality of the world from him. He'd taken the easy way out. He'd mistaken violence for fighting.

Malton was already out of the cell and calling for help. As the emergency alarm rang out over the wing Malton knew what he had to do. He had to clear his name. And to do that he had to break out.

But first he was going to cripple Mickey Farr.

18

It had rained all the way to the caravan park on the coast where Dean now found himself. It seemed like it had been raining for months. Ever since Malton got arrested.

But the act of getting out of Manchester and running down a lead had invigorated Dean. Benton's words had stuck with him. Why was he still doing this? Risking himself for Malton? For the Farrs?

Since Malton had been inside he'd been working sixteen-hour days. Sleeping in the office. Whatever time he had to himself had dwindled to the two hours every Sunday he spent round his mum's for Sunday dinner and his daily call to Vikki. A daily call that now looked to be over and done with. Try as he might, Dean couldn't stop wondering – who else had been there with Vikki? Just off screen. Listening as she gave him the brush off.

That was what he hadn't told Benton. He did this job because, thanks to the job, he didn't have much else left in his life.

The receipt he'd found at the courier's house had been for groceries from a shop Dean didn't recognise. A quick Google and he found out why. It was a chain of convenience stores that existed solely as part of a chain of static caravan parks. It had been easy enough with what was on the receipt to track down the exact shop.

Edge Haven caravan park sat down the coast from Black-pool, nestled between a waste recycling plant and a shipping container storage yard. Once off the motorway Dean had followed his sat nav through a string of scruffy-looking villages filled with squat, grey houses before nearly missing the turning that took him down a long, narrow road that eventually led to Edge Haven.

The caravans were lined up in alphabetical rows. Driving at little more than a crawl up and down the narrow lanes between caravans, Dean spent nearly thirty minutes peering through the dense rain until he found row M and, further along it, the caravan he was looking for – M7.

There was a small, empty parking spot between the caravans. Eager not to get any wetter than he already was, Dean pulled in off the road and got out.

It was less a caravan and more a long, metal box on stilts, hooked up at the back to the site's gas, water and electric. Dean took a look around. A few hundred yards away on the other side of the perimeter fence, stacks of shipping containers, five high, loomed over the park. Even in the rain he could hear the sound of diggers, grubbing through piles of recycling at the plant on the other side of the site.

It seemed like he was the only soul here.

M7's lights were off and the curtains drawn. No matter how hard Dean tapped, there was no answer.

By this point, whatever waterproof qualities his raincoat had were fast becoming obsolete. The rain had got everywhere, matting his hair to his face, running down his cheeks and dripping off his chin into his shirt collar.

The fetid smell of an unloved coastline mingled with the nearby recycling plant and turned Dean's stomach.

Confident the caravan was empty, he took out the keys, crossed his fingers and tried them in the lock.

The door swung outwards and, without hesitation, Dean stepped inside, closing it behind him.

The caravan had been ransacked.

The front portion of the caravan was a large, open-plan living area with built-in seating at one end and a small kitchen at the other. Someone had emptied every drawer they could find into a pile in the middle of the room. Then they'd sliced open every cushion on the seating and pulled the insides out, discarding the hollowed-out covers on the floor.

Spices, pasta, beans, sugar and coffee had all been tipped out alongside the empty containers. Footprints had walked through the mess, tracking up and down the caravan as the studied destruction continued.

Cupboards had come off walls, the sink had been half dismantled. Everything that could be torn apart had been.

In amongst the mess were signs of who had been living here. Beautiful Afghan rugs now crumpled and stained. Photos of what looked like children and grandchildren tossed aside without emotion.

Someone had got there before him.

Dean's first thought was the Farrs. But that made no sense. If they knew about the caravan then why keep it from him? Why go through the charade of sending him off to find the courier's empty house? Carl Farr had kicked the door off the courier's house and left the inside untouched. This level of thoroughness didn't seem like the Farrs at all. It only meant one thing. Someone else was after the courier.

Dean quickly took a look from behind one of the drawn curtains. All he saw was the dark, driving rain hammering down on Edge Haven caravan park.

Whoever had done this could well come back. He didn't have the luxury of time.

The living area gave way to a narrow corridor leading to the back of the caravan, off which came a tiny shower room, a toilet and three bedrooms. The corridor was filled with debris from the bedrooms, which, just like the front of the caravan, had been ransacked.

Stepping over the mess, Dean edged his way into the master bedroom.

It was barely bigger than the double bed, which had been piled with blankets and pillows and other detritus. The cupboards again torn off the walls and tossed aside. It was utter carnage.

He was about to go out and check the other bedrooms when he heard someone unlock the front door and step into the caravan.

Dean froze. He had options. The longer he did nothing the faster those options reduced. He eyed the bedroom window. He could get out and run. Whoever was in the caravan would have seen his car. If they wanted to, they could find him. He kicked himself. If it hadn't been raining he would have parked on the other side of the park and walked. He'd got lazy.

Or he could fight. He quickly looked round the bedroom for a weapon. A few broken bits of cupboard were all that looked even halfway promising. Besides, Dean wasn't a fighter. Fighting was the last resort. There was always another way.

Trying to sound as confident as possible, Dean took a breath and strode out of the bedroom, launching into, 'What are you doing in my caravan?'

Since he'd been working for Malton, Dean had learned the value of projection. If you're somewhere you shouldn't be, make sure you're the one challenging the person who catches you doing it. A little bit of confidence and confusion go a long way.

He got to the front of the caravan and realised no amount of confidence or confusion was going to help him.

'What the fuck are you doing in my dad's caravan?' said Keisha.

19

Keisha had five days to kill in Manchester, holed up in her suite at the Midland, with only Harold Boateng's effects for company. The solicitor had handed over a package of papers. Mainly documents, nothing personal. Nothing to give any clue as to why her father had asked this of her.

As much as Keisha didn't want to care, even more she hated the not knowing. Was this Harold's half-hearted attempt at reconciliation from beyond the grave? Or a final fuck-you from a father who'd noped out on his responsibilities and never stopped running?

There among Harold's effects was the key and an address for a caravan park out on the coast.

The last thing Keisha expected to find waiting for her at Edge Haven caravan park was Malton's protégé – Dean.

The last time she'd seen Dean she was dragging him out of the burning wreckage of his car, seconds after he'd just rammed it into her own car. She'd saved his life that night.

In some small way maybe it had made up for the time she'd shot him in the face. Dean still had a small, round scar where the bullet had gone in through his mouth and out through his cheek. Back then Keisha hadn't cared whether he lived or died. All that mattered was that Craig would find him, lying shot in his office, and know that Keisha wasn't finished with Craig just yet.

That all seemed so long ago. Back when she lived in Manchester and the entire city was her playground. Back then the only toy she wanted to play with was Craig. But Craig wasn't playing.

She had put clear water between then and now. The crystal blue of the Mediterranean to be exact. All she had to do was last five days back home and then she'd be away. Back to Ibiza and the sunshine and the men and the whole new life she had made for herself.

Then she found Dean in her father's caravan.

'My father was a drug dealer's courier?' said Keisha.

They had left the caravan and were now sat in Edge Haven's cabaret lounge, in reality a small bar with a stage and dance floor. A few day drinkers were dotted about but no one was paying any attention to the beautiful, mixed-race woman, her eyes hidden by sunglasses – even at this time of year – and the tall, thin white kid, his hair matted to his face with the rain.

Dean nervously grimaced, and Keisha could see he felt the tightness of the scar tissue around the bullet wound she'd given him.

'Your dad was part of the Farrs' operation to import drugs into the country. He went abroad, put the drugs in tyres and then it was his job to take them out the other end and pass them to the Farrs. They knew him as Ray.'

'Ray?' said Keisha. 'Harold . . . Harry . . . Ray.'

'He was the firewall between the Farrs and the drugs,' said Dean.

'He was their stooge,' said Keisha coldly.

Keisha knew of the Farrs. Back when she'd been married to Paul Bistacchi, the Farrs were just another criminal family who had been lucky enough to stay out of prison long enough to make a bit of money. While her husband Paul had made a couple of million from drugs, back then the Farrs stole diggers off building sites and fenced them overseas. It was a profitable business but high risk. Mickey Farr and his son Carl worked together. Mickey was the brains; Carl was the muscle.

From what Dean said, it looked like the Farrs had finally got the message that if you were going to break the law then drugs was the only game in town.

'Where did he deliver the drugs to?' asked Keisha.

83

'A house in Langworthy,' said Dean, looking around the mostly empty cabaret bar. A young woman in a caravan park uniform was wiping tables while another stood talking to the barman. 'But I don't think the Farrs killed your dad.'

Until she'd seen the caravan, Keisha had no reason to believe her father's death was anything other than a tragic accident. But now things were starting to look a lot more complicated.

'Who do you think murdered my father?' said Keisha.

My father. The words sounded strange in her mouth. Harold had been nothing but a distant shadow all these years but in a few short days he'd taken form, first on the slab and now in the words she could hear herself uttering.

For the longest time Keisha had been alone. Even when she was married she felt it. It was her against the world. That's what made Craig's rejection hurt so much. She always thought he was just like her. Maybe that was the problem – he was too much like her. Another lost soul who couldn't ever let their guard down.

From his expression Keisha could tell Dean was thinking, working out what he would and wouldn't tell her.

'If you don't tell me everything, I'll find out. And you don't want that,' she said.

Dean breathed out and began. 'Firstly, the Farrs are paying me to find him. Or rather, the drugs he was meant to be delivering. I don't think they knew he was dead. I think they thought maybe he'd robbed them himself. Secondly, they didn't know about this caravan park.'

'So who ransacked my dad's caravan?'

Dean shrugged. 'Good question. But thirdly, Mickey Farr's in Strangeways right now. I get the sense the Farrs don't do anything without Mickey's say-so. Even if they had a reason to bullshit me, it doesn't feel like something they'd do without Mickey guiding things.'

Dean's words lit a fire in Keisha. Suddenly life was being breathed into that cold, grey body she'd seen on a slab at MRI. Part of her had always wondered how her mother, a devout, law-abiding Catholic who never once in her life had put her own needs above others, had raised such a ruthlessly criminal daughter. Now she had her answer. She was her father's girl. Keisha was quietly surprised how much that thought thrilled her.

'All you've told me is what you don't know. You're not stupid. If you were, Craig wouldn't have given you a second thought. So stop fucking me around and tell me what you've found out,' said Keisha, watching as Dean pulled up short.

'I'll tell you what I know,' said Dean. 'But first I need something from you.'

Keisha couldn't help but smile. Dean didn't react to her gentle push. He simply held her gaze. He was deadly serious. He almost sounded like Craig.

'Go on,' said Keisha, trying to keep the pleasure from her voice at seeing Dean radiating Craig's tutelage.

'I found blood in your dad's car. Someone had broken the window.'

'The people who robbed him?'

'Maybe. Either way I'm getting that blood checked out. If you promise to hold off until I know whose blood that is then I promise to let you know as soon as I do.'

Dean kept his eyes trained on Keisha. Waiting for her response.

'Craig really did a number on you, didn't he?'

Dean frowned. 'Until he gets out, I'm running things.'

'When did you last speak to him?' said Keisha, avoiding answering Dean's question.

'He's not seen anyone. Not since he's been inside.'

Keisha felt a twinge of sadness for Craig.

She remembered when she had first met him. A shy, mixed-race kid with a white dad and a dead mum. Shunned by white Moss Side, and with no way in to black Moss Side. She'd found him hovering outside a local youth club. Too scared to go inside. She'd taken his hand and led him in. Shown him what the world could look like if you stopped thinking your face didn't fit anywhere and realised instead that it meant you could go everywhere. For Keisha, being mixed race meant she was beholden to no one. Black or white, she made her own rules, lived her own life. That was what she'd taught Craig.

Now all those lessons had come to nothing. Craig was broken and in prison. All that was left was Dean.

Keisha wondered what would have happened if she'd managed to persuade Craig to leave it all behind and go with her to Ibiza.

But Keisha didn't do regrets. Regrets were for people too weak to get back up and keep fighting.

'You've got a deal,' she said to Dean. 'You want to shake on it?' She offered her hand and was impressed to see him smile, realising she was taking the piss.

Even so, he reached over and shook her hand. His grip was light but firm.

'And if you screw me then next time I'll aim a few inches to the left,' she said.

Dean stopped smiling. Keisha didn't care; she was in the game now.

Harold Boateng was no longer a blank slate. Now he was a tantalising mystery. A life that was far closer to Keisha's than she could have ever imagined. Finding that unexpected connection to her father left Keisha hungry for more. And of course there was the question of who had killed her father. And why.

When she'd first arrived at his caravan, before finding Dean waiting for her, Keisha had been feeling something dangerously close to grief. Now she had something better. She had revenge.

20

Ruth had already nearly finished her article, typing on her phone as she walked. Helen had given her two hours out of the office to visit the new café in town where customers were served by young girls dressed up as comic book characters. Ruth had nodded along as the owner explained how it was actually really empowering for the girls working there and their customers (who Ruth noticed were overwhelmingly male) were attracted by a shared love of the comics the costumes were based on and not the chance to ogle young women as they bent over tables.

Ruth already knew exactly what was expected of her. The café had taken out advertising with the site and so the unspoken agreement was that they could expect a nice puff piece to go along with the paid advertising.

The only way Ruth didn't feel too dirty about the whole thing was to expend as little energy on it as possible. What's more, having wound up her interview in under thirty minutes, that left her with over an hour before she was expected back. She knew exactly where she was heading.

It had been over a day since she sent the message on Jake's phone and still no reply. The incoming messages had slowed to a trickle and news that a young man's body had been found in Piccadilly Basin was in that morning's *Manchester Evening News*.

Ruth bristled. She could have written that story. She was right there. But dead bodies weren't the kind of thing *Mancunian Ways* covered.

The café she'd been sent to review was in the Northern Quarter and so, while her new destination was nearby, she still didn't have time to linger. She was already out past Angel Meadow and heading towards the Green Quarter when she stopped, gave herself five minutes to proof her story and then put her phone away. She could have uploaded it to the website remotely but if she'd done that then Helen would know she was finished and ask why she wasn't back in the office.

Ruth pocketed her phone and started walking quicker. Ducking under the railway arches, past the discreet door that led to Hidden, the claustrophobic underground dance club that she'd first discovered in her freshers week all those years ago, she turned north out of the city centre and headed uphill past the reclaimed office building where a grassroots food market had made its home.

There'd always been rumours of a Manchester serial killer pushing people into the canal. Not only was pushing people into a canal a very inefficient way of killing someone, but it also didn't fit any of the serial killers Ruth had read about.

It was all about power. Power and sex. Serial killers weren't the Machiavellian evil geniuses you saw in films. They were sick men driven by perverted desires and a sociopathic disregard for others. The eight dead sex workers fitted exactly into the kind of victims a serial killer would choose. Itinerant and on the edge of society. Boys who no one would miss.

She had already lined up several true crime podcasts to listen to later on to get more insight into the serial killer angle but for now she thought it was worth going straight to the source.

Her pet theory had put Craig Malton as the killer. Now that there was a new body, he was out of the picture, at least for number eight. Despite repeated requests, Malton hadn't agreed to meet. Without his permission there was no way to get inside Strangeways to talk to him.

But that didn't mean there was no one she could talk to.

At the top of the hill Ruth paused to get her breath. It was broad daylight but she was on high alert. Cheetham Hill was still a rough area. Weeds growing through the pavement and large empty plots of land, secured by fencing and padlocks. This part of the city was mainly warehouses and minicab offices. A smattering of African evangelical churches had spied cheap rents and set themselves up in empty industrial units. Ruth passed the Mountain of Fire and Truth Ministry – a windowless building hung with a large canvas banner onto which was printed a photograph of its beaming preacher bedecked in gold.

Finally, she arrived at her destination.

Ruth checked her watch. There was no way she'd be back in the office on time. But she was here now. There was no point in going back.

Holding her head high and doing her best to imagine what her dad would do in this situation, Ruth confidently marched into the offices of Malton Security.

21

'It's no longer safe for you on S Wing,' said Cunningham. Any trace of meeting Malton halfway was gone from her voice. She wasn't his friend or his guardian; she was the governor in charge of safeguarding and right now there was no bigger threat to the safety of prisoners in S Wing than Malton's very presence on the wing.

Malton sat quietly in Cunningham's office, taking it in. Only half listening as his mind spun through everything that he now needed to do.

Connor would live but he would never be the same. His beautiful face was burned clean off. Long bouts of plastic surgery and rehabilitation stretched out into his future.

But Malton hadn't seen Connor lying there in the cell. He'd seen James. He'd seen what happened when he let go of his grip. When he embraced even the sordid happiness of a prison bunk-up. The world wasn't there for Malton to enjoy it. It was there for him to go to war with. To beat and trick and tame. These past few months he'd lost sight of that. The fight had finally broken him but now he felt renewed. Now he saw things for how they really were.

He was locked up for a murder he didn't commit. An investigation headed by an inexperienced young DCI raised the very real risk of putting him away for double digits thanks to someone's obvious frame-up. James's killers were still out there. The entire world was still out there. Outside, he knew Dean would still be going, still keeping on, just how Malton taught him. Working alone.

But not for long.

Cunningham was still talking.

'. . . so in light of all of that, I've applied for you to be transferred to the VPU.'

Malton saw her wait for his reaction. Previously the VPU had simply been a dumping ground for nonces and grasses. But now it was much more dangerous. Malton had been giving serious thought to how he was going to escape from Strangeways. It would be hard enough to escape as a member of the general population. Once he was in the VPU he'd be classed as a vulnerable prisoner. That meant more attention from officers, closer supervision and a whole different set of protocols.

Moving to VPU would change everything.

'Right now I'm transferring a body out of VPU and then you'll have a nice, cosy cell waiting for you.'

Whatever time Malton had for planning was up. It was time to check out of Strangeways.

22

It was in Malton's office where Keisha had shot Dean in the face. It was in Malton's office where Dean now sat thinking over his encounter the other day. Spread out before him was the paperwork for Illian's upcoming appointment with the licensing committee, but Dean found himself unable to concentrate on anything other than his meeting with Keisha.

When he heard someone coming into the caravan he'd been ready to fight a trained killer for his life. It turned out to be something far more dangerous. Stood there was Keisha, wrapped up against the rain and the cold in a giant parka, yet still sporting her trademark shades. Hiding those eyes that Dean knew could strip a man down to his soul in seconds.

'What the fuck are you doing in *my* dad's caravan?'

The way she said it made his stomach turn. He'd heard Keisha beguile and charm and threaten, but this time there was none of that in her voice when she spoke. She sounded raw, a trembling naked violence in her tone.

Dean had made the call and told her everything. He knew lying to Keisha was a losing game. But in turn he'd learned a few things himself.

Ray's real name was Harold Boateng. And he was Keisha's father. If she was to be believed. It all felt too far-fetched to be made up, but still, Dean knew Keisha, knew that she played a long game. Her obsession with Malton had left a trail of bodies in its wake. If she was involved then there was no telling what might happen.

But if she was telling the truth, if Harold Boateng was her father, then that was just as complicated. Dean had been tasked with finding out who robbed the Farrs' shipment of drugs. Harold was the last person to have custody of those drugs before the robbery.

Now he had confirmation that Harold was dead. Did the robbers get spooked and decide to cover their tracks? If so then it was a good sign that Dean was on the right course. Hopefully Benton would get a DNA match for the blood from the car. Dean thought it was a safe bet that someone who was willing to rip off a violent family of criminals had probably been in trouble with the law at least once or twice before graduating to armed robbery.

He'd made the call that he'd rather have Keisha inside the tent firing out than outside the tent burning it down. He'd promised to share the DNA results. Maybe Keisha would be an asset. If Dean's robber was also Harold's killer then he had Keisha Bistacchi onside trying to track him down. Maybe he could use that.

He looked up at the clock on the wall. It was still early in the morning. Yesterday he'd got himself lost following the trail of the Farrs' missing drugs. But now he was stuck in the office waiting on Benton's DNA results while he tried to figure out how best to manage Keisha. In the idle moments, he found his thoughts drifting back to Vikki. It was only half ten, thirty minutes before their daily call. The daily call Vikki had said she wanted phase out. But did she say that? Didn't she just say not at eleven? Was Dean reading too much into it? Getting his wires crossed. Maybe she just wanted a bit more spontaneity?

Unable to stop himself, Dean turned to his laptop and with a few taps Skype was open and ringing.

Just because Vikki didn't want to always talk bang on the dot of eleven didn't mean she didn't want to talk. He'd been letting his paranoia run away with him. A quick chat would sort everything out.

But as the laptop kept ringing, Dean's hopeful smile faded. Vikki wasn't picking up. Finally Dean gave up and with nothing else to do he closed it down and told himself that it was nothing to worry about. She could be asleep, out of the house, in the library. There were any number of perfectly reasonable explanations that didn't involve her murderous father, or worse, some new man in her life. Whoever had been on the call with her was probably a housemate. A friend. Something totally innocent.

Dean wished his brain would be a little more convinced.

Eager for a distraction, he looked down at the paperwork for Illian's upcoming interview with the licensing committee. There were pages and pages of it. It occurred to him, Malton wouldn't be filling this in. Malton would be making the problem go away before it even got this far. Back at the caravan park, dealing with Keisha, for the first time he felt that he'd handled the situation just as Malton would have done. Guarded compromise, a cautious deal, pulling the danger closer. Controlling it. It gave him a sudden rush of confidence.

He would fill in this paperwork later but before he did that he'd make sure it was already a done deal. Malton bent the world to his will, made the rules work for him and when they didn't work he made his own rules. It was time for Dean to stop trying to be like Malton and start acting like the man running Malton Security.

He was about to get up and leave when Alfie, the office manager, popped his head round the door.

Dean had never got to the bottom of why Alfie still worked for Malton Security, long after Dean had discovered he was stealing from the company. Whatever the reason, Dean's rapid ascent from Alfie's underling to running the company had left relations between them somewhat strained.

'Someone to see you,' said Alfie, his Scouse accent leaning into antagonism.

'I'm going out,' said Dean brusquely.

Alfie seemed not to hear. 'So, should I send her in? You'll like this one. Proper fit little girl she is. Says she's a journalist.'

23

The face looking back at Keisha could have been her daughter. A young girl, not any older than six or seven. Dressed in a leotard, holding a trophy and beaming for the camera, her long, brown, curly hair up in a French plait against her head.

She had Keisha's eyes, her nose. Keisha's lean, powerful body. But she had one thing Keisha didn't. That smile. This little girl smiled like she'd never known suffering or pain. Never watched her mother work herself into an early grave fighting a council who'd dumped her in the asbestos-riddled death trap that the newly built Hulme Crescents housing estate swiftly became. It was a smile that had never sweet-talked a man into killing another man just to see if she could. A smile of someone who belonged and knew they belonged. Someone happy.

She wasn't Keisha's daughter. The first time she'd seen that little girl was when she returned to the caravan and found her photo while sorting through what was left of her father's belongings.

When she'd first come to the caravan the other day she was driven by an open, idle curiosity. Five days to kill. Hearing about her father from Dean had changed all that. Learning about her father's criminal life and suspicious, violent death had bridged all those missing decades. Harold had gone from a question to an answer.

Dean was young, but she knew just how smart and determined he was. Craig had taught him well. If Dean thought the Farrs couldn't be behind trashing the caravan and killing her father then Keisha was ready to go along with that theory.

Inchoate grief wasn't Keisha's style but tracking down his killers? That, she could do.

After speaking to Dean she'd locked up the caravan and taken Dean's copy of the keys off him. Then she'd driven back to Manchester where, after rearranging her return flight, she'd started to make a list of everything she'd need to help find her father's killers.

She'd been on the back foot these past few days. Now she was the one driving things.

The road traffic accident looked little more than a cover story. If you wanted to kill someone, a car was a perfect murder weapon. It was legal to own a car and hundreds of people got run over every day. As long as you were smart a deliberate murder with a car looked no different to a tragic accident or, at worst, fatal negligence.

While she was waiting on Dean to produce the DNA results from the blood on her father's car's window glass, something that despite her extensive contacts in Manchester she was unable to do, she thought it best to try and learn more about the man who was her father.

Sorting through the pile of detritus in the middle of the caravan, she'd found bills and bank statements. Nothing that suggested he was working as part of a major drug-smuggling operation. She'd found heart medication and appointment slips for his GP back in Manchester. Everything was addressed to the house back in Salford that Dean had told her about. It would seem this caravan was Harold's attempt to keep his two worlds separate. Back in Salford he was Ray, a drugs runner, out in Edge Haven caravan park he was Harold, just another retiree by the sea.

But then there were the photos. Harold's new family. There was the little girl in the leotard and there was her mother. A woman in her early thirties, mixed race like Keisha. Harold's other daughter. Keisha found a broken photo frame with the name Rachel on it. Rachel. The daughter he cared enough about to fill his home with her photos. There were no photos of

Rachel's mother. Whoever she was, Harold had clearly cut her out of his life just as surely as he had done to Keisha's mother. So why had he kept in touch with Rachel and her daughter? The smiling girl with Keisha's face.

Briefly Keisha wondered if they were in danger. Would whoever did this to his caravan come looking for them? Or had they already found what they were looking for? Keisha told herself that Harold's absence had taught her to survive. It was only fair that Rachel got that lesson too. Besides, Harold had asked her to bury him. Rachel had Harold her whole life; now it was Keisha's turn.

In the entire time she'd been searching she hadn't found a single trace of her existence in the caravan.

The other photos she found were of Harold and a group of other retirees. Mainly older black men and white women. There were shots of them on nights out, theatre trips. Harold there smiling, a beanie covering his head, a neat suit jacket matched with his jeans and shoes. He looked good for his age, dressed well. In every photo he seemed so alive. Nothing like the body she'd seen on the slab back in Manchester.

A couple of times as she waded through the wreckage of Harold's life she was taken by surprise by that same feeling she'd had back in Ibiza. That small, impossible sense that something was missing. Something that refused to reveal itself yet still made its presence felt somewhere deep in her gut.

Whenever she got that feeling she told herself it was simply her desire to find Harold's killers. To complete the puzzle. This was about her. Not Harold.

She was getting to the bottom of the pile when she found the printout. A single piece of A4 paper with what looked like a colour image printed in black and white. It was an invitation to a Northern soul night at a working men's club back in Manchester.

Looking over the invitation Keisha saw that the date was for tonight.

24

Malton was being escorted back to his cell where Cunningham had informed him he'd be locked in until the VPU transfer. This was his last chance.

His senses were on edge. The stale, fetid smell of the wing. The cacophony of voices bouncing off the walls. The sound of the rain hitting the roof far above his head.

With every step he willed time to slow down. His brain racing to assemble his plan. By the time they had reached the third-floor landing he knew there was only one option.

Luck was already on his side. Normally a prisoner like him would have a two-officer escort. One front, one back. Thanks to massive underinvestment, being a prison officer was no longer the choice career it once was. Getting paid minimum wage to deal with aggressive, violent prisoners wasn't an offer many were keen to accept.

Malton had only one guard. A middle-aged man, with thin, greying hair and a belly spilling over his belt. His arms looked soft and smooth, his hands were small, the nails neat. He was clean-shaven and had no tattoos. Whoever this guard was, Malton could tell this wasn't his world. He wasn't a veteran who had a lifetime of dealing with prisoners. This was someone who never imagined they'd end up here. A midlife career shift in the worst possible way.

That was also lucky.

The officer was behind him. He had the keys to the cell. Malton had been in the office with Cunningham when he had taken them out of the locker where the keys to the wing were kept. Three layers of security. The gates to the wing, the door to Cunningham's office and then the locker itself.

Right now those keys were clipped to the belt of the soft, middle-aged man who Malton could hear breathing more heavily having climbed the final flights of stairs.

Malton knew if he'd have acted out just once these past few months he wouldn't have this chance. He'd been involved in two violent incidents in the past few days. But no one had seen what happened to Mickey Farr's boys except them and Malton, and neither side was talking. Malton hadn't been present when Connor was hurt. He had the ultimate alibi: a recorded police interview. Only the suspicion of violence hung around Malton, who until then had, thanks to his complete mental resignation, been a quietly compliant prisoner.

What he was about to do would change that.

'Stand to one side,' said the officer, and Malton did as he was told. The wing was on lock-up. Every prisoner in their cell. It was just Malton and the officer on the landing. Three other officers were also on the wing. Malton had counted two of them on the way up to the third-floor landing. He hoped that the missing officer was above them on the fourth floor.

The officer raised the keys from his belt and unlocked the cell door. In the moment his attention was on the lock, Malton was up and on him. A restraint that he'd used a thousand times over the years working doors. With one hand he twisted the man's arm up his back, with the other he forced his head down against his own chest. This was as much to disorientate and dominate as it was to control.

In a low voice Malton said, 'I'm not going to hurt you. I'm going to put you in the cell and I'm going lock you in. Do you understand?'

The man was shaking. Malton had been correct. This was a long way from his world.

'Please . . .' muttered the officer.

Malton thought it was worth pushing his luck. 'You're going in that cell and if you make a noise then it won't be you who sees me next. It'll be your wife.'

'Please don't hurt Laura,' he wept.

Malton almost felt sorry for the man. Almost.

'Do as you're told and Laura will be just fine. Do it for Laura. Now unclip the keys and hand them to me.'

The officer fumbled with his one free hand and Malton caught the keys as they fell from his belt.

Keys in hand, Malton pushed the officer forward and he stumbled into the cell, turning to face Malton. He looked terrified. Malton raised one finger to his lips in silent command and the officer nodded as Malton locked him in.

Now the clock was ticking. With every other prisoner on lockdown, the sight of an unaccompanied prisoner on the wing would instantly raise the alarm.

Malton didn't have time to check the coast was clear. He was already on the stairs and moving at speed down to the second-floor landing. To Mickey Farr's cell.

Amongst the noise of the wing, the sound of Malton creeping down the metal staircase barely registered. He was at the landing and heading to the cell door behind which Mickey Farr was waiting.

If there had been more time then maybe he could have come up with something neater. Something that left him utterly clean. As it was, this was planning on the fly. It meant that there was a certain amount of inescapable illegality. Malton would deal with that later. Once he was on the outside he could blow apart the murder case against him. With that out of the way a little prison violence set against time served would be child's play to make disappear.

Malton stopped outside Farr's cell. Farr was watching television. Some daytime property show. Malton could hear a presenter talking about resale values and rental income.

He paused for just a moment to ready himself. Mickey Farr was much smaller than Malton but he was brutally old-school.

He was the one in a thousand that was still standing. An entire generation of Nineties Manchester criminals had ended up dead, in prison or over in Spain. Mickey had hung on. Gone from robbing shops to extorting clubs to drug importation. Mickey was a survivor.

Malton slid the key in the lock and turned it as quietly as he could. He left the key in the door. He needed the cell open; he needed to be found.

He also needed to give Mickey Farr enough time to do what he knew Mickey Farr would do when confronted with the sight of an eighteen-stone Malton stood in the doorway to his cell.

The door swung open. Mickey was sat on the bed, halfway through a Pot Noodle. He was in a prison tracksuit with a blanket wrapped around his shoulders for warmth.

His reaction was almost instant.

He hurled the Pot Noodle at Malton and sprang to his feet, shedding the blanket to face Malton.

'Fucking have it!' he shouted as Malton stepped into the small cell with him.

Mickey smiled and darted to the side of the cell where he slipped one hand down behind a cupboard and brought it back up holding a long, thick piece of wire, with one end wrapped in strips of fabric and tape.

Just as Malton had hoped he would.

'He was such a fucking pretty little faggot,' sneered Mickey, and went for Malton.

Malton moved to dodge but in the cramped confines of the cell he could only move so far. Mickey nicked him with the makeshift weapon but had overextended himself, letting Malton wrap one thick hand around Mickey's wrist and slam him against the open door.

Mickey's whole body was alive, moving like a snake packed into a sack. Malton had barely landed the first punch on Mickey's face before Mickey leaned in and, without hesitation, clamped his teeth around Malton's ear.

Malton staggered backwards, making sure to carry Mickey back into the cell with him. Pain shot through his body as Mickey bit down hard, his teeth going deep into skin and cartilage.

Malton kept a tight hold of the hand with the weapon in it while he slipped the other hand round Farr's neck and lifted him bodily off the ground.

Farr kept his grip with his mouth and began smashing his knee into Malton's torso. The first blow hit a rib and Malton felt it break. Farr was impossibly strong for such a small man. The second blow winded Malton, but before Farr could launch another knee, Malton tore Farr from the side of his head.

He felt a chunk of ear coming clean off and saw Farr's face, stuffed with bloody flesh. The smell of fresh blood filled the cell. But only for a second before, with both hands, he smashed Farr against the back wall of the cell like a rag doll. Again and again until he felt his muscle begin to burn and finally he dumped Farr on the floor.

But Farr wasn't done. The moment Malton let him go he hit the floor and sprung up towards Malton, too quickly to dodge.

Malton felt the shank bury itself in the top of his thigh, the thick wire smashing against the bone.

Malton staggered back. Mickey was already on his feet. He spat Malton's ear on the ground and grinned at Malton. He was having the time of his life.

'It wasn't personal, you fucking cunt. Just wanted to give your boy Dean a nudge.'

Not having spoken to Dean for these past three months, Malton had no idea what Farr was talking about. He momentarily felt wrongfooted but said nothing.

Warm blood was spilling down the side of Malton's face. Any of the guards on the wing would be able to see a prison door open. The officer he locked in his cell would be missed. There wasn't time for this.

Malton raised one forearm as a battering ram and charged Farr.

Farr stabbed under Malton's guard, hitting him in the chest but not going deep. It couldn't stop Malton's momentum. Malton's forearm smashed into Farr's face and he felt teeth, loose from a lifetime of smoking drugs, give way.

Malton's free arm went low and grabbed Farr's crotch hard.

The smile went out of Mickey Farr's eyes as Malton twisted as hard as he could.

Farr howled in pain and tried to stab Malton, but now Malton was on Farr, pressing him back against the wall. Eighteen stone of him holding Farr back.

Malton was sure he could hear shouting outside the cell. There wasn't much time.

He looked Farr in the face and headbutted him as hard as he could.

Farr's nose had already been broken more than once. Malton felt the soft mess of cartilage buffering the blow. So he went again. And again and again. A jackhammer smashing his huge, bald head into Farr's face. Never letting go of his grip on Farr's crotch.

He could feel piss soaking through his fingers. Farr's body was giving up. Malton wasn't.

He gave Farr one last headbutt and released him.

What was left of Mickey Farr slid to the floor into a bloody, broken heap.

Without stopping to savour his moment of victory, Malton bent down and picked up Farr's weapon.

He could hear guards coming. The alarm going.

Malton pressed the shank, sharp end first against his own chest, took a deep breath and pushed it in up to the hilt.

25

For the past ten minutes Ruth had resisted the temptation to ask the young guy across the desk from her where he got that scar on his face. She also didn't ask what all the pins in the map on the wall behind him signified. Or whether the weights bench to one side of the room belonged to his boss – Craig Malton.

Instead she did her best to convince him to talk to her.

'I'm going to do the podcast with or without your cooperation,' she said matter-of-factly.

The guy who she'd been told's name was Dean said nothing.

'If your boss is innocent of Stephen Page's murder, a podcast could really help. You heard of Adnan Syed?'

Dean shook his head.

'Famous podcast? *Serial*?' Ruth got nothing so pressed on. 'Well, he was convicted of murder, then there was this big podcast about it in America and it turns out he didn't do it and he got off. I could do the same for Craig Malton.'

Dean looked bored as he said, 'If I were you I'd probably just leave it alone.'

Ruth didn't. 'Is that a recommendation or is that a warning?'

Dean smiled a bit.

'Honestly?' he said.

'Well, I heard some things about Craig Malton,' lied Ruth. She'd found it almost impossible to find anything out about Malton. She'd hoped that this meeting might change that. 'But the thing is, with this new murder, that's proof he didn't do it.'

Dean screwed up his face but Ruth continued.

'If there is a serial killer – and I think there is – he's killing young guys. Young guys in the sex trade. Now I don't know what connects Malton to young men in the sex trade . . .' She left a pause to see if Dean might fill in the blank for her. She was unsurprised when he said nothing. 'But seven bodies is a pattern – and a pattern that I thought your boss was behind. But then number eight turned up a couple of days ago. A young boy called Jake Arnold. I saw the body,' she exaggerated.

The faintest glimmer of interest flashed across Dean's face.

'Why not go to the police then?' he asked.

Ruth smiled. 'I'd have thought someone in your line of work wouldn't need to ask that.'

'And what's my line of work?' said Dean.

'Security. Doors and that? Hired muscle. Sorting stuff out without getting the law involved.' Ruth was improvising now. Something about Dean seemed softer than he was letting on. Like this silence was all a front. She felt there was something there if she just pushed a little harder.

'Malton Security has a policy of not talking to the press.'

'Have you got something to hide?'

Dean shook his head and laughed. 'Everyone's got something to hide,' he said. 'But in this case it's because a lot of our clients value privacy and so knowing that we simply don't ever talk to the press reassures them that whatever we are involved with, it won't become public knowledge. So I'm afraid that the idea of working on a podcast with a journalist is a complete non-starter.'

'Even one that could free your boss?'

Dean shrugged. 'If you can do that, then more power to you, but right now we feel like it's well in hand.'

'Oh?' said Ruth curiously.

Dean frowned. 'And I wouldn't be discussing it with the press.'

Dean stood up.

'I'm already late,' he said.

Ruth looked at her watch and quietly swore to herself.

'And it looks like you might be too,' said Dean.

***

Ruth was indeed over an hour late and so it didn't seem like it'd make much difference if she took a detour back to the office. After getting nothing out of Dean she'd quickly got on her phone to file her article and headed back into town.

She wasn't sure what exactly she was hoping to find at Piccadilly Basin. The police tape was down already, the white evidence tent long gone.

Manchester was moving on. Another body by the canal. Another young man dead. Nothing to see here. Ruth looked upwards at the skyline that loomed over her. First, the ornate warehouses north of Piccadilly, but then, dwarfing them further off in the distance, the tower blocks, identical glass protrusions thrusting upwards towards the sky.

A dead sex worker seemed very insignificant in the shadow of all that progress and wealth.

She was so wrapped up in her thoughts that she almost missed the black Audi with tinted windows that pulled into the car park. The driver's annoyed horn shook her back to reality.

Ruth raised a conciliatory hand and skipped out of the way. She was about to leave when something made her turn back. As she did she saw the driver get out of the Audi and start briskly walking the perimeter of the car park, his eyes fixed on the ground, looking for something.

He was white, a narrow strip of face sandwiched between his coarse black hair and equally black beard. His eyes were set deep in his face, suspicious slits. He wore dark jeans, black hiking boots with shiny silver fixings and a heavy black chore shirt done up to the neck.

Immediately Ruth's journalistic instincts kicked in and whatever disappointment she felt from her meeting with Dean became a distant memory. She pretended to be checking her phone as she watched him sweep the ground. He moved

106

quickly and systematically, his eyes searching the tarmac. Never going over the same spot twice.

She set her camera to video and filmed him as he passed by where she found the phone, holding her breath as he moved a couple of rubbish bags aside, checking before moving on.

Finally he completed his circuit and, having found nothing, returned to the car. As he opened the door, a cloud of grey smoke erupted from within the car and through the rising smoke she saw that there was someone sat in the back seat.

The bearded man got in and wound down his window. As he did so, the passenger in the back leaned over into the front to say something to him and, for just a second, Ruth saw a face she recognised.

The sunken eyes, the brittle skin, the rotting mouth.

It was the face of the man in the hotel bathroom mirror from Jake Arnold's phone.

26

Once upon a time Belle Vue was a dreamland. A circus, a theme park, a zoological garden, a dog track and speedway. It was Manchester's playground. A garden of delights east of the city where Manchester's workers flocked to escape the grim, industrial reality for a few brief hours.

Now it was just more houses.

Only the speedway remained. Less busy but still regularly filling the night air with the sound of souped-up motorbikes hurtling suicidally fast around the track.

The dreams of Belle Vue were in the past, which was where Keisha found herself.

The working men's club was in the shadow of the speedway, tucked away down a back street but still thriving as everything around it changed. Like so many other similar clubs, it was a single-storey building, a flat roof and heavy grilles over narrow windows. But inside it was beautiful. A parquet dance floor and stage with a bar and a club room. The low ceiling and narrow windows gave the place a warm, relaxed intimacy and the bar prices ensured that regulars and visitors alike were going to enjoy themselves.

Keisha sat at the back of the room watching over the proceedings through her dark glasses. A DJ was on stage surrounded by boxes of old seven-inch records. Each one of them a Northern soul classic. Some Keisha recognised; many others she'd never heard before. Growing up in Hulme, her mum's biggest vice had been pop music. Not the sentimental ballads of her parents' generation back in Ireland or the vibrant underground music that was coming out of Moss Side from clubs like the Reno. No. Keisha grew up to Abba and the Bay City Rollers. She was always embarrassed at how uncool her mum was. She had only discovered Northern soul once she was a little older and started venturing out of Hulme to explore the wider world. She'd been in time to catch the fading days of Wigan Casino. The legendary Northern soul club that almost single-handedly revived dozens of forgotten hits.

The legacy of Wigan Casino was all around her tonight in Belle Vue. The vast majority of the punters were well into their sixties if not older. Still immaculately dressed and still enthused by the music they were hearing. A couple of girls in their twenties were on the dance floor throwing Northern soul shapes, high kicks and spins. Around them the original Northern soul crowd did their best to keep up.

Everyone was having a great time. Everyone except Keisha. That feeling was back. The tiny absence that stole her breath away, refused to let her mind rest for even a moment as she struggled to catch up and unmask whatever it was that was leaving her feeling like this.

Since visiting the caravan all she could see when she closed her eyes were those photos. The family that Harold Boateng hadn't abandoned. The family that could have been hers.

All she could think was – why had Harold kept them in his life and not her? The thought infuriated Keisha. She didn't need Harold's approval for her life. Besides, she would never get it now. He was dead. His final act had been one of cruelty. Dragging her back into the mess he'd made of his life. She told herself that whatever she was doing out in Belle Vue it wasn't about Harold. He didn't deserve any of this. This was about Keisha making sure she could return to Ibiza free of that nagging feeling that there was something amiss.

Once she knew who killed her father then she would hold all the cards. Whether or not she acted on that information, this sense of free fall that she'd been experiencing in the past few days would be over. She would be in control. That was more important than any kind of revenge.

Keisha had arrived back in Manchester mid-afternoon and headed out shopping where she'd bought herself a pair of bright yellow, wide-legged, pleated trousers, a heavy white T-shirt and fitted black leather jacket. She'd decided that if she was going to follow Harold's ghost to a Northern soul night she was at least going to look the part.

Now, she sat at her table and watched the dancers wildly throwing shapes and tried to imagine her father sat in this same room, listening to this same music.

'Rachel!'

Keisha didn't respond at first. An elderly woman in denim bell bottoms and a matching trucker's jacket was shouting in her direction, a worried look on her face. It was only when she reached the table where Keisha was sitting and repeated herself that Keisha took notice.

'Rachel! It is Rachel, isn't it – Harold's Rachel?' said the woman, unsure.

'Yes,' said Keisha with a smile and took off her shades. The old woman's face lit up and, without being invited, she sat down.

Keisha immediately felt more at ease. She wasn't Keisha chasing her father's ghost. She was Rachel.

'I thought it must be you. From your photos. I'm Gerry. Harold's always talking about you. Thank God you're here. I was getting worried. I thought something had happened to him. Is he with you?'

'Harold's dead,' said Keisha with a casual cruelty.

With a worried smile the woman said, 'Sorry, what did you say? I can't hear a bloody thing these days, and with this noise!'

Keisha felt herself enjoying the feeling of power. She had information that could destroy this woman. The past few days she'd been on the back foot, assailed with revelation after revelation, powerless to do anything but soak up the damage. Now she was getting back in control and it felt good.

Keisha leaned in closer and fixed her gaze on Gerry's eyes. Gerry was wearing dark eyeliner, and she looked great for her age. 'Harold is dead.'

Gerry's hand came to her mouth and those immaculate eyes began to quiver. 'They got him,' she said, and began to cry.

Keisha did her best to impassively watch Gerry's tears. But as she did so she felt the older woman's grief resonating with the feelings she'd been holding at bay for the past few days.

As the DJ started a new song and the dancers on the floor began once more to spin and twirl, Keisha reminded herself why she was here. This was about information. She wasn't here for anything as soft and indulgent as grief; she was here to get her life back. She leaned over the table and took Gerry's hand. Her eyes softened and she said, 'I know. He was hit by a car.'

Gerry shook her head and reached for a hankie to dab her eyes. 'I'm so sorry – listen to me going on. He was your dad. How are you and Allie doing?'

Allie, that must be the name of the little girl in all the photos.

'We're getting by. It was such a shock,' said Keisha, sounding a little too convincing for her own comfort.

'I hadn't seen him for a few days but, you know, that was typical Harold. He'd disappear for a couple of days here and there. Never tell you where he was going.'

Keisha kept quiet and tried not to think about how thin the line between this play-acting and her true feelings really was. She let Gerry continue.

'He told you about me though, didn't he? I told him to tell you about me,' said Gerry, inches from Keisha's face, shouting to be heard over the music.

'He told me all about you,' lied Keisha. Then before she could stop herself, added, 'He really loved you.'

Gerry sat back and started crying all over again. Suddenly, as tears pricked at her eyes, Keisha wished she'd kept her shades on.

Steeling herself, she thought about how this woman got more of Harold than she ever had. How Rachel and Allie got more of Harold. Even the people who killed him knew her father better than she did.

Harold gave her nothing and he deserved nothing. Least of all her tears.

'We were planning for me to move in with him. Up at his caravan,' Gerry said.

So the caravan was Harold's official home. Or at least the home where he lived his straight life.

'You said, *they got him*. What did you mean?' asked Keisha, trying to sound the right mixture of worried and urgent.

Gerry stopped crying for a moment and looked worried.

'It's nothing. It's silly. Now's not the time.'

'Was my dad scared of someone?'

Gerry's eyes darted from side to side. Her white hankie was stained with eyeliner.

'Please,' implored Keisha. 'I had to see his body. I've got to bury him. If something happened to him, I need to know.' As she heard herself say the words out loud, Keisha realised she was no longer Rachel. She was Keisha, desperate to know about her father.

Gerry leaned in. Keisha could see she was trembling.

'A couple of weeks ago he started acting really weird. *Really* weird. He said he'd messed up. Wouldn't tell me what that meant. But he told me not to worry. That was when he asked me to move in with him. He said he was retiring and was going to spend all his time on the coast from now on. Wanted me to join him.'

'Retire from what?' said Keisha, her heart racing.

'He never told me. Didn't he tell you?'

Keisha fought back a sudden urge to cry out that Harold had walked out of her life when she was a little girl and never looked back. She simply shook her head and said, 'What had he messed up?'

'That's all I know,' said Gerry. 'I think he was scared but you know what he's like – he never talks about anything if he doesn't want to.'

Keisha nodded silently.

Gerry dabbed her eyes again and noticed her hankie.

'Oh my gosh,' she said looking down at the mess. 'What must I look like? I'll be back.'

She got up and hurried out of the room, heading for the toilets. Alone again, Keisha gladly put her shades back on. The room fell back into the comforting darkness of a world behind tinted glass.

Keisha let the music wash over her. Ringing Hammond organs and deep, skipping bass lines. She felt a long-suppressed grief churn inside. The thought of mourning the man who had fled out of her life enraged her and she fought to control the feelings with the only thing she had to hand – his murder.

Someone was after Harold. He was planning a runner with this Gerry woman. He'd messed up. The dead body, the trashed caravan, it all was leading somewhere. A place where the tables would be turned and Keisha would be the one inflicting the pain.

She felt her phone go in her pocket. It was Dean. The DNA was back.

27

'Malton did exactly what he said he'd do for me. I've heard nothing since I last spoke to him.'

Fauzia Malik MP took a sip of the Starbucks coffee she had with her when she'd arrived to meet Dean above the takeaway on the main drag through Daubhill in Bolton. Dean was already upstairs waiting for her. Downstairs a dozen or so Kurdish men were sat round tables, eating and talking, but upstairs the restaurant had yet to be furnished. The white tile flooring was in place and the walls had been painted but there was only the one table, waiting with two chairs at the far end of the room, by the window looking out over the street outside, illuminated with the light of dozens of takeaways.

This was where Fauzia had asked to meet. Dean arrived early and, upon realising who he was there to see, the men downstairs insisted on giving him three different curries, a huge plate of rice and a large, greasy nan bread as well as a large, metal tumbler full of some kind of yoghurt drink. On the house.

Dean hadn't eaten all day so didn't object. His meal was first interrupted by the news from Benton that she had the DNA results from the blood back, and then after he'd let Keisha know the name that Benton had given him, he was about to resume his impromptu meal when one of the men downstairs had led Fauzia up.

'So why am I hearing from you now?' she asked.

Last time Dean had seen Fauzia she'd been a terrified young councillor whose drug-dealing brother had fallen foul of one of the most dangerous men in Manchester. Now she was an MP and exuded the confident power of her position.

She was short but seemed taller with her long, straight, dark hair and sharp features. She wasn't just an MP; she was still a doctor on rotation at Royal Bolton. One of those people who make everyone else look lazy.

'How's your dad's wedding venue?' asked Dean, avoiding the question.

'Completed,' said Fauzia sharply.

'No more planning problems when your daughter's an MP?' said Dean as innocently as he could.

'You're here for a favour, aren't you? I know all about Malton.'

Dean kept quiet and let Fauzia continue. After three months of not hearing a word from his boss he wished he knew all about Malton.

'I keep tabs on him. Out of curiosity more than anything,' said Fauzia.

'To make sure he kept his end of the deal?' asked Dean.

'To make sure if someone ever came to me asking for a favour that I'd know what was going on. So I'll tell you before you go any further. I can't intervene in Malton's upcoming trial. And I can't find out about what's going on at MRI.'

Dean froze. MRI. Manchester Royal Infirmary. What did that have to do with Malton?

He chose his next words very carefully. 'I thought with you being a doctor and an MP . . . Who better to ask?'

Fauzia slowly turned her cup of coffee on the tabletop. She was thinking. Dean could smell his half-eaten meal. The food here was unexpectedly good. Rich, moreish sauces and generous, soft cuts of meat. He felt his stomach rumbling but he kept his focus on Fauzia.

'I did ask after him. He was in some kind of fight with another prisoner. Apparently he was stabbed multiple times and found passed out. They got him to MRI and he's stable.

As I understand it, they're planning to return him to the prison infirmary in the next couple of days.'

All at once Dean lost his appetite. Mickey Farr had had his word with Malton.

'So as you can see,' said Fauzia, 'there's nothing for me to do there.'

Her moment of doubt had gone. She was back in control.

'So if that's all?'

Dean pushed what he'd just heard to the back of his mind and led with what had brought him to a Kurdish takeaway in Daubhill in the first place.

'I don't care about Malton,' lied Dean. 'I'm here about the licensing committee.'

28

Malton's rib was definitely broken. He could feel the hair-line crack, moving with every breath. His nose too. All those headbutts. So many he nearly lost sense of himself. There was a burning sensation in his upper thigh where Mickey's makeshift blade had gone in. He hoped that wasn't an infection. He could still move his leg but the area felt hot to the touch. Or at least he imagined it would if he could move either of the hands that had both been handcuffed to the hospital bed on which he lay.

Malton had been awake for a few hours now. But he hadn't opened his eyes, hadn't done anything to give away the fact that he was now conscious. Instead he'd been lying there listening. Trying to gather as much information as he could. Where was he? Who was guarding him? How long would he be here? What happened to Mickey Farr?

He knew he was in Manchester Royal Infirmary. He'd heard a nurse mention heading over to meet someone at St Mary's, the women's hospital next to MRI. He didn't know what wing he was on but he was in his own room, and from the conversation he'd overheard between nurses there was at least one prison officer guarding his room. Possibly more.

Malton breathed in, his rib grinding as he did so. With every slight movement he could feel the catheter tube running up into his bladder. But what hurt most was the self-inflicted wound in his chest. He'd pushed Farr's blade all the way in. Left just the handle sticking out. He must have passed out because everything after that was blank. He could feel the wound throbbing. A low, numb pain that spread all over his chest. He'd been aiming to miss anything important. He hoped he'd been successful.

But that was the plan. Fight Farr, get injured, get taken to a hospital. Much easier to escape from a hospital than a prison. To make sure he sold the ruse, he'd finally stabbed himself. Not only did it make the injuries look worse but it could also be useful later on to muddy the waters as to what had happened in that cell.

He still didn't know if Farr had lived. He was just about alive when Malton last saw him collapsed in his own blood and piss.

***

Malton wished he could reach Dean. Or that he'd stayed in contact with him while he was inside. As it was, he was on his own. He'd come this far. He'd have to do whatever it took to get all the way to freedom.

He heard the door opening but he lay still, his eyes closed.

'Wake up,' said Cunningham's voice.

Malton opened his eyes to see the governor stood at the foot of his bed smiling.

'I got you. You locked a guard in his cell, you nearly killed Mickey Farr . . .'

So Mickey had lived. That was important. Farr would never cooperate with charges, and Cunningham would know that any criminal trial would reflect as badly on the prison and her competency as it would hurt Malton.

'Ever since I met you I had your number. You think you're clever, don't you?' said Cunningham.

Malton said nothing.

'Here's clever for you. A day's time you'll be out of here. But you're not going back to Strangeways. No VPU for you.'

Malton listened, hiding his sense of mounting dread.

'See, I think you might have something wrong with you,' said Cunningham gleefully. 'Something up here.' She tapped her head. 'We both know that it's in no one's interest to get the police involved. Strangeways' reputation is bad enough as it is. But that doesn't mean there aren't consequences.'

Malton looked past Cunningham through the window in the door to his room. In the time she'd been speaking he'd seen the same prison officer talking to a nurse and walking up and down. That was all he'd seen. There was only one guard.

'I'm sending you to Ashworth,' said Cunningham with a flourish.

Ashworth Secure Hospital. The Broadmoor of the north. Where people who would once have been described as criminally insane were sent. For treatment. Malton knew exactly what that meant.

'Now I don't know what's wrong with you,' said Cunningham, beginning to enjoy the sound of her own voice. 'But then I'm no expert. At Ashworth they'll make sure you get what you need. Lots of nice drugs to calm you down. And obviously there's side effects. All that muscle, I'm afraid it'll probably go to fat. And that brain of yours. I see you lying there taking all this in. Thinking a mile a minute. Well that'll go too. You'll be a nice, happy, compliant blob. How does that sound?'

It sounded to Malton like he was out of time.

29

Sam Kennard was the last one to leave his house. At half eight his wife Tracey Kennard bustled out, juggling an umbrella and three young children wrapped up in heavy coats against the rain. Then half an hour later Sam appeared, a black hooded top, bearing a band logo, on over his overalls. He was tall and stooped slightly.

He got into the large, dirty blue Transit that filled the driveway of his home on an estate in Fallowfield, hemmed in between Princess Parkway to the south and Wilmslow Road to the north, and after sitting looking at his phone for nearly ten minutes he finally turned the ignition and reversed out of the driveway.

As he drove off he was still juggling his mobile phone. More than enough distraction to completely fail to spot Dean and Keisha who had been parked down the road watching him the whole time.

They'd been sat in silence for the past hour, Dean having sensed that Keisha was in no mood for small talk. He wondered what it was she'd been doing since he last saw her at the caravan. He desperately wanted to ask her about her father. Until Benton had come through with the DNA from the car identifying Sam Kennard, Harold Boateng had been his biggest lead in tracking down who had robbed the Farr family.

But he knew better than to disturb whatever was going on behind those dark glasses.

Besides, he had his own problems. The night before, he'd been so shook up over the news about Malton that he'd called Vikki. She'd answered but Dean got the impression that she'd pressed to receive the call before she had a chance to think about what she was doing.

She was on her way out. All dressed up with black, batwing eye liner and hair in bunches. She had a white T-shirt on under her leather jacket. Riding the nineties revival that had utterly passed Dean by.

She'd been drinking and seemed happy. Several of her housemates were there. They all said hello to Dean and for a moment it felt like he was there with her. Living the normal life of a young, twenty-something. Not walking in the footsteps of killers. But all too soon it was time for Vikki to head out. She'd blown Dean a kiss and swung her phone round to let the room say goodbye. But Dean hardly noticed. All he saw was the young man sat at the kitchen table, silently rolling a cigarette. He had floppy hair and a long Raglan coat over a baggy shirt. Dean only saw him for a second, but he remembered two very distinct things. Firstly, how the fingers that were rolling that cigarette were painted with black nail polish, and secondly, how as the phone passed over him, he looked out from under his fringe and smirked at the camera.

The call over, Dean had found himself alone in his front room in Moss Side with his takeaway meal and knowledge that the next day he and Keisha would be paying a visit to Sam Kennard.

***

At a discreet distance Dean started to follow Sam's van as it meandered out of the estate and began a rat run through back streets that would take it up to the A34.

Sam was passing through Burnage, down a narrow road of shops, most notable for still being home to Sifters Records, the old-school record shop, name-checked by Oasis and still going strong thirty years later. Cars were parked on both sides with pedestrians weaving between them. But Sam didn't pause. If anything he sped up, accelerating through a red light and throwing his van into a right-hand turn onto the A34. Dean had no choice but to follow on behind, narrowly dodging the cross traffic that had already begun to accelerate towards him. He hoped that Sam didn't notice the riot of horns that followed his manoeuvre.

Beside him Keisha seemed unmoved. True to his word Dean had told Keisha about the DNA and she'd insisted they follow up together. They hadn't really discussed what they were going to do with Sam. Dean assumed Keisha wanted him as the man who killed her father. He wanted Sam as the next step in his investigation. He hoped that maybe there was some kind of compromise to be had. One that let him at least have a little time with Sam before Keisha got her hands on him.

What he hadn't told her was that Malton was in Manchester Royal Infirmary.

That morning he'd had a call from Janet Farr. He was almost relieved when she simply berated him about his lack of progress in finding out who had stolen their drugs. At best it meant that Mickey Farr hadn't been involved in the fight with Malton. At worst it meant that news of the fight had yet to reach the Farrs. It was too many fires to fight all at the one time.

Eager to get Janet off the phone, he'd given her the news about the DNA, deliberately avoiding mentioning Sam Kennard's name. He hoped that by the time he next had to talk to the Farrs he'd at least know how much trouble he was in.

And then there was Ruth Porter. He'd looked Ruth up after she'd left the office. She was, like she said, a journalist. One who seemed to think that Malton had been caught up in some kind of serial killer conspiracy. Dean knew better than most that in an age of blanket surveillance from CCTV, mobile phones and GPS metadata it was nearly impossible for an individual to kill a string of victims. Serial killers in America operated in the gaps between law enforcement and geography. Britain was far too small for them to get much past the first couple of victims. Nevertheless, it was clear Ruth truly believed there was a killer out there. But far more interesting to Dean, she was convinced someone had framed Malton for one of the murders.

The thought of strong-arming Ruth into dropping the podcast wasn't something he felt comfortable doing. He didn't want to see her get hurt. That meant he'd need to bring a different kind of pressure to bear.

Sam was driving at speed now. He'd turned off at Parrs Wood and was ploughing down Wilmslow Road towards Stockport. The rush hour traffic was thinning out, leaving Sam free to blow through built-up suburbs at speeds nudging fifty miles an hour. Dean hoped he'd put his phone down.

But all these things paled in comparison to the silent woman sat in the passenger seat next to him, her face unreadable beneath her sunglasses. The longer he went without telling Keisha about Malton's condition the worse it would be when she found out he'd kept it from her. He didn't know how she'd find out but he knew she could and she would. Like Malton, Keisha seemed to have a sixth sense when it came to Manchester's secrets.

He watched her out of the corner of his eye as they kept a discreet distance behind Sam Kennard's van. From the look of her he'd guess she'd been abroad, somewhere sunny. Wherever it was, she was back in town now and the last thing Dean wanted to do was upset her.

That was why he'd picked her up earlier that morning and together they'd waited for Sam to emerge.

They were following Sam as he headed out on the M60. He had just pulled off outside of Stockport when Dean finally broke.

'I need to tell you something,' he said.

Keisha turned to face him, her eyes hidden behind her glasses. Ever since she'd stepped in the car it had been filled with her perfume. With Vikki in London, and running Malton Security full-time, the nearest Dean came to perfume was when doormen came off a shift having broken up a fight between a gang of women. Smelling it on a hulking, six-foot-two bouncer wasn't quite the same.

'Malton's in the hospital,' said Dean, deciding that the best thing to do was just recount the facts.

Keisha turned back to look out the window. 'And?' she said.

'It happened in Strangeways. He got into a fight.'

'Who with?'

'I don't know,' said Dean honestly.

Keisha hadn't moved a muscle. She was obviously thinking. 'Which hospital?' she asked.

'MRI.'

'When did you find out?' she asked.

Dean hesitated. He'd known about Malton when he'd called Keisha the night before. Why hadn't he just told her then?

'Last night,' said Dean with deliberate ambiguity.

'I see,' said Keisha, leaving Dean in no doubt that she knew he'd failed to pass on this information the night before.

Dean didn't have time to come up with an excuse because Sam Kennard had finally arrived at his destination.

A small garage on an industrial estate outside of Stockport. Sandwiched between a WHSmith warehouse and a fireplace showroom.

Farrs' Tyres.

30

'I can't do anything about a hunch,' said the desk officer impatiently.

This wasn't going how Ruth had hoped. After seeing the man from the hotel room in the flesh, she'd spent a sleepless night suddenly all too aware of Jake's phone. In the end she'd turned it off and hidden it beneath her mattress where it lay like a cold, hard pea keeping her awake.

But what did she really have? The phone for sure. To turn that in now would be to admit taking it and hiding it. She could always stretch the truth around that. Claim she'd only just found it. But then there was the message she'd sent after Jake's death. The GPS information that could place it with her. Besides, if she gave up the phone she gave up the whole story.

It was clear that whoever the man in the photo was, he was also after the phone, and from the look of the bearded man who was with him, he had professional help in that respect.

It was the sight of that man scouring Piccadilly Basin that had finally convinced Ruth to pay a visit to her local police station. Lying awake imagining what that man would do if he knew that she had not just him but him and his boss on film. That she had Jake's phone and a working theory that his boss had killed Jake.

The city centre station was just off Albert Square in the council offices. Ruth had been there before, chasing stories back when she was a student journalist. It wasn't really a station though, more a help desk. The real station had moved out to Salford. Right now the person behind that desk was being less than helpful.

'From what you've told me, and you haven't really told me anything, I'm not sure what it is you want me to do?' said the desk officer. He was a young guy, still young enough to have acne.

'I think that the boy who was killed in Piccadilly Basin . . . I think maybe there's a serial killer.'

Ruth instantly knew she'd said the wrong thing. The desk officer smirked a little and launched into what sounded like an already well-worn speech.

'We're very aware how popular true crime podcasts and social media content are at the moment, but we'd ask, at this time, you refrain from doing anything that could jeopardise an ongoing investigation.'

'I'm trying to help,' said Ruth.

'What could really help is to let the police do their job,' said the officer condescendingly.

Ruth felt her fear being replaced with indignation. 'What if I've seen something that I think proves there's a serial killer out there?'

'You can tell me,' said the officer, folding his arms and leaning back, ready to listen.

Ruth looked at the young man across the counter from her. The photo on his ID badge showing his blotchy skin. The tattoos on his forearms at odds with his sensible, workplace hair. He reeked of complacency.

Ruth's dad had investigated dozens of crimes, often finding things out long before the police. They'd respected his input, treated him as an equal. But he'd had to earn it. Right now Ruth could hear what she sounded like. She didn't blame this young officer. From what she'd told him, she had squat.

'It's nothing,' said Ruth, and she turned and walked out.

Maybe it was nothing but she was more determined than ever to turn that nothing into the story that would make her career.

This officer had no idea who she was and what she was capable of. None of them did.

Outside the station she sat for a moment on the war memorial and got out Jake's phone. There was still no reply so she composed a new message.

I FOUND JAKE'S PHONE. WE NEED TO MEET. I KNOW WHO KILLED HIM.

31

Five pieces of hardened, machine-tooled polymer lay on the bed in Keisha's room at the Midland Hotel.

She'd not just locked the door but had put a chair up under it just in case. She didn't want to be disturbed.

After Dean had dropped her back to the Midland she'd made a few calls and headed out to buy some supplies. By the time she'd returned a couple of hours later there was a package waiting for her at the front desk.

She'd been away from Manchester for over a year but she still had her contacts. She might not have any muscle to call on but she could still lay her hands on a gun.

Having a handgun delivered to the front desk of a hotel was a needless risk. Instead Keisha had had a set of keys delivered to her in an envelope. A text message from a burner phone had given her the location of some storage lockers in the basement of Manchester Central Library, just a short walk from the Midland Hotel.

In those lockers Keisha had found the gun, which was now spread out, disassembled, on the bed in front of her. The gun was the easy part. The other thing she'd found waiting for her in the locker had been harder to source at such short notice. Harder, but not impossible.

The name of the man who'd robbed her father was Sam Kennard. That morning they'd followed him to his work. Then things got complicated. Sam worked for the same family he'd robbed. It was entirely possible that Sam had simply over-heard something he shouldn't have and gone into business for himself. But to know the exact time and place where Harold would have been? To be able to find the drugs that Dean told her were hidden in a compartment in the dashboard? From everything she heard it sounded like an inside job.

Dean had begged her not to move on the Farrs until he had more information. She hadn't told him at the time but she was in no position to move on anyone. She wasn't even sure she wanted to.

The night before at the working men's club she'd nearly been ambushed by the crushing sadness of losing a parent. That wouldn't happen again.

Let Dean keep digging. Nothing he found would change the past. Besides, now she had something far more important to occupy her attention.

Craig was in hospital and Dean couldn't tell her whether it was a routine visit or he was at death's door.

The gun on the bed was a third-generation Glock. A light-weight, super reliable handgun favoured by police and military for its ease of use. Keisha wasn't taking any chances. Once she had securely locked herself in her hotel room she'd taken the gun apart. The lower part with the handle where the magazine would go, the slide that formed the top part of the gun, and from within the slide – the spring and barrel. She decided against dismantling the firing pin. If it didn't work now, she didn't have the tools to fix it.

She'd picked up a can of WD-40 while she was out. It wasn't ideal. Long term, WD-40 would gum up the mechanism of the gun and do more harm than good. Keisha wasn't planning on sticking around for the long term.

On the floor beside the bed were the shopping bags containing the other things she'd bought that morning.

Keisha sprayed each piece of the gun with lubricant and wiped it down with a hotel flannel.

For the few minutes that it took her to work over the individual pieces, her mind drifted back to the Northern soul night. She thought about how it felt being Rachel. Gerry had treated her like an old friend. She didn't know if Gerry had met Rachel before or not, but the way she talked to Keisha, it was like she was one of the family. She'd asked about Allie. Harold's granddaughter. Keisha's mind went to her own son Anthony. Harold had never even known he existed. Now he never would. Allie would have been Anthony's cousin. No. Allie *was* Anthony's cousin.

Whatever she was feeling it was far too late to let Harold know. She couldn't risk the same thing happening with Craig.

That whole year in Ibiza she'd hardly thought about Craig. Even the news of his arrest hadn't changed that. Under the dazzling Spanish sun, Craig – like the rest of Manchester – seemed like a dark, stormy, remote dream. Something that happened to someone else a long time ago.

But ever since she'd been back she'd found herself thinking about him. He was there in the rain-soaked pavements and the gentle decay. In the shadows between the skyscrapers and the old city, waiting just beneath the surface. That he was locked up in Strangeways made perfect sense. Craig and Manchester had forever been at each other's throats. Chained together in a battle that only one of them could win. But now he was dying and the thought of Manchester without Craig Malton in it seemed intolerable. Keisha had killed for Craig and she'd been ready to kill him. She'd never loved someone more, yet she'd never felt more visceral hatred for anyone alive. If he was at death's door, she knew she would never forgive herself if she didn't make one last attempt to once and for all know just what Craig meant to her.

Keisha finished wiping down the gun and carefully reassembled the parts, fitting the barrel and spring into the slide before clipping the slide back on top of the Glock and moving it back and forth to make sure everything was clear.

Finally she slid the full magazine into the base of the handle and pulled the slide back one more time, feeling the movement of a 9mm bullet sliding into the breach, ready to be fired.

She laid the gun down on the bed and turned to the other thing she'd found waiting for her in the storage locker.

Something that, in the right hands, could do even more damage.

A police ID.

A Greater Manchester Police warrant card with Keisha's photo and the name of a real officer she found from a quick trawl of Twitter. Karen Marlow was approximately the same age as Keisha. She was mixed race and, in the photos Keisha saw, had her hair braided up in a way Keisha could easily replicate.

It wouldn't hold up under close inspection but for what Keisha was planning it would have to do. And if it failed then there was always the gun.

If Manchester was going to drag her back through her painful past then she would at least make one last visit to the only person back there that still meant anything to her.

It made no sense. It was a stupid risk. Not in the plan.

Keisha didn't care. If there was even a chance that Craig could be lying dying in MRI, then she had to see him one last time.

131

32

Malton kept the arm that was still chained to the bed as stiff as possible. By tensing all the muscle he was able to keep it almost unmoved, making the job of dressing the wound on his chest near impossible for the nurse who was currently doing his best to wrap bandages around his torso.

The catheter had come out earlier that morning and it seemed like Cunningham's threat to move him to Ashworth was in motion.

All through the night, Malton had racked his brains. He'd lain in the dark and summoned all his strength as he tried first to break the handcuffs holding him to the bed, and then when that failed, to break the bed itself. Unable to make a sound without attracting the attention of the prison officer outside, he had to rely on brute power, slowly bending the bed frame back and forth.

It had taken him several hours to deform the frame but he was still nowhere near able to free himself. And so, with dawn breaking, he'd used the remaining time to bend the bed back as best as possible and hope that a chance would present itself in the daylight.

From what he could see, his room faced onto a giant, indoor atrium. Even if he could free himself from the bed he'd have to find his way out of the hospital. But before any of that he would have to get past the prison officer who was stood in the room watching the nurse work.

The odds weren't in his favour but once he was in that transport and heading to Ashworth it would be game over.

So he kept his whole body as rigid as possible, whenever he could, moving away from the nurse as he struggled to change the dressings. The nurse was Portuguese. A softly spoken man with a smile in his voice. At first he'd been reassuring, joking with Malton and treating him just like any other patient. Then as time wore on he'd stopped talking and focused on trying to get the job finished.

But after ten minutes of trying and failing to bandage Malton's wounds he finally snapped. 'You must take off the handcuff,' said the nurse to the officer, a tiny trace of outrage in his voice.

'I'm sorry, I can't do that,' said the officer.

Unfazed, the nurse stood up and folded his arms. 'Then I can't change the dressing, and if I can't change the dressing the doctor won't discharge him. He's going nowhere.'

Malton listened to the exchange going on above him. His chest felt like it was ready to explode. The pain was near unbearable. It distracted from the agony of his broken ribs and shooting pains he'd begun to get up and down the leg where Mickey Farr had stabbed him.

'Well?' said the nurse impatiently.

Malton lay still, trying to look delirious. It wasn't much of a stretch.

He'd spent his whole life staying one step ahead of everyone yet here he was now, badly wounded and chained to a hospital bed. Whatever plan of escape he had went no further than the door to his hospital room. It was all he had left.

The officer was leaning over Malton, keys in hand. As soon as the cuffs were off there would be nothing more to think about. He'd have to go all out.

The officer stopped for a moment and looked down at Malton. He was tall. A foot on Malton easily and packed out with gym-honed muscle. He'd not been picked for this job for his personality.

'You going to behave?' he asked grimly.

'He was a few millimetres away from getting stabbed in a major artery,' said the nurse impatiently. 'He's lucky to be alive.'

Malton hoped he still had a little of that luck left.

The officer put the key in the cuff and Malton heard it fall away.

Do it now. While the officer was still leaning over. Reach up, bring him close, overpower him. Knock him out, get out of the room. Run – don't stop. Just run.

Malton went to raise his free arm and it felt like something in his chest burst. He went to open his mouth to scream in pain but all that came out was a dry, hollow yell as he sank back into the bed.

The last thing he heard was the nurse yelling for a doctor.

Then it all went black.

33

The door to Bea Wallace's office opened and a middle-aged man in dad jeans and a sports jacket walked out. As he passed Dean he stared down at him with flat, dead eyes. Dean wondered what terrible thing he'd done to need Bea Wallace's help.

'In you come, pet,' said Bea from her office. She looked exactly like the last time Dean had seen her a few months ago. Short, blonde and beaming. The perfect disguise for an alpha predator.

Bea's office was lined with photo after photo of terrifying, grizzled criminals. The heaviest, most connected men in the Manchester underworld. If you had Bea Wallace as your lawyer it was a safe bet that you were into something that carried a double-digit sentence. The kind of thing that made you rich enough to be able to afford someone like Bea in the first place.

Bea was based in a newly built block just off Deansgate. She was neatly placed between the Civil Justice Centre and the Crown Court, with several barristers nearby around St John Street. Bea sat at the epicentre of Manchester's legal framework, pulling its levers to get some of the most dangerous and deranged men off scot-free.

'What brings you here?' trilled Bea as if Dean dropping in was nothing more than a pleasant surprise.

The last time he'd worked with Bea was when she'd asked Malton to investigate the murder of the son of one of her clients. Whether it was a set-up or a fuck-up, things had gone badly for the client. His body was still missing.

'I've got some information about Malton,' said Dean.

He knew Malton hadn't contacted Bea and Bea hadn't felt the need to lift a finger to defend her former partner and lover. Dean didn't know what had gone on between them but it had struck him as oddly convenient that no sooner had they fallen out than Malton found himself caught up in a legally airtight murder charge.

There was a fine line between seeing all the angles and drifting into paranoid conspiracy theory. Working for Malton, Dean felt that line getting thinner by the day. Right now he needed Bea onside and so he chose not to dwell on just what Bea Wallace might be capable of when crossed.

Instead he hoped that there was still enough lingering affection to pique Bea's interest.

'Go on,' said Bea, tidying papers on her desk.

'I think someone is maybe killing rent boys,' said Dean.

'A serial killer?' said Bea, her Geordie accent rising in amused delight.

'I know,' said Dean quickly hearing exactly how he sounded. 'But if you were going to kill someone, and get away with it, then rent boys aren't a bad shout.'

Bea shrugged. 'Not my area I'm afraid, pet. Why do you bring it up? Thinking of a career change?' She laughed at her joke.

'Stephen Page was a rent boy,' said Dean without any hint of amusement.

Bea stopped laughing and looked confused. 'So you think Craig was a serial killer?'

'Four days ago another boy turned up dead.'

Dean hadn't had time to properly look into the dead boy that Ruth had mentioned back in his office. From the papers and a quick look on social media he knew his name was Jake Arnold. From the comments beneath the *Manchester Evening News* article, the consensus among the trolls was that he was a junkie and got what was coming to him.

Bea stopped sorting her papers and looked straight at him.

'So you think if there is a serial killer, and he's still killing young lads, that puts Craig in the clear?'

'Could it?' said Dean, hopeful that he was starting to move Bea in the right direction.

Bea blew out her cheeks and shook her head. She came round and sat on the edge of the desk, one leg crossed over the other, her skirt riding up to give Dean a glimpse of thigh that he did his best not to notice.

'Thing is, Craig's DNA was found in the car. His DNA.'

'It could have been planted,' said Dean.

Bea shrugged. 'Well maybe. But by who? Why? How?'

Dean's mind raced but Bea was still going.

'And even if it was, which I don't think it was, there's the police informant. Puts Craig in that car.'

'Informants lie all the time,' said Dean, hearing how desperate he sounded. 'And now with this new body . . .'

Bea smiled kindly.

'I know you care about Craig but the best thing you can do for him is exactly what you are doing. Keep the business going, make sure he's got something waiting for him when he gets out. If he ever does.'

Bea's tone unmanned Dean. She sounded so sure of herself. As if she were the adult in the room and Dean was simply a wide-eyed child regaling her with tall tales. For just a moment he wondered if Malton really had murdered Stephen Page.

'Malton's in the hospital,' said Dean, clutching at straws to find anything that could bring Bea around.

Bea slid off the desk and went back to sorting paper. 'I heard. Really sad. But doing what Craig did all those years, what do you expect? Now if that's all, pet, I got a lot on.'

Bea stopped for a moment and smiled up at Dean in a way that let him know in no uncertain terms the conversation was over.

Stood outside Bea's offices, he thought about what she said. What was less unbelievable? That Malton would kill a young man or that Bea Wallace would set him up for the murder of that same young man? Both seemed wildly improbable, and after talking with Bea, Dean felt no closer to the truth. Whatever that was.

Time was running out and with Malton banged up and Bea uninterested that left only him. Not quite only him. There was one other person in Manchester who could help Malton. A long shot, but she was all Dean had left.

34

'DI Karen Marlow?' said the woman at the inpatient desk, looking down at the fake police warrant card in Keisha's hand.

Keisha had braided her hair up to an approximation of how the real Karen Marlow wore her hair and thrown on a plain black dress under a long grey overcoat. The only thing out of place were the black Nike Air Forces she wore on her feet.

There was no way the receptionist could have known who Karen Marlow was or what she looked like, but it didn't hurt to play the part.

Keisha's only addition to the look was to wear a large, distinctive pair of glasses. Karen Marlow didn't wear glasses but if things went bad Keisha wanted to give herself the quick, messy disguise of being able to take off her glasses, ditch the coat and let down her hair.

'I need to find a patient. Craig Malton,' said Keisha forcefully.

The receptionist looked confused. She was a young woman in a neat, dark green hijab. Her face an immaculate oval looking up at Keisha.

'Is there a problem?' said Keisha, letting a little impatience creep into her voice.

'No. Sorry,' said the woman, flustered. 'It's just . . . you don't know the department?'

'No,' said Keisha.

'Give me a minute,' said the woman, and got on the phone.

'Bloody useless round here,' said a voice from low down.

Keisha turned to see a white-haired woman in pyjamas and a dressing gown sat in a wheelchair smiling up at her.

She gave the woman a quick smile and turned back to wait for the receptionist to finish her call.

Manchester Royal Infirmary was vast. A giant hospital that included a women's wing at St Mary's, an eye hospital and a children's hospital as well as several research laboratories and university buildings. Finding one patient was a huge undertaking.

She was currently stood in a towering, six-storey atrium. Bright white walls and glass rising upwards with walkways criss-crossing through the open space. Glass-walled wards looked out onto the atrium and the ceiling too was glass, flooding the building with light. A large column ran lifts from the ground floor all the way up to the sixth floor.

At ground level dozens of patients clutching bags and provisions hurried along. Some on foot, some in wheelchairs.

Like all hospitals, beneath the dazzling white walls and the colourful posters was the flat, chemical smell of sickness and death.

This was a place where people came to die. Craig was somewhere in here. Dying. Alone.

Her father had died before she ever had the chance to process what he meant to her. She wasn't going to let the same thing happen with Craig. It was a mad risk but, set against the thought of him dying without her getting to see him one last time, it felt like the most rational thing in the world.

Time was passing and the receptionist was still on the phone. Keisha glanced around the atrium and froze. Two uniformed police officers had just emerged from the lift and were walking towards her, talking. Two young women, both deep in conversation. Smiling, laughing.

Keisha saw the receptionist's eyes clock the two officers.

'This is time-sensitive,' said Keisha, dragging the receptionist's gaze back to her own.

'I know, it's just . . . .' The receptionist broke off as someone appeared on the other end of the line.

'Yes . . . yes . . . Craig Malton . . .'

The uniformed officers were nearly level with Keisha. She pulled out her phone and made a show of checking something as they passed.

'DI Karen Marlow, right?' said the receptionist out loud to Keisha.

The uniformed officers stopped and looked over to where Keisha was standing at the desk.

'Yes,' said Keisha coldly to the receptionist.

The officers were coming over.

Keisha looked around the atrium. Plenty of places to run but the only way out was through the officers. She felt the weight of the gun in her pocket and held her nerve.

'You OK, ma'am?' asked one of the officers, a tall white woman with red hair tied up in a bun beneath her cap. Keisha clocked her name: PC Willow. The other officer was tiny and South Asian. PC Ghoshal. Bengali.

Keisha rolled her eyes and went for it. 'You know what this lot are like. Kind of bureaucracy makes us look efficient.'

PC Willow smiled, as did PC Ghoshal.

'What you two doing here?'

'Kicking off in maternity,' said Ghoshal.

'Again,' said Willow.

'Can't beat your days in uniform,' said Keisha, letting these two young officers talk to a senior officer, albeit a fake senior officer, with a seductive familiarity.

'Can we help with anything, ma'am?' asked PC Willow.

Keisha looked back to the receptionist. She was still on the phone and smiled back apologetically.

Keisha took a chance. 'I'm here to question Craig Malton? Over here from Strangeways?'

'Good luck with that one,' said PC Ghoshal.

'I don't follow,' said Keisha, the jovial tone leaving her voice.

PC Willow and PC Ghoshal sensed the shift and both did their best to stand a little straighter.

'Sorry, ma'am,' said PC Ghoshal. 'I just meant that you might be too late.'

'Craig Malton collapsed,' said PC Willow. 'He's back in surgery right now.'

35

Paying nearly half her monthly salary to share a flat out in Ancoats, Ruth made sure to take full advantage of what the city had to offer. Even more so when she had the press credentials of *Mancunian Ways* behind her. While she never explicitly promised anyone any kind of coverage, more often than not event promoters were eager to cram as many members of the press in as possible, hoping that at least one or two might sober up from the free drinks long enough to write something favourable.

Ordinarily she'd have enjoyed something like the exhibition she found herself at. The Castlefield Gallery was hidden just behind Deansgate station at the bottom of a block of flats. It was a clean, modern-looking place. Bare concrete floors and white gallery walls. Tonight was the launch of a new artist's residency.

In between the PR hacks, influencers and hangers-on, Ruth could just about make out collections of found objects dumped in piles around the gallery. It reminded her a little of walking up the canal after the magnet fishers had been busy hauling scrap metal out of the water in search of treasure.

But she wasn't here for the art or even the free wine. Dean had got in touch with her. Or, to be more accurate, he had got in touch with Helen in the office and Helen had simply given up Ruth's mobile number. With evidence of a potential murder still sitting heavily in her pocket and the killer out there covering his tracks, Helen's lack of discretion did nothing to calm Ruth's nerves.

She watched as Dean wove his way through the crowd clutching two glasses of wine. This was clearly not his world. While all around people were dressed in interestingly distressed vintage sportswear and angular, draping clothes from niche designers, Dean looked like a trainee estate agent.

'I nearly tripped over the art,' shouted Dean in Ruth's ear. This was a less than ideal place to meet but she wanted somewhere that was both busy and would feel like home turf.

'You told Helen you wanted to speak to me,' said Ruth, cutting straight to the point.

Dean leaned in. 'I've thought about what you said and I've got an offer for you.'

Ruth said nothing. Whatever had changed his mind from the other day, it felt like she was on the front foot. There was nothing to lose in letting him show his cards first.

'You can't do a podcast about Craig Malton,' he said, as if by just saying it that became true.

'Why not?' she asked.

'Firstly, I'd rather you didn't,' said Dean. 'But secondly, the kind of people we deal with at Malton Security. Trust me, you don't want to get involved.'

'I'm a reporter,' said Ruth indignantly. 'That just makes me want to get more involved.'

Dean smiled. 'I guessed you might say that. That's where my offer comes in. I know Manchester better than nearly anyone.'

'I think I know a thing or two about Manchester,' said Ruth. 'That's my job.'

Dean nodded back. 'Mine too. But I don't do art galleries and bars. I do the stuff you don't see. The people who you'll never hear about. The ones who make Manchester work. The real power.'

'You mean criminals?' said Ruth, unimpressed.

Dean shrugged. 'I mean people who if you asked around after Craig Malton may well decide that they'd rather not risk whatever business they had with Craig Malton becoming public knowledge. The kind of people who wouldn't consider simply having a polite word at a nice gallery.'

Dean gestured to the room filled with Manchester's art crowd. What he said was true, to an extent. Ruth had yet to feel like she'd got under the skin of Manchester. But that was what she was going to do whether Dean liked it or not.

'But what if you did the podcast on the serial killer. Leave Malton's name out. And I help you.'

'You help me? What can you do?'

'There's nowhere in the city I can't go,' said Dean. 'No one I can't talk to. You have me on your side then you can get answers.'

Dean stood there looking a little, Ruth thought, like he'd just delivered a speech he'd practiced a fair few times in the mirror.

She turned his offer over in her head. Right now the phone in her pocket was her major lead. She had nothing on Malton but she wasn't going to tell Dean that.

'And all I have to do is leave Malton alone?'

'Not quite,' said Dean. 'I need you to look into Stephen Page's death.'

'The boy Malton killed?'

'We both know he didn't do it.'

'If you can go anywhere and do anything, what's stopping you looking into it?'

'Good question,' said Dean. 'I can see you're always thinking. I've got a business to run and as much as I'd like to devote myself to clearing Malton's name, that's no good if when he gets out there's nothing for him to come back to. Doing what I do, I've learned the best thing you can do is find the right person for the job. And that's you.'

Ruth wondered if this was how her dad had felt when he got a lead. Here was someone who ran a major security company offering her what sounded like unlimited access to the dark side of Manchester. That kind of partnership could make a journalist's career. And if the price was to keep Malton out of things? If he really didn't kill Stephen Page then there was still a story there. The serial killer thing could still work. And after all was said and done she'd have Dean on the hook for life.

'I need to go to the toilet,' said Ruth with a smile.

She handed Dean her glass and turned to head to the toilets. She needed a moment to think. Clear her head and make the right choice.

As she locked the cubicle door behind her she felt Jake's phone vibrating in her pocket.

She was so excited she nearly dropped it in the toilet.

There was a message. For her. It simply said:

LET'S MEET.

36

To one side of the entrance to Betty's sat James's bright purple mini; on the other side, a long queue of people snaked round the corner and further down the block. Stood on the door dressed in all black, Malton watched as James skipped up and down the queue greeting punters as if every single one of them was a long-lost friend. Huge smiles, shrieks of delight and hugs all round.

Malton couldn't help smiling. Being around James, it was impossible not to. Whether it was James's unstoppable joy or the fact that for the first time in his life Malton no longer felt scared, he didn't care. Ever since he and James had got together it was like life suddenly burst into glorious technicolour.

Stood on the door of the opening night of Betty's, James's brand-new club, Malton saw more than just punters and James's deliberately outrageous car. He saw the future and it was good and warm and happy.

Back in Manchester there was no time for smiling. Just fighting. Him against everyone. Even the girl he left behind. As much as he'd loved her, there was too much of Malton in her. That anxious, wary energy of someone who was ready at any point to simply leave it all behind.

Eventually that's what Malton had done and in doing so he'd found happiness waiting for him in Liverpool.

Somewhere halfway down the queue James had started a countdown. Malton checked his watch. It was indeed eight o'clock, opening time.

'Four . . . three . . . two . . . one!' James cheered in delight and the queue erupted with him.

It was just Malton on the door tonight. That would be more than enough. Everyone knew who James's brother was. No one wanted that kind of trouble in their lives.

Malton lifted up the velvet rope and ushered the first customers through the door. A pair of young men, dressed identically in tight jeans and white T-shirts that barely covered their evidently rock-solid abs. They smiled flirtatiously as they passed, but Malton, ever the professional, simply nodded back, the pride and joy he felt unreadable.

As the queue began to filter in and pay their entrance fee to the girl James had working on the desk, Malton fell into his role. The 'straight' man to the brilliant, gorgeous madness that James spread into the world.

He was so caught up on the door that when he felt a hand go round his waist from behind he was about to spin around and make things very dark, very quickly before he smelled the Jean Paul Gaultier. James's fragrance.

'I'm working,' he hissed, only half serious.

'So am I,' said James. 'We're both on the job.'

He felt James lean in closer and whisper in his ear, 'I love the bones of you. This is us. This city doesn't stand a chance.'

With the queue moving on with its own momentum, Malton broke away and turned to face James, ready to kiss him.

But when he did, James wasn't there. Stood in front of him was Keisha. But she was different. Older, harder. She took off her sunglasses and beneath the dark lenses were two eyes so dark and cold and hard that it took his breath away.

'Where's James? I need to see him.' He heard the panic in his voice, the fear. Out of the corner of his eye he was half aware that the street in Liverpool was somehow losing its shape and form. A darkness swelling around the edges.

Keisha said nothing. Those eyes just kept on him. Pinning him to the spot. Suddenly Malton felt a terrible pain in his chest. He sank to one knee. Looking up, Keisha towered over him as the rest of the world fell away.

His chest felt ready to explode. As if a giant ball of scorching heat was trying to erupt through his ribcage. Malton sucked in a lungful of air, steeled himself and looked up at Keisha and – matching the terrible gravity of her stare – he barked, 'Where. Is. James?'

Keisha said nothing. She simply put her sunglasses back on and stepped to one side.

There was James. Stood looking down at Malton.

The pain was getting stronger now. Malton couldn't move, couldn't stand or reach out. Couldn't even say a word as James smiled softly and said, 'I'm dead.'

37

'I just need a clean break,' said Vikki, wiping the tears from her eyes.

Dean had been woken from messy, stress-filled dreams to the sound of a Skype call on his phone. As he slowly came to, the realisation hit him that only one person would be calling him at this time in the morning. Rifling through his covers, he snatched up the phone and was rewarded with Vikki's crestfallen face looking back at him.

Unable to think of an adequate reply, Dean just listened.

'I've been thinking. About us. About Manchester. About my dad.'

So it was her father! Dean knew something had to be wrong.

'Your dad can't touch you. He's never getting out,' said Dean quickly.

'The other day, I got a solicitor's letter. It was him.'

Leon Walker was doing multiple life sentences for a murderous killing spree on top of the attempted murder of his own lawyer. As part of his sentencing he had a lifetime ban from contacting his daughter. Dean knew no decent solicitor would go against a court ruling like that. Unless something had happened. Something bad.

'What did he want?' said Dean, now fully awake.

'I don't know. I didn't reply. I don't want him back in my life. I don't want any of it. And down here in London, it's like it never happened.'

Dean couldn't believe what he was hearing. 'This is about your dad? Because I can make sure he never comes near you again. I've got Malton Security, I've got Benton. I can reach out to Wakefield Prison. If you want, I can take care of your dad.'

'No!' Vikki shook her head. 'That's not it. That's not what I want. I don't want the solution to be that. I don't want threats and fists and knives. I just want . . .' her voice trailed off. Off screen it sounded like someone said something.

'Who was that?' said Dean, sitting up in bed. 'Who's there?'

Viki sniffed loudly and wiped her eyes.

'I'm not saying forever, and I appreciate what you've done, but for now, at least until I finish my course. I need space. To think about what's happening.'

'What is happening? Is someone there? Are you safe?' Dean's thoughts came tumbling out.

He couldn't decide which scared him more. What Vikki was saying to him or where his mind was going, knowing that Leon Walker had reached out. Never mind his indifference, absence and neglect as a father. The nature of his prevention order meant that only the most dire circumstances would persuade a lawyer to even think of challenging the court. Leon Walker had shot dead half a dozen people. Beaten many more half to death with his bare hands – one of them Dean. He was a six-foot-eight, one-man gang who would never be free again. So why was anyone trying to set him up with his daughter? Whatever the reason, it couldn't be good.

'Look, have you still got the letter?'

'The letter?' said Vikki, momentarily confused.

'From your dad's solicitors?'

'Forget about my dad!' cried Vikki. 'I'm sorry, I'm so grateful for everything you did but I just need some space.'

Before Dean could jump in she was leaning toward the camera and the call ended.

Alone in his bed, Dean's brain finally stopped racing. Everything felt very still and very quiet. He swung his feet out onto the carpet and felt the ground hold him. Putting one foot in front of the other, he headed to the bathroom.

38

MIDDAY ANGEL MEADOW.

OK.

With those two brief messages there was no turning back. Ruth was going to meet whoever it was that Jake had trusted to send that photo to. Ruth had heard of sex workers doing similar things before. Photographing clients and sending them to a trusted friend. She'd done it herself on first dates. Even making it a fun ice-breaker. Just checking you're not going to rape and murder me!

It wasn't a joke for Jake. Whoever was in that photo may well have killed him. If Ruth was going to start putting together the story of what happened, then Jake's friend would be vital. Maybe this wasn't the first time Jake had sent him photos of clients. Maybe other sex workers sent him their photos. Maybe he had other photos of the man in the hotel room.

It was a lot of maybes but Ruth was fired up to turn maybes into solid facts. She'd already finished two of her three articles for the day – *Yeah, We Ate at Manchester's Newest Italian-Asian Vegan Fusion Bar* and *Ten Top Spots in Ancoats for a Post-Tindr Hang* – and was heading out the door when Damion caught up to her.

'You off for lunch?'

'Yeah,' said Ruth, not stopping.

'I'll come with,' said Damion, smiling and heading to his desk for his coat. He had a great smile. Teeth like an American. Straight and white.

'I'm meeting someone,' said Ruth.

'Someone for the story you're working on?' said Damion casually.

Ruth stopped and turned back to Damion. 'What story?' she said.

'You tell me,' said Damion. 'But I've seen you beavering away. Laptop facing the wall, look of concentration on your face. More concentration than you need to write the junk we do at this place.'

He was fishing. It was fine. He didn't know. Yet.

'I'm just meeting a friend,' said Ruth.

Damion nodded, clearly only half believing her. As sweet and friendly as Damion could be, Ruth knew how ambitious he was. The first whiff he got of this story, he'd be trying to take it off her and claim it for his own.

'Well if you ever need help with a story,' said Damion. 'A real story. Let me know.'

Ruth flashed a smile and headed out. She had a real story and it was *her* real story.

***

Angel Meadow used to be the most notorious Victorian slum in all of Manchester. Packed full of deprivation, crime and misery, it had been the inspiration for Marx during his stay in the city. Nowadays, the cost of living in the city centre had pushed all the deprivation, crime and misery a little further out. These days Angel Meadow was a park overlooked by flats and the Co-op's giant head office. Out to the east was one long building site as Chinese construction companies built outwards through Collyhurst and beyond. Expanding the already packed city centre.

Ruth was ready to do some serious people-watching, but as it happened, her contact spotted her first.

The rain had let up and she was sat on a bench at the top of the park scanning the entrances when a man in his fifties with a round face and thinning hair sat down next to her. Ruth instantly noticed that he was dressed well for his age. A plaid overshirt and heavy jeans with Red Wing boots and a Palestinian-style scarf.

'You found Jake's phone?'

Ruth turned to look at the man. He was busy staring out across the railway viaducts at the bottom of the park and out towards Bury. He didn't turn to look at Ruth.

'I found a phone,' said Ruth, following the man's lead and keeping her eyes straight ahead. She felt like she was in some kind of spy thriller.

'And then you pretended to be Jake,' said the man sharply. 'After you knew he was dead.' His voice cracked just a little.

'That's why I wanted to meet. I think I know who killed him.'

The man broke and turned to face Ruth. There were tears in his eyes.

'I thought that was you. I thought I was next.' He hung his head and took deep, deliberate breaths.

'I just found his phone,' said Ruth quickly. 'I think Jake was a sex worker and he'd send you his clients. For safety. Is that right?'

The man looked up. Grief and wariness had given way to anger.

'All the good it did him,' said the man, holding back his tears. 'Jake was a good boy; he didn't deserve any of that. And he didn't deserve you fucking around with his memory. Now give me his phone.'

Ruth's first instinct was to apologise profusely, hand him the phone and get the hell away. But she held fast. Told herself that her dad must have been in hundreds of situations like this. She told herself she wasn't a civilian. She was a journalist. It was her job to get the truth and that was never easy.

'I saw the man in the photo,' said Ruth.

A sudden look of guilt came over the man. Ruth continued. 'He was back at Piccadilly Basin, near where they found Jake.

There was someone else with him. He was looking for something. I think he was looking for the phone.'

The man looked back out across Manchester and thought. Then he turned back to Ruth.

'The person you saw looking for the phone . . . Did he have a beard? Dark hair? Something about him . . .'

Ruth's mouth went dry.

'He looked like he knew exactly what he was doing,' she said.

The man sighed and breathed in the chill Manchester air.

'Come with me,' he said.

39

'What happened was something we call cardiac tamponade. Essentially, due to the trauma in your chest wound there was an accumulation of fluid around the heart, and so the heart is compressed and can't function properly. Sort of like a heart attack.'

The young doctor explaining this to Malton demonstrated with her hands, first a normal heart and then a heart under compression. Malton looked down at his chest where a small plastic tube now emerged from under the bandages.

'You were lucky it happened in front of a senior nurse. Thiago guessed what it was and we were able to drain the fluid manually without surgery. Just using a large needle.'

The bald prison officer who was stood beside Malton's bed guarding him looked pale at the mention of needles.

The doctor caught him blanching and smiled. She was young, maybe in her thirties, with curly blonde hair and large glasses. She had a confident manner and a southern accent that Malton couldn't place.

'Believe me, draining with a syringe is far better than surgery. How do you feel now?'

Truth was, Malton still felt like he'd been repeatedly run over, but that was a huge improvement on how he'd felt just before his aborted escape attempt. The pressing pain in his chest was gone. It had been replaced with the dull ache of a stab wound. His leg still felt tight and hot but the doctor had assured him that the antibiotics he was on would soon clear that up too.

'So he's good to go?' asked the prison officer.

'I don't see why not,' said the doctor breezily.

The bald prison officer smiled. 'I'll put the call in. You'll be in Ashworth in no time.'

'He's going to Ashworth?' said the doctor, a note of concern in her voice. She looked down at Malton and their eyes met. Both of them silently acknowledging just what that would mean.

'I'd like to keep him here for twenty-four hours more. Make sure his heart has settled down.'

The prison officer shrugged. 'It's all overtime.'

The doctor smiled at Malton, who gave a small nod to acknowledge her act of mercy.

Twenty-four more hours. He still had no plan. He was still badly injured. Back when he'd blacked out he thought that he had died. As they pushed him through the hospital, voices raised and doors slamming, he lay there thinking how much the afterlife was like MRI.

Right down to when he'd been wheeled past someone who looked exactly like Keisha.

40

A tangle of dumped bikes greeted Dean outside the Farrs' house. Several youths in full head-to-toe black sportswear were gathered. The balaclavas that covered their faces were pulled up over their chins as they smoked in the front garden.

It didn't matter what kind of criminality a family like the Farrs got up to; they exuded a casual lawlessness that made their house a magnet for all manner of waifs and strays. Teenage lads who knew if they turned up they could hang out with Carl and swap porn on their phones or get Janet to order in takeaways or just lurk in the Farrs' western-themed bar getting pissed and smoking. The Farr home was an open house for anyone who was happy to associate with them.

It was early morning but as Dean knocked on the door he could hear the loud bass line of a karaoke track coming from inside.

As he waited for an answer his mind suddenly skipped back to a similar cold, wet morning over a year ago when he and Malton had got breakfast at a café in Salford. They'd been up all night lying in wait for a gang of small-time car thieves to return to the lock-up where they'd stashed a hoard of stolen guns. After delivering the guns and the thieves to a client, they'd stopped off to get something to eat. It stuck in Dean's memory, less due to the job and more to Malton's mood. Usually his boss was silent, only talking if there was something he wanted to know. But that morning Malton had been chatty, or at least as chatty as he ever got. He'd been with Bea for nearly half a year at that point. Dean didn't ask and he didn't expect Malton to tell. But over a warming plate of hot grease, unbidden, Malton had glanced up with a look of sudden concern and asked Dean, 'Everything OK with you and Vikki Walker?'

After Vikki's call this morning Dean found himself wondering if way back then Malton suspected that a relationship with Leon Walker's daughter would end like this. When he said 'Everything OK?' did he really care how Dean was doing or did he know that by going out with Vikki, Dean was risking dragging the ghost of Leon Walker along for the ride? Or had he just known how doing this job eventually drives away everyone who ever cared about you?

Dean's morbid speculation was cut short by a grim-faced Martin opening the door. He waved past Dean to the youths in the garden and they nodded back respectfully.

'In you come,' he said unenthusiastically, and just like that, Dean was back on the job.

Last night Ruth had slipped out of the gallery without telling him. Dean took that as a rejection of his offer. As much as he felt a strong urge to protect Ruth from herself, his desire to help Malton was greater. If handled correctly then maybe giving Ruth the smallest of glimpses into just how dark the world she was getting into could be would suffice to scare her off. Dean knew that if that didn't work he couldn't very well hold back the hornets' nest she was so intent on stamping all over.

First Ruth then Vikki. Dean felt like he was cursed.

Worse still, he'd failed to find out anything more about the incident in Strangeways. Prison was usually an incubator for underworld gossip. Hundreds of criminals locked up together with nothing to do but talk. But whatever had happened behind those walls, the prison authorities were doing their utmost to keep it under wraps.

With more time Dean was sure he could fill in the blanks. But as Martin Farr closed and locked the door behind him, Dean realised his time was up.

Martin led him into the back where Janet and Carl were sat beneath the giant cowboy mural in the Farrs' western-themed bar area. They were eating McDonald's takeaways while Marie was mid-way through belting out a Miley Cyrus song.

Janet looked up from her Egg McMuffin and said, 'Sit him down.'

Martin guided Dean to a seat and put a heavy hand on his shoulder, forcing him to sit.

Marie had stopped singing. The backing track carried on its tinny rendition but she just stood watching. A look of pure fury on her face.

Janet's hair was immaculate, even at this time of the morning. Without make-up her features looked tiny in her face.

Janet wiped her mouth with the back of her hand and said, 'Your fucking boss nearly killed my Mickey.'

Dean froze. It was exactly as he'd feared. Mickey Farr had had his 'word' and it had left both men beaten half to death.

'I don't know anything about that,' said Dean, trying not to look across to where Carl was cramming takeaway in his mouth. Carl was built like a brickie. His giant fingers almost comically useless handling his food. Dean caught himself imagining what those fingers felt like when they were in a fist swinging for your face.

'He beat my Mickey to a fucking pulp. And that's not on.'

'I was told Malton was in the hospital,' said Dean, trying to remain calm. 'That he was seriously injured. Whatever happened, it sounds like Mickey gave as good as he got.'

Janet smiled for a moment and said, 'That's not the fucking point. Suppose someone did that to your family? What you going to do?'

Dean's thoughts immediately went to Vikki. What did her father want? Who had been on those calls with Vikki, just out of frame? Was there a connection?

'I asked you a fucking question,' barked Janet, and Dean quickly forgot all about Vikki.

'You wanted Mickey to have a word. Sounds like he got more than a word,' said Dean, hoping he sounded more confident than he felt.

Janet flushed with anger.

'You cheeky little cunt.'

Dean had fucked up.

Before he could say another syllable Carl was up, barging away the bar table and laying those giant hands on Dean. He moved far faster than his bulk suggested. One hand grabbed Dean's head and forced him down onto the table. Hard. The other hand gathered up both Dean's arms and held them tight behind his back.

Dazed, with his head pressed on the table facing away from Janet, all Dean could see was Martin Farr, sat drinking from a giant McDonald's cup and looking as surprised as Dean.

'We paid you to find a fucking thief and you've just taken the fucking piss.'

Dean could hear Janet but he couldn't see her. He felt Carl behind him. His weight like a landslide.

'So now you find out what happens when you take the fucking piss.'

'I found the courier. His real name's Harold Boateng. He's dead.' There was anger in Dean's voice. The fear of violence was always the worst part. Now it was here in the form of Carl Farr there was nothing left but to surrender to it.

There was silence from where Janet was sitting. This was all clearly news to her. And then: 'Was it him who robbed us?'

'I don't know yet,' said Dean. 'I went to the address you gave me. It wasn't his real address. I found some keys there, traced them to a caravan park over on the coast.'

'You said you searched his fucking place,' snapped Janet's voice.

'Fucking did,' muttered Carl above Dean's head.

'What else?' demanded Janet.

Carl was still pushing his head into the table but from his folded-up position Dean could see Martin begin to shift uneasily in seat.

'I went to the caravan. Someone had got there first. Ransacked it. I think maybe they were worried Harold could identify them. Maybe it was them who killed him.'

'Fucking hell,' said Janet. 'You saying someone fucking ripped us off and now they killed Ray? He was fucking reliable that one. Nice old black bloke. Fucking hell. Who?'

'I don't know,' said Dean. 'But I've got their DNA.'

At the mention of DNA, Martin stopped drinking his giant cup of soda. 'What fucking DNA?' he snapped.

'They fucked up.' Dean was speaking to the room but his eyes were now firmly on Martin Farr. 'When they robbed his car. Broke his window. Whoever did that, they cut themselves. Got blood on the glass. I found glass with blood on. I've given it to a contact who can run it through the DNA database. Soon as that comes back we'll have a name.'

No point in telling Janet Farr he already had a name. Not when it felt like the tide in the room was turning.

'Fuck,' muttered Martin quietly.

'But unless I walk out of here then that's not happening,' said Dean.

'Get the fuck off him, Carl,' shouted Martin, jumping to his feet.

'Don't you talk to my Carl like that,' barked Janet. 'This cunt's boss nearly killed my Mickey.'

Carl Farr's heavy hand stayed pressed down on Dean's head.

'And when he finds whoever ripped us off then we deal with it.' Martin addressed Dean. 'You're not going anywhere, are you?'

'You pay Malton Security, the job gets done. Everything else is just details,' said Dean. He'd heard Malton say as much. Now he truly understood what it meant. This line of work inevitably got messy. Doing detective work for criminals meant uncovering the kinds of things that usually stay dead and buried under several layers of concrete. If Malton had bailed every time inconvenient facts arose he'd never have got to the bottom of anything.

Dean couldn't see Janet Farr's face but he took the silence to mean she was thinking.

'Fucking get off him, Carl,' said Janet.

There was a brief lull before Carl obeyed his mother's instructions and released Dean.

Dean shot up and shook out his arms. Carl had wrapped a single hand around both his wrists and now the blood came flowing painfully back into his fingers.

'Soon as you get a name, you give it to me and we sort the cunt out. Then we'll see,' she said.

Dean nodded and looked straight at Martin Farr when he said, 'Soon as I get a name.'

41

Keisha knew she shouldn't be here. Yesterday was too close. If those two uniformed police officers had asked to see her identification it would have been over. If either of them had ever met the real Karen Marlow, it would have been over. Everything that Keisha had worked for would have ended in an unseemly chase through a hospital, and even if she had got away then the word would be out. She would have to flee without having buried her father or learned who had killed him. More than that, she wouldn't know if Craig was even still alive.

She had no choice. She had come back to MRI.

Keisha felt the weight of the Glock in the inside pocket of her coat and the lightness of her heart. Finally she realised what it was she was missing in Ibiza. It wasn't Craig, it wasn't Harold, it certainly wasn't Manchester. It was the game. Rolling the dice and defying the odds. That was what Keisha lived for. Not sunshine and ease. She didn't give a shit about the trophy. She was all about the fight.

Keisha came into Manchester Royal Infirmary through a different entrance than the day before. Coming in from St Mary's next door and tacking across. The two entrances were exactly the same. The large, white atrium, the walkways and glass ceiling. But crucially, a different set of staff. Unfamiliar faces unused to seeing Keisha, her hair up in braids, her glasses covering her face and her fake police ID in her pocket ready to make one last bluff.

Yesterday, after waiting for the two uniformed officers to leave, Keisha had rushed to the surgical department in time to see Craig being wheeled through into the ICU. She'd toyed with the idea of hanging around, waiting for him. But the longer she stayed in the one place, the thinner her cover story became. She needed to be in and out before people had time to think or ask questions. Flash the badge and walk.

Now she knew where he was, today would be different.

Keisha got into the elevator with several members of the same family all smiling and chattering about the baby they were on their way to visit. Six of them crammed in the lift with Keisha, radiating excitement. They got out on the floor below the ICU and Keisha watched them dance and skip down the corridor. To Keisha their joy felt like an insult to the wards of the dead and dying they passed by on the way to the maternity ward.

As the elevator reached her floor she took a breath and got ready to take one last chance for the sake of Craig Malton.

The doors opened and the first thing Keisha saw was a tiny blonde woman sashaying into the ICU, her high heels clacking loudly off the hard hospital floor. Bea Wallace had beaten her to it.

42

Dean was back at the office getting ready to go and pay a visit to Farrs' Tyres for a quick word with Sam Kennard about why his blood was inside Harold Boateng's car when Martin Farr saved him the trip and turned up in the waiting room of Malton Security headquarters.

The trip to the Farrs had been unpleasant but instructive. Dean knew that for people like the Farrs, violence was the only option on the table. No matter the situation, the moment there was an emotional trigger then things kicked off. That didn't make getting manhandled by Carl Farr more tolerable. But it had dragged his mind into sharp focus. Whatever else was going on, if he could clear Malton and find the Farrs' drugs then everything else would be simple.

Carl had definitely damaged some of the bridgework in Dean's mouth. After getting shot in the face he'd lost six teeth. Malton had paid for a significant amount of expensive dentistry out of his own pocket. Expensive dentistry that it felt like Carl Farr's giant hand had bent out of shape.

But all the while it was happening, Dean was afforded a ringside seat to the expressions crossing Martin Farr's face, starting with placid curiosity and quickly escalating to full-on panic. Dean had thought that maybe it would take him visiting Farrs' Tyres to push Martin over the edge. As it was, Martin was currently sweating in the waiting room while Dean decided the best way to work the situation.

Ever since he'd seen for himself the hidden compartment in Harold's car Dean had suspected the robbery was an inside job. Now he knew for sure. Martin Farr recruiting Sam Kennard to rip off his own family. Or rather, his in-laws.

Martin who had taken the Farr name. Martin who let his mother-in-law treat him like shit while he ran the business for her. Martin who knew Harold's movements, knew about the hidden compartment and knew exactly when to rob him.

What made less sense was then trashing the caravan and killing Harold. Dean had met enough criminals now to know that there was a very clear line between those who couldn't help themselves and those who genuinely didn't give a fuck. The ones who didn't give a fuck were the ones to watch out for. They weren't master criminals but they had one advantage that most people didn't. They completely lacked humanity. By and large they'd been brought up by parents who shared their sociopathy. A childhood exposed to violence, pornography, drugs and everything else that turns your formative years into a traumatic ordeal. By the time they were adults and strong enough to match their diseased thoughts with physical violence, they were unstoppable.

They sold drugs and stole and all the normal crimes but they also beat up strangers, tortured mates over trivial disputes, fired guns into crowded clubs and generally spread misery and fear whenever the opportunity arose.

Martin Farr didn't strike Dean as one of them. He just couldn't help himself. Despite everything the Farrs put him through it was clear he loved the idea of being a gangster. He saw how much money the Farrs were making and clearly thought he could do better. But he'd got greedy and stupid and now Dean was onto him.

Dean couldn't wait any longer to hear just how Martin was going to talk his way out of this situation and so finally called him into Malton's office.

'Have you got a name for the DNA yet?' asked Martin, settling back into the sofa.

Martin was smiling and light. Doing his best to work the easy charm that got him so involved with the Farr family in the first place. Dean let him think he was still in the clear.

'Where did you meet Marie?' asked Dean, changing the subject.

Martin paused for a second, trying to figure out Dean's angle. 'Lads' holiday. On the plane home actually. We were all shit-faced. Week in Bulgaria with the boys. Just so fucked that we had to keep drinking. You know what it's like?'

Dean nodded. He had no idea. He wasn't a drinker.

'Anyway, on the plane home we got sat next to these girls and one thing led to another and I ended up fucking her in the airport bogs.' Martin laughed and then looked annoyed when Dean failed to join in.

'So you didn't know the Farrs dealt drugs when you and Marie got together?'

Martin shook his head. 'Course not. But fuck it, money's money, right? Besides, I know people. I've done things. Not like I've not dabbled.'

Martin's bragging sounded hollow. This was just wasting time now.

'So that's why you robbed Harold Boateng?' said Dean.

Martin's smile froze. He looked around the room, his brain scrambling to pick a course of action.

'You said the DNA hadn't come back yet,' he said.

'I lied,' said Dean. 'It came back. Sam Kennard.'

Martin looked outraged. 'Sam! Fucking Sam? After everything I've done for that lad.'

'Sam wouldn't know how to find out Harold's routes, wouldn't know about the compartment. To be honest, I bet he wouldn't even know about Harold at all. Someone told him all that. I think that's you,' said Dean, impressed that Martin seemed happy to bullshit until the last. He wondered if he would have tried this if it was Malton sat in the chair grilling him.

Martin's smile left his face. 'What you going to tell Janet?' he said, suddenly sounding more aggressive.

'The obvious thing to tell her is that with Mickey in prison, her son-in-law robbed the family and then killed Harold Boateng to cover it up.'

Martin's face twisted in outrage. 'Fuck off. I never touched the old guy. Except when we robbed him. I'm not going to fucking kill a pensioner. Fuck that.'

'So you didn't go over his caravan?'

'I didn't even know he had a fucking caravan,' said Martin. 'Besides, why would I? I got the drugs.'

'Where are they now?'

'Sam's place,' said Martin after some time. 'So what are you going to do?'

'I'm guessing,' said Dean, 'that you coming here, you have some sort of plan as to why I'm not going to tell Janet what you did and let Carl go to work on you.'

Martin angrily shook his head and swore to himself, 'Fucking idiot . . .'

'Or have I overestimated you?' said Dean, enjoying not being the one on the back foot.

Martin stopped and took a breath. 'OK. I do got a deal for you. But only if you make this all go away.'

'And what do you have that you think is worth that?' asked Dean.

Martin smiled, suddenly back to his usual smirking jack-the-lad. 'I know who it was grassed on your boss over that dead kid. And I know for a fact he was put up to it.'

43

'You should have called me sooner, pet,' said Bea, looking out the window of the private room she'd ordered the nurses wheel Malton into.

Bea Wallace turned to face Malton as he lay in his hospital bed. With her shimmering blonde hair, peachy white skin and bright red lips she looked more like a Fifties pin-up than what she was – the most ruthless person Malton had ever met.

At one moment Bea could be the giggling, flirtatious Geordie cracking dirty jokes and howling at her own punchlines, the next she could drop into a cut-glass RP accent and issue the kind of cold legal threats that made even the most grizzled of CPS lawyers quake in their boots.

You underestimated Bea at your peril. A lesson Malton was slowly learning. Just a few months earlier he and Bea weren't just lovers, they were also working together. Above and below the line of legality. What Bea couldn't fix for you in the courts Malton would fix for you in the street. It had seemed like nothing could stop them.

But these past few months had made it painfully clear that like everyone else in Bea's life, Malton was expendable. She hadn't tried to stop him as he fled to Liverpool hunting for James's killers and she hadn't reached out when he'd been arrested for Stephen Page's murder. As soon as Malton was no use to her anymore Bea Wallace had moved on.

So Malton could hardly believe his eyes when the door to his room had opened and in walked Bea. Beaming away as if the last three months had never happened. He had lain watching as Bea worked her charm to convince the prison guard to take off Malton's cuffs and wait outside while she spoke to 'her client'. Bea had that effect on people. She made you do things you'd never normally consider. Things that maybe weren't in your best interests.

After three months of silence, she had chosen to come and visit him in hospital. That at least let him know that something must be wrong. If Bea was back in his life she needed something. But what?

'If you'd called me sooner maybe I could have done more,' she said, moving to Malton's bedside and laying an immaculately manicured hand on his arm where he let it rest.

Malton looked up at Bea's smiling face and kept quiet. At the time he was arrested there were only two people who knew that he was in Liverpool. One was Dean, the kid he trusted with his life. The other was the deadly blonde stood at his bedside. Dean had made numerous efforts to get in touch. Efforts Malton had rebuffed. Bea had been silent.

Until now.

Whatever Bea's role in all of this, she clearly felt confident enough to be alone in a room with Malton without his cuffs on. Briefly Malton considered what him grabbing her up as a hostage would look like. It would look like a bloody mess and would only end one of two ways: prison or death.

Instead he lay in silence and listened to what Bea had to say.

'They've got an eyewitness. They've got your DNA. You're not getting out of it.'

Malton didn't bother protesting his innocence. Instead he listened to Bea's tone. The confidence in what she was saying. Bea, a lawyer who lived to twist words and chisel loopholes through doubt and uncertainty. And now here she was, talking like these were facts carved in stone.

'But now I hear they're sending you to Ashworth? Oh, pet. Trust me, you do not want to go to Ashworth. The madhouse? They'll drug you up, turn you into a drooling wreck. Way I see it, you've got serious prison time in your future, whether you spend it in a cat-A prison with other cons or a secure mental hospital with the monsters is up to you.'

So that's why she was here. She wanted to do a deal. What he couldn't figure out was what was in it for her. If she was so certain he was going away for murder, what did he have that she wanted? Something he didn't even know he had himself.

'I saw your Dean the other day. He's a good lad, that one. Keeping it all ticking over for you. Like a faithful dog waiting for his owner to get back. He'll be waiting a long time, bless him.'

That was a mistake. Whether she meant to or not she'd just told him that she'd spoken to Dean. What had Dean said to her? Something that stirred a notion in Bea that she ought to come and make sure Malton was going away? Did Dean have something that could get him off? Or had he come to the same conclusion that Malton was slowly reaching – that Bea was somehow more involved in all of this than she was letting on?

As Malton's mind began to trawl through the possibilities he felt a wave of guilt come over him. He'd let himself whittle his entire world down to his quest for James's killers. He'd turned his back not just on what he'd built but on one of the few people who'd stood by him regardless of the cost. Amongst the guilt he felt a glow of pride. Dean had gone from a willing apprentice to the only person on the outside who was still fighting for him. If he ever got out of this alive he'd need to make things right between them.

'I know you,' said Bea. 'This strong silent thing. But trust me, pet, you don't have a lot of time. You know my number. If you want to make sure you're going to do your time with prisoners and not the kind of people who shit in their own hands and try to fuck it, then you need to make that call. OK?'

She leaned in and planted a little kiss on his forehead. Malton could smell the make-up, hairspray and perfume it took to make Bea Wallace into Bea Wallace. For just a moment he saw exactly how he'd fallen for her.

'We could have been great together, couldn't we?' Bea said before giving Malton one final, sad smile and walking out the door.

Right up until that moment Malton had his doubts. But that smile told him everything he needed to know. By risking coming to see him like this, she must know that it was nearly over. Talk of her helping him was a smoke screen. This visit was Bea needing to see the endgame with her own eyes. Malton on the verge of being locked away for the rest of his life.

A sudden sharp clarity came over Malton. He knew exactly what he would do next. When the prison officer came in to put his cuffs on he would make a break for it. Overpower the officer, if he could. Cuff him to the bed and then flee. He didn't have money or clothes or a phone but he knew that if he didn't go now, the next place he'd wind up would be Ashworth. No one ever escapes from Ashworth.

Malton readied himself as the door opened and the bald prison officer walked in.

'Hands out,' he said a little too cheerfully.

Malton got ready to move.

'Hands up,' said a familiar voice as Keisha closed the door behind her and put a gun to the back of the prison officer's bald head.

44

'No names,' said Martin Farr, leaning forward on the sofa in Malton's office. 'You get the names when I get my side of the deal.'

'OK,' said Dean with a shrug. 'But I need to know exactly what it is I'm buying.'

Martin grinned. 'Man after my own heart.'

Considering Martin Farr had just admitted to robbing his own family and was now attempting to throw someone under the bus to save himself, Dean strongly objected to that sentiment. But he kept quiet and let Martin continue.

'So Mickey goes inside and suddenly I'm the boss. Thing is though, I'm not. I got Janet on at me all the fucking time. I got that moron Carl. Fuck me it's hard work. And for what? All the money still goes straight to Mickey and I'm doing all the work. Fucking bullshit. If it wasn't for me that whole thing would have gone to shit the minute Mickey got nicked. So yeah, I'm a bit fucking sore about the whole business. You would be too, right?'

Dean nodded. The lighting in Malton's office was bright enough to shine down through the thin hair on top of Martin Farr's head and reflect off the near-bald dome beneath.

'So you rob them?'

'So, I figure I'm just going to get my fucking share. I'm running things. I'm like a fucking director. You run a company you get a bonus, right? So why shouldn't I get a bonus?'

'Why not?' said Dean, playing along.

'Course, Janet won't do a thing without Mickey's say-so and Mickey isn't saying anything 'cos Mickey couldn't keep his fucking hands to himself and now he's banged up for twatting some fucking policewoman.'

Martin breathed out and shook his head.

'You want a drink?' said Dean, pointing to a pallet of bottled water in the corner of the room.

'Yeah, thanks,' said Martin.

Dean didn't move and after a few awkward seconds Martin got up off the sofa, extracted a bottle and returned to where he was sitting.

'I've met the courier. I know he's older than fucking time. So I figure if I'm going to help myself, that's when to do it. I find out the times and that. But I thought better to have someone else do it. You know, case the courier recognised me.'

'So Sam Kennard?'

'He's got three kids and likes a bit of coke. He's always going to need a few extra quid. Three hundred to be exact.'

Martin looked pleased at how little he'd paid Sam Kennard to help him rip off the Farrs.

'And you killed the courier just to be on the safe side?'

Martin looked hurt. 'Nah. I told you, he's an old guy. I'm not murdering a pensioner.'

'Maybe Sam went above and beyond?'

Martin shrugged. 'If he did, that's not on me.'

Hiding his frustration at Martin Farr's almost flippant tone, Dean said, 'That's all great. But you said you had information about Malton?'

Martin grinned and waved a finger. 'I knew I got you with that one.'

'Cos right now all I have is your confession.'

Martin stopped smiling. 'Right. You want it like that. OK. Thing was we ripped off the drugs and everything was fine. Janet had no idea – that's why she got you involved. But before all that what does she do? Only thing she knows how to do. She reaches out to the seller and tells him that unless they get their money back she'll fucking end him.'

At this, Martin laughed and shook his head. Suddenly it made a lot more sense why the Farrs had reached out to Malton. Dean thought back to the Farrs' house with its broken windows. You didn't need to be in the game all that long to know that threatening a heavily connected drug importer wasn't the kind of thing that ended well.

'Now this guy, he's not like Janet. He's fucking a bit posh. Bit educated. Bit fucking connected. And he's a bit fucking smarter too. Not hard, I know. He wants to know what's happened. Is this a fuck-up on his end? Is Janet trying to pull one over on him? He's the kind of guy who likes to know the facts before he starts dropping bodies. So he riddles it out, doesn't he? Works out that it must be an inside job and works out that that means me. Doesn't even worry about Sam and he's the fucker who did the robbery. Fucking unbelievable.'

For a moment the grating smirk left Martin Farr's face only to reappear seconds later as he leaned forward and fell over himself to say, 'Bet that's who killed the courier. Not me.'

The thought had occurred to Dean but he kept it to himself.

'So who is the supplier?' asked Dean.

Martin shook his head. 'Told you, no names. Not until I got what I want.'

'The supplier approached you?'

'Yeah, he did. I thought I was fucking done for, but turns out he had his own thing going on.'

'What thing?' said Dean, sensing a conclusion to Martin Farr's unending chatter.

Martin Farr finished his bottle of water, tossed the empty bottle towards the bin and missed.

'Says he's looking for an alibi for something a bit fucking dark.'

'How dark?'

'Dead fucking rent boy dark,' said Martin salaciously.

Dean didn't move a muscle. He simply stared down Martin Farr while in his head he raced through everything he knew about Stephen Page and about Malton being framed for his murder. Everything Ruth Porter had told him about her suspicions of a serial killer stalking Manchester's streets. Suddenly it didn't seem quite so far-fetched.

'So he tells me if I can find him someone who'll lie to the police and put someone else at a crime scene then he'll forget all about me ripping off those drugs.'

'You mean the CI who put Malton in the car where Stephen Page was found?' said Dean, barely containing the excitement he was feeling as several major unknowns suddenly revealed themselves.

Martin leaned back and looked pleased with himself.

'That's the fucker I mean.'

'So who did you find?'

Martin shook his head. 'Nope. You've got more than enough of a tease out of me.'

'I want the supplier and the CI.'

'You want names? Here's what I want from you.'

Dean already knew what was coming.

'You need to take your DNA test, say whatever you need to say to my fucking mother-in-law and pin the entire robbery on Sam Kennard.'

45

Malton struggled to do up Keisha's grey overcoat as he hurried along the hospital corridor. The coat was cut large for Keisha but even so it was tight on his forty-four-inch chest. It would have to do. Under the coat he was still in his hospital gown, his feet still bare.

He'd removed his own drips but still had the drain from the build-up around his heart sticking out of his chest. That could be dealt with later.

In front of him he could see Keisha taking her hair down, teasing it out with her fingers so her long, dark curls spilled down off her head and, in one small gesture, radically changing her appearance. She pocketed her glasses and turned right towards the wing that housed the children's hospital.

Back in the private room, they must have found the prison guard by now. Handcuffed to the bed, the gag Keisha had made from a pillow cover stuffed tightly in his mouth.

This wasn't how he imagined escaping.

As far as he knew, Keisha had left Manchester and vanished off the face of the earth. So what was she doing in his hospital room with a gun?

Despite everything that had gone on between them, Malton was in no position to ask questions. He'd watched in quiet awe as Keisha told the prison officer in no uncertain terms that she was kidnapping him and threatened to kill the prison officer if he got in her way.

Keisha knew exactly what she was saying. Now when Malton eventually had to give himself up he had the plausible deniability of being the victim. This wasn't an escape. He was taken against his will. At gunpoint.

The corridor had opened up into a walkway high above the giant atrium that contained the entrance to the children's hospital. Over the side of the banister it was five floors down. On the ground floor people flowed in and out. Malton heard no alarms. No sirens. If they could just get clear of the building then they had a chance.

Keisha turned off left through a door, holding it open for Malton to catch up.

She said one word: 'Stairs.'

In silence they both entered the stairwell and began to descend.

Malton's body still felt weak and tender. His injuries from Mickey Farr and the self-inflicted stab wounds cried out with every step. He could feel his broken rib moving unnaturally beneath his skin, turning even a slight movement into agony.

Keisha had her phone out. Over her shoulder he could see she was ordering an Uber for the back streets just beyond MRI towards Victoria Baths. A small enclave of old Manchester that butted up against relics of an even older time. The ornate baths and the house where Elizabeth Gaskell once wrote her novels now sitting cheek to jowl with a sprawling council estate.

On the second-to-last set of stairs, they were about to head down when the door on the floor below opened and a young doctor in scrubs entered the stairwell, jogging upwards at a clip.

Malton locked eyes with the doctor. He saw the doctor looking at Keisha's coat barely covering him and then down to his bare feet. He passed Malton but then stopped and turned.

'Do you know where you're going?' he called back.

Malton kept moving and nearly bumped into Keisha who'd stopped.

'Silly bastard can't do without a fag. Even after his op,' said Keisha, a smile in her voice.

The doctor sighed in resignation. 'Just make sure you're not right in front of the entrance,' he said, and carried on up.

They were leaving through the children's hospital exit when Malton first heard the sirens.

Two police cars hurtled past, heading for the MRI entrance.

The ground was cold and wet under Malton's bare feet. As he sucked in the damp air he realised this was the first time in over three months he'd been outside under the sky. Between Strangeways, prison transports and hospital, he'd been locked up all that time.

For just a moment he stopped and looked up into the slate grey sky. It was raining. He felt the drops hitting his face, running down his shaved head.

'Don't stop,' hissed Keisha. 'And close your coat.'

Malton remembered himself and hurried after Keisha. He could feel his chest beginning to ache and hoped that whatever the build-up of fluid had done to his heart, the damage wasn't permanent.

They turned away down the side of the hospital and, walking quickly but not running, headed towards Upper Brook Street.

By the time they had crossed the street and headed into the warren of terraces and council houses beyond, they'd already passed at least two other patients out in gowns and coats. At least Malton's attire wouldn't have attracted too much attention.

Up ahead, a minicab with an Uber sticker on it was bumped up blocking the pavement, its engine running.

Keisha held up a hand and the minicab flashed its lights and began to crawl off the pavement and into the road.

As it pulled alongside, Keisha walked to the passenger side and opened the door.

'Karen Marlow?' said the driver.

Malton could hear more sirens now. Looking back over his shoulder he saw a Tactical Aid Unit van tearing down Upper

Brook Street heading towards MRI. They had definitely found the prison officer.

Malton turned back to see Keisha with her gun out, the driver getting out of the car.

'Get in the fucking boot,' said Keisha in a voice that convinced the minicab driver she wasn't kidding. For good measure she added, 'I'm kidnapping him,' and she pointed to Malton.

The driver didn't seem to have any objections to that. He got out of the car, his hands up and, with the gun trained on him, walked round to the boot.

Malton watched as he opened it and folded himself inside before Keisha slammed it shut and turned back to Malton.

'Get in,' said Keisha, heading round to the driver's side.

Malton didn't need asking twice. By the time he was in the passenger seat Keisha was already pulling away.

Keisha angrily shook her head. 'This wasn't the fucking plan,' she said to herself.

Malton said nothing. He simply lay back in the seat and watched as Keisha pulled a three-point turn and drove off at speed down the narrow backstreets and away from Manchester Royal Infirmary.

46

It occurred to Ruth that she was on her way to the apartment of a man she'd met half an hour earlier and all she knew of him was through the phone of a murdered sex worker.

But the walk from Angel Meadow to Canal Street had gone some way to easing her fears.

The man's name was Eddie and it seemed like he knew Manchester inside out. As they'd crossed through Ancoats towards the canal he couldn't help but point out the local colour. The Bank of England pub where he drank as a kid. Now boarded up. The warehouses now flats where he'd lived in a squat with a couple of art students nearly forty years ago.

As he talked, he conjured up a Manchester that Ruth had never encountered. Not in the articles on food trucks or the reviews of new flats. It was a Manchester that didn't rest on money or relentless progress. It was a Manchester that lived in the spirit of those who believed their derelict city would rise out of the post-industrial ruins. They had been right, but as Eddie talked about chasing burglars out of the front room of the New Cross house he shared with a long-dead lover, Ruth got the sense that people like Eddie, who had poured their souls into the city, now found themselves pushed further and further out of the very city they'd created.

They'd walked along the canal into the town centre. Winding past the earliest city-centre flats and past the site of what was promised to be yet another food hall experience where once there was a foundry. It was only as they passed under the city that for the first time Ruth got a glimpse of the Manchester Eddie was describing.

As the canal went beneath the streets, it entered a low-ceilinged passageway, half lit by the daylight, half lit by weak yellow lights. The path became narrow, forcing them to walk in single file.

Half a dozen men were stood in the gloom.

Ruth instinctively froze. Eddie kept right on, raising a hand to greet them.

As Ruth hurried to catch up, she saw them now. They weren't the feral predators she expected. She saw young faces. Lost, bored, empty. All of them had made some attempt at grooming. Despite their scruffy clothes their hair was styled; they'd shaved recently. Ruth caught a whiff of aftershave.

They weren't there to rob anyone. They were there looking for business. The dangerous, desperate free-for-all that had been swept away by relentless development was still there, beneath the streets. Still waiting for anyone who had an appetite they could no longer deny. Whoever they might be.

Even a killer.

Finally they had emerged into the light just short of Canal Street. Beside the Crown Courts.

Eddie's flat was actually in the street behind Canal Street. A narrow alley thrown into the darkness by the closeness of the buildings either side. Bins for Canal Street bars and restaurants crowded the narrow pavement while catering staff on their break squatted by fire doors, smoking or looking at phones. Eddie and Ruth stopped at a scruffy black metal door with a couple of buzzers and no letter box.

Eddie got out his keys and opened it up.

Ruth stopped. Was she really going to follow this man wherever this door led?

Eddie clearly sensed her hesitation.

'Trust me, it looks much worse on the outside. Bit like me.' He smiled and Ruth smiled with him.

'This place,' said Eddie, 'I got it nearly forty years ago. Back when no one wanted to live in town. Back before the IRA did their bit for gentrification by blowing up the Arndale. Back then, if you wanted to buy a flat round here they'd bite your hand off for whatever you offered them. So I bought a couple. The whole building.'

Eddie motioned to the six-storey building proudly. It was stained and dank. The messy backstage to Canal Street's bright lights. But the higher up your eyes went, suddenly the windows stopped being smeared with filth and barred to intruders. There were balconies and flowers and chairs and signs that, high up there, someone was living and living well.

'My laptop's up there with all the photos of that guy. You really think you can match them up to the killings, get a connection?'

'It never occurred to you?'

Eddie looked guilty. 'Thing is, sometimes they sent pictures and never vanished. These boys, they've got nothing. No one cares; no one's waiting for them. I guess I didn't care enough to look into it. Maybe I felt guilty that it happened on my watch. But then more of them started turning up dead and I couldn't look away. I realised that I was probably sitting on a photo of whatever bastard it was killing them. Truth be told, I was scared to look.'

Eddie sucked his lip in. He looked great for his age. It was only now as his mind went back over things that he suddenly looked older.

'What if I'd worked it out sooner? What if I could have stopped them? Then I didn't dare look. Because if I was right, then it's all my fault.'

Ruth wanted to put an arm around Eddie but she held her ground. This was about the story.

'You did what you could,' she said. 'But if I get those photos and I put something together . . .'

'Then you go to the police first,' cut in Eddie.

'I go to the police then I put out the podcast.'

'But police first.'

'They get a day and then I release everything. Make sure they can't just kick it into the long grass. That's the deal.'

Just like that, Eddie lit back up.

'You got a deal. After you.' He pointed to the still-open door.

Ruth looked from Eddie to the open door and made her call.

As they walked up the narrow stairs Eddie gave her a running commentary on all the improvements he'd made. He'd gone from an accidental landlord to a major figure in the regeneration of the whole area. He lamented how all his hard work had now been overshadowed, literally, as Kampus – the giant complex of flats marketed as an upmarket urban community – and the flats along the other side of the canal now towered over Canal Street, turning what was once an illicit address into an over-observed theme park.

As they climbed, bare concrete walls gave way to soft white eggshell. Windows became fancy, metal-framed affairs and touches of domesticity started to intrude in the form of pictures on the walls and potted plants on the narrow landings.

On the final flight Eddie slipped past Ruth and skipped up.

'Nearly there,' he sang as he turned the corner and vanished from sight.

A moment later Ruth heard a gasp come from Eddie. She was up beside him in a flash.

The door to Eddie's apartment was wide open. Looking over Eddie's shoulder, Ruth could see inside. The flat had been ransacked.

Someone had got there before them.

47

Malton wasn't saying anything but as Keisha helped him pull on the clothes she'd bought for him, she could tell he was in pain.

She'd gone all black. Black T-shirts, black tracksuit, black beanie and a black anorak.

The T-shirt wouldn't go on over the drain so he had to make do with the tracksuit top over his bare chest. As Keisha helped him into it she thought how long it had been since she'd touched his light brown skin, felt the absolute solidity of his body. Tight, bunched muscles with no fat or give.

They were in one of Malton's more low-key properties. A large, old house on the edge of Salford. It sat on a four-lane road that ran through fields and scrubland. The house had once been a farmhouse but as soon as the road was built a few metres from its front garden it became an isolated relic. No neighbours and no relief from the constant noise of traffic. Thousands of cars drove past every day but no one ever stopped. Because there was no reason to stop.

It was perfect.

Behind the house was a large garage where a discreet black Series 2 BMW coupe and an unmarked black Transit van sat waiting under dust sheets. Keisha had parked the stolen minicab beside them, having stopped first in woodland where she made the driver strip naked before giving the terrified man a twenty-second head start and quickly sweeping the car as best she could for any kind of tracker.

The house looked derelict from the outside. The front room was still how it was when Malton had purchased it from the family of the previous owner. Tatty carpets, a gas fireplace and peeling, damp wallpaper. But beyond the window dressing of the front room the rest of the house had been totally renovated. Refitted to a luxurious standard. The walls were grey, as were the carpets and the furniture black to match. Not flashy but reassuringly expensive. A bolthole with all mod cons.

Keisha couldn't risk returning to the Midland but she had everything she needed with her. Her passport, her gun and Craig.

She helped him settle down on one of the two large black leather sofas in the back room. After a few false starts Keisha had managed to get the wood burning stove going and now the room was well on the way to being toasty.

Finally able to relax, she kicked off her trainers and enjoyed the feeling of brand-new, untouched carpet beneath her feet.

Something about Craig sitting alone on that sofa called to her but instead she took a seat on the empty sofa and leaned back into the butter-soft leather.

For a moment there was silence. Both of them eyeing the other, trying to decipher the events of the past few hours. She had intended just to see him before slipping away, but when she overhead Bea's talk of Ashworth she knew she couldn't leave him.

'I want you to know, I didn't come back for you,' she said, finally breaking the silence.

The wood burner crackled softly in the background.

'So don't think this was planned,' she added.

Malton gave a slight nod and said, 'So why are you back?'

'My dad died,' she said, and was impressed when Craig didn't immediately do anything as trite as offer his condolences. He knew as well as she did that her dad had abandoned her.

'Died at MRI?'

'No. Someone ran him over. Killed him.'

A subtle note of curiosity came over Craig's face. 'And you came back to find out who?'

'Not at first.'

'You told me you never knew your dad.'

'I didn't. You never knew your mum. If someone ran her over and left her for dead, wouldn't you at least want to know who?'

Malton gave a little smile. 'So what were you doing in MRI?'

Keisha shook her head. 'I bumped into your boy. He told me all about you.'

'Dean?'

'He was at my dad's caravan.'

Malton looked confused. 'Dean's looking into who killed your dad?'

'Someone ripped off the Farrs. I understand Mickey might have had a word with you about that?'

'He tried,' said Malton, deadpan.

'I don't quite know how yet but I think the two things are connected. My dad was a courier for the Farrs. The intermediary between them and their supplier.'

'So you turning up at my bedside with a gun? That was all just a happy coincidence?'

'I'd call it a stupid coincidence, but yes. I just wanted to know you were alive. Find out how you enjoyed Strangeways?'

Keisha smiled, teasing Craig. It almost earned a smile back.

'I'm going to find out who killed Stephen Page,' said Malton.

'So it wasn't you?' said Keisha, still poking the bear.

'Someone set me up,' said Malton pointedly.

Keisha gave a look of mock insult. 'I hope you don't think that was me.'

'It did occur to me,' said Malton. 'But no. Not your style. Besides, why do that and then ride to my rescue, guns blazing?'

'Good question,' said Keisha dryly. 'When I left this place I left for good. I wasn't ever coming back. But then my dad dies and makes me his executor.'

'You came back to visit Anthony's grave,' said Malton.

At the mention of Anthony's name Keisha felt the ground move. She looked hard at Malton, trying to see if this was some kind of trick. All she saw was Craig.

Something was very wrong.

'No. I've never been back. Anthony was cremated. A house I own up in Harpurhey. I torched it with him inside. He's gone.'

She felt Craig bristle too as he picked up on her tone. Both of their minds suddenly beginning to lock on to the same inconsistency.

'Someone left a card on his grave. "From Mummy".'

Keisha felt herself beginning to lose it.

'Not me.'

'Last year, someone was watching me. Sending me pictures. You telling me that wasn't you either?'

'I told you, I left and never looked back,' said Keisha, unable to keep the anger out of her voice. 'After everything I did, you have a hard time believing that?'

'So who would do that?' said Craig. From his voice, Keisha could tell he was still probing. Deciding if she was telling him the truth.

'I'm guessing,' said Keisha sharply, 'the same person who would want to frame you for murder.'

48

'Every week I have to justify every penny of our budget back to London,' said Helen, working herself up to giving a bollocking.

Ruth had spent the night locked in her bedroom in the flat she shared with a trainee management consultant called Clara. Unable to sleep, she'd stayed up, clutching a kitchen knife and waiting for the door to be kicked in.

Someone had broken into Eddie's flat, torn the place apart and taken the laptop containing the photos of the man on Jake's phone. A treasure trove of evidence, all gone. If they knew about Eddie then why wouldn't they know about Ruth?

Staggering into work in a haze of sleepless terror, Ruth had completely forgotten she'd left for lunch the day before and simply never returned. She'd been so caught up, first with Eddie's revelations and then with the fear that someone was on to her.

Like Ruth, Eddie thought there was a serial killer out there. Like Ruth, he'd seen photos of the man who had been with Jake the night he was killed. Eddie had spent thirty years becoming a trusted figure to certain young men. The kind of men who'd send him photos of their clients as a precaution. Eddie had been getting photos for years now. All stored on his laptop. Just in case.

Now the laptop was gone and Eddie was fearing for his life.

'Yesterday you simply waltzed out of the office and never came back. After submitting only two stories. I ended up writing your third story for you. If we don't hit the targets then it's me London comes for.'

Helen was wearing bright green dungarees over a red long-sleeve T-shirt. She looked nearly as tired as Ruth felt. Ruth knew that deep down Helen was only trying to keep the leaky ship that was *Mancunian Ways* afloat. Everyone in the office had grown up dreaming of being a journalist. Now they were all struggling through the stark, unforgiving reality of what that dream meant in a world where they were only a few years away from AI being able to replace every single one of them.

But still, Ruth *was* a journalist. She *was* on the tail of something huge. She was risking her life and now was getting a dressing-down for it.

'You've not said anything,' said Helen sternly.

Ruth realised she hadn't even been listening. She'd been too busy trying to work out how they'd found Eddie. What she'd done the past few days that could possibly lead back to her.

'Well?'

'I've been following a story,' said Ruth defiantly.

'You didn't bother to submit it,' said Helen.

'It's a real story,' said Ruth, somewhere between fatigue and fear finding her courage. 'It's about dead sex workers. It's about a serial killer. It's about a cover-up. It's going on right now. Under our noses. It's not cocktail bars or theme pubs for adults who haven't grown up yet. It's about the real Manchester, the Manchester that isn't money and glamour. That isn't fucking *Mancunian Ways*.'

Helen looked shocked. Ruth's brain raced. She hadn't meant to say any of that. It simply came out.

All she could think to say was: 'Sorry.'

'I'm sorry,' said Helen unexpectedly. 'I did my MA on local press coverage of the miners' strike. I started just as everything fell apart. The internet took all the ad revenue. Then it took all the eyeballs and then it took all the jobs. I wanted to do news. Real news. Truth is no one gives a fuck. They don't want to pay and so the best we've got is *Mancunian Ways*. We're fucking PR. I know that. But I'm thirty-five. I've got a mortgage.

I might still want some kids. Fuck knows how. But this job is the high-water mark for me. And I can't risk that.'

'This story could change all that. Put us on the map,' said Ruth, suddenly energised by Helen's candour.

'No. That won't happen. You'll spend however long putting it together. You'll put it up and an hour or so later I'll get a call from London telling me to take it down. *Mancunian Ways* is a smiling, spotless showroom for anyone with something to sell. Not dead prostitutes.'

Ruth was stunned. First Eddie's flat and now this. It was like the cover-up wasn't just whoever ransacked Eddie's flat. It was the whole city. The world of her dad was gone. The curiosity and the crusading sense of justice and truth. It didn't mean anything.

She refused to accept that.

Ruth stood up.

'So do we understand each other?' asked Helen.

'We do,' said Ruth. 'Which is why I quit.'

Helen paused for a moment then looked down and shrugged. 'OK. I understand. Good luck.'

And that was it. There was no argument. No begging. No accusations. Just resignation. Both Ruth's and Helen's.

As Ruth headed back out the office, Damion called over to her. 'How'd it go with the boss?' he asked.

'I quit,' said Ruth, and as she walked out of the office she suddenly felt an immense sense of possibility come over her. Maybe Helen had given up but that didn't mean she would. She had this story and now it was up to her to break it.

Whatever the cost.

49

Illian sat beside Dean, unable to contain his nerves. He was dressed in the suit that Dean had bought him for the licensing committee hearing. Even wearing the tie that Dean had to tie for him earlier that morning.

As they waited in the corridor outside the committee room, Illian wasn't the only one distracted.

Dean had been so thrown by the depth of what Martin Farr had confessed to that he nearly forgot all about the hearing. It was only when Illian had come into the office that morning asking for help with his tie that Dean remembered the appointment at the town hall annexe where Illian's fate would be decided.

Dean hadn't given Martin Farr an answer. What he was asking was for Dean to lie to Janet Farr. To cover up Martin's role in the robbery and to throw all the blame on Sam Kennard. For sure it was Sam who committed the actual robbery but it was Martin who set it up, Martin's inside information that made it work. Martin was the one who was going to end up with a couple of hundred grand worth of uncut cocaine. Sam Kennard had received three hundred pounds for his trouble. More than that, it looked like the events Martin set in motion were what ended up getting Keisha's dad killed.

Dean would be keeping that to himself for the time being.

Far more pressing, Dean had a choice to make. On the one hand, if he lied to the Farrs he would be betraying everything Malton had taught him about the job they did. Malton never once compromised. He always did the job he was hired to do.

Whether the client liked it or not. He always got to the truth and let the truth speak for itself.

But if Dean did play along with Martin Farr then he'd not only get the name of the CI who had set Malton up, he'd also get the name of the man who had put him up to it.

He racked his brain. What would Malton do?

Illian's knees jogged up and down as he watched various council workers passing down the corridor. Dean could tell each time he was wondering if they were the one who was about to pass judgement on his future.

Farr had said the supplier was killing rent boys. Could that really be true? And if it was true then maybe that young journalist Ruth Porter was right. Maybe there was a serial killer in Manchester. That still didn't explain why frame Malton? With all of Manchester to choose from, why go for him?

Ruth still hadn't got back in touch. After this committee hearing, Dean resolved to track her down with the utmost urgency. Maybe if he had enough pieces he could get to the name without Martin Farr or Ruth. Was Malton the clue? What was it that linked him to the Farrs' supplier?

The committee was late. Dean took out his phone to check the time. He couldn't ignore the dozens of notifications waiting for him. Various searches he always had live. Feeding him as much information as he could get about what was going on in Manchester.

Idly opening the first notification, he was about to read the headline when he heard, 'It's done. You can go.'

He looked up to see Fauzia Malik stood in the corridor.

'Wait!' said Illian, jumping to his feet. 'I can explain.'

'There's no need. There is no hearing. You're in the clear.'

First disbelief and then joy broke over Illian's face.

'Thank you!' he cried, and was about to grab Fauzia and hug her when he remembered himself and turned to Dean. 'You fixed it?' he said.

'It's fixed,' said Fauzia. 'And that's the last time I ever want to hear from you again. Especially after what's just happened.'

Dean looked blankly. 'The committee?'

'The committee?' said Fauzia, incredulous. 'That's nothing. I mean Craig Malton being kidnapped at gunpoint from MRI. Your boss is in the wind and I don't want anything else to do with him ever again.'

She turned to Illian and said, 'Lucky for you I'd already spoken to the committee.'

Dean looked down at the first notification on his phone. He'd been so wrapped up in Martin Farr and then the hearing. The headline read: GUNWOMAN KIDNAPS PRISONER FROM HOSPITAL BED.

Gunwoman. He had a horrible feeling he knew exactly who that was.

50

Stephen Page grew up on the edge of Didsbury just as the suburb was becoming one of Manchester's most sought-after postcodes. His parents Simon and Liz had lived there their whole lives and were delighted to see the tiny semi-detached house they had bought ten years previous suddenly shoot up in value. They were even more delighted when their first child came along and turned out to be a boy.

Stephen attended Parrs Wood High where his early academic promise was quickly squandered after he discovered drugs and fell in with a crowd of children who were a mixture of affluent latch-key kids whose parents had sent their children to a state school as a grand political gesture and kids from troubled families who, like the Pages, had seen where they lived on the edge of Didsbury rapidly gentrified by an influx of new house buyers.

It wasn't long before Stephen was skipping school, having daily arguments with Liz and Simon and going missing for days at a time.

By the time Stephen was sixteen, Simon had insisted to his wife that the only way to bring their son to his senses was to break all contact. Let him hit rock bottom and come back to where they would be waiting with patient love.

Three years later, Stephen's body was found strangled to death and dumped in the back seat of a minicab.

The news had broken the Pages. Even the arrest of Craig Malton, his killer, had brought no relief.

But life went on. Simon was still a warehouse manager. Liz was still a teaching assistant.

Every day they left the house together just after six to head to their work.

Today there was an unfamiliar car parked across the road from the house.

Today Malton was waiting for them.

He'd slipped out before Keisha could wake up and taken the BMW, leaving her the keys to the black Transit. Malton couldn't quite bring himself to believe Keisha's story that she was in Manchester for her dead father and that her rescuing him from MRI was pure coincidence. He'd learned from past experience that when Keisha was involved every situation had a hidden agenda. Keisha lived her life with one eye on the prize and one foot out the door. She would never simply 'turn up'.

Besides, if, as she claimed, it wasn't her who had been spying on him then who had been sending him surveillance photos? Part of him hoped that Keisha was lying to him. That this was all some elaborate scheme and that she had indeed been watching him from afar. Whatever her reasons, it was something he could deal with. It could be contained.

But if Keisha was telling the truth, that meant two things. Firstly that whoever had been watching him was still out there, and that secondly, and much more troubling, in the moment, when faced with impossible odds and no reward, Keisha's first instinct was to draw a gun and ride to his rescue.

If that was the case then everything was far more complicated.

His attempt to untangle Keisha's motivations was interrupted by the sight of the Pages leaving their house.

Connor's face getting melted off was the wake-up call Malton needed. He had finally turned to all the legal paperwork that, without a lawyer, had built up around his case. In the short time he'd had before his 'meeting' with Mickey Farr, he'd committed as much as possible to memory. That included the Pages' home address.

Their road was in Didsbury in name only. In truth it was a couple of miles from the shops and bars that most people thought of as Didsbury. Instead it was tucked away between the A34 and the River Mersey. On a low floodplain, which in recent years had begun to flood more regularly. Their house was at the end of a series of interconnected dead ends. Roads that had nothing but houses. No pubs, no shops, none of the Didsbury sparkle that had made the suburb so desirable.

In the driving rain it could have been anywhere in Manchester.

By the time the Pages had locked their front door behind them Malton was already out of the car. Keisha had bought him head-to-toe black sportswear. A black Under Armour tracksuit with tapered legs and zip-up top with a hood over his bare chest. Black Adidas running shoes with black soles. She'd also bought him a large, black padded coat, the kind football managers wore on the sidelines.

Alone in bed the night before, he'd realised he was in no condition to change himself and so he'd gone to sleep in the same clothes, in which he then woke and left the house wearing.

With his hood up and his tracksuit top fastened right up to under his chin, only his face was visible. Even so, now he was a wanted man he was taking no chances.

He'd driven past the Page house several times that morning and around the block, convincing himself that there were no police lying in wait. It would make sense if they were. He was accused of murdering the Pages' son Stephen.

Luckily whatever GMP's plan for finding him was, it didn't involve the Pages.

By the time Malton was on the driveway they had spotted him. Both immediately reacting to the sight of a large man dressed head to toe in black striding towards them through the downpour.

Malton stopped a few feet away, pulled back the hood and held his hands up to show them they were empty. It was more a gesture than anything. Simon was a slight man with bright white hair, barely five foot eight. His wife Liz was a similar height and build. Neither would present any problem to Malton if that was how he wanted to play it.

'My name is Craig Malton,' said Malton.

'You!' shrieked Liz as Simon stepped in front of his wife.

'You can't be here,' said Simon.

Malton was impressed. Despite everything he wasn't shaking. There was no fear in his voice. He was a man who had already lost his son. What did he have left to fear?

'Do you believe I killed your son?' asked Malton. He saw Simon stop for a moment to think. That was all he needed. The answer wasn't immediate. There was doubt there. He could do something with doubt.

'The police have DNA,' said Liz from behind Simon.

'The police have DNA and the word of a criminal whose name they are refusing to release. The police know that if it went to trial there's only two pieces of evidence linking me to your son's murder.'

'You killed him!' Liz shouted over the rain.

'The police also know there is no CCTV of me at the scene. There are no other witnesses.'

'That's for the courts to decide,' said Simon, squinting through the rain.

'If it goes to court, whatever happens to me, the man who killed your son is still out there. What's to say he won't do it again?'

'That other boy,' said Liz before she could stop herself.

Malton was still playing catch-up. Three months of letting his mind idle. It would take more than a few days to get back on top. Time he didn't have. With no idea what 'the other boy' meant, he decided to bluff.

'That boy and there'll be others. I've been locked up these past few months so you know it couldn't have been me. A predator like that, he's not a normal criminal. He's not doing it for money or power, he's doing it because he can't stop.'

'You know a lot about it for someone who's innocent,' said Simon.

Malton had no choice but to go all the way.

'Before I got arrested I ran a security company. But that wasn't what I really did. I solved crime for criminals. I've tracked down dozens of murderers, rapists and thieves. People you will never hear about because when I find them I hand them over to the people who pay me. Bad people.'

Finally a look of horror began to creep over Simon's face.

'Right now I'm on the run and the best shot I have to not go back to prison is to find out who really killed your son and I can't do that without your help. So if you don't want to help me then I'm going to get back in that car and disappear. They won't find me. Whoever really killed your son will simply go right on killing and you'll never ever have an end to it. But you need to decide. Now.'

Malton felt his weight on his injured leg. The chilling cold of the rain made both stab wounds ache. He was hyper-aware of the plastic drain still in his chest, and his broken ribs. But he stood tall and resolute. Letting the Pages come to their answer.

'I can't wait any longer,' said Malton.

As he turned to go it was Liz Page who cried out, 'What do you need to know?'

51

Even though it was no surprise to wake up and find Malton already gone, Keisha still felt something. Alone in the house, suddenly that empty feeling she'd had in Ibiza was back.

It was the last thing she wanted. This was why she'd gone in the first place. Every day she spent in Manchester, the city got back inside her as sure as the rain soaked her skin.

Just what had she expected? She'd gone to MRI fearing that Craig was at death's door. She wanted to see him one last time. Convince herself that she'd made the right decision stepping away. Instead she'd allowed herself to be dragged right back into the eye of the storm.

Keisha only had the clothes she'd been wearing to visit Malton. Clothes that she'd been seen wearing. And so after showering in a well-appointed en-suite wet room, with a soft white towel still wrapped around her, she went searching the house.

Craig had set this place up. That meant he would have planned for anything. Sure enough, she found a cupboard filled with brand-new clothing. All of it untouched, some even with the labels still on.

Of course all of it was in Craig's size, but she went with a large, hand-knitted gansey jumper, which she wore like a sloppy dress. The wool was dark blue, flecked with tiny dots of colour. She kept the tights from the day before and her trainers.

After heating up a tin of beans for her breakfast, Keisha took the keys to the black Transit van she found left for her on the kitchen table and headed out.

With everything that had gone on the past few days she'd nearly forgotten. Today was the day of her father's funeral.

In the short time she'd been home, Harold had gone from a name pinned to a long-gone memory to something approaching a fully realised person. As much as she resisted, there was something inside her that wanted to do right by the man who abandoned her. She knew it was irrational. He was dead. Even when he was alive he didn't give a damn about her or her mother. But still there was a part of her that held out hope that if she could only do right for him in death somehow that could close the circle.

That was why she found herself on the road back to Edge Haven. Five days ago, burying her father alone and unknown into the Manchester soil made total sense. Now it seemed unforgivable. She wanted something to put on the grave. A photo, a memory. A reminder of who Harold Boateng really was.

The pile of Harold's belongings would still be where she'd left them. Dumped on the floor of his caravan by someone she had yet to track down.

Everything was a mess. Keisha had lost control of the situation. Craig was off God knows where. She was probably a wanted woman and she was no nearer finding who it was who had run over her dad. As if it even mattered anymore.

But the funeral – that was something she could handle. Keisha could do funerals.

As she arrived at Edge Haven caravan park the rain was coming off the sea and lashing the silent, sodden rows of mobile homes. Driving the black Transit along the narrow lanes of caravans, it felt like the world was finally coming to an end.

She would get a photo. She would get back in the van and she would drive to Southern Cemetery for the funeral. See what her twenty grand had bought her. With her father in the ground maybe things would seem clearer. It felt like a great time to cut her losses. Leave Manchester and leave Craig.

Struggling through the door of the caravan and out of the rain, she found a letter waiting for her on the floor. It was addressed to Harold and had a red FINAL DEMAND printed on it. There was no stamp.

Soaked from the short walk from where she'd parked to the caravan, Keisha wiped a sleeve of the heavy gansey jumper across her face. The smell of wet wool snatched at a childhood memory she couldn't quite place. As she opened the letter, her wet hands turned the envelope to pulp.

It was a bill for the rent on Harold's caravan.

A cold fury seized Keisha as she looked down at the invoice in her hands. Her father was dead, his caravan had been broken into and ransacked, and all Edge Haven could do was send him a bill?

She felt the tears coming but held them at bay. What was she crying for? That some office drone at the caravan park wasn't aware of every movement of Harold Boateng? Until a few days ago, neither was she. The insult of sending a bill to a dead man? A dead man who, from the contents of his caravan, had made clear that as far as he was concerned it was as if Keisha had never even existed.

Her father didn't deserve tears. He'd already taken more than his share since she'd been home. Harold Boateng was going in the ground and Keisha was going back to Ibiza. Craig was on his own. Just how he liked it.

She was about to screw the letter up when a line on the invoice caught her eye. There was M7, Harold's caravan, but beneath it another line for an identical amount. For M8.

Keisha dove into her pocket and pulled out the keys she'd taken from Dean. There was the key for M7, labelled with the tag. But there, next to it, was an identical key. No label.

Keisha looked through the rain-smeared windows at the next caravan along. Caravan M8.

52

'If you have been in contact with Craig Malton and don't report it, that's assisting an offender. If you're providing assistance to Craig Malton, that's assisting an offender. If Craig Malton contacts you and you fail to report it, that's assisting an offender.'

Dean sat in silence listening to DCI Priestly laying down the law in Malton's office.

The news that Malton had escaped suddenly dragged everything into the here and now. The longer Malton was on the run the more chance there was of him committing some new crime, which would render Martin's information meaningless.

Priestly's suit fit him in a way that Dean's never did. Of course it didn't help that Dean used every pocket of his suit jacket to carry random items – pens, phones, keys, change and a toothbrush. But even without all the baggage he would never look as good as Priestly looked. Dean wondered if he should ask Priestly where he got the suit from.

Since learning that Malton was on the run, Dean had been expecting one of two things: either to be contacted by Malton himself or for the police to get in touch. It turned out the police were the first off the blocks.

'. . . and the same goes for the woman seen helping him escape,' said Priestly, coming to an end.

There was only one woman Dean knew that fitted the description of the mixed-race woman with braided hair who had led Malton out of MRI at gunpoint. From the blurry CCTV that had been released, under the glasses and the coat, Dean would put money on it being Keisha.

Like Malton, Keisha had spent a lifetime flying under the radar. Unlike Malton, she hadn't been arrested for murder and brought into the system. For all the harm she'd done, Keisha was totally clean. It meant she had a head start.

'If I hear anything, I'll be sure to let you know,' said Dean, knowing that both he and Priestly knew that was bullshit. The very first lesson Malton had ever taught him: never, ever, ever call the police.

Dean was less worried about the police and more worried about Keisha. Was Harold Boateng really her father or was it all a story to get close to Dean? Was he somehow responsible? He'd told her about Malton being in MRI. Next thing, Malton was kidnapped. Just what was Keisha playing at?

Dean saw Priestly out. He could see from the faces of the Malton Security staff watching him that they'd heard the news about their boss. First a murder charge and now a jailbreak.

Things were going from bad to worse.

Back before he got involved with Bea Wallace and then took off to Liverpool, only to return in the back of a police van, Malton would never have been anywhere near the police. What Malton did was so far beyond the law that they never even knew he existed. He had shown Dean how he enforced something bigger than the law. A bespoke criminal justice that adhered to his own private code. Malton saw everything that was wrong with the world and he chose to use it to his advantage.

But he could only do that under the cloak of anonymity. To acknowledge that a man like Malton existed was to admit the entire system was a farce. Now that he had been dragged into the light, Dean wondered just how long his old boss could survive.

There was nothing for it. Back in Malton's office, Dean locked the door and got out his phone.

He put in a call to Martin Farr.

53

One whole side of the Pages' front room was given over to shelves of vinyl records. A turntable had pride of place beneath a giant, wall-mounted television. The whole set-up running to a large pair of floor-standing speakers in the corners of the room.

Everything was neat and clean. The pale blue IKEA sofas, the dark beige carpet and the sage green walls. There were a couple of framed film posters and in one corner a large, ornate plant pot sprouted a giant cheese plant.

It was all so unremarkable.

The Pages were still in their sixties. They'd grown up through punk and the Eighties. They were old but not in the way that Malton remembered old people. Back in Moss Side growing up, old meant white hair and house coats and a language that belonged with the bomb sites, slum clearances and the Windrush generation.

But there, on the wall, was the photo of them all together. Simon, Liz and Stephen. All three of them wearing plastic rain ponchos at some theme park. Stephen too young to be on the path that would lead to his murder, and Simon and Liz basking in the joy of finally reaching the stage where their child was a small, articulate, loving human being who still needed them but very soon would be forging his own life.

Simon's white hair had been misleading. Inside and out of the rain, he looked a lot younger. He was slim and Malton noticed his clothes fit well. He still cared.

No one had offered him a drink and Malton didn't ask. He didn't want to be friends with these people. He wanted information.

'We thought what was the harm with a bit of pot?' said Liz. 'We even let him smoke in the house.'

'We thought better that than out somewhere else doing it,' said Simon before hearing himself and hanging his head.

'It all just happened so quickly,' said Liz.

'We made the right decision,' said Simon, fixing Malton. 'What else could we do? It got to the point he was stealing from us. Selling my records, selling your jewellery.'

Liz Page looked ashamed to hear her son being talked of as a thief. Like her husband, she was neatly dressed. Fashionable but reserved. She was in a long-sleeved floral dress with black tights underneath and Doc Marten boots on her feet.

Malton took them both in. Both of them still youthful. The kind of parents who would be your friend first and your parent second. People with no tools to deal with a kid like Stephen.

'We said he couldn't stay here. I changed the locks.' For the first time since they'd sat down, Simon faltered.

'Did you know how he was making money?' asked Malton.

Liz let out a little sob.

'He was spending that money on drugs. Either he stole from us or he got it somewhere else. But I'm not having my money going to drug dealers,' said Simon angrily.

In Malton's life he rarely met people like the Pages. People who would never have any reason to dive into the filth and deprivation that Malton had made his speciality. They would never meet someone who could beat a man to death with a tyre iron and sleep like a baby. They'd never come across a woman paying thousands of pounds to run kidnapped women into the country or a businessman who in reality owned a string of cannabis farms staffed by indentured immigrant workers. They had no idea how close to the surface it all ran.

'He was a rent boy,' said Malton plainly.

For a moment Simon seemed ready to leap to his son's defence but then realised the futility of it all.

'That's what we heard,' he said.

'And did you know who he saw? Where he found his clients? Where he took them?'

Liz shook her head and covered her mouth.

'I don't know you,' said Simon, 'but I like to think I'm a good judge of character. That world, that's your world, isn't it? Bad people, doing bad things. We're just regular people. Boring even. I don't know and I didn't ask. Maybe I should have done but, to tell you the truth, I didn't want to know.'

'Wait,' said Liz, her eyes lighting up.

Malton said nothing and let her continue.

'He came back once. He was drunk or on drugs.'

'We didn't let him in,' said Simon sternly.

'But he had something for us. A present. In the end he left it on the doorstep.'

Malton felt the gears in his head begin to move.

'What was it?' he asked.

'A handbag. A really expensive one,' said Liz.

'He stole it?' asked Malton.

'No,' said Liz. 'That was the strange thing. He turned up with one of those yellow Selfridges bags.'

Malton could feel it getting closer. All those months locked away languishing in self-pity couldn't dim it forever. That instinct that told him he was on the right track.

'Do you still have it?' he asked.

Liz shot out of the room, leaving Malton alone with Simon. The two men stared at each other. Simon not giving an inch.

Malton sat in the silence. Simon was right: he wasn't from their world but he saw in Simon something he recognised. The refusal to let the darkness win. A willingness to not flinch, even in the face of the ultimate tragedy.

Liz came hurrying back in with the shopping bag.

'Did you mention this to the police?' asked Malton.

'The police haven't been in touch since they arrested you,' said Simon. 'It was like it was all over and done with.'

Liz handed Malton the bright yellow store bag and sat back on the sofa.

Malton reached in and took out a handbag. It was black and cream leather with a large, golden YSL clasp.

Malton flicked the clasp and looked inside the handbag. The smell of fresh leather filled his nostrils.

'Did Stephen have a credit card? A debit card?'

Simon laughed. 'He went overdrawn on all of it. I cancelled them. He had nothing. We thought he'd come back once he realised he couldn't support himself.'

That's exactly what Malton wanted to hear.

Sat in the bottom of the handbag was a credit card receipt.

54

Keisha had never tasted salmon before. She'd watched her mum put the tin on the highest shelf in the kitchen and then warn her in no uncertain terms not to touch it until the day of the wedding. Keisha knew it must be a special occasion as her mum usually didn't buy any more food than was absolutely necessary. Having food in the house attracted the cockroaches.

Keisha had read in the papers about street parties happening all over the country in celebration, but when she'd asked her mother whether or not they would be having a party her mother told her that they would have their own party in the flat.

Outside she could see the usual faces gathering in the communal area in front of the Crescents. It used to be that all her friends lived in the Crescents but one by one the families moved away. Keisha's mum refused to move out. She said that it was her who'd convinced so many of her neighbours to move there in the first place. If she left the sinking ship what would that say about her?

The flat was immaculate. Her mum constantly scrubbed away at the damp and mould and fought a losing battle against the rats who they could hear scurrying around in the various ducts that ran throughout the estate.

Each building was a giant, curved concrete structure. Six storeys high and joined together by walkways and bridges. When Keisha had first moved in it looked like a space-age paradise. Then the whole thing fell apart.

The flats were cold and damp. In the winter Keisha wore her coat indoors. The communal heating systems failed and infestations of pests became commonplace. When the council had stopped collecting rent and abandoned the whole estate, Keisha watched as school friends and their families moved out only to be replaced with problem tenants, artists and students. Suddenly the space-age paradise became a modern slum.

Whether out of pride or guilt, her mother had hung on in there and in doing so Keisha had seen first-hand just what a woman could achieve if she refused to take no for an answer.

Her mum had hung their ground-floor flat with bunting that they'd both made and spent the morning making a feast for the two of them. There was a trifle, iced buns, lots of crisps and, pride of place, a pile of salmon and salad cream sandwiches on fresh, white sliced bread. Her mum had even cut them into little triangles.

From early morning the television had been on, competing with the noise of the music coming from the flats above. Keisha had been glued to the screen watching the crowds gathering in London bedecked in Union Jack flags. Her mother was far too Irish to cover her front room in Union Jacks and so their bunting was multi-coloured. Keisha thought their bunting looked much prettier.

She couldn't wait to see the princess. She'd read in the paper about the carriage and the dress. Keisha was always reading the paper. She read it more than her mother. Cover to cover.

On the TV the carriage had begun to make its way up the Mall and her mum had just laid out the salmon sandwiches when there was a knock at the door.

Before her mum could stop her, Keisha was up and running to answer it. She liked answering the door and talking to the adults on the other side. Adults were more interesting to talk to than kids and they always seemed pleased to be talking to a little girl full of questions.

Living surrounded by the chaos of Hulme Crescents had quickly made Keisha fearless. As far as she was concerned this was her home and she had every right to be there.

She opened the door to find a black man with a neat afro and beard smiling down at her. He was wearing a long, brown leather jacket and had a carrier bag in one hand.

'You're even bigger than the last time I saw you,' he said to Keisha.

She tried to remember who he was.

'That's because it's been nearly two years,' said her mum from over her head.

'Not today,' said the man, shaking his head wearily. 'I come over for the wedding.' He peered past her mum to the food and the television. 'I bought your favourite,' he said, holding up the carrier bag, which gave the tell-tale clink of glass bottles.

Keisha stood between these two grown-ups, trying to work out what was going on.

'And I bought this!' said the man, holding up a camera. 'I don't have any pictures of my little girl.'

'Dad?' said Keisha, and the man's face lit up.

'See? She remembers me!' he said and stepped in the flat.

Keisha's mother said nothing, closing the door behind him.

'Here,' he said, handing her mum the camera. 'Me and my little princess.'

He put an arm around Keisha and hugged her close. Keisha wasn't sure how she felt about that but she knew that if someone was taking a photo you ought to smile and look your best. So that's just what she did.

★★★

M8 was neater and less personal than M7. There were no rugs or throws and the kitchen was piled high with palettes of cans and large sacks of rice and pasta. It was more a storeroom than a home. An overspill from Harold's other caravan.

Only one of the three bedrooms had a bed. The largest had a desk and was set up as a study. The other two were storerooms filled with cardboard boxes and bags of random clutter.

In fact, the only thing that said Harold Boateng had ever been here was the photograph that had pride of place on the wall.

It was a young man with a neat afro and a beard. He was wearing a brown leather jacket and in one hand he had a carrier bag. The other hand was resting on the shoulder of a five-year-old Keisha McColl.

55

Ruth hadn't meant to get this drunk.

After the adrenaline high of quitting her job on a point of principle she had the awkward shuffle of returning to the office when she'd realised she still had to clear her desk.

Damion was all over her, asking questions. Helen had the decency to stay in her office and pretend to be on the phone.

It didn't take Damion long to get the full story out of Ruth. Whispered in the corner of the office so the rest of the room didn't hear what a fool she'd been. She had expected disbelief, but to her surprise Damion couldn't stop talking about how much he admired her. What integrity she had and how he'd never have the nerve to do anything so brave.

She left the office feeling like she'd made the right decision.

The feeling lasted until she was stood outside shivering in the shadow of the giant glass tower block across the street. The rain funnelling down between the buildings and running into small, filthy rivers in the road. Pooling in the potholes and burbling up through Victorian drains, which were never intended to cope with the sheer volume of waste now passing through them daily.

All at once Manchester felt very big and Ruth felt very small.

Fleeing the rain, she found herself in a pub just opposite Shudehill coach station. It was one she'd walked past hundreds of times yet never once set foot inside. As the rain got heavier she'd ducked in with her sopping wet box of office supplies and found herself taken back in time about thirty years.

The bar was a traditional, wooden affair in the middle of the pub serving three distinct rooms.

Ruth headed for the front room, dumped her box, and after being asked to prove she was indeed over eighteen, ordered herself a drink. Warm and dry, she instinctively checked her phone for new updates. There it was. Craig Malton was a wanted fugitive. On the run after being taken out of Manchester Royal Infirmary at gunpoint. A naked taxi driver had been found in the woods near Bolton but neither his car nor Malton nor his kidnapper had been seen since.

Something between fear and exhilaration came over Ruth. Now the whole world was watching but it was only her who knew the real story. This was no longer about hunches and suspicions. This was current news and she was going to be the one to break it.

Ruth got out Jake's phone and, safely ensconced in the corner with a pint of Strongbow Dark, she began systematically poring over it. Putting together a story that would make her career.

Ruth pulled out a notepad and pen and, in the shorthand that her dad had finally taught her after endless nagging, she began in earnest to follow the trail that she hoped would lead her to discover the identity of not just Jake's killer but also the man who'd killed at least eight other boys including Stephen Page.

As Jake's life unspooled in front of her, the drinks kept coming and so did the rain. Hammering against the front of the pub and flooding into the sewers.

She searched every name in the phone. Trawling social media and beyond. Cross-referencing names, building up an idea of Jake's social circle. Where he lived, where he ate, who he loved and who he was scared of.

Jake lived through his phone. And it wasn't just photos – there were voice notes. He had a habit of talking to himself. Recording his thoughts. There were dozens of them, some running to nearly twenty minutes long.

Ruth slipped on her headphones and began to listen.

She was so caught up in Jake's voice messages she barely noticed the pub filling up as the lunchtime crowd started arriving.

A mixture of older regulars and younger guys from offices and building sites. It was time to go.

By the time she was walking home the rain had died down to a slow dribble. Manchester glistened, the whole city washed clean once more.

Ruth, too, felt suddenly renewed. Maybe it was the booze, maybe it was the memory of Damion's gushing praise or maybe it was the thrill of a story that was now unfolding in front of her.

She was surprised to find the fear of the night before had gone too. Now this was her full-time story, suddenly it all felt very different. She wasn't an amateur dabbling where she shouldn't be dabbling. She was a journalist and as a journalist she should be prepared to take risks. She'd once asked her dad had he ever been scared doing his job. He'd told that of course he had. He'd exposed criminals, dragged conspiracies into the light. He'd pissed off a lot of powerful people. But he'd told her that every time he felt the fear, that was his way of knowing that he was doing his job.

Ruth felt just the same.

Right up until she opened the door to her flat and found her flatmate Clara sat in their living room cowering in terror.

Clara didn't say a word. In silence her eyes moved to the other side of the room where a giant, shaved-headed man dressed entirely in black was sat watching her.

56

She looked younger than Malton was expecting. Dark hair framing an almost childlike face. Smooth skin and large, brown eyes. He knew she would be scared and that was a problem because right now Ruth Porter knew more than anyone about the murder of Stephen Page.

She sat across the room from him, weighing him up. It was a typical city-centre flat. White walls; rough, beige carpet and small flourishes of individuality from the people living there. Malton guessed the framed newspapers were Ruth's. Front pages from old *Manchester Evening News* editions. He'd had some time to inspect them before Ruth got there and noticed a theme: the journalist's name – Glen Porter.

It must run in the family.

'You know you're a wanted man?' said Ruth.

Malton noticed she'd got out a notepad and pen. He let it pass. In the kitchen just off the front room, Ruth's flatmate was hovering nervously.

'You kept asking to see me,' said Malton. 'Here I am.'

Ruth gave a little smile and nearly dropped the pen she was holding. Malton could tell she had been drinking but at the same time the booze gave her a candid intensity. If she was scared she wasn't going to let that get in her way.

'Did you kill Stephen Page?' she asked.

'Is that your opener? To put me off balance? Catch me out? Hope I might confess?'

Ruth suddenly looked less sure.

'You're not going to butter me up first?'

'You're on the run,' said Ruth. 'I don't think you've got time to be buttered up. If it helps, I don't think you killed him.'

Malton hid his surprise.

'So what did you want to talk to me about?' he asked.

'I used to think you killed him but then another boy turned up dead.'

Malton leaned forward and in a low, commanding voice said, 'Tell me about him.'

Ruth hesitated. She was thinking. Finally she set down her pen and paper and said, 'I spoke to someone at your company. A lad called Dean.'

Malton nodded. Once again it seemed like Dean had stepped up and been doing all the things Malton himself ought to have done the moment he was first charged with Stephen Page's murder. He wondered what Dean had made of this woman.

'He offered to help me research my story. So long as I left you out of it. Said looking into you could be dangerous.'

Malton felt a flush of pride. Dean knew his job.

'So what's the story if I'm not in it?' said Malton.

'Someone's killing sex workers. Stephen Page was a sex worker.'

'So I hear,' said Malton.

'Another boy turned up dead a few days ago. Jake Arnold.'

'And you think he was murdered?'

Ruth didn't answer.

'Let me put it another way,' said Malton, 'I don't think you just come to conclusions out of thin air. I think you understand what a journalist does. Well, what a journalist used to do. Like your dad.'

He saw her react to him mentioning her father. Eventually she'd work out he must have seen the name on the framed newspapers but for now it served Malton's purpose to let her think he was already ahead of her.

'So what I should ask is, why do you think he was murdered?'

There was a long pause and finally Ruth said, 'I found his phone.'

Malton went very quiet. Left Ruth hanging. He needed more.

'There's a man who lives in town. Some of the sex workers send him photos of their clients. As a safety thing.'

She was talking now. Malton could see the story she was telling excited her so he let her continue.

'Jake sent him a photo of his final client. Then a few days later I saw the same man, where I found the phone. Looking for it. Well, the man he was with was looking. I think he was a bodyguard or something. He had that look about him.'

'It sounds like you're good at this. So did you take Dean up on his offer?'

'I haven't got back to him.'

'Did he tell you what would happen if you make the story about me?'

'He made some threats.'

'No,' said Malton firmly. 'Dean doesn't do threats. What he told you is true. Because of what I do, there's a lot of people with a vested interest in keeping it quiet.'

Behind Ruth's head her flatmate had her phone in her hand.

'Please put that phone down,' said Malton, talking past Ruth.

Ruth turned to see her flatmate frozen and guilty.

'He's on the run. He killed someone,' she said desperately.

'No,' said Ruth. 'He didn't kill anyone. I don't know why he got arrested but I'm going to find out.'

'When Dean offered to help did he tell you what he could do?'

'I'm doing pretty well on my own, I think,' said Ruth defiantly.

'I just escaped from MRI in broad daylight. When I leave your flat, I disappear. I can go wherever I want, see whoever I want and I won't be caught until I want to be caught. Now imagine what your story would be with me helping you. Not Dean. And in return, I'm a footnote.'

'I still don't see why I need your help.'

Malton went in for the kill.

'Whoever framed me for murder knew that they were taking a huge risk. They took that risk because they stood to lose even more if they got found out. That means there's nothing they won't do to keep their crimes secret. I know that you'll find out who they are. But I also know that without me helping you, that when you do find them there's nothing to stop them pulling you off the street into the back of a van and making sure no one ever sees you again.'

Malton stopped and let his words sink in. The flatmate was crying in the kitchen.

It was more than a bluff. It was the truth. After Bea Wallace had turned up at MRI, Malton had begun to slowly start to piece together what had previously seemed like totally unrelated events. Bea slipping him the lead that took him to Liverpool. His arrest and her subsequent silence. Framing someone for murder was no small job. To start with, you needed a murder. And that meant you needed to be the kind of person who could not just lay their hands on a killer but could convince that killer you knew just the right fall guy to take the heat.

Ruth looked at Malton. Weighing him up.

'How do I know I can trust you?'

'You're a journalist. It's your job to make that decision.'

Ruth breathed out, reached into her bag and handed Malton a phone.

'This is Jake's phone. The last photo he took is the man I saw looking for this phone, the day after he was murdered.'

Malton turned the phone on and went to the gallery.

There was a photo of a toned, middle-aged man walking into a hotel bathroom. The bathroom mirror caught half his face in the reflection.

A face that looked like it had been to hell and brought a great deal of hell back with it.

The face of Jake's killer, the face of the man whose crime Malton had taken the fall for. A face that, under all the wreckage, Malton immediately recognised.

57

From across the road, Keisha could clearly see into the front room of the house on the other side of a terraced street in Chorlton.

She stood in the rain, beneath her umbrella, wondering what the right words would be.

Keisha spent her life knowing exactly the right words. Growing up around Hulme and Moss Side, she knew everyone and everyone knew her. From her mother she learned that any community was both good and bad. Far more of the good and far fewer of the bad, but she quickly discovered that deep down they were all from the same place. All on the same journey. Some took paths that were more dangerous or cruel but they all ended up at the same place in the end.

She never forgot that. When Craig had left her thirty years ago and she found herself alone for the first time in her life, she resolved to take what she'd learned and apply it to the whole wide world. There was no one Keisha was scared of. The volatile North Manchester hardman or the pampered Cheshire housewife. Keisha saw them as people just like anyone else. She could befriend them, she could comfort them, she could charm them and she could exploit them. All with her words.

Keisha had talked herself into wealth and power. She'd been in the kind of places that, growing up, she would never dream even existed. She'd held the world in her hand and made it look exactly how she wanted it to look.

There were always words.

So why was she stood silently in the rain watching as, across the road, a young woman dressed in black was plaiting the hair of a little girl who looked just like Keisha?

Keisha was ready to have Harold buried alone without fanfare and move on with her life. After finding all the photos of Rachel and her daughter Allie, it had given her grim satisfaction to know that Harold would be buried without them even knowing he was dead. They'd had him their entire lives; now it was Keisha's turn.

The photo had changed everything.

Now she knew that whatever else Harold did, he hadn't forgotten her. She would never know why he hadn't reached out. Perhaps he was ashamed of how he'd treated her mother. Perhaps he simply couldn't find her. Whatever the reason, he had remembered that day in the flat in the Crescents. When all three of them sat and ate salmon sandwiches and watched Charles and Diana getting married.

It bothered her how many memories of Harold had simply hidden themselves from her. They were there somewhere inside but for whatever reason she had let them slip into the shadows of her mind until Harold was neatly scrubbed from her life. She let go of the father who'd abandoned her.

Now she couldn't simply walk away. Harold had two daughters. And both of them were going to watch his final act.

With the funeral scheduled for that afternoon, Keisha had driven at speed all the way back from Edge Haven. On the way she called the number she'd found in Harold's caravan and delivered the message with as little emotion as possible.

'Harold Boateng is dead. He is being buried today at half four in Southern Cemetery.'

Then she'd hung up.

But as she drove back to Manchester she realised that letting Rachel know her dad was dead wasn't enough anymore. She had to be there herself.

Summoning up every last bit of her courage, Keisha crossed the road and knocked on the door.

She saw the little girl rush to the window to look out. Keisha turned and peered from under her umbrella. She clocked the look of shock on the little girl's face when she saw herself staring back through Keisha's eyes.

Her half-sister Rachel answered the door and took a step back.

Both women stared at each other. Keisha knowing exactly who Rachel was, Rachel feeling the uncanny sense that this stranger was at once familiar.

Rachel was definitely her father's girl. She and Keisha both had the same beautiful light brown skin, the same thick, dark hair that fell down in curls. While Keisha had her father's face, Rachel looked a little different. Keisha imagined Rachel must have got her tiny nose and wide mouth from her mother. Whoever she had been.

She was stunning in mourning. A black trouser suit, with wide, boot-cut trousers that tapered up around her hips. A clean white shirt under a short jacket and her make-up equally sober save for the dark burgundy of her lips.

'Can I help you?' asked Rachel, her tone uncertain as she ran through her head looking for where Keisha fitted.

Rachel's accent was softly Mancunian. The faint, middle-class trace of Manchester. Keisha's accent could dive hard into Moss Side but if needed she could correct it, leaning into her blackness or her whiteness. Whichever served her best. Her mixed-race heritage was like a superpower for her. A licence to be whoever she needed to be wherever she found herself.

But right now she was lost.

The rain was bouncing off her umbrella. It had rained all the way back from Edge Haven. It was beginning to feel like it would never stop.

'It was you who phoned, wasn't it?' said Rachel. Then out of nowhere she said, 'Keisha?'

Before Keisha could say a word Rachel rushed forward and threw her arms around her.

Keisha was taken completely by surprise. She barely kept hold of the umbrella as Rachel held her tightly.

Over Rachel's shoulder she saw Rachel's daughter, Allie, stood in the hallway watching her with a face that could have been her own. A glimpse into a life that she'd never had. A world of family and kindness and light.

Keisha dropped her umbrella and hugged Rachel back as hard as she could.

58

Martin Farr's phone had gone straight to voicemail but when, a few hours later, he did get back to Dean it was to insist that they meet in person.

Nothing about what Dean was preparing to do felt right to him. He'd seen first-hand what happened when people had tried to play Malton. It always ended badly. Usually for whoever it was trying to fold Malton into their plans. He knew that if Malton was presented with the choice of compromising the integrity of his reputation or getting the information that would free him from prison, then Malton would somehow work out a way to both get that information and walk away unscathed.

Malton's reputation was the one thing that had kept him alive all these years. Dean had witnessed just what Malton would do to protect it. To suddenly simply throw that away felt almost sacrilegious.

But driving north to the address in Kersal where Martin had asked to meet, Dean was drawing a blank. Martin Farr would demand that he tell his mother-in-law Janet that Sam Kennard had robbed the courier alone before giving up the names of the supplier and the informant on whose word Malton had been charged with murder.

Once he'd lied to Janet then it was over. If she found out the truth then Malton's reputation would be shot, and if once he had Martin's information he told Janet himself that he'd lied to her then it would be exactly the same.

Kersal in the rain was a warren of twisting streets and Sixties council housing. It was surrounded with undeveloped land.

Some beautiful, some not so beautiful. It was only a few miles from the middle of town but it felt very much like its own territory, removed in every respect from Manchester.

Where the houses bled into the scrubland you could find derelict buildings, lock-up garages and odd little homes built out in the middle of nowhere. Their windows barred and the doors sealed up but still showing signs of life. CCTV cameras, lights that came on in the middle of the night.

Dean had made it his business to know every inch of Manchester. Kersal still struck him as uncharted postcodes.

As he pulled up to the address Martin had given him it felt like he was stepping blind into enemy territory.

The address was a two-storey building at the edge of a concrete hardstanding where once a much larger building had stood. Weeds grew up through the concrete footprint of whatever had been standing there. The old fencing was still up in places; in others it had been torn down or was simply missing.

Fly tippers had dumped hundreds of black bags, mattresses and broken furniture all over the site. The endless rain had turned it all into a damp layer of chaos. It looked like hell.

And there, quietly watching it all, was a squat, flat-roof building a little like a clubhouse with a canopy extending from the first floor, shading the front of the building. Metal shutters covered the windows, but the heavy metal shutter that had been screwed over the door lay ominously ajar. Someone was inside.

There were two vehicles already parked up. Dean recognised them both. One was the battered Jag that he'd seen parked up outside the Farr house. The other was Sam Kennard's van.

Leaving the warm, dry interior of his car, Dean picked his way between the puddles that formed in the broken concrete and made his way towards the open door.

He paused for a moment beneath the canopy, glad to be out of the rain.

That's when he first heard the sound. It was muffled and wet but unmistakable. Someone was screaming. It was the sound of someone terrified for their life.

Right then it struck Dean – he had come here alone. He'd not told a soul he was here. He'd fucked up.

Before he could do a thing about it the shutter over the door opened fully and Martin Farr was stood before him with a smile on his face.

Dean clocked that he was wearing blue mechanics' overalls. The overalls were covered with blood.

'In you come,' said Martin with a grin.

Dean knew he had no other choice. As he followed Martin inside he racked his brains as to what Malton would do in this situation.

His train of thought was derailed as he came into what was once some kind of clubroom. A bar at one end of the room and a broken-up parquet dance floor. Lying in the middle of that parquet floor – naked, bound and bloody – was Sam Kennard.

Carl Farr was stood over him, stripped to the waist with sweat pouring off him. In his hand he held a blowtorch, the blueish-yellow flame piercing the gloom.

'Martin says you got something for us.'

Dean spun round and saw Janet Farr as she emerged from a back room, a cigarette in her mouth, utterly unconcerned by the scene before her.

'That's right,' said Martin quickly. 'Dean here's found our thief.'

59

Keisha was drowning. The rain was relentless. Stood out in the open in the far corner of Southern Cemetery, the downpour bounced off the tarpaulin that covered the grave like some kind of giant funeral drum, beating an unending tattoo for the death of Harold Boateng.

A little way away on the tarmac path stood a black horse-drawn carriage, two black horses and a rider. Keisha's money in action.

The ground was saturated with rainwater. Keisha's trainers sank into the mud, every step uncertain.

Beside her stood Allie and Rachel, each under their own umbrella, each similarly drenched. Allie and Rachel had brought wellington boots with them. Allie's were pink and sparkly. A flash of colour amongst the black of mourning.

Keisha had the photo of Harold she'd taken from his official caravan. It was an old photo. She guessed taken a few years after the one she'd found of her and her father. Harold was still young, his hair dark, his features handsome. He was stood next to a silver Mercedes, arms folded, mugging for the camera.

The priest was shouting to be heard. He'd been expecting a solo funeral but was delighted when Keisha, Allie and Rachel had appeared in the distance, tramping through the foul weather towards their father's final resting place.

'Harold Boateng leaves behind people who cared. People who remember him. And it is in those cherished memories that Harold will live on,' yelled the priest over the downpour.

Did Keisha care? She was here. She'd brought the photo and her half-sister. She'd dropped twenty thousand pounds.

She clearly felt something. But what memories did she really have? That morning of the royal wedding? A few hazy half-remembered images. Childhood memories as unreliable as a faded Polaroid picture.

Beside her Rachel was crying. As if she wasn't wet enough. Allie held her mother's hand and did her best to look solemn but brave.

Keisha wondered what they remembered of the man they were burying. How would Harold Boateng live on for them?

As Keisha felt the emotion of the moment rise up inside her, she realised she wasn't mourning Harold at all. She was mourning everything she'd never had. The Harold who would live on in her mind was the dead body on the slab. He was the empty caravan. The absent father. He was the hollow feeling that kept her awake at night. The itch she couldn't quite put her finger on.

Harold was dead but he was still one step ahead of her. Just around the corner and out of reach.

'Would anyone like to say a few words?' bellowed the priest. He was a young man, soft and white. His blonde hair plastered around his face, which glowed red with the cold. He had the perfect smile. Sympathy and warmth. Keisha wondered how you grew up to smile like that.

Rachel shook her head. Allie put her arms around her mother and hugged her tight. The priest turned to Keisha expectantly.

Keisha looked down at the tarpaulin-covered grave but nothing came.

60

'How long are you staying here?' asked Damion.

Ruth looked around the Airbnb. It was a flat in a large Victorian apartment complex just beyond the Gay Village. On Malton's advice she'd left her own flat on the edge of Castlefield and moved to a new location. One that there was no way anyone trying to find her could know about.

Her flatmate Clara had straight up refused to be chased out of her home. Ruth had finally given up and, after extracting a promise not to call the police, had left her to fend for herself.

Ruth's new place was small, a bedsit really, but situated in the large, high-ceilinged proportions of an older building, it was much bigger than the place she had just fled.

There was a bed, a small kitchenette with a sofa and television that separated the two areas. From her window, Ruth could see the trains going over the viaduct from Piccadilly to Oxford Road.

'As long as it takes,' said Ruth. In truth, she had no idea. The meeting with Malton had been as thrilling as it had been terrifying, but now it was time for the comedown. Part of her was still energised at the thought of diving so deep into a story. With Malton's help she was sure that she would be able to blow it wide open. She told herself that all journalists have contacts. That's all Malton was. A contact who she would protect with anonymity in return for his information.

It felt like a lifetime ago she was sat in Helen's office arguing her case.

But alone in the Airbnb, the enormity of the task had begun to overwhelm her. She thought about calling her dad, asking for his help. She could imagine how that would go. He would already be driving at speed back to Manchester to scoop her up and take her home and never let her out again.

So she called the only other person she could think of – Damion.

He'd arrived bearing a takeaway and now they sat on the sterile Airbnb bed, eating Korean barbecue while Ruth built herself up to telling him the whole affair.

'You said this is about a story?' said Damion, licking sticky barbecue sauce off his fingers. 'I'm guessing not a *Mancunian Ways* story?'

Ruth shook her head and smiled. 'Fucking hell no. This is . . . this is a proper story.'

She saw Damion trying to conceal his interest. Talking to him would be a risk but the bigger risk was that, alone, she'd drown under the weight of it all. She needed a sounding board, someone who could help her wade through it all and make everything she was going through worth it.

'And where do I come in?'

Ruth didn't know.

'Because, whatever you decide, this is *your* story.'

Damion flashed a perfect white smile. She'd never noticed how tall he was before. Sat across the bed from her, it was really noticeable. He was larger than life. His features as they smiled at her, his hands as they held his food, his long legs folded under him as he perched on the bed. She hoped she could trust him.

She knew she didn't really have much of a choice.

'I just need to pick someone's brains. Make sure I don't lose sight of what I'm doing.'

'Of course,' said Damion. 'Anything I can do to help you make this work. It sounds intriguing.'

He ferreted the last of the food out of its cardboard carton and dropped his chopsticks into the empty container.

'For you to be on the run like this, it must be big. I knew you were too good for *Mancunian Ways*.'

Ruth flushed with pride at the compliment.

'It is big,' she said. 'It's huge and it's happening right now and if I get it right then . . .' She wanted to say it would make her career; it would define her. To say it out loud felt scarier than whoever it was Malton thought she should move flats to avoid. But that's what was at stake. If she could expose a prolific Manchester serial killer then she could pick whatever job she wanted. She would be a real journalist.

She just needed to make sure she got it right.

'It won't be easy. And it's going to take some time. Not a three stories in a day thing.'

Damion smiled. 'That sounds perfect. Something meaty. So what is it?'

Outside, a train rumbled past on its way to Oxford Road Station and on out west to Liverpool.

Ruth set down her half-eaten takeaway and told Damion everything.

61

The smell of burning flesh filled the room, quickly followed by Sam Kennard's muffled howls as Carl Farr held the blowtorch to his foot with one hand while with the other he held Sam down.

Dean felt his stomach clench as he struggled not to throw up.

He focused on the wall beyond Carl and Sam. A darts scoreboard hung there. The dartboard had been taken down long ago so now all that remained were the barn door chalkboards either side where the players kept a tally.

The score from the final game ever played on that board was still there. The player on the left was down to seventy-six while the player on the right still . . .

Sam Kennard made a sickening retching sound and began to wildly shake. His whole body twisting and squirming so much that Carl could barely hold him.

'He's thrown up – get that rag out of his mouth,' said Janet calmly.

Carl tore away the duct tape gag that had been wrapped around Sam's mouth. Out came a rag as well as a torrent of vomit.

Sam screamed into the fresh air, gasping in pain and shock.

Carl's reaction was simply to take this opportunity to catch his breath. He bent double, his giant hands on his knees as he sucked in air. Dean couldn't help notice how unbalanced his body was. His upper half was an enormous slab of muscle but his legs were spindly and slight. He would have looked comical if he wasn't in the midst of torturing a man to death.

'Looks like you came good after all,' said Janet, turning to Dean. 'DNA proof,' she shouted over to where Sam was whimpering and hacking up. Carl stood over him, the blowtorch on a low flame waiting for his next instruction.

'The blood in the car was Sam's DNA,' said Dean feeling himself spiralling.

The rain pounded on the building. In a couple of places it was coming through the roof and pooling into buckets. Whatever this room used to be, now it was cursed. These past ten minutes, after Martin had drawn Dean out about it being Sam Kennard's DNA in the courier's car, he had watched as Carl Farr first kicked Sam around the dance floor like a bloody football before dragging him to his feet and holding him up while he punched him again and again in the head until Sam went limp, at which point he'd dumped him back on the ground and started with the blowtorch.

Dean knew exactly what Martin Farr was playing at. He'd already told Janet about the DNA. They had already snatched up Sam before he'd even arrived. It was a done deal. This was a demonstration for Dean's benefit of what Janet Farr would do to Martin if Dean pointed the finger at him. Carl would kill him and Dean would never learn the identity of the CI who fingered Malton. He had no choice but to go along with Martin's lies.

Martin Farr had played him perfectly. Malton would never have found himself in this situation.

'And we found the drugs at Sam's place,' said Martin for Dean's benefit.

'So Sam *was* the thief?' asked Janet.

Dean heard the moment of doubt in her voice. It was clear Martin heard it too. They both looked to Dean. Two men's lives were in his hands. Not just Sam Kennard's but Malton's too.

Dean looked Janet in the face. It was now or never.

'He was the thief,' said Dean.

The words were barely out of his mouth before Martin had the gun in his hand. He walked across the room to where a mutilated Sam Kennard lay dying, bent down, put the barrel to his temple and pulled the trigger.

The gunshot echoed off the bare walls, and Sam Kennard's brains, along with a good part of his skull, erupted across the floor in a livid red splash of gore.

***

'It was me,' said Martin Farr proudly.

Inside the building Carl Farr was tidying up. Outside, Martin had walked Dean to his car and now, as they stood under Dean's umbrella in the rain, Martin was fulfilling his side of the deal.

'You?' said Dean, incredulous.

'Yep,' said Martin. 'I'm the CI. I told the police I saw Malton in that car. I was given the time and the date and I told them what they wanted to hear. All bullshit.'

Dean felt his fist bunching. He'd never felt this kind of anger before. Martin Farr hadn't just played him, he'd played Malton too. He was the informant who'd put Malton behind bars. Having been caught stealing from his own family, Martin Farr had thrown Malton under the bus to save his own skin.

Dean breathed in the cold, wet air and did his best to keep control.

'OK,' he said coolly.

'I'm sure I don't need to tell you to keep it to yourself. See those?'

He pointed to the CCTV cameras on the building. Dean felt sick.

'We'll get rid of poor old Sam but if I ever think you've told anyone about me then the film of us arriving with Sam, and then you rocking up, will start doing the rounds. Clever, eh?'

Dean had to admit, Martin had thought of everything.

'Even got the drugs back. We found them under one of his kid's beds. Can you believe that? Some people are fucking sick.'

Dean couldn't tell if Martin was making some kind of black joke or if he genuinely could compartmentalise his morality so completely.

'Who asked you to do it? What's the supplier's name?' said Dean.

That's the part that didn't make sense. There were lots of people who might want to see Malton behind bars, but what about the man selling wholesale product to the Farr family made him want to undertake such an elaborate charade? Surely if he had a grudge against Malton it would be quicker to simply kill him?

Martin pulled a face. 'Thing about that. I might have led you on a little bit.'

Dean stiffened. 'If you don't come through on your deal, whatever else I do I'll make sure your mother-in-law knows what you did. That'll be you lying there with Carl going to work on you.'

'Calm down,' said Martin condescendingly. 'I just mean I don't know the name of the supplier. But I do know the name of his right-hand man. Ex-services guy called Wormall. Hairy bastard. Big black beard. He's the one I talked to so technically he's the one who asked me to do it.'

'It was him that trashed Harold's caravan?'

Martin nodded. 'He's fucking thorough that one. After Janet went off at the supplier this Wormall turns up and goes through everything. Turns out Harold was onto me. Clever old fucker guessed it must have been me put Sam up to it. Even said he had proof. So when that hairy-faced prick's done with poor old Harold, he shows up looking for me. I thought I was fucked.'

Martin stifled a laugh and lowered his voice as if taking Dean into his confidence.

'Turns out I wasn't the only one with a little something on the side. Whoever the supplier is, he's got a bit of a thing for young boys.'

Martin guffawed like a schoolboy and Dean wondered if he could hate him any more than he already did.

'Things are getting a little edgy for him on the bum-boy front and so he's fixing to set someone up. A fall guy to take the heat. And could I give the police a bit of a nudge in the right direction?'

Working with Malton, Dean had met psychopathic killers. He'd dealt with men who'd sold out their own families and gangs who treated human life as utterly disposable. None of them had a patch on Martin Farr.

'You pointed the police at Malton?' said Dean, doing his best to keep his cool.

'I know,' said Martin. 'Small fucking world. Can you blame me though? You've seen what Janet feels like about forgiveness. And that Wormall had me bang to rights.'

'He found the proof Harold was talking about?'

Martin shook his head. 'Wormall said the old boy was just bluffing. He'd guessed it was me. Was trying it on. Still, Wormall offed him anyway. Can't be too careful.'

Martin Farr wasn't just a killer, he was a coward and a grass to boot. The lowest of the low. Yet Dean had underestimated him. He'd thought he was a harmless braggard out of his depth. He was nothing of the sort. He was a grinning sociopath, making whatever decision kept his head above water and fuck everyone else.

Maybe that was why he'd been able to so comprehensively outplay Dean. How could he out-think someone who thought like that? Maybe he did need to get out of this game.

Dean played through what he'd just learned. Martin robs his own family. The Farrs accuse their supplier and their supplier launches his own murderous investigation only to stop short of outing Martin in return for a false witness statement. And in the middle of it all Harold Boateng gets permanently shut up.

With nothing left to say, Dean simply turned and walked to his car.

'So are we square?' shouted Martin after him.

237

Dean looked back to see Martin stood, still in his blood-spattered mechanics' overall, soaked to the bone. He was smiling like he'd just won a fiver on a scratch card.

Dean didn't answer. He got in his car and drove away, his brain going into overdrive as to how exactly he'd make Martin Farr pay for what he'd just done.

62

The Metropolitan was a short ride from Southern Cemetery and filling up with a lunchtime crowd. Home workers and retirees. It was a large pub housed in a grand Victorian building. Downstairs was open plan with high ceilings and high windows. Keisha, Rachel and Allie sat at a table in the corner waiting for their food to arrive.

'But that was dad all over, always mysterious,' said Rachel, taking a sip of her Americano.

After the shock of Keisha's arrival and then the ordeal of the burial, Rachel's whole demeanour had changed. It was like now that the two of them had been through the shared trauma of burying their father, the past forty years were nothing more than a blip. Rachel spoke to Keisha like she'd known her all her life.

Keisha sometimes spoke to people like that. People she wanted to get onside, manipulate and use.

'We always knew he had other children. I asked him all the time. Told him, if I had siblings out there, I deserved to know about them. Course, he never said a thing.'

'Back at the house,' said Keisha, 'you knew my name.'

Rachel smiled. 'Lucky guess. Sort of. Dad wasn't a talker but he was a drinker. Just after Allie was born he turned up one time worse for wear. A happy drunk. Kept looking at Allie in her cot, saying to himself over and over 'My Keisha . . . my Keisha . . .'

Keisha felt lightheaded. It wasn't just a photo in a caravan. He'd never forgotten her.

'I play basketball,' said Allie, obviously bored of the adult conversation.

'We're talking, Allie,' scolded Rachel.

'Basketball? Who with?' asked Keisha, glad to change the subject.

'Stockport Lapwings,' said Allie proudly. Keisha looked at the little girl and imagined her moving up and down the court. Then she saw herself sat courtside. Watching. Part of something.

'That's great,' said Keisha. 'You must be very strong and fit.'

'I am,' said Allie proudly.

'I just can't get over how much she looks like you,' said Rachel. 'One thing Dad was right about. She's like your little mini-me!'

Rachel's over-familiarity was brought up short by Keisha's unreadable expression.

Sure, there was the photo and Rachel's cute story of a drunk Harold seeing Keisha in Allie. But then there were the forty years of nothing. Harold's complete absence from her life.

Now Rachel was talking as if suddenly that was all forgiven and Keisha was going to become part of their lives. She really did have no idea who Keisha was. Rachel sounded posh and soft and nice. Her daughter was eager and charming. Their home in Chorlton tidy and loved. Keisha was none of those things. She was a force of nature. Born in a place where weakness was punished and you knew from the start that not everyone would make it out in one piece.

Keisha's world would suck Rachel and Allie in and spit out their bones.

'So where *have* you been?' asked Rachel, keen to change the topic.

Keisha looked from Rachel to Allie. This wasn't her world. And it never could be. It was time to end this charade.

'My son died the day he was born,' she started. 'Then I decided the only way to never ever feel that kind of pain again was to be the one inflicting it. I've spent my whole adult life hanging around criminals. Gangsters, drug dealers, men who simply can't control their temper. I play with them. Use them. Like trained animals. My last husband was tortured to death over a gun sale gone wrong. The man who went on a shooting spree last year? He was a junkie I rehabilitated just to have him kill as many people as possible. And for the last year I've been living in Ibiza, spending my dead husband's millions and enjoying myself.'

She watched as the light went from Rachel's face. Keisha held herself tight against the urge to take back her words. Tell Rachel she had been joking and tell her some comforting lie. She finally understood Craig. His determination to stand alone. His refusal to take her back. She and Craig were both the same. Neither of them could trust anyone but themselves. They could linger and they could pretend, but deep down there was the fear that she felt now. The fear that something soft and good would be taken away. Just like when they were kids.

They were the ones who got away, but they took the damage with them. Craig wore his scars on the surface; now Keisha realised she had just as much pain. She had simply made sure it was harder to see.

But in the moments since Rachel had thrown her arms around her on the doorstep, Keisha had been in free fall.

Now she saw what she had to do. What she always did. Burn it down.

'I don't know what to say,' said Rachel, stunned.

'You got a dad; I had to look after myself.'

'I'm so sorry.'

'Don't be. It was his fault, not yours.'

Keisha stood up. She was done.

'Someone killed Harold. He worked for a family of drug dealers and he was killed for it. The people who killed him ransacked his caravan. He has a second caravan next door. You might not know about that.'

Keisha couldn't bring herself to look at Allie. She dropped the keys to Harold's caravan on the table. She was never going back.

'Please,' said Rachel. 'I don't care what you've done. You're my sister. I've already lost my dad. I can't lose you too.'

'I'm not your sister,' said Keisha. 'I'm the person you were lucky enough not to turn into.'

She turned to go.

'Where are you going?' asked Allie after her.

Keisha turned back to answer but realised she was about to say, *I'm going to kill the men who murdered my dad,* and so she said nothing.

Instead she walked out into the rain, took a deep breath and left the past buried in the damp soil of Southern Cemetery.

63

Night-time couldn't have come soon enough. After meeting Ruth, Malton didn't want to risk getting spotted driving out of the city centre. So he'd been laying low in a multi-storey car park. Waiting for the cover of darkness to slip out of the city that he once walked about as if he owned it – lock, stock and barrel.

That wasn't the only risk he was taking. He'd set up a meet with an old police contact. A Detective Benton.

Malton was a wanted man. An escaped killer. But he was banking on his decades-long relationship with Benton to count for more than the facts on the ground. Facts that, if he had anything to do with it, would very soon be changing in his favour.

Benton had crossed the line for Malton enough times in the past that he felt that what he was about to do was an acceptable risk. But it was still a risk.

In the hours since he'd met Ruth Porter, he'd been slowly putting it all together in his head. Stephen's parents' doubt as to his guilt was what had convinced them to talk to him in the first place. Hearing them talk about how the police had simply cut them off after arresting Malton made sense when he thought about Priestly's visit to Strangeways a few days earlier.

GMP had put all their eggs in one basket but as the case proceeded through to trial it must have become more and more clear that they had a whole lot of nothing. Now they were getting desperate.

Malton vaulted the iron railings that surrounded Platt Fields park and rushed into the darkness. Platt Fields sat just outside the city centre between Moss Side and Fallowfield. It had once been the grounds of a grand hall; it was now a large, well-used park with a boating lake and skate park. Families from Moss Side and students from nearby Fallowfield both used the park, and in the daytime it was reliably busy.

At this time of night it was locked and deserted. Or at least Malton hoped so. He'd arranged to meet Benton in the park on the bridge between the playing fields and the boating lake. A small walkway that crossed over a trickle of a stream but which was shielded from view on all sides by trees. If he had to make a quick getaway, the bridge was only five or six feet high. He could easily vault over the side and disappear into the trees.

Or at least he hoped he would be able to do that. His wounds were still there. Still nagging at him. A reminder that he was running on empty. He no longer had Malton Security at his back. He'd frozen Dean out for all these months. Now that things were on a knife edge he couldn't risk finally reaching out for help. If the boy was caught assisting him then that was a criminal record and probably a prison sentence.

Malton was alone.

That suited Malton. It meant that if things did go badly then he knew he could go all out. There was nothing left to lose. He'd left Keisha sleeping as he headed out early that morning. Whatever her reasons for springing him from Manchester Royal Infirmary, he couldn't risk her turning on him. His only chance was to find the real killer of Stephen Page and find them fast.

Failing that, it looked like he'd finally have to say goodbye to the city that had made him. Flee Manchester and possibly the country.

In a strange way the thought gave him a thrill. Starting again. Doing it all over. Malton had always been ready to walk at a moment's notice. Despite relationships and his business, he'd never felt that anything had ever got under his skin enough to not be cast aside if it was a matter of survival.

Platt Fields was one large inky black void. The perimeter of the park was surrounded by roads and back alleys and houses and cut-throughs. Plenty of places to run to. But first he had to meet Benton.

He lurked in the shadows, watching the path that led to the bridge.

The other reason that GMP could be so eager to pin Stephen Page's murder on the wrong man was that Ruth Porter was correct. There was an individual out there killing young men. If that was true and GMP knew about it then there would be uproar. It was only a couple of years since one of the most prolific rapists in criminal history had been arrested in Manchester. A monster who'd preyed on young men without hindrance for years. That case was one of the many reasons why Greater Manchester Police had gone into special measures and found itself with a new, no-nonsense chief constable who, as far as Malton could make out, was slowly turning the ship around.

Not fast enough for Malton. The photo he'd seen on Ruth's phone was a man he recognised. But that didn't mean he had killed Jake, the boy whose phone it was on. Nor did it mean he had killed Stephen. To make that connection Malton would need Benton's help.

The sound of raised voices coming from the other side of the bridge ought to have been reason enough to turn and run.

A man shouting and a woman's voice. Shouting back. Louder. Benton.

Malton was halfway across the bridge when he saw, under a sodium light, a sturdily built middle-aged woman in a purple anorak wrestling a skinny man in grey tracksuit bottoms and a dark top to the ground.

By the time he was on them DI Benton had already thrown handcuffs on him and was kneeling on his back.

'I would ask if you need a hand,' said Malton dryly. He had only run a short way but his body had felt it. He wondered how far he'd get if he had to flee for real.

'Fuck me,' said Benton. 'It's come to something when a DI can't take a stroll in a deserted park in the middle of the night without some bin lid trying it on.'

'I didn't know you were filth,' said the skinny man from the ground.

'Don't think flattery will help,' said Benton, pressing the man's face down into the wet tarmac of the path with her boot.

'We need to talk,' said Malton.

Benton finally turned to look at Malton. Her hair was a little longer than when he last saw her and her face a little more drawn but she was still the same Benton. Her expression always caught between sarcastic disbelief and professional severity. It was the face of a proper cop.

'Give me a minute,' she said, and hauled the skinny man to his feet, taking care to keep his head pointing away from Malton, who in turn sloped back into the shadows.

★★★

With Benton's assailant handcuffed to a railing and waiting for her return, Benton joined Malton in the darkness at the edge of the playing fields.

'You know how risky it is me being here?' said Benton.

'I think you know I didn't kill Stephen Page.'

'Course I know that. Bumping off rent boys doesn't seem your style. You're a lover not a fighter,' said Benton with a smile. 'I also know after you went inside you cut off all contact. If you'd spoken to Dean then maybe I could have done something. But as it was, you went silent so I figured I'd leave you to it.'

'I had some things to deal with,' said Malton.

'I heard about Mickey Farr. They say you very nearly castrated him.'

'He gave as good as he got,' said Malton truthfully.

'So now you've decided the best thing to do is go on the run? I have to say, Craig, it's not a great look.'

'I need your help,' said Malton.

'We all need help,' said Benton leadingly.

Malton's bolthole out in Salford had a safe under the carpet in the corner of one bedroom. Before he'd left that morning Malton had opened it and taken out several thousand pounds in cash. Now his hand went into his coat and brought out a thick roll of notes.

Benton smiled. 'I wondered if you thought maybe I'd do you a favour for old times' sake.'

Malton knew that she would do just that if push came to shove. But somehow keeping things as they always were, the quid pro quo of it all, made both of them feel a little better about the chance they were taking.

Benton kept talking as Malton peeled off notes. 'I guess you don't need me to tell you to keep your head down. And on a side note, say hello to Keisha for me. She's got her hair up and glasses on in those CCTV shots but I don't know any other woman who'd march into a hospital and pluck you out at gunpoint. You two really need to just get a room.'

Malton handed Benton a couple of thousand pounds.

'You have no idea how expensive a teenage girl can be,' said Benton, pocketing the money. 'Plus you'll never guess what, my fucking ex-husband's only getting maintenance. Turns out 'cos I was earning more than him before the divorce, now he's *my* dependant. Absolutely unbelievable.'

'I only need one thing from you,' said Malton.

'Well that's good of you,' said Benton.

Malton dug in his pocket and brought out the receipt he'd found in the handbag Stephen Page's parents had showed him.

He handed the slip of paper to Benton.

'I need you to trace the card details and get me a name.'

'Is that it?' said Benton in surprise.

'That's it. That's all I need.'

Benton grinned. 'You've been on the run just over a day and you've already solved the case. Just as well you're on the other side. No place for that kind of efficiency in the Greater

Manchester Police.' For a moment she was serious. 'So this receipt? This is Stephen Page's killer?'

'We'll see,' said Malton, and left it at that.

'You know the other year I was looking at a dead kid. He was a rent boy. Body dumped up near Belle Vue?'

Malton remembered it well. At the time it had meant nothing to him but since he'd begun to dig into Stephen's real killer it had been playing on his mind. He thought it best to see if Benton brought it up unprompted. He hid his satisfaction that she had.

'I thought there was something off. He'd been strangled. Had meth in his system. But someone had dumped him there and I don't mean like out of a car after a struggle. I mean he was killed somewhere else entirely. There was no trace anywhere on the scene. Just the body. Never did get an answer on that one.'

'If I'm right about this,' said Malton, 'then you might get your answer. But first I need to clear my name.'

'Priestly seemed like such a promising young lad too,' said Benton. 'Then he goes and backs the wrong horse. Oh well, can't win them all.'

'I need those details quickly,' said Malton.

'You'll have them by tomorrow,' said Benton.

'And stay clear until I let you know,' said Malton.

'You paid me for a favour,' said Benton, suddenly stern. 'I'm a copper who takes money from fugitive murderers but I'm still a copper. If I need to act to stop people getting hurt then I'm going to act.' She paused and added, 'So whatever you're about to do, do it quickly.'

With that, Benton turned and headed back to where she'd locked up her attacker.

Alone in the dark, Malton doubled back on himself and left Platt Fields on the other side to the one he entered before circling back around the park to his car and heading to the safehouse in Eccles.

By tomorrow, either he'd have confirmed the name of the killer or he'd be leaving Manchester for good.

64

Vikki wasn't answering Skype so now Dean was ringing her number. Driving back from Kersal in the rain, everything having suddenly and violently unravelled, all he could think about was Vikki.

Martin Farr had murdered Sam Kennard in front of him. Knowing full well that Dean would keep quiet and let him. He'd made Dean an accomplice to his act of cowardice. Behind all the mind games and the manoeuvring, this was the reality of what Dean was involved in. Maybe Malton had somewhere cold and dank in the depths of his psyche where he could toss memories like the sound of Sam Kennard's screams. Dean did not. The screams rang out in his head. Loud enough to shake him into action.

If Vikki was in some kind of trouble with her father then it didn't matter whether she wanted his help or not. It didn't even matter if she'd found someone else and was never going to come back from London. After seeing what happened to Sam Kennard, Dean couldn't simply pretend everything was OK.

The Farrs' missing drugs, Keisha's hunt for her father's killer, Malton's imprisonment. None of that meant anything if Vikki was in danger.

Dean was stuck in crawling traffic on the inner ring road when finally a man's voice came through the Bluetooth and onto the car's speakers.

'You need to stop calling,' it said curtly.

Dean felt his pulse quicken.

'Who is this? Where's Vikki?'

'She's safe. Safer than she'd be with you.'

Dean's mind raced. He spent his days hearing the colourful cacophony of Mancunian accents. Janet Farr's scooped-out staccato vowels; Keisha's strong, black Moss Side lilt; even Priestly's lower-middle-class south Manchester lisp. But this voice, this was nothing like any of them.

'I asked who is this? I don't think you realise how serious the situation is.'

Confidently, the voice ignored his question. 'Vikki's told me all about her father and about what you do and she agrees with me that the best thing is to not get involved.'

And then he hung up.

By the time Dean had redialled, his number had been blocked.

The traffic inched on through the rain while Dean sat in his car, incredulous. What now? Should he drive down to London? Call the police? Call Leon Walker's prison?

Then he remembered the young man in Vikki's house. Rolling a cigarette with his painted black nails. Glancing out from under his floppy hair. Suddenly it all made sense. Whoever was on the other end of the line wasn't a criminal. It wasn't an associate of Leon Walker, or worse, someone with a grudge against the brutal giant. It was the boy from the Skype call the night before. He'd been the one just out of frame all those times.

Dean's relief was over before it started. Vikki *had* found someone else. Some posh-sounding boy with floppy hair who slotted perfectly into her new world. Not someone like Dean in his awkward suit with his inconvenient loyalty to Malton. Someone who could take her far away from the world that Dean had chosen to inhabit. Someone who could be by her side. Listening, talking, bringing a little normality to her life.

But whoever he was and however much he thought he was in control of the situation, the moment Leon Walker came into the picture, then all bets were off.

Dean realised he had finally taken the baton from Malton. The job had not just pushed away the people he loved; it had put them in dreadful danger into the bargain.

The revelation made him feel sick.

The traffic continued on, dragging itself through sheets of rain, headlights and traffic lights indistinct in the midday gloom. Manchester had a hold on Dean and whether he liked it or not he wasn't going anywhere.

With Vikki hundreds of miles away and out of reach, Dean turned his thoughts to exactly what he was going to do to Martin Farr.

65

An invisible force field radiated out from Keisha as she sat in the canteen at Malton Security. As one by one, doormen came in from the night shift to debrief, log their walkie-talkies and take advantage of the free breakfast, they clocked her sat in the corner of the room, staring through the dark lenses of her glasses, and they gave her a wide berth.

Craig wasn't at the safe house. She'd gone back there after leaving Rachel and Allie only to find it empty and Craig nowhere to be seen. It didn't matter anymore. Whatever she thought she would achieve springing him from MRI, it was clear Craig was far too caught up in his own mess to play along. It was time to get back on track. Sam Kennard had robbed her father but most likely one or all of the Farrs were in on it too. Either way the result was the same. Harold was dead and that meant that before she could leave Manchester for good she was going to have to kill them all. But to do that she'd need help.

She'd left her rain-soaked, mud-caked clothes at the safe-house, showered and once again raided Malton's wardrobe, this time selecting a grey tracksuit top to serve as an oversized dress.

Sat in the canteen at Malton Security she looked relaxed, wrapped in her parka and sporting her sunglasses. She wore her hair out in curls, if only because in the CCTV images of her that she'd seen from MRI her hair was still up.

The gun was secure in the inside pocket of her coat. Every bullet still present and correct.

Keisha knew that every second she spent in Manchester was a risk. She also knew how poor most people were at cross-racial identification. To a white person one black person looks very much like the next and vice versa. When that black person is in a grainy CCTV photo with different hair and clothes and wearing glasses, then that felt like enough leeway for Keisha to take the chance.

She didn't have a choice. Dean was her key to finding her father's killers. He already had the DNA from the car and had found Sam Kennard. But he'd withheld information once already when he'd delayed telling her about the DNA. Now she would lean on him however she could, to find out everything he knew about the Farrs. Names, dates, places. What she would need to put down her father's killers and then get out of the country.

Thinking about revenge meant she didn't have to think about Rachel and Allie. The look of surprise and sadness on Allie's face as she walked away. How Rachel had heard everything she'd said and still wanted her to stay. Grief did funny things to people. It had made them blind to who Keisha really was.

She could already feel the light touch of the Ibiza sun on her skin. In a few days' time she'd be back at her villa, drinking gin, planning her next conquest. Living in the moment, looking to a future free from the clutter of the past.

All that stood between now and then were a few well-placed bullets.

When Dean walked into the canteen, from the look on his face Keisha knew he'd been forewarned he had a visitor.

As she followed him to Craig's office she wondered where Craig was now. Was his quest to clear his name of murder any less unhinged than her quest to murder her father's killers? Each of them still out there, fighting alone against a world that seemed determined to chew them up and spit them out.

'Martin Farr had your father killed,' said Dean before he'd even sat down.

Keisha had expected to need some back and forth but Dean was in no mood to play games. He seemed drawn, almost haunted.

253

'He was behind the robbery. He put Sam Kennard up to it. Paid him three hundred quid. The rest of the Farrs had no idea. The man who supplied the Farrs found out about it and reached out to Martin. Gave him an ultimatum. Either Martin fingered Malton for the murder of Stephen Page or he'd tell Janet Farr it was him who ripped them off.'

'Wait, what?' said Keisha. This was an avalanche of information. The last time she'd seen Dean he'd tracked down Sam Kennard and now this? Craig was right to hire this kid. He wasn't much to look at but since the last time she'd seen him he'd got that same distant look in his eyes that Craig had when he was in the thick of it.

'Martin Farr was the CI who put Malton away.'

'But why Craig?' asked Keisha.

'I don't know. I think that's the key to all of this,' said Dean. 'I had a visit from a journalist a few days ago asking about Malton. She seemed to think someone was killing male prostitutes.'

Keisha was already there. 'You think the same person who's selling drugs to the Farrs is murdering rent boys?'

Dean shrugged. 'I know. It sounds crazy. But what if that's why he wanted someone to go down for Stephen Page's murder? Break the connection to him? Suddenly all the other killings look just like unconnected random events again. That'd explain needing to frame someone for Stephen Page's murder.'

'Just not why you'd pick Malton,' said Keisha, finishing his sentence for him.

The last time they were in this room together she'd shot him in the face. She could still see the small, round scar on his cheek. Now the energy was very different. Now Dean felt almost like Craig.

'So Martin Farr killed my dad?' she asked.

'I wasn't the only one looking into the missing drugs. The Farrs' supplier was running his own investigation. I think he thought maybe the Farrs were trying it on. Either way his hired muscle found out that your dad was on to Martin.'

254

'And if the whole point of Martin fingering Malton is to avoid trouble with the Farrs then you've got to take care of Harold?'

'Exactly,' said Dean, smiling for a moment only to see Keisha's stern face looking back at him.

Dean looked down, suddenly sombre.

The cacophony of feelings and thoughts in Keisha's mind suddenly faded to a calm clarity. The simplicity of seeing the whole picture overwhelmed her with a feeling of intense relief. Finally she was getting names.

'Martin Farr started the ball rolling; the supplier found out my dad was involved. That just leaves who did it,' said Keisha.

'Far as I can make out, someone called Wormall. I think he's the supplier's bodyguard or something. Ex-military guy. Farr said he had a beard and didn't fuck around. If this supplier's been killing rent boys and has the kind of money that someone moving that quantity would have, then my guess is that this Wormall has been running interference on the killings. Dumping bodies in different places, messing with the evidence.'

'Planting evidence,' said Keisha. 'Someone put Malton's DNA in that car.'

Dean shrugged. 'Right now I'm prepared to believe anything.'

'Still doesn't explain why pick Craig.'

Dean shook his head. 'You've got Martin Farr in your pocket, you've got an ex-military guy who can apparently get to anyone, all you need is a fall guy.'

'So why pick the most dangerous man in Manchester?' said Keisha, unable to keep just a hint of a smile from her face.

She could feel something passing between her and Dean. Two minds on the same path now. Both navigating through the dark with a murderous instinct.

'Maybe,' said Dean, 'someone else picked Malton for him.'

Keisha sat back and gave voice to her thoughts: 'Who would you go to if you were a major drug importer with a trail of dead bodies and the money to make it go away? Who would take on that kind of client? More to the point, whose solution to the whole mess would be to frame Craig Malton?'

Keisha knew Dean was thinking exactly the same thing as her. Someone with brains and connections. Someone five foot tall and blonde.

Bea Wallace's name hung in the air unspoken. For a moment, neither Keisha nor Dean dared say it out loud. Knowing that if they did then suddenly everything would become infinitely more complicated. It was Keisha who broke the silence.

'How do we get to Wormall?' she asked.

Dean leaned forward and said, 'We? I don't work for you. I work for Malton. Whatever you're planning, that's on you. Not me.'

Keisha was surprised by his boldness. This would take a little more of a push.

'How do I know I can trust this information?' she asked.

'It came from Martin Farr's own mouth,' said Dean proudly.

Keisha had hoped he'd say that.

'And what did you do to get him to say it?' she asked. As much as Dean could follow in Craig's footsteps, he wasn't an eighteen-stone ex-bouncer. However he went about getting information, it wouldn't involve the same level of 'leverage' that Craig could bring to bear. Whatever Dean had done to get this information he must have given Martin Farr something very, very precious.

Dean looked away and Keisha knew she was on the money.

'I watched Carl Farr torture Sam Kennard while Martin stood by smirking. Then I watched Martin blow Sam's brains out. Right in front of me.'

Now the distant look made sense.

'You told them it was Sam, didn't you?'

'It was the only way he'd give me the information,' said Dean sadly. He stared off, looking agitated.

'And you've been awake all night trying to forget the look on that man's face when he saw that he was about to die?'

Dean turned to Keisha and she knew she was right.

'You won't ever forget that look. So what you do is this – you put it alongside the look on Martin Farr's face when he realises the exact same thing is about to happen to him,' said Keisha, and she reached into her coat and laid the gun out on the table.

She saw Dean flinch for a moment at the memory of the last time he saw her with a gun in her hand.

'We're going to lift Martin Farr off the street at gunpoint. We're going to zip-tie his hands and feet, stuff him in the back of my black Transit van, and then we're going to drive him somewhere quiet and I'll get everything I need to out of him to find this Wormall and his boss. Unless you've got a better plan?'

Keisha looked across the table at Dean. All he said was: 'Let's do it.'

66

The opening riff to 'Mother' by post-punk band Idles echoed tinnily around Ruth's Airbnb, dragging her out of her sleep. The song had been her ringtone ever since catching the band at one of their early gigs a few years back.

Last night had gone late. Finally saying out loud all the thoughts and theories that had been going round her head these past few months, Ruth had felt the story taking flight. As Damion questioned and probed, she forced herself to interrogate her thinking, discarding dead ends and making new deductive leaps as the pieces came together.

It was as if she hadn't dared think about what she was sitting on, but explaining it step by step to Damion and seeing his reaction, she was filled with the absolute certainty that she was onto something big.

She'd told Damion everything. From the bodies to the phone she found and the man searching for it. She'd told him about Eddie and his ransacked apartment and about Dean's threats and Malton's unexpected visit. That had Damion sitting up and paying attention. Like everyone else in Manchester he'd heard about the brazen kidnapping of a prisoner on hospital release. He couldn't believe that same prisoner was the subject of Ruth's investigation and had tracked her down, no less.

By the time Damion had left, it was getting light.

Ruth found her phone, the battery nearly dead, and she lifted it up to see who was calling. A number she didn't recognise. As a journalist, that wasn't all that unusual. For every number she stored in her phone there were four more she simply forgot to put in.

'Hello?' she said, hoping that whoever was on the other line would introduce themselves and spare her blushes.

'What have you done?' cried the voice on the other in such panic that Ruth forgot all about her coyness and asked:

'Who is this?'

'Eddie,' said the voice. 'You gave me your number. I trusted you and you do this?'

Ruth was awake now. Warning sirens going off in her head. She sat up in bed.

'What's going on?' she said. 'What's happened?'

'What do you mean? When I spoke to you, you said you wanted to get to the truth. You said you'd go to the police once you had something concrete. Before you published anything.'

'And I will,' said Ruth, desperately trying to catch up.

'So why am I looking at this shit?' spat Eddie.

Ruth already had her laptop open and booting up. *Mancunian Ways* website was still her homepage. The first article she saw – THIS MAN SAYS THERE'S A SERIAL KILLER IN MANCHESTER. COULD HE BE RIGHT?

There, under it, was a photo collage. One shot of the crime scene at Piccadilly Basin and the other a picture of Eddie that looked like it had come from his Facebook page.

Ruth's eyes began to spill down the page and she felt sick. Everything she had discussed last night, all her leads and theories. They were all there, whipped up into the frothy, clickbait prose of *Mancunian Ways*. The meeting with Malton and the meeting with Dean, all of it there on the page. Written as if it had happened to Damion.

'This wasn't me,' Ruth pleaded. 'I didn't do this.'

'Fuck you,' spat Eddie and hung up.

Ruth had quit her job, she'd fled her home and now it was all for nothing?

If Damion thought he could do this and get away with it then he didn't know Ruth Porter.

67

This was madness. But to Dean it all made sense. This is what Malton would have done. He would have taken up Keisha on her offer. Aligned someone else's bloody vendetta with his own and kept his hands clean of any of it.

Keisha's black Transit van tore round the M60, heading towards Stockport and the Farrs' tyre garage. Dean was at the wheel, Keisha sat beside him, the gun she had shown him safe in her coat pocket.

Despite his size and appearance, Dean had rarely seen Malton raise a hand in anger. Instead he'd watched as Malton moved the players like chess pieces, turning one side against the other in furtherance of whatever unknown, long game he was playing.

That, Dean told himself, was why he was driving Keisha to find Martin Farr with the plan for her to kidnap him at gunpoint.

He didn't know what he'd do if Martin didn't play along. He had no idea whether Keisha would simply rely on her gun or had some other plan to get Martin into the van. Dean would be sat behind the wheel, waiting. Just removed enough to feel like he wasn't descending into the bloody fray.

Malton had stayed alive by never sinking to the depths. He somehow managed to lower himself into the filth without ever getting dirty. But Dean wasn't Malton. Seeing Sam Kennard getting shot had changed him. Something inside felt like it had been set adrift. He felt it even now. Rattling around inside him, slowly wearing him away.

In the moment, Keisha's offer of bloody revenge had seemed like a lifeline. Now, as they drove to the Farrs' garage it felt like it could be a death sentence.

'There's still Craig's DNA,' said Keisha as Dean turned off the M60 just past the giant brick viaduct that loomed over Stockport.

Dean had been thinking the same thing. It wasn't just Martin Farr's false testimony that had put Malton away. There was DNA evidence.

Malton wasn't a man who did anything without extreme care. The idea of him letting someone take DNA from him didn't add up.

'Before he was arrested Malton had kind of . . .' Dean trailed off. Kind of what? Lost his mind trying to find James's killers? It felt deeply disloyal to talk about Malton like that but, in truth, that was what had happened. The invincible, immovable, omnipresent Craig Malton had rushed headlong on a wild chase that had ended with him getting arrested and charged with murder.

'Kind of what?' said Keisha from behind her dark glasses.

'He had gone to Liverpool following a lead about James. I think it was all he could think about.'

'Where did he get the lead?' said Keisha.

That was another thing Dean had never quite got to the bottom of.

'I don't know,' he said.

Keisha said nothing.

They were at the start of the industrial estate where Farrs' Tyres was located. A brewery, a retail depot, several small showrooms for bathrooms and fireplaces and the like. Traffic was quiet. Dean slowed down.

'What's your plan?' he asked.

Keisha turned to him and smiled. 'I can be very persuasive if I want to be,' she said.

Dean pulled to a stop a few hundred metres up the road from Farrs' Tyres. He could see the battered Jag parked across the road from the garage. He was surprised at how calm he felt about all of this.

He wondered if he was still in shock. He had been attacked and even shot working for Malton. But he'd never seen someone murdered up close. So close in fact that he could remember the smell that filled the air. Now whenever he closed his eyes all he could do was see that moment again and again. The bang of the gun, the vivid red of the viscera emerging, the casual nonchalance of Sam's killer.

Suddenly he began to feel very scared.

'Something's wrong,' said Dean.

'I'm going to make it right,' said Keisha firmly.

Martin Farr appeared outside Farrs' Tyres. The garage was a typical tyre garage. A large, square building, the front open to the street and a workshop within. Jacks to raise up cars and rows of tyres lining the walls.

It looked like Martin was mid-conversation with someone inside the garage. He was laughing and joking with Sam Kennard's workmates. He didn't look like a man who the day before had murdered Sam in cold blood to save his own skin.

Dean saw Keisha clock Martin.

'Don't go anywhere,' she hissed to him and opened the van door.

Martin finished his conversation and stepped into the road to get to his car. As he did so a deafening roar filled the industrial estate and a scruffy white Audi came howling out from behind the buildings opposite, turning at speed into the road. Before Martin Farr could respond, the Audi clipped him, knocking him several feet down the road, bouncing his body off the tarmac.

Keisha froze.

The dirty, white Audi caught up to where Martin had landed. People were coming out of the garage, drawn by the sound.

The driver of the Audi seemed not to care. Pulling up just past Martin, he got out and strode over to Martin's prone body, opening the boot of the car as he passed. He was a compact man with a black beard. Martin tried to raise himself up, but as he turned to face the driver, the driver smashed him across the head with what looked like a wrench, before grabbing him and with seemingly no effort at all, hauling him back to the car and flinging his limp body into the boot.

The driver didn't even look back as more people began to emerge from the garage. He simply got in his car and drove.

'Follow that car!' screamed Keisha as the white Audi hurtled past them.

Dean was pointing the wrong way but he fired up the van and pulled a long, looping U-turn, bumping up on the pavement and back onto the road as he turned the bulky Transit van before slamming his foot down.

The van's two-litre engine flooded with power as they quickly began to catch up on the Audi.

'I'm guessing that's Wormall,' said Keisha.

As much as Dean had thrilled at seeing Martin run over, he knew that Martin was his only link to get to the supplier. A link that right now was stuffed in the boot of a car racing away from them.

Up ahead the Audi emerged from the industrial estate, pulled right at a T-junction and headed for the motorway.

They were approaching the edge of the M60 as it came out of Stockport. On all sides were fields and motorway embankments. No people, no traffic, just a clear run for Martin's kidnapper.

Dean did his best to keep up, feeling the weight of the van as he tried to make the same turns at a speed that matched the car ahead of them.

He could see Keisha clutching the door for support but saying nothing. Her eyes were firmly on the white Audi as it curled around the roundabout that led off onto the motorway.

The roundabout circled a large, grassy hill, making it impossible to see more than the road ahead. If the Audi pulled away there was a chance Dean would lose sight of it on the wrong side of the hill and risk the car disappearing down an exit before he had a chance to see it.

Dean put his foot down, eager to close the gap and stay on the white car.

The car pulled into the left-hand lane. It was taking the next exit. Dean stayed closed on it and prepared to come off and onto the motorway.

He gripped the wheel as the centrifugal force of the van threatened to pull him too far to the left and off the road entirely.

'Wait!' Keisha's warning came too late.

As the exit appeared the Audi suddenly put on a burst of speed, pulled across into the right-hand lane and vanished round the other side of the roundabout and out of sight.

Before he could react Dean was already on the exit ramp. The speed and weight of the van making it impossible to come out of the turn.

Unable to stop they carried on down onto the motorway. The white Audi with a half-dead Martin Farr was already long gone.

There was a silence in the van as Dean pulled into the middle lane and slowed down to match the speed of the other traffic.

'Plan B,' said Keisha tightly.

'Plan B?' said Dean.

'We go and have a word with the little blonde lawyer about DNA.'

68

Malton could barely hear himself think as loud dance music shook the entire building. Even in this back room the beat was inescapable. The heavy DOOF DOOF DOOF DOOF of the bass dragging his thoughts into four-four time. Next door thousands of bodies filled the old mill, jumping, writhing and dancing to the sound. Sweat dripping off the walls as low, red lighting lit up the pitch-black. It was 2002 and this was Martyrdom, the place to be seen in Manchester.

But here in this back room a boy was dying. Outside in the darkness of the club he could have been any age, but in the back office, under the unforgiving strip lights, he was no more than sixteen. If that.

He lay on the filthy carpet tiles, his trousers and pants around his ankles, his flesh a limp greyish blue. Livid marks already blossomed around his neck as Malton went from chest compressions to blowing into his lungs and back again. Just like he and everyone who worked for him had been taught to do on the first-aid course they had to complete to become licenced as security staff.

Luke Gannon perched in one corner, smoking, looking bored. A diet of cigarettes, vodka and stress kept him thin. His hair was bright blonde and cut short. Martyrdom was Luke's club. He was the promoter who'd turned a derelict mill into a thriving nightclub. He'd brought over internationally renowned DJs and made stars of local talent. Inside the walls of Martyrdom, Luke Gannon was a god.

If God told you to bring the boy he'd just strangled back to life then you did what God asked. Malton Security had only been going a few years and so getting the contract for Martyrdom was massive. It meant they went from pubs and bars to doing security for one of the biggest clubs in Manchester. A club with a nation-wide presence. If Malton could handle Martyrdom, then there was nowhere that his firm couldn't take on.

'Come on, this is getting boring,' said Luke over Malton's head. 'I've got a night to run.'

Malton held his tongue. He knew enough about Luke Gannon to not want to risk getting on his bad side. Luke was a whip-smart kid from Sheffield who'd come over to Manchester for uni and never left. He had great taste in music and, when he wanted to be, was magnetically charismatic. But what made Luke Gannon so successful was his utter ruthlessness. He was the kind of promoter who would hire criminals to fly-post for him and make sure they beat up rival fly-posters while they were at it. He'd give gangs a couple of hundred quid to attend rival nights and cause havoc. Luke seemed to enjoy destroying the opposition almost as much as he enjoyed running his own club.

'He can't die here. If you can't do anything, then I want him taken elsewhere. I can't lose my licence over this bullshit,' said Luke, gesturing to the boy with one hand.

The door opened and for a moment the sound got even louder and the thick, dank smell of thousands of sweating bodies filled the office as a stunningly attractive girl stumbled in laughing. One look at Malton doing CPR on the boy on the floor and she stopped.

'Fuck's sake, Luke. Not again.'

'Don't know what happened,' said Luke with a grin.

The girl smiled back. 'You fucking deviant,' she said, and kissed him.

Malton kept his eye on the boy. He told himself this was his job. He had to make this problem go away. Either by saving this kid's life or covering up that Luke Gannon had a love of violent sex with boys who couldn't fight back. Something his fiancée – whom he was currently in the corner kissing – seemed more than OK with.

The boy's body jerked beneath Malton's hands and, twisting to one side, the kid heaved in a huge lungful of air and began to cough wildly.

266

'I knew you could do it!' said Luke, and applauded sarcastically. 'Finish up here,' he said, and led his fiancée back into the club, leaving Malton alone with the boy.

Malton handed the kid a bottle of water and watched as he slowly came back to life.

Malton had visited enough saunas, been to enough sex parties to know just how rough things could get. Sometimes that was all that could clear his head of the nagging thoughts that plagued him. Feeling another man's body beneath him, Malton's hands around his neck, grabbing at his hair, bending him to his will.

But that was very different to Luke Gannon. Luke Gannon did; he was never done to. He wasn't part of the scene. Luke Gannon was the straight, white promoter putting Manchester on the map.

As Malton helped the boy into a taxi, he thought how money and success could buy you a seat at the table but nothing washed your sins clean like being white. But that wasn't going to stand in Malton's way.

Watching the taxi head off into the night, a couple of hundred pounds stuffed in the young boy's jeans, Malton promised himself that one day he'd be bigger than all the Luke Gannons in Manchester. All the ones who had it easy, who had people look the other way and make excuses. Malton would smile and take their money and clean up their mess, and in return he would soak up their secrets, learn every weakness until there was no one in Manchester who could touch him.

***

'It's a company credit card for INK Leisure,' said Benton's voice over the phone.

'Luke Gannon's company,' said Malton mechanically.

'Do I need to know what Luke Gannon's got to do with this?' said Benton.

Malton was parked up on a back street in Bury. He'd slept in his car, waking up late to find his body screaming in pain. His injuries weren't healing. The dressings soaked in blood and pus. But until he'd got this phone call from Benton all he could do was wait. Now he had the confirmation it was time to move.

Luke Gannon had long ago stopped promoting. He'd retired young, got out with millions of pounds in the bank and retreated to a manor house out in Knutsford. The last club job Malton worked for Gannon, he was being leaned on by some heavy characters from Salford. Malton had brokered a sit-down, Gannon had paid them more money than they could dream of and then decided to get out while the going was good.

Since his retirement, Malton Security guarded Luke's house, and when his wife had nights out in town, Malton provided an escort to follow a discreet distance away. Luke's final brush with Salford had obviously spooked him.

'Well?' said Benton. 'Is Luke Gannon killing rent boys?'

Malton thought back to that night at Martyrdom. The utter disdain Gannon had shown for the boy who nearly died. Back then he was just starting out. Retired and with all the money in the world, what would stop him endlessly indulging his hobby?

Malton had seen up close just what Gannon was capable of. It made perfect sense that if he was looking for a fall guy to drag focus from his crimes he'd pick Malton. Killing two birds with one stone. Shattering the idea of a serial killer and putting away one of the only people still breathing air who knew what Gannon was really like.

But if Gannon really was framing him for murder he'd need more than money and muscle. He'd need someone who knew their way around the law. Someone who'd do anything for the right price.

'I'm going to find out,' said Malton and hung up.

69

'I trusted you. As one journalist to another and you betrayed me. No. You lied to me. You took the research I shared in confidence and rather than help me develop it into a story – my story – you stuck it together into a clickbait article and slapped your name on it. You sold out my sources. You chopped up my work. You fucked me, Damion. You fucking fucked me.'

Striding through the rain, Ruth practised her speech in her head. She was so angry that she'd forgotten to take an umbrella and so now was soaking wet. Her hair clinging limply to her face, the water dripping down into her collar and soaking her T-shirt.

Safe and warm beneath her coat, she felt the reassuring press of her notebook. Filled with all her arguments written in shorthand. Like a real journalist.

Ruth had spent the last couple of hours going over Damion's article line by line. Making sure she knew where every last piece was stolen from. She'd pulled it apart and could cite her sources for every quote. She wanted to be absolutely watertight when she finally confronted him.

For sure she was angry, but anger wouldn't do her any good without facts behind it. Her dad had always told her that. A journalist should be driven by anger, but unless you know your craft then that anger will turn whatever work you do into nothing more than a rant.

After confronting Damion she'd have to go to the police. There was no other option. The story was out there. Eddie was running scared and whoever it was who was killing those boys would be forewarned.

She was just glad she hadn't given Damion the phone or the photo of the man in Jake's bedroom. Without that he hadn't been able to name a suspect in his article. Instead, without hard facts, he'd filled the space with innuendo and speculation.

The sloppy journalism was almost as much an affront as the betrayal.

The *Mancunian Ways* office was on the other side of town. It was nearly midday by the time she crossed Piccadilly Gardens, still cluttered with half-built fairgrounds and speculative food carts, and made her way up Oldham Street to the Northern Quarter.

As she approached she could see the tall, glass tower opposite the offices, looming over the Victorian workers' cottages and even the old warehouses.

Rounding the corner, she stopped for a moment and composed herself. She had the facts. She was in the right. All she had to do was state her case with passion, but not too much passion. She didn't want to give him the chance to start accusing her of being hysterical. Wave away her concerns with some misogynistic slight.

Ruth gritted her teeth and started to walk towards the office. That was when she heard the scream. It sounded odd at first. Bouncing off the walls, as if coming from far away.

She turned, momentarily unsure if it was coming from behind her.

She turned back just in time to see Damion end his fall from somewhere up above.

For a split second she saw him, flailing in mid-air, and then the pavement turned his tall, handsome body into a pile of broken meat.

Ruth was already turning to flee. Her notebook with all her arguments and thoughts fell out of her coat, landed in a puddle and turned to pulp.

But she didn't look back. She just kept on running.

70

This was too easy.

Keisha had simply walked past the front desk of Bea's office, into the narrow elevator and straight up to her floor.

Heading down the corridor, she stole a glance out of the window to where Dean was sat waiting in the black Transit. Ready to leave at a moment's notice if things went south.

But there was no security. The office wasn't even locked.

Bea was no fool. Once before, Keisha had underestimated Bea. Thought she was a nice, middle-class girl playing at it. After the last time their paths crossed Keisha now knew that Bea was every bit as dangerous as the most deranged criminal. Worse. Bea was smart, sane and driven by a ruthless ambition.

Whatever she'd been doing in hospital speaking to Craig, she clearly knew that the narrative of Craig being a killer was unravelling. Whatever her part in it all, now that Craig was in the wind, she must have considered he'd figure it out and pay her a visit.

But as Keisha pushed open the frosted glass door that led to Bea's waiting room, lined with a who's who of Manchester criminality, she was met with an empty room. The sound of typing coming from Bea's office beyond.

'Come in!' sang a voice from the office. Bea's Geordie accent was light and inviting.

Keisha raised a hand to her coat and felt the weight of the gun in her pocket. Martin Farr was already as good as dead. But without the name of whoever it was who had leaned on him to frame Craig, then she couldn't rest. Keisha's grieving process was measured in dead bodies and right now she was a couple short.

If there was anyone in Manchester who could frame someone for murder and get away with it, it was Bea Wallace. That the man she'd framed was her former lover only made Keisha more sure that she was on the right track.

Bea looked up as Keisha came in the room. She was smiling. This was too easy.

'Hello, pet, I don't think we've met. Least not in person,' said Bea, getting to her feet.

Keisha noticed a pair of heels lying on the carpet beside Bea's desk. In her stocking feet Bea seemed smaller, more child-like. Keisha towered over her but yet Bea seemed unfazed by her showing up unannounced.

'Unless you count when you tried to kill me that one time.' She smiled as she walked over to her shoes and slipped first one then two black, stockinged feet into the heels and rose up, her hips coming forward, her shoulders back. She suddenly seemed much larger.

'Doesn't look like it worked,' said Keisha from behind her sunglasses. It was true, she had groomed a violent criminal – Leon Walker – to first hire Bea as his lawyer, and then when she was alone with him in counsel, to murder her with his bare hands.

Ironically, the person who'd saved Bea's life was waiting outside at that very moment behind the wheel of her getaway vehicle.

'Why did you frame Craig for Stephen Page's murder?' said Keisha. She had no time or inclination for niceties.

'I'm sorry, pet, I don't follow you,' said Bea.

'Martin Farr is dead. Before he died he grassed you up. Let me know that he was the CI who put Craig in that minicab. That he was asked to do so by someone who had dirt on him.'

Keisha knew Bea would see her bluffing, but after bluffs all she had was the gun.

'And did he tell you who that was?' asked Bea with a look that told Keisha she knew she had nothing.

'That's why I'm here. To find out.'

'How could I possibly know that?' said Bea, all innocence.

'Because whoever it was, had enough access to Craig to get his DNA and enough fucking nerve to use it to stage a crime scene.'

There was no more time. Bea was a professional bullshitter. She was a lawyer who could get confessed killers off. She had kept countless drug kingpins out of prison and let them hold on to their ill-gotten gains. She was unflappable.

Keisha drew the gun.

Bea took a step back. 'What have you got that for, pet?' said Bea sweetly.

'I'm not your fucking pet,' said Keisha darkly, and started moving towards Bea.

Bea moved quickly for a woman in three-inch heels. She scuttled around her desk, putting it between her and Keisha.

'I thought I knew what Craig wanted,' said Bea. 'Turns out he didn't want to be a respectable member of the Manchester business elite. He thought he did. He told himself he did. But what he really wanted was to go chasing ghosts.'

'James,' said Keisha.

Bea gave a little nod. 'Aye. That poor, dead boy. I think deep down Craig knows he'll never get an answer for that. But it doesn't mean he'll stop looking. I just gave him what he wanted.'

'You're why he was in Liverpool when he got arrested?'

'I'll give him one thing, he doesn't quit.'

'So why set him going in the first place?'

Bea shook her head. 'I knew he was half in, half out working with me. I thought maybe if he thought I might have some kind of new information on his poor, dead boyfriend then he'd stick around. I needed him to need me. Turns out needing people isn't Craig's style. But I think you've found that out yourself. Right, pet?'

Keisha gripped the handle of her gun a little tighter. Bea was baiting her. Daring her to make a move. But even so, what she said rang true. If all Bea was doing was playing for time, then why tell her all this?

This *was* too easy.

Keisha raised her gun and barked, 'What have you done?'

Bea's mouth opened in delight. 'Aren't you the clever one? Soon as I heard you come in I pressed the panic alarm I had rigged up the other day. Straight to the police. They said five minutes tops. That was three minutes ago. I thought it was you on those CCTV photos. I think it's sweet you came back for Craig. Bet he didn't thank you for it though, eh?'

If Keisha had any more time she would have shot Bea but she could neither spare the time nor the bullets.

She was already out of the door and running through Bea's waiting room to the corridor outside. She could swear she could hear sirens.

Bea's office was slap bang in the middle of town. There was no way out.

Rushing down the corridor, she looked out the window.

The van was gone. She hesitated, double-checking, looking up and down the street. The black Transit had vanished. Dean had deserted her.

Gun in hand, she started back, running towards the elevator.

She should never have come home. She should never have seen her dad's body, gone to his caravan. She should never have risked it all to see Craig one last time, much less revealed herself to Rachel, or let Dean tell her all about how her father was murdered.

Stupid, stupid, stupid.

A lifetime of being smart and being careful and this is how it ended. Her, six bullets, and the GMP.

Craig was right. The moment you need people, you stop thinking about yourself. People make you soft; they make you weak. You're so busy thinking about them that you make mistakes. And living like Keisha did, you can't make a single mistake.

As she was level with the elevator, she heard a voice she would recognise anywhere.

274

'They're already in the lobby; come this way.'

Further down the corridor, holding open the fire escape, she saw the one person who could make her make the same mistake again and again.

Craig was stood in the open door.

'You can come with me or you can go down that elevator and take it up with a firearms team,' he said.

Keisha didn't need asking twice.

71

'Martin Farr's dead,' said Keisha.

Malton was sat with her in the back of the black Transit waiting for Dean to arrive with some hot food. In the meantime, he was demolishing the emergency supplies he kept in the back of the van.

If this wasn't an emergency then what was?

Malton hadn't realised how hungry he was. He hadn't eaten for nearly a day. The chase had been all-consuming. Tracking down leads and slowly getting to the truth had pushed out any thoughts of food. But now that oversight was catching up on him.

He'd arrived at Bea's offices to the sound of approaching police cars only to find Dean parked outside, nervously waiting.

Upon learning Keisha was in the building, Malton sent Dean round to the back entrance and headed inside.

'You killed him?' asked Malton, his voice devoid of judgement.

Keisha shook her head.

The back of the Transit van didn't just have supplies. It had cupboards filled with anything you might need to go on the run. Changes of clothes, money, weapons. Three different false plates for the van and a passport bearing Malton's photo but the name of a minor gangland figure who'd gone missing nearly twenty years ago. Someone Malton could say for sure wasn't coming back anytime soon.

It also had a single bed on which Malton and Keisha were sat, side by side.

'It was your boy Dean who worked it out. Martin robbed his own family then made Dean throw his accomplice to the Farrs.'

Malton frowned.

'To save your arse,' said Keisha, clocking his reaction. 'That's how he learned it was Martin who grassed you up.'

Malton was genuinely surprised. Without any help, Dean had exposed the CI. It was just a shame that CI was almost certainly dead.

'So if you didn't kill him, then who?' asked Malton.

'The man who put Farr up to it all. Well, his goon. Bloke with a beard called Wormall. Ran Farr down outside his own garage, snatched him up and fucked right off.'

'So you don't know he's dead?'

Keisha sighed and went back to the very start. Malton listened as she told him the whole story. About her father acting as a courier and how he realised it was Martin who had robbed him, and how Martin had been offered a way out. A way out that included Wormall keeping things neat and tidy by murdering Harold.

Keisha came to the end of her story. Malton couldn't help but smile. He was impressed.

'You're not the only clever fucker, Craig,' said Keisha. 'I taught you everything you know.'

She was teasing him. If Malton couldn't feel his broken ribs and his infected wounds then he might even have laughed.

Luckily, among the van's provisions there were antibiotics. They were no substitute for a doctor but they would have to do.

'That's why I was at your girlfriend's place.'

'She's not my girlfriend,' said Malton coldly.

'Cos I reckon your girlfriend was the one who set the whole thing up. Got hold of your DNA and coached Martin Farr. Which means she knows the name of the Farrs' supplier. The one who's responsible for all of this fucking mess. If I'd just have had a few more minutes . . .'

'Luke Gannon,' said Malton, cutting across Keisha.

He enjoyed the look of astonishment on Keisha's face.

'Scrawny club promoter?' she said, surprised.

'He killed Stephen Page, probably a lot more boys besides.'

Keisha was shaking her head. 'That doesn't make sense. The guy who leaned on Martin Farr, he sells drugs to the Farrs. Dean said he was a heavy-duty supplier.'

Everything suddenly came together in Malton's head. Luke Gannon hadn't retired. He'd moved jobs.

Luke's brush with a Salford gang had taught him a very different lesson to the one Malton had thought. He hadn't got out of clubbing; he'd moved sideways into drugs. His decades promoting meant he had contacts all over the world. He had the capital to get started and, more than that, he was a clever fucker who made sure to cover his arse.

Malton wondered if someone even higher up the chain had realised Luke's weakness for killing young men and ordered him to get his house in order. Pointed him in Bea's direction.

'Looks like Luke Gannon had a late career change,' said Malton as the doors to the back of the van opened and a soaking wet Dean stepped inside holding two large McDonald's bags.

Keisha and Malton took the bags off him. Malton devoured the food in huge bites, barely chewing as he shovelled fuel into his body.

'This is the last time you can see me,' said Malton to Dean through a mouthful of chips.

'I'm here. I'm in it,' said Dean.

'He's the one who got us this far,' said Keisha.

'And I'm on the run,' said Malton. 'I beat Mickey Farr half to death and I'm still wanted for murder. Until that's done, if they catch you with me then that's game over for you. You're too good for that.'

'I'm not scared,' said Dean.

Malton looked him up and down. He could see it was true. The callow, enthusiastic boy he'd taken on a couple of years ago was long gone. Dean was every bit as much of this world as he was.

'I know you aren't. And I still need you, but from here on in, you're arm's length. 'Cos I know you can do the job. I'm trusting you with my life here. If this goes south, then it's over. You understand?'

Malton saw the look of pride in Dean's face. Watched as he quickly squashed it and did his best to look professionally nonchalant.

'I understand,' said Dean. 'What is it you need me to do?'

Malton swallowed the last of his Quarter Pounder with Cheese and licked his lips clean.

'We're going to take down Luke Gannon. And this is how we're going to do it.'

72

Whatever doubts Dean had harboured seemed like distant memories. Malton had trusted him with his life. Dean wasn't going to let him down.

Malton and Keisha had gone off with the van, leaving him to get an Uber back home. After picking Keisha and Malton up at Bea's office, Dean had driven slowly and carefully all the way out to the edge of Chorley. The whole time checking his mirrors, convinced that at any moment he'd hear the roar of sirens and see the lights of the police coming to arrest them all.

By the time he'd got back to his place in Moss Side, Dean was exhausted. Eager not to dwell on Vikki and the voice he'd heard when he'd last called her, he'd spent the evening reading up everything he could about Luke Gannon.

Dean had never been big into clubs. Spending several hours packed up against hundreds of other people listening to loud, repetitive music in a darkened room was his idea of hell. Through working for Malton Security he'd got a unique view of Manchester nightlife. From the doors to the back rooms. The hard graft that went into making everything go smoothly. Club promotion was a cut-throat world at the best of times but everything he'd read about Luke Gannon made it seem like he'd elevated it to some kind of art form.

Gannon hadn't just been successful. He'd been successful enough to shed all the infamy of his early rise and become a local celebrity. But, while other promoters used their profiles to boost the city's nightlife and twist the arms of politicians, Gannon had simply revelled in his notoriety. He was known as a party animal. A raconteur and the kind of man who made things happen. He arranged parties for footballers and pop stars. He was the man to turn to if you wanted a venue to open with a bang. Luke Gannon had lived as hard and fast as he could.

Then he simply disappeared.

After only a few hours' sleep, Dean had spent the morning attempting to match up any deaths of young men he could find with Gannon's movements. It helped that Gannon was so publicity-hungry. Knowing where he was on any given day was simple. Until a couple of years ago when he'd stopped running clubs and gone dark.

Again and again, dates that Luke was in the city tallied with reports of young boys turning up dead. It wasn't proof but it was enough to reassure Dean that Malton's theory was on the money.

His first stop had been the address of the Airbnb Malton had given him. As expected, he found it empty. A Spanish cleaner was in the middle of giving the place the once-over when Dean arrived. She told him that no one was booked to stay for the next week.

That was how he found himself heading up in the elevator to Ruth's flat. He already knew she wouldn't be there, but that wasn't why he was visiting.

He'd knocked enough times to be considering breaking in when, finally, he heard movement from the other side of the door. Dean stood back and smiled at the peephole. Someone was sizing him up.

'I'm a friend of Ruth's,' said Dean.

'She's not here,' said a curt voice from the other side of the door.

Dean pulled a worried face and kept talking. 'It's just. Well, we've only just started seeing each other. And I know it's really soon and this feels super weird, but . . . I just got this vibe, you know? That something was wrong and I'm probably massively over-reacting and she's going to be scared off now, but I wanted to check she was OK?'

Dean stood and listened. Whoever was behind the door was still there. Debating. He needed to get into that flat. Malton's entire plan depended on it.

'If you could just have her shout out to me? So I know? I don't know what else to do.'

There was another long pause and then the sound of someone putting a chain on the door.

Dean tried his best to look pitiful as the door opened a crack and a girl with curly strawberry blonde hair peered out.

'She didn't mention seeing anyone,' she said.

'I know, like I said. Super early. We went to a gallery opening the other night.'

'Castlefield Gallery?'

'She told you? Did she say anything about how it went? Did she talk about me?'

The strawberry blonde girl looked like she was thinking. 'I think she's in trouble.'

'What kind of trouble?'

'Did you hear about that guy who fell off a building yesterday?'

Dean had indeed caught up on events. He suspected it was no coincidence that Damion Carter worked at the same place as Ruth. 'Yeah, fuck, that was awful.'

'She knew him.' The girl lowered her voice conspiratorially. 'I don't think it was an accident.'

'Shit,' said Dean, feigning surprise. 'We should go to the police.'

The strawberry blonde looked unsure.

'I could go,' Dean offered. 'But I don't know what to tell them. Do you think she's in danger?'

The strawberry blonde took a second then shut the door and Dean heard her taking the chain off and opening it up.

'I think she's in real danger. She said she was leaving town. Heading home.' As Dean stepped inside the flat, before Ruth's flatmate said another word, he already knew he had everything he needed.

It was there on the wall of the flat. A framed newspaper story about a reporter who was retiring to run a pub.

73

Ruth had lied. When she'd turned up unannounced on her parents' doorstep the other evening she'd said it had been a spur-of-the-moment thing. She wanted to see them and so just hopped on a train and here she was.

Whether she was convincing or whether her parents were just glad to see her, neither of them had questioned her story. Instead they'd spent the evening in the pub. Her mum and dad behind the bar and Ruth sat in a corner, glued to her phone while various locals got her up to speed on just how often her dad boasted about his 'journalist daughter'.

How could she ever tell her dad that her dream was dead? She'd tried to follow in his footsteps and instead she'd found herself in the middle of a nightmare.

She knew that eventually her dad would spot the story of Damion's death and start to wonder. How it was she hadn't mentioned someone she worked with falling to his death from a great height? It was being written up as a tragic accident, but Ruth knew better.

She'd seen Eddie's flat and heard the fear in his voice. She'd seen the bearded man searching for that phone and the man from the hotel room sat in the back directing him through a cloud of smoke.

Everything Malton and Dean had said was true. This was a world she had no experience of. She was hugely out of her depth.

Fleeing Manchester, she'd stopped at the Airbnb to grab her laptop with all her work on it and what few possessions she'd brought with her.

Now all that was left of the story was stashed away in her parents' spare room. Waiting like an unexploded bomb.

Ruth couldn't decide what would be worse when they caught up with her – if she still had the phone or if she'd thrown it away. At least with the phone she had something to bargain with, but as long as she had that phone she knew whoever had killed Damion was still out there looking for it.

That morning she'd been unable to stand it any longer. She'd headed out into the driving rain for a walk, taking the phone with her.

Her parents' pub was in a little village high up in the Peak District. Over one side sat Sheffield, on the other, Manchester. But in between were miles and miles of uninhabited land. Perfect for losing an unwanted phone.

An hour's solid walking later and Ruth was exhausted. The rain had turned the ground to slop and left every hard surface treacherously slippery. Walking any distance required her entire body to be at attention. Every muscle ready to keep her upright and balanced.

Standing atop the rocky outcrop she could look down and see her parents' pub in the distance. An indistinct shape through the rain. They were there getting ready to open up. Oblivious to what she'd left behind in Manchester.

Up here, in the pouring rain, alone in the middle of nowhere, Ruth could almost feel safe.

She took out Jake's phone. The battery was dead. It sat lifeless in her hand. A tiny, inert object radiating all the pain and suffering contained within it.

Beneath her, the outcrop fell away to a cliff scattered with gravel and scrub. It carried on for a couple of hundred metres down into a river at the bottom of the valley. Nowhere near roads or paths or anything that would give anyone any reason to ever come to this part of the world looking.

Then she remembered the sound Damion made when he hit the pavement.

Was this phone the only thing standing between her and ending up like Damion?

She looked out through the impenetrable rain and made her decision.

74

Keisha didn't know exactly what it was she was looking for but she knew that she would find it in caravan M8. Her father's second pitch at the Edge Haven site.

Hammering up the motorway through the driving rain, she realised that she was singing along to the radio. She was in the midst of an organised attempt to murder the man who'd killed her father. She was carrying a loaded gun and working with a known fugitive, and if things went south she might lose not just her freedom but also her life.

Keisha hadn't felt this carefree in as long as she could remember.

She was so busy belting out tunes that she nearly didn't see the car that suddenly barrelled out of the deluge, headlights on full beam. It hurtled up the narrow road heading away from Edge Haven, swerving at the last moment and forcing Keisha to do likewise. The sound of hedgerow scraping against the side of the van shook Keisha to her senses as she pulled back on the road and saw, in her mirror, the car she'd very nearly collided with vanishing into the gloom.

She was slowly crawling up the row of caravans towards Harold's twin pitches when she saw the one thing she had been dreading ever since Craig had told her he needed her to go back to Edge Haven.

There, outside Harold's caravan, was Rachel's car.

It was Allie she found first. She was on her hands and knees in M7, sorting through the pile of trashed belongings in the middle of the floor of the caravan. She had a black bin liner and was ruthlessly chucking everything that couldn't be saved.

Allie looked up as Keisha came in out of the rain, quickly shutting the door behind her. Keisha pulled back the hood of her coat and wiped the rain from her face with the palm of her hand.

'Who is it?' said a voice from the back of the caravan. Rachel was in the bathroom.

Allie and Keisha stared at each other in silence. Each one privately marvelling at seeing themselves reflected back across decades in time.

Then, at once, they both spoke.

'It's Keisha,' said Keisha over Allie who said, 'It's Auntie.'

A hurried flushing sound came from the toilet and Rachel emerged looking worried.

'What's happened?' she said, unable to hide the fear in her voice.

'Nothing,' said Keisha. 'I just had to come back for something.'

Keisha was sure that she hadn't looked as shocked as she felt to hear Allie use that word: Auntie.

Relief passed over Rachel's face.

'Not us then?' she said with a hopeful smile.

From down on the floor, Allie watched Keisha expectantly.

'I told you,' said Keisha, 'you don't know me. I'm not someone you want in your life.'

'You don't know me,' said Rachel. 'You have no idea who I do and don't want in my life.'

Keisha had been dreading this. Craig got the easy job. He just had to go and risk getting killed by Luke Gannon's hired goon.

'I'm just here to collect something and then I'm gone.'

'What?' demanded Rachel.

'I don't know,' said Keisha.

'I've been over this caravan all morning. You tell me what it is you're looking for.'

'It's not in here,' said Keisha.

Keisha and Rachel left a reluctant Allie in M7 sorting through Harold's broken junk and, on Rachel's insistence, went into M8 together.

287

Inside, they had to raise their voices to be heard over the rain smashing down on the thin metal roof of the caravan, echoing around the space.

'Typical of Dad. He wants a secret bolthole but he's too lazy to stick it more than six feet from his front door,' said Rachel as she looked around M8. 'The plan was to clear this place this afternoon. So what is it we're looking for?' she asked with an enthusiasm that threw Keisha off balance.

'I told you, I can do this alone.'

'This is my dad's caravan. Besides, you gave me the keys. You said you were done.'

Keisha started going through cupboards. She really didn't know exactly what it was she was looking for. Half expecting Rachel to be here, she'd steeled herself for fear, anger and rejection. She hadn't planned on Rachel picking right back up as if they were in the Metropolitan, chatting over soft drinks and waiting for their food.

Instead of letting it throw her off balance she focused on going through the caravan. Everything had the instantly recognisable smell of old age. A polite decay.

Taking Keisha's lead, Rachel started going through the nearest box of possessions.

The photo of Keisha and Harold was still there on the wall.

'That's you, isn't it?' said Rachel as she sorted through neatly folded bedding. 'Up on the wall with Dad.'

'Yes,' said Keisha, not turning away from her search. Rachel was still looking at the photo.

'When me and Allie first came in here we couldn't believe it. You look so much like her. I don't know why Dad never reached out but it looks like he never forgot you.'

Keisha pulled open a new drawer. It was full of receipts.

'I'd forgotten him. Right up until he dragged me back here to bury him,' said Keisha. She dug into the drawer and hundreds of neatly packed receipts exploded all over the floor.

'Dad could be a complete prick,' said Rachel, 'but I think maybe he was scared.'

'I already knew he was a coward,' said Keisha.

'Don't get me wrong, he wasn't a good dad. Or even really a dad. But in his own pathetic way, he tried. I don't think it makes it right what he did but I think he was scared. He knew deep down he couldn't ever make it right with you.'

'And so he gets me to arrange his funeral?' shot Keisha.

'Maybe he knew you'd find out about me and Allie. Maybe he hoped you'd reach out.'

Keisha looked up from where she was gathering receipts. Stunned that the thought had never crossed her mind.

'Maybe he knew it was too late for him to make amends. But he hoped that maybe it wasn't too late for you and me.'

'I shouldn't have called you. But then . . .' Keisha's eyes went to the photo on the wall.

'But then something changed, didn't it?'

'What does that matter?' said Keisha sharply. 'Soon as I find what I'm looking for I'm gone.'

She tried to look busy searching a drawer. Were Rachel and Allie her dad's way of trying to make things right? It made more sense than any other reason he had for dragging her back into his life.

'You still haven't told me what it is we're looking for.'

Keisha looked up at Rachel.

'There is no you and me. Let me tell you why. I've found the man who killed Dad. Now I'm going to lure him out and kill him and then I'm going back to Ibiza for good.'

Rachel didn't turn away. Instead she matched Keisha's stare. Both women looking at each other through shared eyes. Finally, Rachel spoke.

'Good,' she said. Then added, 'But not the part about going to Ibiza for good. I'd miss you. Allie would too. We've only just found you.'

Rachel turned away and began to search again. 'So what is it that you need?' she said.

Keisha took a moment and repeated, 'I'm going to kill him.'

'I heard you,' said Rachel. 'You never knew Dad,' she added.

289

'I never had the chance,' said Keisha curtly.

'He was a right bastard. Into all sorts of dodgy stuff. He'd nick things. He'd lie. He'd disappear for weeks on end without telling anyone. When you said someone had killed him, I was only half surprised.'

Keisha couldn't believe what she was hearing.

'Hearing you try and scare me off. You sound just like him. He always tried to be the big man. Take it all on himself. Never let anyone in. Hiding it all away in his secret caravan.'

Keisha felt a lump rise in her throat. She turned away and pulled open a drawer, her back to Rachel as she fought the emotion.

'Whatever happens, whatever you do, if you want a sister I'm here,' said Rachel softening. 'I'd like to at least try.'

Keisha focused all her attention down into the drawer. She thought about Harold's dead body. About Martin Farr flying through the air and landing in the middle of the road. About what she'd do to Luke Gannon. Anything except the words she was hearing from Rachel.

Then she saw it. What she was looking for.

There, written on a tatty scrap of paper at the back of the drawer. The thing she needed to make sure there was no escape for Luke Gannon.

75

Luke Gannon lived in a fortress. To be more exact, he lived in a timber-framed Tudor mansion on the outskirts of Knutsford, a wealthy commuter village. Luke Gannon's money and paranoia had turned it into a fortress.

The extensive grounds, which included a small wood and a decent-sized lake, were encircled with a ten-foot-high, rigid mesh fence, which was monitored with twenty-four-hour CCTV. Within sight of the house, that fence became a brick wall topped with ornate iron spikes.

The only way in and out of the grounds was through the main gate, a large, reinforced metal and wood affair, which was controlled remotely, requiring not only the possession of a key fob but authorisation from the house itself.

The house had a twenty-four-hour security presence with at least one man on the grounds at all times.

If somehow an intruder got past the fence and the gate and the security guard, there was an internal panic room and closed-circuit alarm that went straight to the police.

Luckily for Malton he was the man who had set all this up.

When he rang through from the gate directly to the security guard on duty, the gate was swiftly opened and he was met by Illian, to whom Dean had allocated the morning shift.

Whether or not Gannon knew Malton was onto him, he hadn't risked showing his hand by beefing up the security detail. Maybe he thought he'd got away with it.

Illian only said two words to his boss: 'He's out.'

Malton headed up the long, curving gravel driveway, around the lake and up to the house. Every step hurt. His injuries were getting worse. The stiff, burning sensation was back. Only by tensing every muscle in his chest could he half-prevent the agony of his broken ribs bringing him to his knees.

He and Keisha had spent the night back at the safehouse. Separate rooms. Conversation kept to a minimum.

He still had the drain in his chest, and that morning, in the privacy of his ensuite, he'd turned the small valve at the end of the plastic tube and to his horror a thin stream of clear liquid had flowed out into the sink. The relief he felt was tempered with the knowledge that as long as he was on the run he was risking doing serious damage to his heart.

Walking up Luke Gannon's driveway, Malton told himself that there was no time to think about that now. He had been on the run for three days. In an era of CCTV and camera phones he knew he would only stay lucky so long. He needed to wrap this up and quick.

The front door had been retrofitted with a biometric lock that only Luke Gannon and his wife could access. Fortunately for Malton there was a bypass code. A code that he himself had programmed in.

After tapping in the code, he was inside.

Malton hadn't been in Luke Gannon's house since he finished installing the security several years back. Since then he'd kept an eye on the roster of men doing security duty. Making sure only those Malton Security employees who could be trusted to behave themselves were allocated to such a high-value client. Malton knew just how challenging Luke could be. The last thing he wanted was for an employee to lose his rag and stick one on him.

The ceilings were low and the house asymmetrical. The Tudor beams visibly warped from the passage of time. Slowly petrified. The floors buckled and bowed. It cost millions to have a house this lopsided.

The first thing he noticed was how hot it was. Outside, the rain had briefly let up but it was still freezing cold. He felt it right down into his stab wounds.

Inside, the house was oppressively warm. He opened his coat and let the heat into his body and for a moment felt a little more human. He realised his drain was visible beneath his tracksuit top and zipped it up to under his chin.

Malton hadn't decided exactly how he was going to play things but when a strikingly beautiful, middle-aged woman with shocking silver hair came out of the kitchen holding a plate of food and saw him standing there, the decision was taken out of his hands.

Luke's wife hadn't lost any of her looks. If anything, age had enhanced them. Given her a more relaxed air. She was barefoot in a sloppy tracksuit. Alone in her house. Yet the sight of Malton's giant, battered body stood in her hallway seemed not to faze her.

You didn't stay married to Luke Gannon if you scared easily.

'He's not here,' she said casually and walked across the hallway, past Malton and into another room.

Malton followed her into a vast sitting room. The walls were wood-panelled and the windows all came with benches set into the thick Tudor walls. Art was hung on every surface. Malton didn't recognise any of it but he knew it would have been expensive. At the far end of the room were built-in bookcases filled with antique books. Malton guessed the Gannons had never read a single one. Like so much about Luke Gannon, it was just for show.

A giant fireplace dominated the room, throwing out heat. It was piled high with the white ash from hundreds of previous fires.

Luke's wife sat down on one of the large sofas and started eating what she'd been preparing in the kitchen.

'I know you,' she said. 'You set up our security.'

'That's right,' said Malton, walking over and sitting down across from Luke's wife. 'We met before too,' he said.

Luke's wife looked up.

'At Martyrdom.'

Malton saw the memory come storming back into her head. That night at Martyrdom. The back room and the boy, half-undressed, half-dead.

Luke's wife shook her head and went back to eating. 'What's he done now?'

'You know, don't you?' said Malton plainly.

She kept eating but slowed down. When she looked up she was angry. 'Know what? About the meth? About the drinking? About how he spends all his time either off his head, fucking some young kid, or in the gym desperately trying to stave off his own mortality?'

Malton said nothing. He just listened.

'Of course I remember that night. You should have let that boy die. At least then maybe he would have stopped.'

Her voice cracked and Malton knew he had her.

'It's because of people like you that he's the way he is. He gives you money and you look the other way. You help him get away with it. He used to be a bastard, but now? Now he's a fucking monster and it's people like you who made him into that.'

'He's been killing boys,' said Malton.

Luke's wife began to quietly cry. She set her plate down and put her hand to her face to stop herself. When she looked up, her eyes flashed with rage.

'And what am I meant to do? How can I stop him? No one has ever said no to him.'

'He framed me for the murder of one of them.'

She laughed. 'So this isn't about the murder? This is about him fucking you over? What did you expect? Whatever else Luke is, he's never lied about who he is. He tells you to your face what he'll do to you. But people think they know better. That he's joking or it'll be different with them. He charms you, lets you think somehow you'll be the one who gets away. No one ever gets away.'

She sucked in the warm air through her nostrils and swallowed hard. Her eyes went back to their dull, glassy stare.

'I agree,' said Malton. 'No one ever gets away.'

A strange look came over Luke's wife. Her eyes darted away guiltily.

'You know he has a bodyguard. Not one of your lot. Some-one proper. Wormall,' she said. 'He was in the Paras. He's killed more people than you've had hot dinners.'

'I know about Wormall,' said Malton.

'He knows about Wormall,' she sang to herself. 'Well if you know about Wormall just what do you want from me?'

Malton watched her for a moment, trying to weigh up whether or not he could trust her. Would she relay this meet-ing to Gannon? Would he even listen if she did? It sounded like money and leisure and a touch of madness had destroyed Luke Gannon. The sociopathic promoter Malton first met was now a monstrous predator, out of control and with no one to stop him.

Until now.

'All I want from you,' said Malton, 'is Luke's private number.'

76

'You're a fucking liar! He's not dead. Say that again, I dare you!'

Dean attempted a look that sat somewhere between sincere condolence and a readiness to start throwing hands. Across the table from him, in the corner of the Farrs' western-themed bar room, Marie Farr was coming apart at the seams.

A country song Dean didn't recognise played over the PA, the twangy, upbeat vocals lending the scene a hysterical air.

Next to her sat Janet, her hair straight, black and immaculate; her permanent Botox scowl scouring Dean for any sense that what he was saying was anything other than the complete truth.

Carl was back behind the bar, on his phone, seemingly uninterested in the drama unfolding on the other side of the room.

'It happened right in front of me,' said Dean.

'So why didn't you stop it?' howled Marie. Her eyes were black and smudged, her thick foundation smeared across her face and the back of her sleeve from where she'd tried to wipe away the tears.

'Good question,' said Janet.

'I tried,' said Dean. 'I saw Martin get run over and then dragged into the back of a car. I followed, but whoever was driving the car was faster. They lost me.'

'It's your fault!' shouted Marie. She turned and grabbed her mum, sobbing into Janet's glossy black tracksuit top.

Janet Farr eyed Dean over her weeping daughter's shoulder. As always with Janet it was hard to know what she was thinking. Botox, fillers and a touch of sociopathy had given her the unreadable glower that was currently trained on Dean.

'I want a word with you,' she said.

The rain had let up so they stood outside the Farr house, amongst the piles of scrap, next to a stack of garden furniture that was quietly rotting in one corner of the yard.

Janet had produced a spliff from somewhere and held it daintily between two manicured fingers.

Dean shivered in the damp air. Malton's plan was ingenious but it required every single part to work in unison. Keisha was away doing her bit, as was Malton. It fell to Dean to be the one to break the news to the Farrs.

'He was the one who nicked the drugs, wasn't he?' said Janet after a silence, which Dean didn't dare try and fill with small talk.

This wasn't in the plan.

'You knew?' Dean said, desperate to avoid showing his hand.

Janet took a long drag and held the smoke down. The sour smell of cannabis filled the air. Dean did his best not to gag.

'Course I fucking did. When it went missing we went straight to the supplier. Told him what'd happen if it didn't turn up. Got our windows put through. That's fucking nothing. That's an invitation, that is. But next thing Martin's pissing his pants telling us to let it go. Start with, I thought that was just him being a fucking pussy. But then something about the way he was so keen to just write off a couple of hundred grand.' Janet shook her head. 'That fucking prick.'

Dean couldn't believe what he was hearing. 'If you knew, why did you hire me?'

'Cos the little shit got away with it, didn't he? Covered his arse and I couldn't prove it. Course, if it wasn't for her in there I'd have just had Carl smash the cunt to bits. He got to you too, didn't he?'

Janet was smiling through her frozen face. Dean was lost for words. Was he really this transparent?

'Yeah,' Dean admitted sheepishly. 'He had something I wanted and told me that unless I put all the blame on Sam then he wouldn't play ball.'

Janet spat on the wet grass. 'Absolute bad news, that one. Sam was a sweet lad. Could just about change a tyre. Shitty taste in music, but harmless. Then that fucking weasel Martin gets in his head and now look what's happened.'

Janet seemed sad. As if somehow Sam Kennard's death was an avoidable tragedy and not a horror show she herself had conducted.

'At least you don't have to deal with him now,' said Dean.

Janet frowned. 'You fucking dense, son? I needed proof so that I could let that dickhead know I was on to him. I wasn't going to actually do anything. Not as long as that girl in there loved him. She comes first. But if I had a bit of proof then maybe I could have convinced her what a shitbag he really was or at least kept him on a short leash. But now he's gone and got himself killed, she's in bits and he's Saint fucking Martin.'

'What if I said I could give you proof?'

'Bit fucking late for that,' said Janet, sucking the spliff down to the nub.

'You said yourself your daughter's in bits. Could be a closure?'

Janet dropped the spent joint onto the grass and warily asked, 'And what do you want in return?'

Dean had come hoping to appeal to Janet Farr's professional pride. Give her the chance to tidy up her operation. Now it turned out he was playing with something far more dangerous. He had the white-hot rage of a mother protecting her daughter.

Dean walked Janet through the chaos that had surrounded Martin Farr, and when he had gone over every sorry detail he made Janet Farr his offer.

77

Craig wasn't built for the country. He was still larger than life in the city but a lifetime of living in its concrete folds had left him with the ability to blend into his surroundings. Become part of the backdrop. Out in the country, surrounded by fields, stone buildings and endless hikers, Craig looked exactly like what he was – an eighteen-stone one-man army.

When they'd first walked into Ruth's parents' pub it was like a bad movie. That moment of silence as everyone looked up at the black woman in shades and the black man with a scar down one side of his face.

Keisha could tell Craig was in a bad way. He was moving far more slowly. It was clear every step was costing him. He hadn't changed his clothes either and was starting to smell. A sour, wet stink of rain and sweat and blood. From Keisha's reckoning he didn't have much longer left in him.

She left him sat in the corner and went to the bar, taking off her shades and flashing a beaming smile at the older man behind the bar.

'Two pints of Coke, please,' she said.

'Right you are!' said the man she assumed must be Ruth's father as he started getting the glasses.

'This is a lovely little pub, isn't it?' said Keisha.

The man grinned and shook his head.

'This is my idiot idea of a retirement.' The ice tumbled noisily into the glasses as he set them down on the bar. 'Thought after working for the *Manchester Evening News* for thirty years this would be a piece of piss.' He caught himself. 'Sorry. Language.'

'I've heard worse,' said Keisha, her eyes locking with his as he started pouring out the drinks.

'You here on holiday?'

'Oh no. Just passing through,' said Keisha. 'Fancied a change of pace. Actually, we're here to speak to your daughter Ruth.'

The man finished filling the glass to the brim with sparkling, brown liquid, put the soda gun down and just like that, all his light, friendly affect was gone.

'Who are you?' he said.

'She came home, didn't she? The other day. Has she told you why?'

'Like I said, thirty years at the *Evening News*. Whatever your game is, I don't scare.'

From the way he held her gaze, Keisha knew he wasn't bluffing.

'That's good. We need that. You see, your daughter's been following in your footsteps. Looking into things that other people might think were best left alone.'

'I'm calling the police,' he said and dug for a phone in his pocket.

On the other side of the bar Keisha could see Malton about to get to his feet. One look from her and he sat back down.

'Don't. Because we're here to help her. Your daughter uncovered a killer. Hiding in plain sight. She found out things no one else had. But she made the mistake of trusting the wrong people and now she's in a lot of trouble.'

'Then I'm definitely calling the police.'

'This isn't the kind of trouble the police can deal with. You've read, haven't you, about the boy who fell out of a window where your daughter worked? You've wondered, haven't you? Is that connected? Is that why she's back?'

The man had his phone out and was getting ready to dial. Keisha changed gears.

'I remember you. You came to Moss Side back when it was a no-go area. Young guy, had hair back then.'

300

The man stopped and looked up from his phone. Keisha had him. So she continued.

'You did a piece about a local café. Lorrayne's. About how she did a Christmas dinner for whoever wanted to turn up. Back then all we ever heard about was how bad it was and how we were living in hell. I was there, and it wasn't easy, but there were good people. Not me, not him either.' She nodded to Malton in the corner. 'But they were there and you found them. That's how I know that when I tell you this you're going to think long and hard before doing anything stupid.'

'Tragedy what happened to Lorrayne,' he said. 'I used to go there sometimes when I was passing.'

Keisha didn't tell him that when Lorrayne who ran the café was shot dead, the man sat in the corner of his pub was right there moments later. Or that he had mutilated the kid who'd killed her.

'What are you going to tell me?' he asked.

'The man in the corner there? He's on the run from Strangeways. Actually, I kidnapped him.' Keisha's face let him know that she was letting him in on her scam.

'What does he have to do with my daughter?'

'The man your daughter was about to expose framed him for a murder. But now that man's plan is unravelling and he's killing everyone he can think of who might get back to him. That's why your daughter left Manchester.'

He was quiet now. Keisha could see he was still hiding behind his professional sangfroid but beneath the mask was the red-blooded fear of a parent.

'And how can you help her?' he asked, his voice firm. He still wasn't decided.

'I need her to come back to Manchester and help me draw him out.'

The man's front finally broke and he shook his head, almost laughing.

'Not a chance. If he wants to kill her that's the last place she's going.'

'If I could find you out here, then he can find you too,' said Keisha coldly.

Ruth's father went quiet. She could tell he knew she was speaking the truth. All he had to do was let himself be carried along. Take the first step and let Keisha in.

Finally he said, 'What happens when you get him?'

'Do you want to know?' asked Keisha sternly.

He was silent. Neither of them were in any doubt that he already knew exactly what happened next.

At that moment the door to the pub opened and out of the howling rain stumbled Ruth Porter.

78

Ruth realised she'd stopped listening to what Dean was saying. Instead she was looking over to the bar of the Stanford Hotel where an elderly man in a well-cut suit was struggling to stay balanced on a bar stool while talking to a woman no older than Ruth, who, despite it being the middle of a wet March afternoon, was wearing a bright white, tight-fitting bodycon dress that barely covered her backside and a pair of terrifyingly high, high-heeled sandals.

The Stanford Hotel was a Manchester institution. One of the few old-school bastions of money that had kept going as the city changed around it. The bar had been done up in the past few years and now the high ceilings of the Stanford were hung with giant, glittering disco ball chandeliers and the bar was now a large, space-age-looking circular structure. The giant windows were just a touch above street level, allowing patrons inside the bar to gaze out while the hoi polloi at street level could only crane their necks and wonder at what could be going on within such a grand, old building.

It was here that Malton wanted to lay the trap for Luke Gannon.

It was two days since Ruth had returned from her walk at her parents' to find Malton and a woman who looked a lot like the CCTV images of the woman with a gun walking Malton out of MRI.

Immediately she knew she'd made the right decision keeping the phone. As scared as she was to see them in her parents' pub, knowing that she still had Jake's phone as leverage was just enough of an edge to give her, if not courage, then at least the appearance of it.

It was that feigned bravado that had seen her agree to be here today.

'There are men on every exit. Our men,' said Dean.

Ruth snapped back to attention as, at the bar, the young woman put one manicured hand on the elderly man's arm.

'Where's Malton?' she asked.

'For obvious reasons he's lying low until we have Gannon.'

'So you're running this?'

'That's right, but this is Malton's plan. You contact Gannon, let him know you have the phone and that you want to meet here, at the Stanford Hotel.'

The opulence of the surroundings added to Ruth's sense of unreality. She wondered when it was that she suddenly cut adrift from her old life. From worrying about clickbait articles and dreaming about journalism to here and now, bait in a trap for a deranged murderer who wanted her dead. This felt wrong.

'What if he sends that man? The one with the beard?'

'You need to be clear; he needs to come alone.'

'He'll know it's a trap.'

'It doesn't matter. He doesn't have a choice. As long as you have the phone he can't risk it.'

Ruth was again overcome with relief that she hadn't hurled the phone into that gorge.

The elderly man at the bar finally slipped off the bar stool, barely managing not to lose his footing completely and tumble to the floor. The young woman, surprisingly agile in her heels, was up and catching him, just about holding his weight.

This was a bad idea.

'So he comes here, I give him the phone and when he goes to leave you snatch him up and then what?'

'You don't need to know.'

'Oh, but I do. Because if I'm going to do this, I need to know everything. Who comes to this bar at this time of day? Who

304

are the staff? What is the CCTV like? Does this guy Gannon know them? Could he get to them? Will I get out OK? I've never been in here in my life and now you're asking me to risk my life?'

'The plan will work,' said Dean firmly.

Ruth watched as the elderly man was helped back onto his bar stool, his wandering hands now all over the younger woman.

'I can't do this,' she said and meant it.

79

Keisha slipped her hand into her coat and wrapped her fingers around the cold, firm handle of the gun. She squeezed the weapon hard, letting its solidity press back against her as she desperately tried to keep focus.

Right now she needed to be exactly where she was – sat in a car across the road from Rachel's house in Chorlton keeping watch. Malton was taking care of his end of the plan, but Keisha needed to know that, whatever happened, none of what was about to blow up could possibly affect Rachel and Allie.

The unexpected novelty of fear was bad enough but on top of that she knew that Craig was dying. The past couple of days had been agony to watch. She also knew he wouldn't accept help and so she didn't insult him by offering it. For Craig it was never enough. He would never let himself rest until every last fire was out. But Craig lived in a world that was burning down around him. Whether it was his upbringing or a cruel trick of God, he would never stop moving forward. Even as his injuries were beginning to bring him down. He was a wounded animal, stalked by his own insecurities. All that was left was for him to eventually tire and fall.

When he did, then forty years of demons would come for him.

She held the gun tighter and listened to the rain. It was heavy today, making it hard to see through the car window, across the street and into Rachel's home.

One way or another this was nearly over. Her father was in the ground. Soon Luke Gannon, the man who'd put him there, would be too. It was all a mess. This is what happened when you got involved. When you stopped fighting and made the mistake of just trying to live.

Keisha held the gun tightly. Lost in her thoughts and soothed by the mesmeric sound of the rain, she didn't even notice as, a few spaces behind her, the car that had nearly run her off the road the other day at Edge Haven parked up and killed its lights.

80

Every breath was a battle now. Sat in the back of the black Transit van, parked a few streets away from the meeting point, Malton knew his time was almost up. In the two days since they brought Ruth Porter back to Manchester, his condition had gone rapidly downhill. The antibiotics weren't working. His wounds were burning hot to the touch. He'd already opened up the drain in his chest twice that morning, draining at first clear fluid and then fluid with the tell-tale pink tinge of blood.

Everything was moving forward. If he stopped now then it was all for nothing. Connor's face, Keisha's rescue, Luke Gannon's own wife giving him up. But more than even that. The years of grind, hauling himself up from the streets of Moss Side. His company, his reputation and the reach he enjoyed into every dark recess of Manchester's underbelly.

Between them, Luke Gannon and Bea Wallace had nearly cost Malton all of that when they framed him for murder. All these years, all the hardened criminals Malton had dealt with. All the bad blood he'd been keeping at bay, constantly fighting against a deep reservoir of stored-up vendetta. In the end it wasn't a psychopathic drug dealer or a hardman with something to prove who had brought him low. It was a club promoter turned junkie killer and a lawyer who he once called his lover.

Luke Gannon had long ago lost his soul. According to his wife he'd fallen down a terrifying abyss of addiction. Taking meth to supercharge his already violent sexual desires and using his money and reach to ensure he remained utterly untouched by his terrible actions.

Bea Wallace was altogether different. The lead into James's killer was nothing more than a red herring to keep him on the hook. But when that had backfired she'd tossed Malton to the wolves. Luke Gannon turning up needing a fall guy was just good timing. Malton knew that if it wasn't Gannon then Bea would have found some other ingenious way to make sure he was out of the way for good. Between her criminal contacts and her legal ruthlessness Bea Wallace was one of the most dangerous people he'd ever met. Malton had grown up somewhere that constantly dragged people under. He knew that most criminals were simply people who'd taken a bad path. People who started the game with rigged odds. If your family are all in it and they bring you up to despise weakness and to take what you want by force then how on earth do you become any different?

Malton had only ever met a handful of people who had been born in the light and had chosen to walk into the dark. Most of them, like Luke Gannon, came to regret that decision. Malton would make sure that someday soon so too would Bea Wallace.

But today was all about Gannon and while Malton was still a fugitive, the most he could do was sit and wait.

He wore headphones that connected to a tiny, in-ear receiver on the other end of the line. On the bed beside him were two rolls of duct tape, a bag of zip ties and a brand-new, stainless-steel hatchet. That was everything Malton would need.

The only thing left undecided was what happened to Luke Gannon.

In all his time playing policeman, judge and jury to the underworld, Malton had never once taken on the final role of executioner. Malton was there to mediate, to investigate and to drag the truth out from under whatever rock it was hiding.

As soon as he killed someone then there was nothing to separate him from the criminals he had worked so hard to rise above.

Luke Gannon felt different. He had tried to destroy Malton. He had killed at least eight young men, almost certainly more. He had crossed a line a long time ago.

If Malton was still alive by the time this day was over then he'd have to find out whether or not he would be joining Gannon on the other side of that line.

In the meantime, all he could do was sit and listen to the sounds coming from the headset as he waited for Luke to arrive.

81

Affleck's Palace was the last place in Manchester Dean would have chosen to set up the sting.

A true Mancunian one-off, Affleck's, as it was locally known, was a large, former department store a short walk from Piccadilly Gardens, in the heart of Manchester. Ranging over four floors, the store had been subdivided into a thriving indoor market comprising dozens of small independent shops.

From vintage clothing to handmade cosmetics, second-hand records to collectible action figures, there was nothing you couldn't get at Affleck's. All four of its floors were always crammed full of customers. Students, goths, punks, second-hand dealers and the just plain curious all jostled for space among the tiny shops.

The smell of joss sticks and sometimes more always hung in the air while dozens of different, small sound systems merged with the shoppers' voices to fill the building with a constant, benign white noise.

Stepping into Affleck's felt like a brief glimpse into how Manchester once was. A scruffy, innovative culture thriving in the ruins of its former glory days. A world away from the gleaming skyscrapers and giant flagship stores that now filled Manchester city centre. Affleck's had survived bombings and recessions and was still very much the same as it ever was.

For teenagers in Manchester their first trip to Affleck's was a rite of passage.

Now it was to serve as the backdrop to Luke Gannon's final act.

The problems were immense.

Dean had half a dozen men from Malton Security. The names he could trust. That morning they'd all met him in the canteen, having been rostered on a morning shift. They were the hardcore. The ones who had been shot at, beaten up or worse. Men who had given as good as they got and knew that, as long as Craig Malton was running Malton Security, someone had their back. They looked like what they were – dangerous men. Muscle packed over brutal genetics. The steady, unflappable faces of men who'd spent their entire lives surrounded by violence and through their own strength had stood in the middle of the storm.

This was who Malton had handpicked.

Of course, Dean hadn't mentioned Malton's name. On Malton's insistence Dean had to operate with absolute plausible deniability. Whatever the case, Dean knew full well that what he was doing now was aiding an escaped prisoner. This is what Priestly had been warning him about.

If anything went wrong today then that would be the end of everything. Not just Malton and Malton Security but Dean too. He'd never work in security again and he'd very possibly be joining Malton behind bars.

The thought gave him an extra spring in his step. Nothing would go wrong. He'd make sure of it.

Three sides of Affleck's faced onto the street, with the fourth side butting right up against another four-storey building. There was a narrow alleyway between the buildings that ended in a small door that led underground to a bar filled with arcade machines.

Every side of Affleck's had an entrance. The entrance on Oldham Street was the main entrance, a covered parade of shops that led to a staircase up to the first floor. Round the corner the entrance was much smaller, a single door that led onto the ground floor as well as to a staircase that carried on up to the very top of the building.

There was a door on the corner of the alley that too led to the ground floor, opening straight into a large shop filled with goth and anime fashion, as well as leading to a second, steeper stair-case that also led right to the top, going past each floor in turn.

Further down the alley were a couple more fire doors. Far too many ways to escape.

Dean had put a man across the road from each of these entrances and told them to remain unseen. As desperate as Luke Gannon was, there was every chance he wouldn't walk into an obvious trap. Dean needed to let Luke at least feel he had the upper hand. Right up until he didn't.

Two of the men were parked a little way down from the alley. Their job would be to take delivery of Luke Gannon and drive him a couple of streets over to where Malton was waiting in the van.

Once Luke had entered Affleck's it would be a case of wait-ing until he emerged, at which point he would be grabbed by whichever man was on the door he came out from. That man would use the element of surprise to march Luke at speed to the car. If he made a scene then each of them was more than capa-ble of moving a man Luke's size. Keeping his head down and his mouth shut. It would be messy but that couldn't be helped.

Once in the car, Luke would be put in the back with a man either side of him and restrained while the driver moved quickly and safely to the back street where all three of them would move Luke to the back of the van. Once in the van one of the men would drive while Malton stayed with Luke in the back. The other two would disappear.

That just left the final man. He would be waiting, hidden in the cubicles of the toilets in the café on the very top floor of Affleck's Palace.

The café that was the only place in Manchester where Ruth would agree to meet Gannon.

She was sat there now. Waiting for the most important meeting of her life.

Dean was on the Oldham Street side of Affleck's Palace, opposite the main entrance, when his headset crackled to life.

'Corner entrance. It's Gannon. He's inside.'

82

The man across the table from Ruth couldn't have looked more out of place if he had two heads.

At the very top of Affleck's Palace, tucked away in one corner of the uppermost floor, was the kind of café that no longer existed. There was no theme, there was no hook, there was only what you'd expect to find in a café somewhere like Affleck's Palace. Cooked breakfasts and milkshakes. Cakes and coffee and sandwiches. Café food. The food wasn't the point. The place meant everything. One of the final holdouts of whatever was left of alternative Manchester. For those who had braved every floor of Affleck's it was a hidden refuge with what were once views out towards Affleck's straighter, more corporate twin – the Arndale Centre.

Now that view was blocked with the inevitable flats.

Two dated arcade machines guarded the entrance and inside, amongst the smells of fried food and sugar, Ruth felt safe.

Or at least she had until Luke Gannon had walked in and sat down opposite her.

He was dressed in a loose, lime green double-breasted suit with a scoop-neck T-shirt beneath, revealing his toned chest. His skin was even more tanned in person. Immaculate. Ruth couldn't help but notice how clean it was. Scrubbed and shaved and neat. His hair was grey, but short and fashionably cut. So tidy that it was as if he had only just emerged from the barber's. It was only the face that let it down.

The lines around the eyes, the skin so thin that the light from the windows of the café almost went straight through it.

From the minute he sat down, his eyes, red and watery, had never left Ruth's. They sparkled in a way that, despite herself, Ruth found mesmeric. And when he spoke it was as if they were old friends.

Ruth was expecting to meet the devil and, in a way, she had.

'You are one hell of a journalist,' said Luke, sitting back looking proud. 'I could have done with someone like you doing my press back in the day.'

Ruth said nothing. This wasn't what she had prepared for. She was ready to be brave, to resist. Not to be charmed.

Luke leaned in and took a quick look around. 'Love this place. Great choice. It's ages since I've been here. You got good taste.'

He smiled and in an instant the spell was broken by the fetid wreck of his mouth. Gums black and grey, shrinking away from filthy, rotten teeth. Luke Gannon's mouth was like a window on his soul.

'Did you kill Damion?' asked Ruth calmly.

Luke laughed and looked around theatrically as if to demonstrate to an unseen audience his delight at this line of questioning.

'I've never killed anyone,' he said, his voice floating the proposition.

Ruth thought she saw his sparkle flicker for a second. But only a second.

'But now you have something I want,' said Luke. 'A phone.'

Ruth held firm. 'And what happens when I give it you?'

Luke shrugged. 'I walk out of here and you never see me again. Of course, I'd like to know that you don't have the same mad ideas as your late friend Damion.'

Luke breathed in and Ruth heard his lungs rattle. The money and the gym had held Luke Gannon's lifestyle at bay, but inside it was all catching up to him.

'Manchester,' said Luke, looking out the window. 'It's changing. Getting bigger, taller. Lots of things you could fall off.'

He laughed and sounded like a delighted child. He wasn't performing for Ruth anymore; now he was indulging his own twisted internal pleasure.

'I'm bored now,' he said suddenly.

Ruth felt the tide turning.

'Where's Malton? I saw a couple of his goons trying to look inconspicuous outside. I'm guessing he's covered all the exits?'

Ruth said nothing but she felt her face giving her away.

'Has he stuck a couple in here too?'

Luke looked to the toilets and back to Ruth.

'Is he in there? Classic Malton. So here I am just walking into his trap. Like a fucking idiot.'

Luke scowled and finally his face made sense. Ruth saw the expression that Jake must have seen just before he died. The look that had greeted God knows how many young men.

He lowered his voice and spoke in a feral hiss. 'I'm not here to fuck around. I'm here to get that phone and then I'm going to walk out of here and maybe your dad's pub won't get burned down. Maybe you won't get scooped up one night and found beaten and raped on some towpath. Maybe Craig Malton might even have the fucking common sense to fuck off out of Manchester before the police catch up with him and he spends the rest of his life in prison for murdering that poor young rent boy.'

Gannon was shaking with rage. Little trails of spittle came from the corners of his mouth and lay on his immaculately tended skin as if something dark was trying to crawl up from inside him and escape into the light.

Ruth tried to look away but she couldn't. She was caught in his stare. His manic energy holding her firm to the spot.

All she could say was: 'I still have the phone.'

Gannon spat on the floor in disgust and said, 'Give me that fucking earpiece. I'm done speaking to the monkey; I want the organ grinder.'

He leaned over and, before Ruth could stop him, reached beneath her hair and snatched out the earpiece that Malton had given her.

Luke kept his eyes trained on Ruth as he held the earpiece to his mouth and began to speak.

'Listen, Malton, let me tell you why I'm walking out of here with my phone.'

83

A voice Malton knew all too well filled his headphones as he sat alone in the back of the van.

It was whispered, low and harsh but with an unmistakable certainty.

'Who the fuck do you think you are?' said Luke Gannon in his headphones. 'A fucking jumped-up bouncer who thinks he can tell me what I can and can't do? How dare you?'

Malton said nothing. He felt the fluid around his heart pressing in. He tensed every muscle in his body, straining to stay awake. In a few hours' time he could lie down and die, but right now he was needed.

'You fucking imbecile. I've seen your men outside. You think I'd just walk into your fucking trap? You know what I learned from running all those clubs? That criminals are thick as fuck. The dealers who tried to lean on me? The ones who wanted to leech off my success? Well now they're all dead or in prison. And I'm doing what they could only dream of. That's what people like you never understand. It's all a business. It's about money. If you can make money then everything else is bullshit.'

Malton gripped the single bed he was sitting on. His eyes fell on the as-yet-unused steel hatchet. It gave him clarity.

'I know you're there. And I know you can hear me,' continued Gannon. 'Now I want you to tell this little bitch to give me my phone and then I'm going to walk out of here and no one is going to even look at me funny or else you know what happens?'

Malton held his breath.

'I asked you a question, you fucking moron.'

'What happens?' said Malton quietly into his headset. Every single word hurt.

'I'm glad you asked,' said Gannon. 'If I don't get what I want, then after I've had your girlfriend's family murdered. I'm going to have her beaten so badly that you won't be able to tell her from fucking meat. Then I get nasty.'

Malton felt his chest becoming unbearably tight. He bent forward, fumbling for the drain as dark red fluid leaked out of the tube, spilling onto the floor of the van.

With his last breath he picked up the walkie-talkie that went straight to Dean, squeezed out, 'Stand down,' and then everything . . .

84

Keisha felt both barrels pressing into her back. The bearded man Craig had told her was called Wormall had taken her by surprise, shattering the passenger-side window with the butt of his gun and getting the drop on her. He'd take her weapon and now both guns were trained on her as she crossed the road through the rain. Every step taking her a little closer to Rachel's front door.

Rain ran down her face, with her hands behind her head she could only blink and splutter as it filled her mouth and eyes. She could taste her conditioner, orange and sweet, melting off her hair and into her mouth. But she dared not make any move lest the guns at her back fired and left her to die in the street.

She hadn't been quick enough. When Malton suggested his plan she had insisted that, whatever his part, she would be here watching Rachel.

Back in the caravan when Rachel had talked about their father it was as if she was describing Keisha. A man constantly on the move. At once charming and ruthless. But, while her father had never managed to pull his talents together, Keisha had taken his genetic inheritance and perfected what he couldn't. She came out on top and knowing that made her wish her dad was still alive so that she could tell him. She wanted him to be proud.

All at once the unceasing upward direction of her life made total sense. She was her father's daughter.

She promised herself she wouldn't die here.

They stopped at the front garden wall of Rachel's terrace. It was less a garden and more a strip of land little wider than a wheelie bin. A small barrier between the front window and the street outside.

She felt the bristles of Wormall's beard against her neck as he leaned in to speak to her. Shouting over the rain.

'You ring the bell and as soon as the door opens you move inside. I'll be right behind you. You try anything and I shoot all three of you here and now.'

His voice was flat with just a trace of what was left of a Welsh accent.

'This was Gannon's plan?' said Keisha. 'Get you to kill women and children?'

'This is what he pays me for,' came the deadened voice from behind her head. 'Now please ring the bell.'

Keisha stepped through the front gate and stood on the doorstep. She was soaked through, her clothes heavy with rain. But as she rang the bell her heart was beating so fast it felt like she was about to lift off from the ground.

The guns pressed into her back as, behind the door, locks were being undone.

Keisha took a small step forward, so she was right up to the door. She felt the gun barrels follow her and the bearded man take a step to keep close behind.

And then the door flew open.

Keisha seized the split second she had and dropped down moments before Carl Farr's giant fist sailed over her head and straight into Wormall's face.

Keisha dived sideways into Rachel's front garden as, before Gannon's goon could raise his guns, Carl Farr was on him, pulling Wormall close to him, wrapping those huge arms around him, pinning both guns harmlessly downwards.

Carl's outsized head shot forward and smashed into the dazed face of the bearded man before he took a step backwards and dragged him into the house.

Keisha looked up from where she'd landed and saw Janet Farr looking down at her.

'Don't do it in the house,' said Keisha.

Janet gave a small nod and shut the door behind her.

Several miles away in Trafford, Rachel and Allie were enjoying their morning at a trampoline park. Auntie Keisha's treat.

85

Ruth was still shaking five minutes after Luke Gannon had stood up and walked out of the café at the top of Affleck's Palace.

He had the phone.

Over the headset she'd heard Malton give the order to stand down. She'd seen the mountain-sized man emerge from the toilets and without a backward glance head out of the café, leaving her alone with Gannon.

Whatever had happened, all Dean and Malton's promises had, in that moment, evaporated. She was sat opposite the devil holding only a single card. Jake's phone.

Coldly, mechanically, she'd taken out the phone and handed it over. Watched the look of glee spread over Gannon's face as he pocketed his prize before pulling out a stainless-steel vape and taking a huge breath full of smoke that gave off a sickly sweet smell Ruth couldn't quite place.

She could barely remember what he'd said as he rose to leave. It didn't matter. Without the phone she had nothing. Gannon had outmanoeuvred Malton so what chance did she have against him?

Then it struck her. She was a journalist. She only had one chance. The truth.

The only weapon she had against Luke Gannon was the story of Luke Gannon. The dead boys and the debauchery. How one of the men who built Manchester's nightlife was consumed by it.

If Luke Gannon was going to kill her then at least he would kill her doing the job she loved.

This whole set-up had been a mistake. It was on Malton's terms. This was about springing a trap on Gannon. Ending his life. That wasn't Ruth's world. Ruth wanted Gannon alive to see the truth being built up brick by brick. She wanted to peel back his rotting façade and let the light in.

She remembered the late nights when she'd found her dad awake. Sat downstairs with his notes and a glass of whisky. She'd known even then that he was scared by the work he was doing. Now she understood why he kept going. It wasn't bravery. Nothing like that. He was a journalist and that meant to do anything else was physically impossible. It was the truth or nothing.

Ruth rose from her chair and started off in the direction Gannon had left.

One way or another she was going to get some answers.

86

Dean gripped his walkie-talkie and watched as Luke Gannon walked out of Affleck's Palace and into the rain. Gannon threw up an umbrella and took off towards Stevenson Square.

Across the road a Malton Security guard watched Dean shake his head. Malton had given the order. Stand down.

Something had gone badly wrong. Luke Gannon had the upper hand.

As Gannon crossed Oldham Street, Dean stood waiting for the next instruction from Malton. An instruction that never came. Into his walkie-talkie he hissed, 'Hold your positions. Do not approach Gannon. I repeat, Gannon is to be left loose.'

Then he holstered his walkie-talkie and, keeping a good distance between him and Gannon, he started off after him.

Gannon was headed up Dale Street towards Piccadilly Station. This part of town was home to dozens of Victorian warehouses, now used as flats and businesses. For every road there was a back alley, smaller roads that wound between the old buildings revealing hidden courtyards and discreetly placed doorways. A thousand different places to hide.

Gannon sailed past the hoardings behind which a cluster of giant, mature trees had been allowed to grow to the height of several storeys. A strange anomaly so close to the heart of the city.

Dean was far enough back to see Gannon turn right and dart down a narrow side street. There was no way he could follow Gannon down there and not be seen. Betting that Gannon would continue away from town as Dean passed the entrance to the alley where Gannon had turned, he broke into a run. If he could get ahead of Gannon then maybe he could get the drop on him in the back alleys.

Dean had no idea what had happened. As far as he knew, Malton was still waiting in the van parked up towards the inner ring road. Dean was currently walking away from the van. He'd already left behind all the men he'd brought with him from Malton Security. He was alone.

Worse than that, deprived of contact with Malton he had no idea what Gannon had said or done to walk out of Affleck's untouched. Something had gone badly wrong and until Dean knew what it was he couldn't risk letting Gannon know he was in pursuit, much less try and apprehend him.

Still running, Dean turned right and nearly lost his footing on the wet pavement. With no time to fall he let his momentum keep him upright as he drew level with the other end of the alley down which Gannon had vanished.

The alley was empty. Somehow Gannon had got away.

Out of breath, Dean stumbled into the alley. Buildings rose up on either side of him, funnelling the rain down in a concentrated shower. Wet, mouldering brick and Victorian metal fire escapes. It was no coincidence that Hollywood used these back alleys when filming scenes in 1920s New York. There was a strange smell in the alley. Sickly sweet, like candy gone bad.

As the rain fell around him Dean felt the phone in his pocket vibrate. Still stood in the middle of the alley, he pulled it out. It was the burner phone that connected him to Keisha.

'What happened to Malton?' he whispered frantically as he neared the bottom of the alley where he'd seen Luke pass by.

'Have you got him?' said Keisha urgently.

'Malton said to stand down,' said Dean, keeping an eye on the bottom of the alley.

'And then he told you it was back on,' said Keisha on the other end with a hint of nerves in her voice.

Dean's head spun. Something had gone wrong. Just not the thing he thought. 'No, he said stand down, then went silent.'

For a moment there was nothing on the other end of the line. Gannon still hadn't appeared at the end of the alley. Maybe he'd doubled back on himself.

'Malton didn't tell you the full plan,' said Keisha, breath-less. 'He would get you to back down, make the girl think it was a done deal and give Gannon the phone. Then when Gannon was on his way out he'd tell you it was back on. No way Gannon was leaving without the phone and he couldn't risk that reporter not giving it him.'

Dean stared down at the phone in his hand. His brain racing to catch up. Malton had hedged his bets. Made sure that only he knew the full story. But something had gone badly wrong and now Gannon was free.

'Wherever Gannon is,' shouted Keisha, frantic now, 'he's on his own.'

There was that smell again. Sweet and rotten. Stronger this time. And white smoke, floating into the air from somewhere behind him.

As Dean spun round he felt an exploding pain in his arm and the sound of something breaking. He stumbled backwards in agony to see, there amongst the bin bags and broken-down boxes, Luke Gannon facing him, his umbrella discarded on the ground, a vape pen in one hand, an extendable baton in the other.

'It's like Malton wants her dead,' cackled Gannon, sucking on the vape.

The smoke smelled soft and sweet and Gannon's whole body moved as he inhaled it into his lungs.

Dean's arm was in agony. He knew straight away it was bro-ken. Still, he remembered Keisha's call. *He's on his own.*

'Fuck off then,' said Gannon. 'Or I kill the girl.'

Dean held fast. 'It's over. She's safe,' he said, still unsure exactly which girl Gannon was talking about. Malton had dropped the ball. It was up to him now. He'd given up so much to be here, on the ground in agony in the rain, facing down a deranged killer. He had to make this moment count.

327

Gannon stared down listlessly. The rain was drenching him through, his suit clinging to his body.

'Oh fuck,' he muttered to himself, dropped the vape and pulled out a small gun.

Dean was already closing the gap. He only had the one arm but it would have to be enough. His good hand shot out and grabbed at Luke's wrist. Luke was stronger than he looked but Dean had fear on his side. The gun flew up and Luke fired into the air, the bullet ricocheting off a metal fire escape somewhere above their heads.

Dean wasn't finished. He kept hold of the arm and twisted it round behind Gannon who let out a shriek of pain. There was no time for measured restraint.

With his free arm Gannon brought his baton down on Dean's leg, catching him on the side of the knee. Dean felt the knee buckle. His feet slipped in the sodden slime of the alleyway.

Gannon was constantly moving. Like an animal caught in a trap, he squirmed this way and that. Dean felt himself losing his grip on Gannon's wrist just as Luke stepped in front of him and performed an immaculate trip that unbalanced Dean, sending him crashing to the ground.

Gannon howled with glee. He tossed the baton away and ran a hand through his wet hair. His eyes were pinpricks, his mouth a cackling maw.

Through the rain Dean saw him raise the gun. For a moment Dean thought how odd it was that he didn't flinch away. He wasn't scared. Sure, he didn't want to die, but somehow with the idea of his inevitable death, suddenly everything was calm and easy.

He wondered if this is how it felt to be Malton.

THUD.

Not a gun, a duller, wetter sound. And Luke Gannon falling to the ground onto the filthy alley floor.

Stood there behind him was Ruth Porter, half a brick in her hand and a look of grim determination on her face.

87

'You awake?'

Malton opened his eyes to see a filthy, bedraggled Luke Gannon sat on the floor of the van, his hands behind his back. His green suit was smeared with damp brown stains, which merged around his lapels with the still-wet blood from a fresh head wound. His silver hair matted with gore.

Despite all this, Gannon was grinning, his rotten mouth wide with mirth.

Malton sat up on the narrow single bed and very nearly collapsed straight back down. His head felt light and his mouth dry.

His first thought – the plan! Having met her he knew there was no way Ruth would give up the phone unless she thought she had no other choice. If she really believed Gannon had the upper hand and that Malton had failed to protect her then what other choice did she have? And to make her believe that, he had to make Gannon believe it too. Let Gannon hear him give his men the order to stand down but then before Gannon left Affleck's, carrying the phone, give the command to step back up.

But he'd passed out before he had the chance to close the trap. So how was Gannon lying bound and beaten in the back of his van?

'You look as bad as I feel.' Gannon laughed. 'Or is it the other way around?'

The van was moving and Gannon clocked Malton noticing the motion of the vehicle.

'Big, tall guy at the wheel. Polish maybe? Doesn't say much. Found you passed out on the floor of the van. You should have seen your boy. Beside himself. It was like you'd died. That's the key to a successful business. Good employee loyalty.'

Malton tried to breathe but the air in the back of the van was thick and stale. Gannon smelled of wet sewage and blood.

He'd fucked up. But Dean had somehow made it good. He'd never doubt the boy again.

'Well that was fun, wasn't it?' said Gannon. 'You had a plan; I had a plan. Seems like you just edged it.'

Malton lifted one hand and realised his trousers were wet with blood from his wound. His head swam. Something inside him felt like it was slipping away.

'If I were you, I'd have stayed in that hospital,' said Gannon. 'But then we wouldn't be here if you did that, would we?'

The van swung to one side and for a moment both Malton and Gannon slid along with it before it straightened up and continued driving.

Malton closed his eyes tight and focused. He thought about Strangeways and Connor and James. He thought about Keisha telling him about their son Anthony. The boy who was born and died on the same night, and then his thoughts took flight and began to cascade. He saw faces. The dead and the dying. The guilty and the innocent. People he'd met over the past few decades. Some bad, some worse. All of them passed through on his way forward. To where? To here? Trapped with a crazed, sadistic murderer? To die here on the floor? Or wherever it was they were ultimately headed?

His eyes snapped open. It had been less than a second but his mental audit was complete and the world reduced down to the size of the back of a van. With its steely chill and damp stench of blood.

'You killed Stephen Page,' said Malton.

Gannon smiled and said, 'Yeah. I got a problem. Hard to run a club and not bump into drugs. Hard to say no, isn't it? You ever tried meth?'

Malton said nothing.

'I know, I know,' said Gannon. 'What if I called it chems? That make it any better? I know you like the boys as well as the girls. You never spent a weekend off your face with some nice young men and some crystal?'

Malton didn't even smile.

'You're no fun, Malton.'

'You used to be someone,' said Malton.

Gannon shrugged. 'I'd say I still am. I do whatever I want. And sometimes, just sometimes, I want to take a nice young man somewhere private and fuck him and kill him. And I know, before you say it. It's not guilt or self-loathing.'

Gannon shook his head.

'It's 'cos it's fun. That's what money does for you. You try all the usual things. And then you try the unusual things. Fuck me, I know how I sound. But you should try it. Just once. It's like the world is moving a million miles an hour and every single atom in the air is singing to you and you close your eyes and fall into it and you don't ever want it to stop. Thank God for Wormall, there to tidy up afterwards. Scatter the bodies, change up the causes of death. He's been invaluable. Ex-para. Done some fucking dark shit. I imagine working for me is something of a relief.' Gannon burst out laughing.

'Wormall's gone,' said Malton.

Luke looked unsurprised. 'I figured as much when your boy started following me. RIP Wormall. I remember back when you were my security, you always could see five moves ahead. You remember those days, don't you? Back when Martyrdom was the biggest thing this city had ever seen. They called me the next Tony Wilson. Only difference, I made money.' Gannon fell back into his deranged laughter.

'Why did you frame me?'

Gannon stopped laughing. 'You think I picked you? I told her this would happen. Said, pick someone else. Anyone but him. But she was adamant that it had to be you.'

'Who?' Malton already knew but he needed to hear it from Gannon's rotting mouth.

Gannon looked pleased with himself. Savouring the moment. 'Your friend and mine, Bea Wallace.'

Bea Wallace had been Malton's ticket into the above world. The respectable sunlit bars and restaurants of Manchester where the clean money was flaunted and the overt power was flexed. Malton could turn Manchester any way he wanted if he so chose but up until he'd got together with Bea those rooms had been closed off to someone like him.

Because being accepted by those people was his greatest desire and his greatest weakness, he'd let Bea get way too close. Get inside him and use him. She'd seen him coming.

'Maybe you're more live-and-let-live than I am,' said Gannon. 'But if I were you I'd maybe want a word with Bea Wallace. Now that's something I could help you with.'

The van stopped moving.

'Cos you and me, we got history,' said Gannon. His tone just a touch more urgent.

Malton marvelled. Even now, Gannon thought he could talk his way out of this. He had been wrong. Framing him hadn't been Bea's original plan, but in Luke Gannon she'd seen the chance to box Malton away for good and, just like that, she'd taken it.

'Before those doors open and this situation runs away from you,' said Gannon, 'right here, right now, we can fix this. Us two. The smartest guys in the room. I just want you to know, none of this was personal.'

The back doors opened and light flooded the van. They were in a large warehouse space. Bare concrete floors and the deafening hammering of rain on asbestos sheet roofing. A deep chill hung over everything.

Keisha stood framed in the van doors wearing a black rain poncho, silhouetted by the headlights behind her.

'Killing my dad,' she said. 'I call that pretty fucking personal.'

88

'You should go to hospital with that,' said Ruth in the back of the Uber.

Beside her Dean was clutching his arm and wincing with every pothole.

He hadn't told her where they were headed, but she'd insisted on coming with him. Now, as their Uber came down off the Mancunian Way and headed west towards Old Trafford, she was beginning to wonder where exactly they *were* going.

'Everything you said would happen happened,' said Ruth.

Dean looked up, grimacing with pain. Every inch of him was daubed in the filth from the alley floor. Rotten food, mud, rain and shit. He was beginning to smell but neither of them cared.

'I'm not going to say I told you so,' he said. 'But this world, it's dangerous.'

'You're still here,' said Ruth.

She saw Dean think for a moment as the cab shot past an out-of-town shopping centre, cutting through the rain as it hit sixty miles an hour.

'This is what I do,' he said finally.

'Get beaten up by meth heads in back alleys?' said Ruth playfully. 'That was the plan?'

She was flying. The cold fear she'd felt after Gannon had left her in Affleck's was long gone. The sudden sense of purpose, the last-minute chase. Catching sight of Dean following Gannon and then looping round to get the drop on him. In her head she was armed with a barrage of difficult questions for

Gannon – why are you on Jake's phone? What's your connection to Stephen Page? Do you know Martin Farr?

In the end she was armed with half a brick. She'd seen Luke put Dean down and draw his gun. She acted in the moment. No sooner had the brick hit Luke's head than the reality of what she was doing hit her.

Luckily it was a reality that Dean was more than used to. Before she could even process what she'd done he was on his feet shouting into a walkie-talkie and in what seemed like seconds several large men appeared along with a black Transit van. When the van doors opened they had found Malton lying unconscious on the floor of the van.

While Ruth panicked, the men jumped into action as if this is what they'd been training for their whole lives. Between them they tied up Gannon while a couple of them performed CPR on Malton.

There in the filthy back alley, in the driving Mancunian rain, she'd seen a miracle. Craig Malton return to life, coughing, shaking, and growling in pain. But alive.

The men didn't stop to savour the moment. Malton was laid out on a bed in the van, Gannon was put in on the floor next to him, the doors shut and the largest of the men got in the van and drove away.

Next thing she knew they had simply melted away. It was just her and Dean.

'When I started this,' said Dean, 'I don't think I understood it. I thought it would be like playing detective. Finding things out, following clues.'

'Like being a journalist,' said Ruth firmly.

'But then I realised, Malton's world, it's not like that. When you work with drug dealers and killers – people who don't operate like normal people – you have to start thinking like they do. Doing the things that they do.'

'Killing people?'

'No,' said Dean quickly. 'I mean, the longer you spend with the darkness, the longer the darkness spends with you. Some people can't do that. That makes sense. This isn't how anyone should live. But some people, this is what we were born to do.'

Dean finished his speech. There was a gleam in his eyes. He looked as noble as a person can look when they're smeared in alley filth and blood.

The cab had turned off towards Sale. Out of the window the houses began to pile up and more and more trees lined the roads.

'That's me,' said Ruth defiantly. 'I always saw my dad working on a story and I wanted to be like him. I don't think I ever really knew why. 'Cos I loved him obviously and he was my dad and I looked up to him and wanted to be just like him. But now I know what it was underneath it all. He chose to be in that darkness because if he didn't then no one would see what it was hiding. And it scared the hell out of him but he did it anyway. That's what I want to be.'

The Uber turned into a pretty street of detached Victorian houses and pulled up.

'I'm going to write this story,' said Ruth. Before Dean could speak she carried on, 'I'm going to leave you out and Malton. I can do it without you. Besides, why would I burn two amazing sources?'

She hopped out of the car into the rain and ran round to Dean's side. She opened up the door and Dean struggled out, doing his best not to bash his broken arm.

They stood for a moment in the rain. Under all the filth and bravado she was amazed how young Dean looked.

'Are you going to be OK?' she asked.

As if on cue, the door to the nearest house opened and an older Asian man waved frantically for Dean to come in.

'Don't worry. He's a doctor. Malton Security health plan,' said Dean with a smile. 'You did well today. You saved my life.' Before she could answer him he had turned away and was heading inside.

Ruth watched the older man usher Dean inside and then she got back in the Uber.

'Where to?' asked the driver.

'Home,' said Ruth without thinking.

'Where's that?'

She barely had to think before she said, 'Manchester.'

89

Luke Gannon was on his knees on the concrete. The first blow he'd taken from Carl Farr had loosened a few teeth and now his mouth wept blood. But still he seemed unbowed.

Keisha had seen this before. Gannon was deep into his drug addiction. By this point she doubted he even felt the high anymore. Instead the meth had simply scooped out the middle. Left him a blank, dead shell. While this would have broken most addicts, Luke Gannon had something most addicts didn't. Millions and millions of pounds. His money, boosted by his drug dealing, had not only insulated him from the fall, it had emboldened him. Luke Gannon's humanity was long gone; all that was left was monstrous ego.

'I never killed your dad,' he said, looking up at Keisha. 'Take off those shades and look me in the eye.'

Keisha reached up and took the shades away from her face. Gannon smiled at his little victory.

She was stood in a small pool of water. The rain dripping off her and puddling on the hard concrete.

'You can see I'm telling the truth. It was Martin Farr who killed your dad. Well, technically Wormall, but you dealt with him already. You see? We're square.'

Gannon started to cough and shake. A stuttering wet rattle rose out of him, growing solid and viscous until he spat out a mouthful of blood, phlegm and teeth.

'Been meaning to get some dentist work done,' said Gannon.

'You killed my Marie's Martin.'

Janet Farr stepped out of the light and came into focus beside Keisha.

Gannon seemed unsurprised to see her.

'You should be thanking me,' spat Gannon. 'He robbed from you and was doing everything he could to lie and cover it up. If it wasn't for me you wouldn't even know about it. This is the game. Or now Mickey's banged up, have you gone soft?'

'It's not a fucking game,' said Janet, and threw a scrap of paper on the floor in front of Gannon.

'What's that supposed to be?' said Luke.

'I found it in my dad's caravan,' said Keisha. 'I don't know where he got it from but that's Martin's handwriting. Instructions for Sam Kennard of how to rob Harold Boateng. Your courier.'

'Like I said, it was Martin. And I dealt with him for you.'

'Look at it,' said Janet. 'It tells Sam about the hidden compartment, the amount of drugs to expect. And it tells him Harold's route and times. Martin didn't know the routes and times. Even I didn't know that. That was between you and him. That was the whole point of Harold. He was the buffer between us and you.'

'Oh shit,' said Luke softly with a smirk.

'The only person who knew Harold's movements was you. Somehow you passed that information on to Martin. You set him up.'

'You needed someone to come forward and grass on Craig,' said Keisha. 'So you got Martin all twisted up and then he would do whatever you wanted.'

Luke looked down at the paper and shook his head.

'I told Bea to pick someone else.' Gannon turned to the van where Malton was sat watching this unfold. 'But she had such a hard-on for it being you. Anyone else and this would have worked a treat.'

He turned to glare at Janet.

'Your precious Martin was already trying to work out how to rob you.'

Janet shook her head. Gannon laughed.

'You don't believe me? Unlike you, I like to keep an eye on my investment. Wormall monitored every step, my end and yours. So this exact sort of shit doesn't happen. He reported back that Martin Farr was sniffing round. Trying to track the courier back. Work out his routes. Bad news for him, Harold knew what he was doing. Knew how to lose a tail.'

'Fucking Martin,' muttered Janet.

'So you told Martin what he needed to know?' said Keisha.

Gannon shrugged. 'I might have "accidentally" slipped some information in a shipment of tyres. Somewhere Martin might come across it. What he did with that information was up to him.'

'But why Martin?' asked Janet.

'Simple,' said Keisha. 'You want an informant to lie for you? You pay him. Someone pays him more and now he's changing his story. You threaten him. Someone tells him they can protect him and now he's pointing straight at you. Bea's no fool. She knew she'd need an informant who really believed that lying to the police was in his own best interests.'

Gannon turned back to the van where Malton sat watching. 'You want to give this one a job.'

Keisha's hand shot out. A fist crashed into Gannon's face sending him tumbling to the ground. He shot back up a look of furious indignation.

'None of this was my idea. This was Bea Wallace. She insisted it was Malton we framed.' He turned to the van. 'You hear that? Your crazy ex-girlfriend set all this up. Chose you. It was her who gave the orders. Got Martin killed, got Harold killed. About to get me fucking killed. And for what?'

Keisha looked to Craig but from his face she could see he was just as baffled as she was. Both of them had underestimated the lengths Bea would go to in keeping her hands clean.

'So come on, what is killing me going to achieve?' said Gannon, looking from Keisha to Janet to Malton. Blood was weeping from his mouth, staining his suit lapels.

'It's going to make me feel better,' said Janet Farr coldly.

At that moment Carl Farr stepped into the light and suddenly all hope left Luke Gannon's face.

'Malton,' he called back into the van. 'Are you happy with this? You going to let this happen? What about all that shit about not getting involved? You kill me then what the fuck is the difference between you and all the other thugs out there? A fancy company logo and a credo that means fuck all?'

'Stop.'

Craig's voice came from the back of the van. The voice Keisha remembered. Deep and calm and commanding.

Out of the van stepped Craig. Slowly but solidly.

Gannon sighed impatiently. 'Finally, someone who I can talk to. OK, I'm sorry, I should have insisted that Bea pick someone else. But you of all people know just how persuasive she can be.'

Keisha held her tongue.

She felt the air around them growing thick and cold. Craig was doing his thing. Imposing himself on the situation with sheer physical will. Through injury and doubt and betrayal he hadn't changed. He was still the brilliant, mercurial prospect she'd met that day outside the youth club down in Moss Side.

'It's over,' he said.

'It's never over,' said Luke. 'I'll tell you why. Ten million pounds. Cash. Split however you want. Martin's dead. That's the case against you dead. The DNA? That doesn't mean a thing. You get to walk. And you,' he said, turning to Janet Farr, 'we pick right back up. You were one of my best customers. Why go through the hassle of throwing it all away for a little shit like Martin? And what's more, you get your share of that ten million.'

Keisha looked from Malton to Janet to Carl. She put her sunglasses back on. Craig was right. It was over. Everyone except Gannon knew it.

'Take him to the pit,' said Janet.

'What?' screamed Gannon as Carl half carried half dragged him across the concrete floor.

'You fucking idiots. You have any idea what happens if you kill me? The people I work for? You think I'm the top of the chain. You're going to cost people much bigger than me. People who aren't nice like I am.'

'When that happens,' said Keisha, following behind, 'I'll tell them you said you were very sorry.'

Carl stopped at the edge of what was once an inspection pit. A steep concrete grave. Next to the edge of the pit was a plastic jerry can.

Carl held Luke up so that he could see what was lying in the pit. The broken body of Wormall. Very definitely dead.

Finally Gannon's courage left him.

A hollow shriek burst forth from him. 'Nooooooooo!' High-pitched and self-pitying. Again and again like a petulant child. 'No! No! No!'

He squirmed and wrenched but Carls' grip was like steel.

Craig had stayed back at the van. His work was done. Keisha watched as Janet squared up to Luke. Her face bent out of shape with Botox and rage.

'Martin was a piece of shit and my little princess could do so, so much better. But he was her piece of shit and you killed him and broke her fucking heart.'

'That's what this is about?' said Luke, incredulous.

'You were wrong,' said Keisha. 'Craig does have a code. He'd never kill you. He doesn't have it in him.'

'He's not a mother,' said Janet.

She nodded to Carl and he threw Luke into the pit.

Luke landed hard on Wormall's body but scrambled to his feet as if it was nothing. 'Twenty million. I can get you twenty million.'

Carl simply picked up the jerry can and began to pour its contents into the concrete hole.

The smell of petrol filled the air.

'What do you want? What the fuck do you people want? Everyone wants something,' screamed Luke.

'I wanted my dad,' said Keisha. 'I never realised I did until you got him killed.' She turned to Janet. 'I'm bored now. This is what you paid Craig for. Enjoy.'

She turned and walked back to towards the van, towards Craig. Behind her she could hear Luke Gannon still screaming, begging, crying and pleading.

Then she heard the hollow thud of an empty plastic jerry can being tossed in the pit and a second later the unmistakable whoosh of oxygen being sucked in as the pit erupted into flame.

Luke's screams bounced around the empty warehouse. Before she could stop herself, Keisha took a look back over her shoulder. As she did she saw a flaming body half haul itself up out of the pit before Carl Farr kicked it back into the inferno.

She didn't look back again.

90

Malton lay in bed, the sheets still damp with perspiration. His broad, heavy chest uncovered to the air, he felt a slight chill running through his body as James's warmth slipped away.

He could hear James in the next room. He always wanted a cup of tea after they had sex. Malton could have just lain there in his arms for hours, marvelling as his mind, which the rest of the time raced on ahead of him, gently floated in a sea of contented nothingness.

He'd never felt like this before. Or rather, he had once. Back in Hulme when he was with Keisha. But back then he'd been terrified of it. His whole life was spent in constant readiness. Assessing everyone he met, who they were, what they wanted, how he could neutralise them, use them, slot them away somewhere neatly in his mind. Another tool to be selected at a later date. With Keisha, just like with James, all that fell away. The only thoughts in his brain were formless shapes of what he now knew was contentment.

In Hulme he'd been young and scared. He was so unused to happiness that he took it for something dark and awful. An undoing of his mental defences. He felt exposed to the world.

Now he had James, he realised he wasn't exposed. He was invited. Permitted to feel what he felt without fear or doubt.

The bedroom door opened and James came back in. Only it wasn't James. It was Connor. And his face was missing.

★★★

The movement of the van shook Malton awake. He was lying on the narrow bed in the back of the van. Looking up, he saw

Keisha silhouetted in the dim interior lights. She was sat beside him, holding his hand.

He licked his dry lips and tried to speak but it occurred to him he didn't know what to say. Luke Gannon was dead. Bea's plan to frame him had unravelled. A committed, relentless young journalist had all the facts of the case and Dean was more than capable of making sure that whatever she wrote protected everyone involved.

He couldn't think what the next move was, where his energy was required. It almost felt like he was happy.

Keisha squeezed his hand.

'It was Bea all along,' she said.

Malton wanted to tell her that he knew. That Gannon had told him everything. But he didn't have the strength so instead he simply lay and let Keisha talk.

'She framed you for Stephen Page's murder. Gannon asked her for help and that was her solution.'

Keisha was wearing her sunglasses. Malton could see his reflection, fish-eyed in the lenses. He looked half dead.

He squeezed her hand back and said, 'I know.'

'No,' said Keisha, shaking her head. 'You don't know everything. You don't know why.'

Malton's brain skidded into neutral. Bea had got close to him. Bea had betrayed him. Deep down he always knew she would. So when she finally did, he'd never stopped to ask himself – why?

'You were in Liverpool chasing down a lead on James?'

Malton nodded weakly.

'She gave you that lead, didn't she?'

A dark, heavy dread settled over Malton. He knew what was coming next.

'She made that lead up. She wanted something to keep you close to her. Something that would keep you on a short chain. But you leaned on her, made her give it up to you.'

Keisha spoke without emotion but her hand never left him.

'The reason she helped Gannon frame you, she knew you were getting closer to finding out the truth. That she'd lied to you. She knew what you'd do, so when Gannon approached her, it was too perfect to resist.'

Malton felt his strength leaving him. He lay back on the flimsy bed and let his weight pour into it.

He was no closer to finding James's killers. He'd been betrayed, imprisoned, and now he was dying.

Maybe this feeling of ease wasn't happiness after all. Maybe it was the end. His mind finally running out of road.

'Craig! Open your fucking eyes!'

Keisha's voice was full-bore Moss Side. Rich and beautiful and strong and coming from a place you absolutely do not want to fuck with.

The sound of it dragged him back into that van, onto that bed, his hand in hers.

'I was wrong,' said Keisha.

Malton looked up, bewildered.

'I always thought the whole world was against me. I didn't care. I was bigger than them all. I could hit them before they hit me. I was smarter and stronger and I had something they didn't have. I was Keisha McColl.'

Keisha's words darkly resonated with Malton's own feelings.

'And almost all the time I was right. I went looking for the worst people I could find and I tamed them. I wasn't scared. I found the richest people, the people with power and I showed myself time and time again that I could run rings around them. It made me feel like nothing could touch me. But then my dad died and everything changed.'

Malton thought he heard her voice waver but she continued.

'My dad was a shit dad. He left me and my mum. But that wasn't the worst thing he did. He left me expecting everyone else to do the same. As long as I was one step ahead then it didn't matter. But now I'm exhausted. I can't keep running so hard or so fast all the time.'

She smiled.

345

'Listen to me. I sound like a fucking wet cunt from Chorlton. Next thing you know I'll be doing yoga and talking about my trauma. Fuck that. What I mean, these past few days I found out I got a sister and a niece and neither of them need me. But they want me. Me. I think I was wrong. I think maybe there are one or two good ones out there. Not many. Hardly fucking any. But there are a few. Do you understand?'

Malton did and it hurt him more than any of his wounds. He thought he'd spent his life looking for them but in reality he'd never even started. He'd found people who he knew he could control, or who he thought he could control. People who he could put under glass and protect. Both from his world and from ever realising who he really was.

The last time he'd felt this vulnerable was when he was lying in bed, waiting for James to return with his tray of tea.

The van was slowing down.

'But now, I got to make sure you don't go to prison for the next twenty years. You understand?' said Keisha.

Malton's brain kicked back into gear. He knew this moment was coming. It meant it really was over and now they were going their separate ways. Just like always.

Every time they met it was like the world was coming to an end and then, just at the point of oblivion, they would hold back and at the last minute miss each other by millimetres before carrying on off into their own lonely orbits.

It was that time again.

Malton sat up with Keisha's help and held his hands out in front of him. The effort was agony. His broken ribs crunching in on themselves in protest.

Keisha opened the bag of zip ties and pulled one tight around his hands, biting into the flesh.

'Feet,' she said, and Malton swung off the bed, holding his ankles together.

'Got to make it look real,' she muttered as she knelt down and tied his ankles with another zip tie.

The van had stopped now.

Keisha helped Malton to his feet and held him as he shuffled towards the doors at the back of the van.

She opened one door. It was somewhere in town. Rain was hammering down. The streets filled with umbrellas. The cold air shook him awake.

'I love you,' said Keisha. She gave him a kiss on the cheek and then pushed him out of the van, slamming the door behind him.

Malton hit the pavement hard but he was beyond pain now. Lying in the gutter, bound and bleeding, he watched as the van and Keisha drove away into the heavy Manchester rain.

91

Ruth had never been more nervous in her life. She sipped at the dregs of her coffee and tried to look at her phone while across the table from her, Eddie sat with her laptop open reading the final draft of her story.

They were in a coffee shop in the Northern Quarter. It ground its own beans and the smell filled the small café. Eddie looked immaculate in a pristine, heavy maroon chore shirt and black drill-cord jeans. He'd grown a little moustache since Ruth last saw him. Like everything else about his appearance, it was neat and stylish.

She'd already done a deal with a national newspaper to publish it. A deal that included hiring her on a semi-permanent basis as an investigative reporter based in the north. Her dad had helped her hammer out the contracts as well as working on the story with her for the past couple of months.

She'd told him everything. Watched as her dad did his best to be a professional fellow journalist and not a terrified father as she described meeting Luke Gannon, what happened in the alleyway, and how, thanks to Malton and Dean, she'd been given a look behind the curtain at the dark underbelly of the city she thought she knew.

With her dad's help, she told the truth without exposing her, Malton or Dean. He'd used every trick in the book to ensure that she neither lied nor omitted anything relevant, nor put any of her sources at risk. Ruth was confident that every single line she wrote would hold up in court.

That meant Bea Wallace was conspicuously absent from the tale. Between what Dean had told her and what she'd managed to piece together, it was clear that the celebrated criminal lawyer was intimately tied to the whole affair. But with Luke Gannon missing and Malton freed from prison after charges were dropped, there was neither the appetite nor the leads to go after her.

That didn't mean Ruth would forget her.

Eddie had one hand over his mouth. He started crying early on in the story and had been dabbing his eyes and gasping ever since. Finally he blew his nose and closed the laptop.

'Thank you,' he said with deep sincerity.

'I couldn't have done it without you,' said Ruth.

'If it wasn't for me you wouldn't have had to do it,' he said sadly. 'I let them down. All of them.'

'No,' said Ruth firmly. 'You were a friend to them when no one else would be. Luke Gannon let them down. The police who couldn't be bothered to join the dots let them down. The Manchester that builds hundreds of feet into the sky but is happy to let lost, broken boys sell their bodies on the streets let them down.'

Eddie reached over and clutched Ruth's hand.

'This is going to the police,' said Ruth. 'But I can't give them the phone. If I did then I'd be guilty of withholding evidence, interfering with a crime scene.'

'The police had no idea what was going on,' said Eddie, outraged. 'They would have put Jake down as another dead rent boy. If it wasn't for you that bastard would still be out there killing them.'

'I thought you should have it,' she said and took out Jake's phone, sliding it across the table.

Eddie looked down at the phone and his eyes filled with tears.

Now Ruth knew why her dad had all those sleepless nights. Why he was so scared but he did it anyway. Asked questions that got you in trouble, told stories that made bad people very angry.

She had exposed a serial killer and lived to tell the tale. Compared to that, Bea Wallace would be a piece of cake.

92

Manchester on a Saturday night was every bit as wild, exciting and unpredictable as Keisha remembered it. Traffic crawled through the Deansgate rain as crowds of half-dressed revellers staggered across the road, spilled off pavements and clustered in the promising half-light of club doorways.

From where she sat in The Wren she watched as minibuses of drinkers from out of town pulled up and disgorged excited people from Leigh and Wigan and Warrington and Bolton and all the other distant suburbs that now turned towards Manchester for their joy.

Staying in Manchester was a calculated risk. She knew Craig would never cooperate with the police other than to say that he'd been taken at gunpoint, leaving them with only their blurry CCTV to go on. She hoped that any old faces recognising her would keep quiet if not out of a sense of residual loyalty to her then out of a belief in the threadbare code of keeping your fucking mouth shut.

It was a risk worth taking because there was one thing left to do before she disappeared. A score to settle. One big enough that she was prepared to be in Manchester on a Saturday night, sat in the wood-panelled warmth of The Wren, nursing an untouched cocktail and waiting.

She'd been in Manchester long enough to lose her Ibiza glow. Now her skin was a light brown against the black of her diaphanous playsuit. The bejewelled purple of her nails an elegant shout of colour. Hidden beneath the flared legs of the playsuit she wore her black Air Force Nikes. Ready to run when the time came. Hidden beneath her sunglasses she saw everything.

The Wren on Deansgate was once an insurance building, then offices and finally a cocktail bar that embraced the elegant interior that harked back to the time of Cottonopolis. Back when Manchester was more than just a drunken playground. Heavy crystal chandeliers and staff dressed in buttoned-up shirts and trousers lent it an air of authenticity. Still, the downstairs bar where Keisha now sat was only half the story. Anyone could wander into The Wren. Smile at the giant on the door (not a Malton doorman Keisha noticed) and be led inside to spend a fairly indecent amount of money on cocktails. The real cash was in a room two floors up.

To one side of the dimly lit bar there was a lift door, operated via a key, which would take you up to a private function room built in what was once the chairman of the insurance company's personal office. Heavy curtains, gilt lighting, original paintings with signatures any schoolkid would recognise. It was a little time capsule of the kind of wealth Manchester once had. A wealth that, thanks to the property boom, it was now enjoying once more. And with it came a new class of wealthy. The kind of people who were up there right now being wined and dined to within an inch of their lives.

Keisha felt the hard metal shape of the key to the lift in her hand. She was pleased to see that her old bait-and-switch skills were still sharp. It had been easy enough to distract the barman as she leaned over the bar gawking at the bottles of spirits while in reality one hand was behind the bar grabbing up the key.

From where she sat, the lift door was five metres away across the room. It was a small lift. It only held at maximum two people. If when it opened there were two people inside then all this would have been for nothing.

As the sodden hordes continued to besiege Deansgate, wetly trailing off towards what was left of Spinningfields, Keisha saw the light above the lift illuminate. Someone was coming down.

This was the third time this had happened. Both times a false alarm as the lift had opened to disgorge faceless property speculators. Nevertheless, Keisha was on high alert. She slipped her feet from the footrest of her bar stool onto the floor and gently reorientated her body towards the lift. Once the doors started opening she'd have to move.

The barman was serving a small group. The giant on the door was talking to a PCSO. Keisha clenched her fist and let the sharp bite of the key bring her into focus.

She told herself – this is worth the risk.

The first thing she saw as the lift opened was the blonde hair. That was enough. She was moving. Crossing the room. A black shadow in her playsuit and shades. Already at the door as it opened to reveal Bea Wallace who, before she had time to react, was pushed back into the lift by Keisha who turned and put her stolen key into the hole by the lift's controls and jabbed the door closed.

With her other hand she slipped the blade out of the folds of her playsuit and held it to Bea's throat, blocking the view of what she was doing with her body as the door swung shut, only for Keisha to immediately pull the key out, stalling the lift in place.

Keeping the blade at Bea's throat, she turned her body to face her.

'I love the playsuit,' said Bea, smiling calmly. 'Less keen on the knife.'

Keisha looked down at Bea. Blonde and tiny and not retreating an inch. The two of them filling the lift with their presence.

'You killed my father,' said Keisha.

'No. I didn't,' said Bea definitively. 'I advised a client and that client decided it was in his best interests to kill your father. And I'm fairly sure you killed my client. Were you close?'

Keisha held herself tightly, pressing the blade harder against Bea's soft, white throat.

'So you've come for revenge? Haven't you jumped your turn? As I recall, it was you sent poor old Leon Walker to kill me?'

Keisha almost smiled. Bea was right. But still, that wasn't personal. It was just her trying to get Craig's attention.

'Was this really your plan? Catch me in The Wren and stab me to death? I'd expect more from you.'

'Sorry to disappoint,' said Keisha.

'Keisha Bistacchi,' said Bea out loud. 'I think you should know there's cameras here. With sound. You understand that, don't you, Keisha Bistacchi, née McColl?'

Bea held the blank stare of Keisha's sunglasses.

Kiesha smiled. Bea had no idea.

'I'm not here to kill you,' she said.

'Knife at my throat in a private lift? You could have fooled me. Did you just want a drink? It's a free bar upstairs. Let me take you up. I could introduce you to some very dull, very rich men.'

'You set Craig up.'

Bea looked a little crestfallen. 'Is this really about him? Still? Pet, I can't be the first to tell you, I just don't think he's that into you.'

Bea seemed relaxed. Like she felt she had the measure of the situation. Keisha let her go on thinking that.

'I know, but there's something about him I can't quite shake. And I want him to know just what he means to me.'

The smile left Bea's face. Her accent hardened down to something closer to a Home Counties sneer. 'Whatever you do next, my advice, free advice, would be to kill me. Because if you don't, then you're finished.'

Keisha shook her head. 'I told you already. I'm not here to kill you. I want to give *you* some advice. So you think twice next time you try and fuck with me and mine.'

Before Bea could open her mouth Keisha raised the blade and slashed it across Bea's left cheek. Bea let out a gasp of shock, her hand shooting up to her face where blood was cascading down.

'Now every time you look in the mirror maybe you'll remember that,' said Keisha with a smile.

She dropped the knife to the floor, turned the key back in the hole and slipped out the doors as they opened. By the time the screaming started she was already heading down the alley beside The Wren and away into the filthy Mancunian night.

93

Dean would be lying if he said he simply stopped thinking about Vikki. But after Luke Gannon was packed away and with his arm well on the way to healing, Dean simply let the irresistible clutter of life carry him along.

From time to time he found himself missing their eleven o'clock catch-up. Sometimes he'd wonder what was behind her father reaching out from behind the walls of HMP Wakefield. Sometimes he'd think about the young man with the painted nails. The one he'd glimpsed rolling a cigarette in Vikki's kitchen. But most of the time he simply got on with life.

It was made all the easier by his promotion to head of Malton Security. Even after Malton had been cleared of all charges, and even with an injunction covering the reporting of his 'kidnapping' from MRI, it had been decided that Craig Malton was too high-profile a figure to be running a legitimate security firm.

So now it was Dean's role. Malton's position, his office and all his responsibilities running the company. They were all Dean's.

After his arm finally healed he had his old cast signed by every single member of Malton Security and mounted on the office wall. Marking his territory.

Even though it was now officially his office, Dean couldn't bring himself to change a thing. The collage of maps, dotted in pins, was still there – as was the battered sofa and the weights bench. Only the continued presence of Dean's laptop suggested that Craig Malton was no longer in residence.

The Farrs had done a solid job of disappearing Luke Gannon off the face of the earth. The strangest thing, for a man who had left such a mark on Manchester, no one came looking for him. His wife had reported him missing and that was the end of it. The world carried on without Luke Gannon.

Upon learning the entire story, Mickey Farr, from his hospital bed, had ordered Janet Farr to settle the balance with Malton Security. Whatever bad blood there had been between him and Malton, Mickey wasn't the kind of man who held a grudge. Not once there'd been a bit of mutual bone-breaking.

That side of the business had been quiet. Something about Malton's imprisonment, kidnap and exoneration felt a little too public, and for now Manchester's underworld were solving their own problems. That didn't mean Dean wasn't keeping himself informed of the currents passing through the city.

The council's coordinated push to decimate the counterfeit district had driven several organised crime gangs online, and with the market in fake designer goods no longer the money maker it once was, they had turned to fake prescription medication. Salford and North Manchester was still a free-for-all as various upcomers vied for supremacy with guns, grenades and knife attacks. Whatever blip Luke Gannon's death had caused in the supply chain was rectified almost immediately and, if anything, the Farrs had moved up in the world, with Janet Farr taking the reins from her dead son-in-law Martin.

As for Malton himself, Dean hadn't seen him in nearly four months. But he knew better than to go looking. Malton had trusted him to run the company. That meant, wherever Malton was now, he was relying on Dean to keep things moving forward.

Not just that. Along with the promotion, Malton had suggested that he move out of the house in Moss Side where he had been living and into somewhere more fitting.

Malton's old home in Didsbury.

Dean was already hardly ever at the two-up two-down terrace in Moss Side. Without Vikki to keep him indoors and with all of Malton Security under his watch he spent most of his time all over Manchester. Meeting clients, interviewing new staff, dealing with all the usual issues that cropped up when you ran security. While a larger house in Didsbury was of little use to him domestically, he liked the idea of feeling like suddenly he had arrived. And with Malton's blessing he moved his mum out of her old one-bed flat and into his house in Moss Side.

Malton's Didsbury house was huge. A five-bedroom detached Victorian mansion on a tree-lined road scattered with similarly vast homes. It had a giant garden and boasted the most tastefully discreet security that money and a lifetime of enemies could buy.

It was far too big for Dean alone. He had been living in the one room. Eating over the sink. Treating it as little more than a place to crash every night.

That was until three hours ago when, out of the blue, Vikki had called him up and told him that she was coming home.

Dean was so shocked to hear her voice that he couldn't think what to say when she told him she was already at Euston and getting ready to catch a train and that she needed to see him.

With three hours until Vikki arrived, Dean was a whirlwind of domesticity. Firstly he'd driven to the nearest supermarket where he'd bought new bedding, plates and cutlery. A few frozen pizzas, some milk, eggs, orange juice. A random assortment of food. Enough, he hoped, to dispel the impression he'd been living on tap water and takeaways.

The past few months he'd been on ruthless autopilot, doing everything he could to fill Malton's shoes. But now Vikki was coming home, suddenly he felt less like the acting head of Malton Security and more like the lanky, baby-faced lad who was still a little unsure just what Craig Malton saw in him.

Vikki hadn't stayed on the phone long. She didn't say why she was coming home or what she needed to see Dean about. But something about her voice lingered at the back of Dean's mind. He didn't let himself dwell. Vikki was coming home.

Whatever the reason, it meant that he had a second chance. He wasn't going to blow it.

Three hours later he was wrestling with duvet covers when, glancing out of the upstairs window, he saw Vikki's taxi pulling onto the sweeping brick driveway in front of the house. He'd left the front gates open especially but had been so busy making sure things were just right that he'd lost track of time.

He saw Vikki step out and stand gazing up at the house. As the taxi driver retrieved her luggage, Dean hurried downstairs in time to open the front door just as the taxi was pulling away, leaving Vikki stood with her suitcases and bags.

She was even more beautiful than he remembered her. She stood in every inch of her near six-foot height wearing a long leather overcoat over a faded, vintage tracksuit top and shredded jeans. Her hair held back with barrettes.

Unsure what else to say he simply gestured to the house and said, 'Welcome home!'

Something was wrong.

Vikki stood on the driveway, a deathly serious look on her face. Dean had seen her scared, happy, relieved, hopeful and filled with joy. But he'd never seen her like this before. He felt a familiar dread welling up.

'What's happened?' he said, instantly wiping everything he'd planned for their reunion from his mind.

'It's my dad,' she said.

Dean had quietly hoped that the edge in Vikki's voice had been all to do with the boy with floppy hair, or rather the boy with floppy hair no longer being in her life. But no. It was far worse. Leon Walker cast a long shadow.

'Last week, I got this weird feeling, like I was being followed,' said Vikki.

Dean froze.

'This guy. I kept seeing him. I told myself it was nothing. London's a big place. A long way from Manchester. But then last night I got home. There was no one in. I thought there was no one in.'

Dean listened with mounting horror.

'That's when I found this.' She bent down and handed Dean a shoe box that had come along with her luggage.

Dean looked to Vikki for some kind of clue as to what could possibly be inside. She looked away, wrinkling her nose in disgust. So, very carefully, Dean lifted the lid.

Inside, surrounded by ice packs, was a human hand. Dean couldn't help but notice the fingernails. They were painted black.

On top of the hand was a note. It simply read.

TELL YOUR DAD. I WANT IT BACK.

Epilogue

Keisha closed her eyes and let the warmth of the villa encircle her body. The dazzling Ibiza sun streamed in through the narrow windows of the villa's kitchen, unimpeded by the flat, dead air.

It fell over her body, her bikini revealing toned dark skin. Her hair was braided back into thick, shimmering cornrows, her dark glasses shielding her eyes from the sun's glare.

Condensation dripped from the glass of gin in her hand and ran down her fingers. The chill of the ice felt utterly different to the freezing cold of the Manchester sleet she'd left behind. The past few months seemed like an indistinct vision. A collection of grief and horror and revelation that no longer made sense within the walls of her beloved villa.

The sound of laughter interrupted her silence and she heard footsteps on the spiral staircase from below.

Allie and Rachel were back.

Keisha didn't have to consider the smile that came across her face as her niece ran upstairs, her hair still wet from the sea. Even now, it still threw Keisha just how much the little girl looked like her. When Allie had seen Keisha's braids she had begged her mother, Rachel, to do the same to her hair and now, side by side, Keisha and Allie were indistinguishable save for the thirty-something years between them.

'How's the beach?' asked Keisha.

'You should come!' said Allie, water pooling at her feet and onto the warm tiles.

'I don't do swimming,' said Keisha.

'How about just sitting on the beach and drinking gin?' said Rachel, appearing from below. 'This place is amazing. I would ask you how on earth you could afford it.'

Rachel had a sarong over her bathing suit. She was younger than Keisha by over a decade but, of the two women, Keisha had the muscle and the tone. Rachel had curves and a softness that at first had misled Keisha.

'Trust me, you don't want to know.' Keisha laughed.

It had gone from a cagey evasion to an in-joke. No one was more surprised than Keisha at how quickly Rachel and Allie had slotted into her life. Before she left Manchester she'd taken them away for a couple of days to a cottage in the Lake District. A chance for them all to get to know each other, and then late at night for her and her half-sister to make up for lost time. Filling each other in on the details of their lives. They talked into the early hours, both women thrilling every time one of them talked about their own life and yet again the other chipped in with an identical recollection.

There was so much lost time to catch up on.

Keisha was fixing her sister a drink when she heard the sound of the car.

Her villa was hidden off the main road, nestled in an alcove facing the sea. Steep hillside surrounded the building with the only approach being via a dirt track that came off the main road. The entrance to the track was partially hidden amongst the trees. It was easily missed. That was how Keisha liked it.

Keisha didn't get visitors.

She put down her drink and went to the window.

'Is everything OK?' said Rachel. Keisha could hear the note of caution in her voice. Wrapped up in a sing-song insouciance for Allie's benefit.

Keisha said nothing but watched from the window as a white hire car pulled up and a middle-aged woman wearing a baggy T-shirt, shorts and action sandals got out of the car and peered up at the villa through airport-bought sunglasses.

She was so focused on the arrival she didn't hear the sound of Craig coming down from the bedroom on the top floor.

'Benton,' came his voice from over her shoulder.

***

Hot weather didn't suit Benton. Even within the cool walls of the villa sweat was dripping off her face. She constantly had to stop to wipe it away with the back of her hand. Her feet were red and swollen in her sandals and she wore a hairband to keep her hair off her face.

Malton had only meant to come out for as long as it took to recover from his injuries. After Keisha dumped him in the street he had been hospitalised for weeks. Long enough for his wounds to heal and the case against him for Stephen Page's murder to collapse. Having already been inside for nearly three months the charges were dropped and it didn't take much pressure from Malton's new lawyers to have reporting on the case stifled.

No one cared that much about Malton anyway. Not after Ruth Porter's devastating exposé of Luke Gannon came out. Officially, GMP were still looking for Gannon. Unofficially, Malton knew that they'd never find whatever was left of him. The Farrs had seen to that.

Still, when Keisha made the offer, it had seemed a good time to leave the country for a few weeks. That was nearly four months ago.

Dean was now fully in charge of Malton Security and from what Malton could tell was running a tight ship. The Manchester underworld was churning away same as it ever had. Even James's killers were still out there. Everyone having the gall to keep on without him there to watch over them.

For the first time in a long time Malton had let go.

But now Benton was here he could feel the muscle memory returning. The sense of something dark on the horizon. A feeling that filled his long-recovered body with readiness.

363

Rachel had taken Allie back to the beach and left Keisha and Malton alone with Benton. They sat round the small table in the kitchen. Malton and Benton with iced water. Keisha with her gin.

'Fuck me, I don't know how you do it out here. I'm sweating buckets,' said Benton.

'How did you find me?' asked Keisha coldly.

Malton watched as Benton swerved the question and said, 'You're looking good, Craig. Not being a murderer suits you.'

Malton had never noticed Benton's accent before. Plucked from its northern setting it suddenly struck him. A no-nonsense confidence passed down from one strong, northern woman to another across generations. Manchester was a city of women used to rolling up their sleeves and working alongside the men.

'You two can talk shit on your own time,' said Keisha. 'This is my house and I asked you a question.'

Benton took a breath, her whole face battling the heat as her eyes closed and her brow furrowed. When she opened her eyes again she was all business.

'I need you,' she said to Malton.

'You need me?' said Malton.

'Greater Manchester Police need you,' she said.

'You're here to arrest him?' said Keisha, an edge to her voice.

Benton shook her head.

'This is between us three and only us three,' she said, her voice lowering. 'And if this goes wrong I've been reliably informed I'm the one who'll be thrown under the bus.'

Before she spoke she took a look round as if unsure they were alone. Seemingly happy, she continued, 'Two years ago Greater Manchester Police inserted an undercover officer in north Manchester. They were given the time and resources to establish themselves in the community and make contacts with a number of organised crime gangs. Their ultimate mission

364

was to spearhead an intelligence-led operation to neutralise organised crime in North Manchester.'

Keisha laughed at the very thought of ever taming North Manchester.

'Don't start,' said Benton, 'I know. But Manchester Council saw the amount of foreign property money sloshing around and decided next bit of the city to be sold off was north of the city centre. But first they wanted to give it a quick clean-up.'

'What are you here for, Benton?' said Malton, cutting her off.

'A week ago that undercover officer went dark. The emergency extraction plan failed to find them and now it looks like they've vanished off the face of the earth. GMP could tear North Manchester apart looking for them. But that would tip off too many people, flush two years of intelligence down the drain. And so . . .'

'You want me to find him?' said Malton.

'I want you to find *her*,' said Benton. 'And I want you to bring her home alive.'

Acknowledgements

When you start writing a novel you imagine it's just you and the inside of your head. But in between that first page and seeing it emerge as a fully formed book there are a hell of a lot of people helping things along. Like all creative endeavours, a little bit of collaboration with the right people always makes everything far better than you could ever have done on your own.

With that in mind I'd like to thank my literary agent Gordon Wise who took on the first novel, sold it and got this series moving. I can't think of a better person to have in my corner. As well as Gordon I'd have to thank Michael McCoy, my TV agent, who stuck with this idea when it was a spec script and watched it emerge into a novel, and was kind enough to put it across Gordon's desk.

Next up is my former editor Bethany Wickington who guided the first three books, taught me a great deal about what goes into producing a book and was responsible for getting these books out into the world and into the hands of readers. Working alongside Bethany has been Helena Newton, a free-lance proofreader whose job has not just been to catch the hundreds of typos but to also back up Beth in giving notes, making sure everything tracks and most importantly – it all makes sense.

Bethany has left for new challenges and so I also would like to thank my new editor Cara Chimirri for picking up the reins and diving in on Settle the Score. I'm always impressed how people in publishing can be across several books all at the one time. As well as Cara I'd like to thank Phoebe Morgan for supervising the changing of the guard.

367

Closer to home it's inevitable that you end up consulting friends and family. It's no small ask to get someone to read an entire book so I'm hugely grateful to Dr Hughes for all her suggestions and thoughts as well as being able to zero in on the smallest discrepancy in timelines or logic. Thanks to the incredibly exciting author Elliot Sweeney (*The First to Die*) who has been more than generous with his time and feedback. It's always great to get notes from another author, especially one whose work you enjoy as much as Elliot's.

I'd also like to thank anyone who I've managed to miss out here.

Two final thanks and I'm gone.

Firstly Manchester. It's such an amazing, infuriating, mercurial city. It's changed so much in the past few years I've been writing these books. Hopefully in some small way I've captured the sense of a city in a state of breakneck flux.

Finally I'd like to thank all my readers. Writing in a genre with so many amazing, established authors, it's been really heartening to see how many people have got involved with the Manchester Underworld series. I hope it's as much fun to read as it is to write.

For more information about what I'm up to, head to www.samtobincrime.com. See you there!

Go back to where it all started with book one in the series!

There's only room for one boss in this city . . .

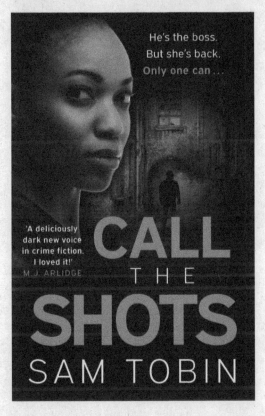

He's the boss.
But she's back.
Only one can . . .

'A deliciously dark new voice in crime fiction. I loved it!'
M J ARLIDGE

CALL
THE
SHOTS
SAM TOBIN